The town of Kymlinge exists on the map to roughly the same extent as Burma, Ragnhild's Mountain Guest House and Our Lord.

THE AXE WOMAN

HÅKAN NESSER

THE AXE WOMAN

Translated from the Swedish
by Sarah Death

MANTLE

First published in the UK 2022 by Mantle
an imprint of Pan Macmillan
The Smithson, 6 Briset Street, London EC1M 5NR
EU representative: Macmillan Publishers Ireland Ltd, 1st Floor,
The Liffey Trust Centre, 117–126 Sheriff Street Upper,
Dublin 1, D01 YC43
Associated companies throughout the world
www.panmacmillan.com

ISBN 978-1-5098-9233-4

Originally published in 2012 as *Styckerskan från Lilla Burma*
by Albert Bonniers Förlag, Stockholm

'Aubade' extract from *The Complete Poems* © Philip Larkin, courtesy of Faber and Faber, Ltd.
'Anthem' from STRANGER MUSIC by Leonard Cohen. Copyright © 1993 Leonard Cohen and
Leonard Cohen Stranger Music, Inc., used by permission of The Wylie Agency (UK) Limited.

1 3 5 7 9 8 6 4 2

A CIP catalogue record for this book is available from the British Library.

Typeset in Dante MT by Palimpsest Book Production Limited, Falkirk, Stirlingshire
Printed and bound by CPI Group (UK) Ltd, Croydon, CR0 4YY

Visit **www.panmacmillan.com** to read more about all our books
and to buy them. You will also find features, author interviews and
news of any author events, and you can sign up for e-newsletters
so that you're always first to hear about our new releases.

ONE

29 April 2012

1

Just another morning.

He woke up, and even if there could possibly have been any discernible change in the room itself, he did not discern it.

The stillness was as usual. The grey light of dawn cautiously filtering through the thin curtains was as usual. Everything was as usual – or *seemed to be*: the low stone seat running along under the window and the wicker chair in the darkest corner, the clothes on hangers, the sparse leaves of the potted palm, the photographs of the children in a row on the wall beside the door; everything the same as it had been when they moved in, four years ago.

And within him: the fragment of a dream – an interview room with a table and a faceless elderly man who had just said something important; it faded away, vanishing into its own secret landscape.

And the heaviness and fatigue in every joint and limb: that, too, the same as usual, and gradually worsening; he was in his fifty-first year, after all, no cause for concern, merely something to register and live with. He turned his head and looked at the clock. Twenty past six. The alarm would go in ten minutes. He stretched out a reluctant hand and switched it off. With some effort he turned over and then reached out to put his right arm over Marianne. He burrowed under the covers, too, to make contact with her skin. It didn't matter where.

For one second more, it was the most ordinary of mornings.

Then he was jolted awake by something like an electric shock, running from his hand via his arm and his whole body. It exploded in his head like a flash of ice-cold lightning.

The chill. The absence.

The utter lack of sound and movement. Every atom of every cell in him knew what had happened, before the viscous membrane of his consciousness was ripped apart by a silent scream and a No.

It had happened.

It *has* happened. For a whole series of moments it was only those three words that presented themselves. Nothing else.

It has happened. It has happened.

And after a while, something more.

This is real. It's not a fear. Not something I'm imagining. It's really happened.

I'm lying here.

Marianne's lying there.

It's morning.

We're lying here after a night like any other.

But I'm the only one here.

She isn't lying by my side. She will never lie by my side again.

It has happened.

It has actually happened.

Once more he let his hand rest on her body. It didn't matter where.

Her body, yes, possibly. But not her. No one is that cold. Dead.

It was 6.26 in the morning. It was 29 April 2012. Marianne was dead. That was how it was, there was no escaping it.

No escaping it.

Her eyes were not quite closed. Or her mouth. As if she had somehow taken one last sight with her. As if she had intended telling him something in that final second.

Perhaps she actually had. Told him something; uttered a few words that might conceivably have found their way through the heavy carapace of his sleep. Or not.

Or perhaps death had caught her unawares. He would never know. He would never stop wondering.

So far it's just me, lying here, he thought. So far, I'm the only one who knows. It's still just about possible to convince myself everything's normal. Maybe I'm actually asleep and this is merely a dream. It makes no sense for it to have happened so fast. It's absurd. From one second to the next. It simply isn't . . .

But all these thoughts were flimsier than the surface of a soap bubble as it bursts.

And they burst. Everything burst apart.

Marianne? he whispered.

Marianne?

And somewhere inside him, her voice answered.

I'm not here.

I'm sorry.

I'm so sorry for you, but I have moved on.

Sorry for you and the children.

Look after the children. I love you all. It's hardest for you and them, but we shall be reunited one day. I know that.

He took her hand and even though it didn't belong to her any more, he held it. He felt its rigid chill, held it close and closed his eyes.

At a quarter to seven he got up. He had heard one of the children moving about, and it was time to tell them their mother was dead.

That she had died in her bed during the night.

An aneurysm, presumably, like the last time. A little blood vessel in her brain that had burst. Eighteen months ago. He had not been unprepared. The possibility of it happening had been embedded in him like a poisoned barb. Now that barb had gone.

Before he even reached the door, grief felled him with a single blow. It came from behind with the force of a hurricane and hurled him to the floor. He lay there as if trapped in some kind of spasm until he finally managed to put his hands together and ask God for strength.

Strength to get himself down to the kitchen, gather the children round the table and tell them.

TWO

May 2012

June 1989

2

Eva Backman knocked and came in.

She stopped just inside the door and scanned the room. Asunander was standing at the window with his back to her, talking on the phone. Behind the desk there were cardboard boxes piled against the wall – she estimated there were eight or ten of them. She wondered if he really needed that many. When the time came for her to vacate her office, she would probably be able to make do with one. At some distant future date.

Or even a couple of paper carrier bags.

But then Asunander was a chief inspector and the boss, so of course there was a difference. He had presided over this spacious office for more than fifteen years and had accumulated a lot of stuff in the process. He kept quite a well-stocked bookshelf, for example; presumably most of the books were his own private collection. She had noted the fact before and, as she ran her eyes along the shelf while waiting for him to finish his call, she noted it again. A policeman who read books. History mostly, both general and of the criminal variety. Dictionaries and encyclopaedias. Half a metre of fiction.

And who could say: perhaps he kept fine whisky and other such things behind the rows of books? Or in his desk drawers? There were sides to Asunander that she had never really been able to explore and, now that he had barely two months left in post, he must presumably be allowed to take his secrets with him.

So thought DI Backman, taking a seat in the visitor's armchair.

Asunander ended his call, turned and nodded to her. He rocked from his heels to his toes and back again a few times before he sat down at his desk.

'You've started packing up?'

She indicated the boxes. He glowered at her. She reflected that she had never got close to him in all those years, and that she wouldn't be doing so in these final weeks, either. She was in good company. Asunander was as he was: a lone wolf.

'Toivonen had some spare boxes. He moved house in March, you'll recall. He brought them in this morning.'

Backman nodded.

'But it wasn't my departure for the hereafter I wanted to discuss.' He cleared his throat and rummaged among the pile of papers on his desk. 'It was Barbarotti. How in heaven's name is he doing, honestly? Is there any improvement to speak of?'

Eva Backman sighed and wondered what she ought to answer.

Improvement? She contemplated Asunander's heavy face for a few seconds. Was there some understanding behind the frown lines and elephant-like folds of skin? Was there a drop of warmth and humanity, or had the years, the tedium and the solitude worn away the last traces of empathy?

It was hard to say.

It was three weeks since Marianne's death, and just over a week since the funeral. Backman had spoken to Barbarotti more or less every day. Often twice or three times. Well, *tried* to speak to him. Most recently that very morning. She didn't know if the word 'improvement' was in any way appropriate, in the circumstances. She couldn't detect any herself, but she had no idea what lay concealed beneath Barbarotti's robotic exterior.

Like dark water under the crust of ice on a lake in the forest: that was the image that had come to her that morning, and it seemed a reasonable description.

'He's coming in this afternoon.'

'Yes, I know,' said Asunander. 'The question is, what can we use him for?'

'Use?'

'Don't pick me up on my choice of words. You know what I'm talking about.'

'I think it's important for him to get back into his work,' said Eva Backman.

'We can't set ourselves up as therapists here,' said Asunander. 'Not even in a case like this. Don't misunderstand me; even I have a heart, you know.'

'I've never doubted it,' said Backman. Though I have, actually, she thought. On several occasions.

'Well?' said Asunander.

Eva Backman thought for a moment. 'I don't really know how he is,' she admitted. 'Or how much use he'll be at the moment.'

'He's a damn good police officer,' said Asunander. 'An odd customer, but good.'

And you're pretty damn odd as a boss, Backman continued her inner monologue. Good perhaps, but definitely odd.

'You're right there,' she said.

'And having your wife drop dead on you doesn't make

you any better, of course. In fact it's likely to make you even odder.'

He leant back, clasped his hands behind his neck and stared up at the ceiling, apparently weighing his next pronouncement.

No better, but even odder?

Eva Backman just sat there in silence for a while, wondering what Asunander really wanted from her. Whether he did in fact expect her to make an assessment of Barbarotti or had simply called her in because the situation called for some sounding out.

But Asunander rarely contented himself with sounding things out for the sake of it and he didn't care for small talk. She decided that behind all this, he was really seeking some advice on the matter. He wanted her considered opinion on what sort of task could be put in the hands of a good, if odd, detective inspector whose wife had died at the age of only forty-seven and left him alone with five children, mostly still adolescent, and a . . . a burden of grief so all-encompassing that it was simply impossible to imagine. Yes, she assumed that was the nut he was hoping she could crack for him.

'Maybe we shouldn't expect him to jump straight into Fängström,' she said. 'That wouldn't be right.'

Asunander gave a curt nod but kept his eyes fixed on the ceiling. Eva Backman involuntarily found the Fängström case forging its way up to the surface of her mind. It was hardly surprising, of course; it was only two days old and she had been in on it from the word go.

Raymond Fängström, twenty-nine and single, had been found dead on his kitchen floor on Sunday morning by his loving mother when she came round to lend a hand with the housework. Cleaning and ironing, and so on. She had found him lying on his stomach with his arms trapped beneath him in the space between the cooker and sink on one side and the refrigerator and freezer on the other, and it didn't take long to establish that he had been lying there since late the previous evening. He had thrown up quite extensively and his head was resting in a patch of his vomit. On the table were the remains of a meal; by the look of it, two people had dined on spaghetti with bolognese sauce and had shared a bottle of red wine.

They still had not established who his dinner guest had been, but the pathologist, one Herbert Lindman, who tended to be right three times out of four, had examined the body for a few minutes and then declared that it looked more than likely to be a poisoning. Samples of the wine, pasta and bolognese sauce, and of the contents of Fängström's stomach – both the vomit and what he had retained – had been sent off to SKL, the National Forensic Laboratory in Linköping, and the answer would no doubt be with them before long. In the course of the coming week, hopefully.

The problem was not only that Raymond Fängström had died in murky circumstances. The problem was also that he was who he was: a local councillor in Kymlinge, elected in 2010 for the Sweden Democrats. Voices had already been raised to claim that it was a case of politically motivated murder. That Fängström had fallen prey to malicious forces from the political left. Maybe an immigrant, maybe a homosexual; there was no shortage of opponents to the policies and xenophobic opinions that Fängström represented and was attempting to ram through the local council, where he had to some degree held the balance of power.

The fact that these voices were greater in volume than in number seemed less important; the media had made a big splash of the story, both nationally and locally. Sweden was rather short of political murders and more than fifty journalists had turned up to the press conference at Kymlinge police station.

Eva Backman had so far interviewed six people who had all had dealings with the dead Sweden Democrat; she had a further twelve on her notepad and she was not looking forward to those conversations. Late the previous day she had sat eye-to-eye with Sigmund Stiller, second on the party's list for the local elections and the man expected to take over Fängström's council seat. She was still clenching her jaw at the very thought of it.

Stiller had not asked to have a lawyer present, but he had insisted on a bodyguard. He considered himself under threat from left-wing terrorists, and had made the fact very public in every possible media outlet. He also demanded that each and every Sweden Democrat in the country be allocated a bodyguard, a proposal that had immediately been toned down by the party leadership in Stockholm or Skåne, or wherever it was. After just a few hours on the case, Eva Backman had started feeling that she would gladly be a traffic cop or a narcotics investigator, or virtually anything else. Anything but a DI embroiled in the fate of a dead racist.

Admittedly the Sweden Democrats had stopped calling themselves racists once they started wearing ties and getting elected to parliament, but at the local council level – at least in Kymlinge – no one was left in any doubt about their views on that score. In his barely two years in post, Raymond Fängström had successfully shown the electorate two things: he hated every individual born south of the Alps, and he did not have the sharpest brain in the land.

And Sigmund Stiller (Eva Backman had uncovered the fact that his real name was Jan Johansson, but that he had changed it after being bullied at school) had soon proved that he was more than a match for his party leader in both respects.

'What makes you think Fängström's death has a political dimension?' Backman had asked.

'It's bleeding obvious,' Stiller had replied. 'They're after us.'

'And who are *they*?'

'Them, of course. The Islamers. The immigrants. Raymond was murdered; this is the beginning of the big race war, geddit?'

'Dead right,' added the bodyguard, who was called Hank and looked as if he weighed about 150 kilos. In English he added, 'The hit has shit the fan.'

No, it didn't seem fair to let Barbarotti anywhere near Fängström.

'We'll have to keep Barbarotti well away from all that,' said Asunander. 'Hot air really isn't what he needs, eh?'

'Not in overly large doses,' said Backman.

Asunander lowered his hands onto his desk and rummaged some more. Then he seemed to change his mind and extracted a brown folder from his top right-hand desk drawer.

'What do you think of this?'

He did not let go of the folder, but turned it round so that she could read what was written on the front:

Arnold Morinder

It was just a name and she did not immediately recall the circumstances. It certainly rang a bell, but she had not been involved. Except perhaps in a very peripheral way. Asunander opened the folder and muttered something she could not catch.

'I don't entirely remember,' she admitted. 'He was the one with the blue moped, wasn't he?'

'Spot on,' said Asunander. 'Coming up for five years ago. We didn't ever really get to the bottom of it.'

'No, I remember,' said Backman. 'Though I wasn't actually on the case. It was abandoned fairly quickly, wasn't it?'

'It was,' confirmed Asunander, a look of dissatisfaction settling around his mouth. 'Uninvestigable. It proved impossible to draw any conclusions. But the wretched fellow never turned up.'

'Disappearances,' observed Backman. 'Always difficult to get anywhere.'

'You're telling me,' said Asunander.

Backman reflected for a moment. 'What did you have in mind for Barbarotti to do with it?'

Asunander shrugged, pretending he did not already know. 'It would keep him occupied. Wasn't that what the doctor ordered? And if he doesn't get anywhere, at least it will do no harm.'

Backman made no reply.

'I'd like you to run an eye over the material before he does,' said Asunander with an expression that was presumably meant to illustrate they had come to a joint decision. 'Then you can take him through it this afternoon. But he'll have to do the work on his own, remember that. A one-man investigation – we can't allocate any real resources to this. A week or two, so he starts getting back into the swing, what do you think of that, Inspector?'

'I don't think anything at all,' said Eva Backman.

'Right then,' said Asunander. 'The prosecutor has been

informed, but there are to be no formal interviews. Just some cautious soundings, and I want you to make that clear to Barbarotti.'

Cautious soundings? she thought irritably, once she had closed the door behind her. One-man investigation? If you were going to work, it was best to make a proper job of it, wasn't it?

And Barbarotti was bound to see through Asunander's ploy, wasn't he? To realize that all it amounted to was easing him back into the job. That he wasn't considered capable.

But then again, perhaps that was exactly what was needed? The medicine Barbarotti himself would favour, in the current situation? A sheltered workshop in a corner while all the real police activity went on around him?

If he were to be asked, that was.

Always assuming that he felt any sense of will at all. There had been little enough of it in evidence in the phone calls Backman had had with him to date. None at all, in fact.

Bereavement, she thought as she went into her room. That's what this is about. The permafrost of the soul.

3

The Morinder case involved Arnold Morinder, naturally enough. But he could hardly be called the main character.

It was his wife who featured in the leading role, and there were specific reasons for that. It took Eva Backman twenty minutes to read through the summary of the case; it had been written by DI Borgsen – generally known as Sorrysen because of his grave demeanour – and even though she had not had a great deal to do with the investigation, the story came back to her quite vividly, now that she had it in front of her again.

It was August 2007. A little under five years ago, just as Asunander had reminded her. Arnold Morinder, fifty-four years of age and an employee of Buttros Electrics in Kymlinge, had vanished from his summer cottage out on the northern shore of Lake Kymmen. He had set off on his moped to go to the Statoil petrol station to buy an evening paper. When he still had not returned three days and three nights later, his partner, a certain Ellen Bjarnebo, phoned the police. Inspector Sorrysen and Assistant Detective Wennergren-Olofsson went to her place to interview her. Suspicions were aroused almost immediately that a crime had been committed.

Not that there was much evidence pointing in that direction – neither initially nor later on, in fact – but it was because Ellen Bjarnebo was who she was.

The Axe Woman of Little Burma.

At the end of the 1980s she had experienced brief notoriety under that title. Little Burma was the name of the medium-sized farm about five kilometres north-east of Kymlinge where she had lived with her husband and their one child. There was a Great Burma too, and the track that led between the two farms was called the Burma Road, a borrowing from the infamous construction project in Asia that was completed about the same time as the farms came into being in the late 1930s. The new settlers were two brothers, Sven and Arvid Helgesson, and it was Arvid's son Harry who was butchered with an axe fifty years later.

But first he was killed by a blow from a sledgehammer; that was in early June 1989, and about five months later his wife Ellen Helgesson, née Bjarnebo, was found guilty of murder and desecration of a dead body and sent to Sweden's only women's prison, Hinseberg just outside Frövi, in the region of Bergslagen. And there she stayed until her release eleven years later.

The Axe Woman of Little Burma?

She had been released from prison in November 2000. She had moved back to a flat in Kymlinge and eventually got a job at the Post Office. There she had worked until the incident in the summer of 2007 – latterly for its offshoot, the Swedish Cashier Service. Backman wondered if her colleagues had known that they had a murderess among them. Maybe, maybe not; someone must surely have been aware of her background when she was first appointed to the job? Even if the Royal Swedish Post Office was not what it had once been.

Ellen Bjarnebo – she had reverted to her maiden name by the time of the trial in 1989 – had moved in with Arnold

Morinder about a year before he disappeared on his moped. Sorrysen's summary did not reveal how they had met, but they had lived together in a flat in the suburb of Rocksta from June 2006 onwards. Morinder had been married once before but had no children, and had owned the cottage out by Lake Kymmen since the mid-1970s, when he inherited it from his father.

They had started looking into the electrician's disappearance. The preliminary investigation was led by Prosecutor Månsson, known in police circles as Fusspot Månsson and still a very active member of the HQ team. Backman wondered why he had agreed to more or less reopen the case – if that was the way to describe it. Maybe Asunander had not informed him; it wouldn't surprise her. In their many years as colleagues, the chief inspector and the prosecutor had worked about as well together as a fish and a bicycle.

Anyway, it was pretty soon established that Morinder had bought his evening paper at the filling-station shop in Kerranshede as planned, but what had become of him after that remained a mystery. Just over a week after he vanished into thin air his moped, an old blue Zündapp, was found in a boggy area about eight kilometres west of his summer cottage. The bog, called Stora Svartkärret, was known for its vast numbers of mosquitoes and was searched for a week by a sizeable group of police officers and technicians with a wide range of expertise, but nothing came to light that offered the slightest hint as to what had become of the missing Morinder.

After a week of squelching around in mosquito hell they were presumably pretty sick of the whole thing, thought Eva Backman. So it was hardly surprising the case was abandoned. Written off as uninvestigable.

Eighteen years had elapsed between the murder at Little Burma and the disappearance of Arnold Morinder, she reminded herself. Now a further five had gone by.

A suitable task for a detective inspector in the grip of raw grief? Suitable for anyone in fact? What was going on in the back of Asunander's mind? Anything?

Good questions. Eva Backman looked at the clock. It was time for lunch.

Time to prepare herself for her meeting with Barbarotti, who would be setting foot in Kymlinge police HQ for the first time since Marianne's death. That, too, was a task.

No better, but even odder?

She felt a sudden wave of queasiness.

4

Gunnar Barbarotti switched off the engine and unclipped his safety belt, but did not get out of the car.

This was a moment he had been dreading. Back at the police station.

Or not dreading, really, because there was nothing left to dread.

But a moment of stone. He was afflicted by those from time to time, he had noticed. A kind of paralysis that came over him without warning; it could catch him mid-step, or still sitting at the kitchen table, and render him incapable of moving from the spot. Incapable of thinking a single forward-moving thought.

The petrifaction of grief. It was the kindly therapist he had seen a couple of times who had been able to put a name to the condition.

Bereavement counsellor. What a hopeless profession, because he genuinely was a specialist in that affliction, he had admitted as much.

Or maybe it wasn't so hopeless? Maybe Åke Rönn really did manage to help one or two of his wretched patients? Little by little. Grieving always takes time, he had explained. It is a sluggishly flowing river, but it is still possible to travel along it in the right direction, and sooner or later you emerge into the sea. The current is feeble, you can't be in any hurry. You have no oars and there is no wind.

Gunnar had nodded, but made no comment. There were so many words. So many clichéd images. Well-meaning, but clichéd.

You've got to try to focus on the children, Eva Backman had told him when they were on the phone the night before.

I know, he had answered. That's what I am doing. Focusing on the children.

Do you want me to come over?

No, there's no need.

Are Jenny and Johan back from their dad's?

Yes, they got back this morning.

How are they?

All right, I think, considering.

And you?

Not so good.

Are you sleeping?

Not much.

Have you tried sleeping tablets? I know you're against them, but . . .

No.

Questions and answers. In the end he said he couldn't talk any more, cited some domestic chore that was waiting, and hung up.

Once this conversation, too, had left his head, Barbarotti took two deep breaths and climbed out of the car. It was raining as he cut across the car park to the main entrance, but it didn't bother him.

Time to start work. Time to face everyday life.

★

'Thank you.'

'What are you thanking me for?'

'For her. An axe woman. I wasn't expecting a welcome present.'

Eva Backman attempted an apologetic smile, but it wouldn't stick. 'I think it's one of those old cases playing on Asunander's mind. He's only got about six weeks to go. It was his idea, at any rate.'

'I get the point.'

'Eh? What point?'

'He doesn't think I'm really fit for work.'

She thought quickly. 'And *are* you fit for work?'

Barbarotti shrugged. 'I'm no worse than usual. As far as I can tell.'

'I liked what you said at the funeral.'

'Which bit?'

'About looking forward, yet still having her in a room inside you.'

'Saying it is one thing. Living it is another.'

'A guiding star surely can't do any harm?'

'No, you're right. It goes on hanging there, even when you're not looking at it.'

'What are we actually talking about here?'

'I don't know. Tell me about the axe woman instead. I still drink coffee, by the way.'

She got up to go and fetch some. Gunnar Barbarotti looked out at the rain.

'You didn't have anything to do with the investigation, either?'

He shook his head. 'No. It must have been while our letter-writing friend was keeping us busy. All I remember is something about a blue moped in a lake.'

'A bog,' Backman corrected him. 'But you're familiar with Ellen Bjarnebo, I assume? Or Helgesson, as she was at the time.'

Barbarotti nodded. 'When was it again?'

'In 1989. I was on maternity leave after I had Viktor.'

Gunnar Barbarotti contemplated his coffee cup with a frown. 'It was that year when I was redeployed. To a narcotics investigation in Eskilstuna, whatever the point of that was. I got back for Christmas, and by then she'd confessed. But we read about it in the papers, of course.'

'We certainly did,' said Backman. 'The Axe Woman of Little Burma. Hard to forget. I wonder how things are going on that farm nowadays?'

'Hmm,' said Barbarotti.

Eva Backman just sat there for a while, saying nothing. The rain came down harder.

'Do you want us to talk about Marianne?'

He shook his head. 'Not yet. Not in this building. But thanks for asking.'

'I don't want you to be all pig-headed and macho about it and keep everything bottled up inside.'

'I know you don't want me to. There's no need to remind me. Not too often, anyway.'

'OK,' said Eva Backman. 'I'll accept that for now.'

'Good,' said Barbarotti. 'Then let's turn our attention to the man on the blue moped. What happened?'

Eva Backman cleared her throat and launched into her recapitulation of the case.

'So she waited three whole days before she reported it, is that right?'

'She did indeed.'

'Why?'

25

'She thought he would turn up. Or that was what she claimed, at any rate. You'd better talk to Sorrysen, I think he was the one who interviewed her. Once or twice anyway, but it was mostly that Gunvaldsson who was the lead investigator. Remember him?'

Barbarotti nodded. 'Have you read the interview transcripts?'

'No. Only a summary. Asunander gave me the task of briefing you. I've only had two hours, lunchtime included.'

'Hmm,' said Barbarotti.

'And what does "Hmm" mean this time?'

'Not much,' said Barbarotti. 'Maybe that there seems very little point in what we're doing here. There seems very little point in most things now, mark you.'

'I can understand that,' said Backman. 'Anyway, I think we can conclude that Ellen Bjarnebo wasn't particularly happy about having to contact the police. Given her background.'

'Remind me, will you?' said Barbarotti. 'Was she the one who reported her husband missing in the Burma case? It took them a long time to find him, didn't it?'

'Two questions,' said Backman. 'But yes, she was the one who raised the alarm. And they started finding him after about two months, but I think it took a little while to complete him – as it were. A few days, but I could easily be remembering wrong.'

'Female murderers who butcher their victims?' said Barbarotti. 'They don't exactly grow on trees, do they?'

Backman grimaced. 'She worked at an abattoir in Gothenburg in her younger days. Developed quite a skill, evidently. And they kept beef cattle and pigs at Little Burma. Not when this happened, but earlier on.'

'That explains it,' said Barbarotti.

'Maybe,' said Backman.

'But they found no trace of the man on the blue moped?'

'Not so much as a foot,' said Backman.

'Were there any genuine suspicions that it was her the second time? Apart from her CV, obviously.'

'I don't really know,' said Backman. 'A couple of witnesses turned up, I think. Claiming to have seen a few odd things . . . an incident at a restaurant or something. But you'd better read it for yourself. Talk to those who worked on it, of course, and go through the interview transcripts.'

'Where is she now, Ellen Bjarnebo? If we're reopening the case, she should probably have her say, too.'

Eva Backman pushed a slip of paper across the desk.

'Number forty, Valdemar Kuskos gata,' read Barbarotti. 'Where's that? Who the heck is Valdemar Kusko, anyway?'

'It's in Rocksta,' Backman informed him. 'But I don't know who Kusko is. Or *was* – normally you have to die before they call a street after you.'

'Yes, you're right,' said Barbarotti. 'But that's where she lives, is it?'

'Yep,' Backman confirmed. 'All by herself and one hundred per cent alone, I'm given to understand.'

'Maybe she's had enough of men,' suggested Barbarotti.

'And they of her.'

'Best for all concerned,' said Barbarotti.

They sat in silence for a while, staring out at the rain, which gave no sign of either intensifying or easing. Backman tried to think of something to say, but couldn't come up with anything worthwhile.

'Thanks for the briefing,' said Barbarotti, picking up the files. 'I shall go and sit in my room and look through these. I presume the intention is for me to work on this on my own?'

'If I understood Asunander correctly,' said Backman.

'I've no doubt you did,' said Barbarotti.

He was just getting to his feet, but Backman put a hand on his arm.

'Wouldn't you like to come round to mine for dinner one evening? I don't want to force you, of course, but . . .'

'I'd have nothing against it,' said Barbarotti. 'But I've got at least four kids to look after. Give me a few days; I'm finding it difficult not being at home, for some reason.'

'OK,' said Eva Backman. 'It probably isn't to be wondered at. I'm here in the building, don't forget that.'

'Thanks,' said Gunnar Barbarotti, slinking out of the door.

5

He had not been unprepared.

Much could be cited and many wounds of grief were bleeding, but not that. It was a year and a half since Marianne had suffered her first aneurysm, and the time since then had been perforated with those thoughts. *She was a millimetre from death. It could happen again.*

He had thought it and he had dreamt it. Imagined it and tried to picture the worst: one day she would not be at his side. That possibility had been his shadowy and dogged companion, walking beside him these last eighteen months; once or twice he had woken from a dream and been convinced it had really happened. They had talked about it, several times and without any real fears. With a kind of accepting calm, which in retrospect he found hard to understand. Hard to find his way back to.

The only certain thing in life is that it will end one day. We are not made for eternity, not here on earth. Make the most of the days and the hours. A time will come – those are the terms.

No, he had not been unprepared.

And they had made the most of them, they really had. Standing close to death had sharpened their senses, honed their perceptions; however you looked at it, their last times had been their best.

And we shall wait for one another on the other shore.

Or the alternative, those stubbornly recurring lines of Larkin's:

The sure extinction that we travel to
And shall be lost in always.

It was meagre consolation, particularly Larkin of course, but he had known it would be. For that, too, he had been primed. For that, too, he had been prepared.

The children, she had said. If one of us is gone, the other has to pull them through.

She said it more than once.

They had five, but none of them together.

His own: Sara, Martin and Lars. Sara was twenty-four and had flown the nest. She was studying law and had been living in Stockholm since last winter. She'd had a new boyfriend for a while now, but Barbarotti still hadn't met him. He was possibly called Max. Or Maximilian.

The boys were seventeen and fifteen. They each had their own room up under the eaves of the rambling old house that had been the family home these past four years. He felt he was getting to know them better all the time. The years they had been in Helena's care were now past, years in which he had felt that they were slipping away from him. They had loved the new mother they had just lost, there was no doubt about it, but it had not hit them as hard as it had him. They were secure enough to keep their heads above water, or so he liked to think. They had school, friends and leisure activities. Handball and geocaching. There was something so healthy and uncomplicated about the two of them; he hoped it wasn't merely him making excuses and wearing blinkers.

Marianne's eldest, Johan, had turned twenty. He still lived at home, worked in an espresso bar in the centre of Kymlinge and knew more about coffee than anyone else Barbarotti had ever encountered. He would be going away to university in the autumn, to Lund, Uppsala or Linköping. Something media-related – Barbarotti hadn't really listened properly. Johan was the one he felt least close to.

Jenny was seventeen. When he found himself able to raise his eyes from his own grief, he saw that she was the one finding things hardest. She was emotional, torn up by the roots. She was possibly closer to him than any of the others; perhaps she was clinging to him so that she wouldn't have to move back to live with her real dad. The man had proposed as much at the funeral, and subsequently in a couple of phone calls, but Barbarotti couldn't judge whether he meant it seriously or was simply afflicted by a guilty conscience. Trying to compensate. Jenny and Johan had spent the weekend with this Tommy and his doll's-house family in Halmstad, but neither of them seemed keen to say anything about the visit.

One thing he *could* tell for certain was that Jenny wanted to carry on living at Villa Pickford. She didn't have much time for her actual father, and that comment about helping the children through had applied to her, above all. Jenny was also the only one he could sit and grieve with, late into the night.

Raw grieving – she was the one who came up with the term. *Come on, Gunnar, let's sit here and do some raw grieving for a while. Just you and me.*

Tea, a lighted candle. The house silent, or as silent as an eighty-year-old wooden house ever could be. A few words now and then. A few memories of Marianne. Tears and a bit of laughter as they sensed her listening from up there on her puff of cloud, telling them to buck up.

Yes, that sort of thing. They were moments of healing and it seemed rather strange that this was so.

On the way back from police HQ on this Day of Return, he stopped at the little ICA supermarket in Rocksta to lay in supplies. Lars and Martin had promised to cook a pasta recipe and they were a few ingredients short. It was only half past five by the time he emerged into the car park, and he decided he might as well locate Valdemar Kuskos gata. Seeing as he happened to be in Rocksta, where Ellen Bjarnebo lived these days, according to the paperwork.

His first assignment since Marianne's death.

The Axe Woman of Little Burma.

Was that how people still thought of her? Was that how she thought of herself?

More than twenty years had passed, but presumably it was not a title you could shed very lightly.

And Arnold Morinder. What had happened to him? Vanished after buying an evening paper at the petrol station in Kerranshede. Five years ago. That was the part of this tangle he ought to try to unravel first, of course. That was the case he had been told to investigate; what happened at Little Burma had been laid aside long ago. But putting a bit more meat on the bones, so to speak, before he found himself face-to-face with the axe woman presumably wouldn't hurt.

And he really did wonder why Asunander had tossed him this particular old bone to chew over, but on reflection he decided it would be as well to put it out of his mind.

To leave the question unasked. Words like 'faltering capability' and 'retraining' sprang all too readily to mind for him to want to engage at closer quarters. For now, surviving was enough. Surviving and, as previously underlined, getting the children through all this.

Yes, that was the main thing.

There was a map at the entrance to the housing area and he found Valdemar Kusko right away. It was one of the banana-shaped roads enclosing the whole development, with the forest to the east. He climbed back into the car and drove round there; number forty was the final staircase in a row of three-storey blocks, 1970s-style. They were red-brick, with inset balconies. He did not know which floor Ellen Bjarnebo lived on and was not intending to find out today. Today it was just a question of cautious soundings, a preliminary manoeuvre of no importance whatsoever.

He thought about Rocksta as he turned the car and started making his way back.

It had been a typical problem area for the first ten or fifteen years of its existence, but it had calmed down now. It was still top of the league in the Kymlinge crime statistics, of course, and there it would remain for the foreseeable future, but Barbarotti could not remember them ever being called out specifically to Valdemar Kuskos gata. No grievous bodily harm, no drinking binges that got out of hand, no domestic abuse, as it was termed.

But more than 5,000 people lived in Rocksta. More than fifty different nationalities were clustered together in this one district; it was a piece of Sweden that was a significant part of the country's demographic map at the start of the twenty-first century. He knew that at least three of his colleagues lived here; passing its little shopping precinct again, he wondered why the place made him feel like a fish out of water.

Spoilt? Perhaps.

On the other hand, it wasn't only Rocksta that felt alien. It was everything. The police station. Villa Pickford. The entire town, where he had lived for thirty-five years.

The people, the times, the thoughts.

In the washed-out evening light, his own hands on the steering wheel looked as if they came from another planet. I have got to start talking seriously to Our Lord, thought Inspector Barbarotti.

He had thought that before.

It was almost midnight by the time he got to bed. Meals tended to be quite long affairs, now Marianne was no longer among them. Though they seldom managed to express their sense of grief and loss in words, the very fact of sitting together, being gathered round the big oak table, was clearly important. For every single one of them; no one wanted to be the first to leave the circle; and perhaps there was even an element of torturing themselves, but he never asked. They no longer laid a place for her. Initially they did, setting out a plate, a glass and cutlery at her usual place, but after the funeral Jenny decided it was time to stop.

Afterwards they sat there in the window alcove for a little while, raw-grieving, he and Jenny, while the three boys disappeared into their rooms. But around eleven she gave him a hug, saying she had half an hour's maths homework to get done, and then he sat at the computer paying bills, until fatigue got the better of him and all the numbers and codes started to swim before his eyes.

Being tired was one thing, falling asleep was quite another. He remembered his resolution to start a conversation with Our Lord, but there was something blocking the way. It had been like that ever since catastrophe struck; he knew the problem lay with him, but also that God was a gentleman who had all the time in the world to wait. Perhaps it was surprising that he had not instantly thrown himself, his shock and despair into the hands of a benign higher power – particularly as he was now convinced of its existence, and he and Marianne had talked about it a lot. About putting things in other hands, trusting in them. Not bearing all those burdens alone.

But something else was missing, too. Something was in the way.

Perhaps he was waiting for a sign.

Waiting for Marianne to get in touch. She had sort of promised she would, but of course there was no way of knowing whether such promises could really be kept. And what the process would be, if so. What form the contact would take. The most natural way would probably have been for her to crop up in his dreams – or at least that's how he would have approached it, if the boot were on the other foot – but so far, a good three weeks after her death, she had not shown herself.

It might be, of course, because he routinely slept poorly and was extremely short of dreams. There were no pictures left in his head when he woke up in the mornings, so he couldn't be completely sure. Maybe she had been with him during the night, maybe he had just forgotten? It could be as simple as that.

It was a frightening thought, on top of all the general distress – that Marianne could be trying to reach him, but he remained oblivious to it – and he decided to give it no credence.

He resolved instead to be watchful, alert to every sound, and not to make unreasonable demands of either his dead wife or Our Lord. That would be a presumptuous tactic and there was no reason to.

After this delicate deliberation process, and while he waited for elusive sleep to put in an appearance, he started looking through the material on the Arnold Morinder case. He had read the summary at the police station that afternoon, but at some speed, and if Asunander really did want to test his capacity for work, it would be as well to take the bull by the horns and do it properly.

Arnold Morinder was born in 1953. At the time of his disappearance, therefore, he was fifty-four years old. Or nearly, anyway, and his life to that point had been a far from glamorous one. If DI Sorrysen's concise phrases were to be relied on, that was, and they undoubtedly were. Sorrysen was not prone to exaggeration, but in striving to be objective and correct, he seldom missed a detail.

Arnold was born in Kymlinge, the only child of Alfons and Anna Morinder. His father was a smith, his mother had various jobs in Kymlinge, predominantly as a cleaner, and they had died within two years of each other when Arnold was just past twenty. His parents had both been in their forties when he came into the world; there was no further information about them.

Arnold completed his nine years of statutory schooling in 1969 and then did two years at Samsö Upper Secondary to qualify as an electrician. He was employed by four different electrical firms in the course of his working life, three in Kymlinge or the surrounding area, plus one in Gothenburg in the 1990s. At the time of his disappearance he had been working for six years at Buttros Electrics, a local firm with a decent reputation, based out on the Gripen industrial estate and employing ten to fifteen people, depending on how business was going.

In March 1983 Arnold Morinder married a woman named Laura Westerbrook; they had no children and filed for divorce just eighteen months later. Between leaving his parental home and moving in with the former axe woman, Morinder lived in a small flat on Norra Kyrkogatan. He and his first wife also lived at that address for the short time they were married. While he was working in Gothenburg – from 1989 to 1996 – he had sublet the flat.

Then back to Kyrkogatan and ten years later, a move to 40 Valdemar Kuskos gata.

So she *did* hang on to the flat, thought Gunnar Barbarotti, wondering what this might indicate. Probably nothing at all.

Laura Westerbrook? Whoever she was, she must be of non-Swedish stock. British maybe, or American. He made a note to look her up.

The summer place out by Lake Kymmen, from which Arnold subsequently vanished, had been acquired by his parents back in the 1950s and was always referred to, even by Ellen Bjarnebo, as *Fisherman's Cottage*. Fishing was Morinder's only known leisure interest and in his case, according to the report, it consisted of taking a battered flat-bottomed rowing boat out onto Lake Kymmen and trying to catch perch or pike with a casting rod, or even a simple hook and line – the latter for preference.

Exactly how Ellen Bjarnebo and Arnold Morinder met was not described in any detail in Sorrysen's presentation, beyond the fact that they happened across one another in a pub in town and started talking. Sorrysen's account indicated that the former axe woman had not been particularly forthcoming on the topic. She and Arnold had started seeing each other and a year later they had moved in together, that was the long and the short of it. They lived in a free country, didn't they?

Barbarotti sighed and turned the page.

Information about the day Morinder went missing was almost as sparse. Good weather had brought the couple to Fisherman's Cottage for the weekend, both of them still with a week of their holiday left – and at around one o'clock on Sunday afternoon Morinder had taken the moped, the old blue Zündapp, headed off to the petrol station in Kerranshede about three kilometres west along the 272, filled up and bought an evening paper. He had left the petrol station just before one-thirty, never to be seen again. According to the girl on the till, he had behaved as normal, not been particularly talk-ative, but she seemed to recall they had agreed they'd been having an unusually nice spell of weather lately. She recognized both Morinder and his moped; he was a sporadic but loyal customer in the summertime. Things had been that way ever since she first started work at the petrol station at the end of the 1990s.

Ellen Bjarnebo called the police three days later, on Wednesday 8 August, to report her partner missing. About a week later the blue moped was found in the aforementioned mosquito-ridden bog, some five kilometres west of Kerranshede and eight kilometres from Fisherman's Cottage, and that was where the trail went cold.

That was basically it. They had interviewed Ellen Bjarnebo, and a dozen or so other people had provided information, but that transcript was filed separately, and DI Barbarotti decided that enough was enough.

He switched off the light, turned on one side and stretched out his arms to the empty space beside him in the bed. He so longed to convince himself there was still an impression there, still something left, and what is the world, after all, but our conception of it?

6

2 June 1989

Drive straight past! Don't stop at Burmavägen!

For almost as long as she could remember, she had had the voice. Perhaps other people had one, too; she didn't know, she so rarely interacted with anyone else. There were six other passengers on the bus with her; she recognized four of them, three elderly men and a teenage girl, but she had never so much as said hello to any of them. She thought how typical it was; here they were, with metres of space between them, as if solitude was something fragile, something to nurture and cherish.

Drive straight past?

Over the years she had increasingly come to identify it as a real voice – a voice she had heard once, long ago, yes, that was it: Mutti, the caretaker. He was a terrifying figure at Hallinge school, where she was a pupil for her first three years in education, and was seemingly the only child in the whole town who wasn't petrified of him. Which was strange, really, because she was generally known for being scared of most things. Scared and different.

Mutti was different, too, but in another way: people called him a cross between a cobra and Adolf Hitler, and said he had at least a dozen dead children on his conscience.

But that wasn't true, of course. When she met Mutti face-to-face, that one time in his office, he had a single sentence of advice for her: *Go and tell Miss Bolling what Annika Bengtsson really had to do with your bike disappearing.* And once she did so, everything resolved itself for the better, exactly as he had promised. No, not promised, because he hadn't done that, but exactly as she had understood from his voice that it would.

A quarter of a century later, she had forgotten what the bike incident was actually about, but she had not forgotten the voice. It was a most peculiar thing, but it grew more and more distinct with every passing year.

Don't stop at Burmavägen?

Nor had she forgotten the fact that she was different, but then her father had made sure to impress it on her, long before Mutti came into the frame: That girl's got a screw loose, there's no doubt about it.

But then her mother was the same, he generally added. It's passed down the female line from generation to generation.

She sighed and glanced out of the grimy window of the bus. She saw that they still had some distance to cover – it would be at least seven or eight minutes. Time enough for a quick plunge into the muddy waters of memory. Whether she wanted to or not.

She had never understood that last bit as a child. Down the female line from generation to generation? What did that mean? She had grown up with her dad and her brother Gunder, six years older than she was. Her mother had drowned when she was only four. An accident, people said. Later she had come to understand that this was not the case. It was the voice inside her that had said so, and when she thought about it later in life, she was pretty sure that was the first time she heard it. Or the first time she associated it with Mutti, at any rate, because it must have been shortly after her encounter with him.

Your mum killed herself, just so you know.

It was one evening, when she was trying to get to sleep. She must have been eight or nine. And sleep had not come readily.

Just so you know?

The next day, when she asked her father about it, he would not answer, but she could see from the way he looked that it was true. Her mother had no wish to live any longer and she had put her wish into action.

A screw loose – that was the phrase, wasn't it? She had never discussed it with her brother Gunder. But then Gunder always thought the same as Father, so it would have made no difference.

She had never been afraid of the voice, because it was exactly like with Mutti; there was nothing frightening about it. Not really; it was always dry and matter-of-fact, rather like a public-service announcement on the radio. And it was rarely wrong, interpreting the situation precisely as it stood and making a single statement, plainly and clearly. The message was seldom hard to understand. Sometimes it was a piece of advice, but not always, and when that happened, it never felt like a demand that she was obliged to obey.

She was also aware of the voice being distinct from her normal thoughts, completely unmistakable. It was sparing in its visits, too; when it spoke today, on this early June evening, she recalled how long it was since she had last heard it. A couple of months at least, earlier in the spring, perhaps even longer ago than that.

What was perhaps a little strange about it was that it seemed to be addressing the driver, at the wheel of his bus. A big, burly chap with a back like a barn wall.

And it said: *Drive straight past! Don't stop at Burmavägen today. Let her sit here and rest a bit longer instead.*

Her? Yes, it really did sound as if it was speaking to the driver – but out of concern for her. She was the one who mattered: Ellen Beatrice Helgesson, née Bjarnebo. Thirty-five years old.

In the middle of life, but already lost.

It didn't take an inner voice to bring that home. Fifteen years of marriage to Harry Helgesson had taught her well enough. And the time of expectations was long gone. If life had any sort of flowering, it was a stage that she had personally now passed. Or even skipped entirely.

But now this *Don't stop!* It might as well have urged her not to get off, or not to press the Stop button, but it didn't. It transferred the responsibility to the bus driver in some way. The question was: why?

She blinked wearily a few times, realizing her eyelids were drooping. Which would have been one solution in fact. You could guarantee that Ellen Helgesson would be the only one to get off at the Burmavägen stop. No one else would alert the driver to stop, if she happened to have dozed off. What was more, he was new; she hadn't seen him before and he would certainly have no idea where the various passengers lived.

She looked at her watch. It was just before five-thirty. It should have been shortly before four-thirty instead, but she had missed the bus. The shopping had taken longer than she had expected, both in the off-licence and at the ICA supermarket, and that meant she wouldn't have dinner ready until getting on for half past seven. She could assume Harry would be hungry and petulant. Irritable and out of sorts, that was guaranteed. He would get through three or four beers before the meal and that wouldn't help. The evening lay mapped out before her like a hopeless sheepfold into which she would be herded; over dinner they would share one of the bottles of wine she had bought, four glasses for him and one for her. After the meal she would clear away and wash up; Billy would be sent to bed around nine, or at least to his room; husband and wife would watch TV to an accompaniment of cigarettes, cheesy snacks and another bottle of wine, or maybe a couple of beers and a whisky and soda – she had bought everything on her list at the off-licence – and maybe Creedence Clearwater Revival instead of the television. There were variations, depending on his mood and the atmosphere and what had happened during the day. His hand would eventually start groping its way up her thigh and then it would be time for the Friday fuck. There was no variation to that.

Drive straight past! Don't stop at Burmavägen!

There were only a couple of hundred metres to go now. She raised her hand and pressed the button.

7

Gunnar Barbarotti spent the whole of Wednesday holed up in his room on the third floor of Kymlinge police station. Eva Backman stuck her head round the door just before lunchtime to ask if he wanted to come to the King's Grill, but he said he'd brought his lunch in with him and declined the invitation.

He hadn't brought a proper lunch to heat in the microwave, only a sandwich and a banana, but that was plenty. If there were two things in the world that didn't go together, it was bereavement and appetite.

But before he got as far as his cheerless lunch, he read through all the material and briefed himself fully on the case. Or he tried to convince himself that was what he was doing. He was plugged into his iPod and had fado music in his ears, and it was hard to shake off the feeling that it was more of an occupational-therapy session than anything else. Of course he could go in to Asunander in a week or ten days' time and say that he hadn't found anything to bring the puzzle of Arnold Morinder's death any closer to a solution – and Asunander would simply shrug and say, Ah well, in that case the matter is closed and we shall turn our attention to other things.

Wouldn't he? You never really knew where you were with Asunander. If he asked someone – anyone – to take a closer look at a case when he only had a month left to retirement, there could be something else behind it. Perhaps he was genu-inely expecting Barbarotti to come up with something? Find some detail or another that would allow them to make progress.

Solve the case even? Perhaps there was some kind of pres-tige at stake here? A personal interest on Asunander's part?

Hard to tell. There was nothing in the documentation to indicate more than peripheral involvement on his part. The lead investigator was called Gunvaldsson and he had only made a relatively brief guest appearance in Kymlinge. He would have to be contacted, of course, but it would be better to give it a few days – wait until Barbarotti knew more about the matter himself.

But what about Asunander? Were there any hidden twists and turns in this business? He couldn't rule it out. The chief inspector had always been a rum customer. And when it came down to it, there was no reason to do a bad job just because you had suffered a personal tragedy.

Once that constellation of words had gone through his mind – personal tragedy – he found himself paralysed again. He just sat there, staring out of the window. Incapable of going any further, in thought or in physical action. The sky outside was lowering and restless and the wind tugged at the newly unfurled birch leaves. He had changed rooms six months ago and had a new view. More open space and sky, designed for reflecting one's soul, you might have thought, but today there were no such ways in for him. The reflection of his soul was as it was. The fado music changed track, from Lucília do Carmo to Fernando Mourinho.

Will I ever be happy again? he thought. Will I ever feel expectation or desire? And what for, if so?

This is the phase when you need to focus on getting through one day at a time, Rönn had instructed him. The bereavement counsellor. Don't look forward, not more than a few hours. Your heart is still bleeding copiously, but with time you'll reach another state.

Will I? Barbarotti had wondered, though he said nothing. What sort of state is that? And how do you know, incidentally? Have you got a wife who's just died, eh? A woman you loved above everything else on earth and who's left you all alone and abandoned, though she was only forty-seven? Have you in fact got the first idea what you're talking about?

Feel free to be angry with me, Rönn had invited him. It can be a healthy part of the healing process.

Christ almighty, Barbarotti had thought.

But today, behind his desk, there was no anger to grasp hold of. Just rigid despair and hopelessness. He turned off the music, clasped his hands and started to pray.

Dear God, I'm sorry I haven't been in touch, but things have been so hard. You know that as well as I do. But give me a sign now – I can't bear this any longer. A straw to clutch at, a few words from the Bible, anything. This is my darkest hour; I simply don't know if I can live without Marianne. I don't know if I have the strength. Where is she? Are You looking after her?

Then he closed his eyes and strained his inner sense of hearing.

Initially, for the first fifteen or twenty seconds, he detected nothing. Then there was a discreet clearing of the throat, and then the familiar voice, the proper one, the one that was not his own.

Hebrews 11:32–40, perhaps that could offer some guidance?

Inspector Barbarotti unclasped his hands, opened his eyes onto the still-restless sky and gave thanks. He didn't keep a copy of the Bible in his office, but he made a note of the reference on his pad. He tore out that page and slipped it into his wallet.

Then he leant forward to his desk, returned to the Portuguese blues and reapplied himself to the Arnold Morinder files. The acquaintances of the missing electrician who had given their opinions of his character were pretty unanimous.

Morinder was – or possibly had been – the shy and retiring type.

The woman who had been his wife for a very short period in the 1980s – Laura Westerbrook – had had nothing to say about the marriage other than that it had been a mistake from the word go. She was from England, born and bred in Birmingham, and had come to Sweden because she felt drawn to living in a country where someone like Ingmar Bergman had made his name – and was still working. She had interpreted Morinder's sullen diffidence as profound thought and existential melancholy, but soon discovered he was a much simpler soul than that. They parted as easily as a skilled chef separates the yolk of an egg from the white.

And Morinder was not the yolk.

Those were the exact words recorded in the interview report, and Barbarotti was aware that the slight pulling sensation he could feel in his cheeks was the start of a smile. It was over in fractions of a second, but it was the first time since 29 April.

That was something, he supposed.

It was abundantly clear from other statements that Arnold Morinder was not of a sociable disposition, and the question of how he and Ellen Bjarnebo had formed a relationship remained unanswered across the hundred pages or more that Barbarotti ploughed through on that oppressively grey day.

They had met at the pub, or to be more precise at Brasserie Långe Jan on Heimdalsgatan one evening in September 2005, but that was simply a location and a point in time, and derived from Ellen Bjarnebo's own statement. It was, incidentally, the same restaurant where the alleged altercation had taken place, just a few months before Morinder's disappearance. There were three statements from witnesses of that little incident, one of them a waiter, and the other two customers who were there the same evening. No one could say exactly what it had been about, but voices had been raised, Morinder had violently thumped the table with his clenched fist, and his companion had marched out of the door with a furious look on her face. One of the two diners also claimed that she had muttered through clenched teeth, 'An eye for an eye, a tooth for a tooth!' This was categorically denied by Ellen Bjarnebo; she did, however, admit that she and her partner had had a difference of opinion, the details of which she refused to divulge. But she solemnly swore it had nothing to do with his disappearance.

The couple seemed to have had no friends or acquaintances, so there was no one to provide any insight into their relationship. Their neighbours on Valdemar Kuskos gata described them as quiet people who never bothered anybody. They would say hello if they saw you in the laundry room or bumped into you in the street or at the shops, but that was as far as it went.

They knew who she was. Of course they did. The Axe Woman of Little Burma. It didn't make anyone particularly keen to form a closer acquaintance, not that they were prejudiced or prey to preconceived ideas. Absolutely not, God forbid.

The forensic reports from Fisherman's Cottage, the blue

moped and the mosquito-infested Stora Svartkärret ran to twenty pages and had about as much real content as an interview with an emotional Swedish sports star. Barbarotti had no idea why that particular analogy should pop into his head, but it did. Perhaps it had something to do with the white and yolk of the egg, and that was the moment at which DI Backman put her head round his door and was rebuffed. After his lunchtime banana, he sneaked along the corridor to fetch a cup of coffee. He got back to his room without seeing a single colleague and plugged his ears with some more fado, but instantly regretted it and turned it off. He stowed his iPod in his right-hand desk drawer and extracted the material on the Little Burma murder from the left-hand one.

It would be just as well to read up on that case, too, he thought. Especially as he would shortly be encountering the protagonist herself. He was not looking forward to the meeting; he disliked meeting anyone at all at the moment, apart from his children, but if you had been told to investigate the deeds and misdeeds of an axe woman, he presumed you would inevitably have to meet her. Sooner or later.

What with her still being very much in the land of the living and as fit as a fiddle. Or whatever.

Postponing the encounter in order to do a little preparation was no more than good practice, surely?

He was some way into the report of the court proceedings when his mobile rang. He saw that it was Sara and he was surprised to find himself hesitating for a second before he answered.

'Dad?'

'Yes, it's me. Hello, Sara.'

'Hello. How's it going?'

'OK, thanks.'

'Be honest.'

'Not great. How are things in Stockholm?'

'It's raining. I'm busy revising.'

'Have you been to a lecture?'

'Yes. How are you, Dad, really?'

'I don't know what to say.'

'What are you doing at the moment?'

'I'm back at work. Sitting in my room at the police station.'

'Good. It's good that you're back at work.'

'Yes, they tell me so.'

'They?'

'Yes . . .'

'Are you sleeping all right?'

It was only five days since they had last seen each other. They had spoken on the phone the day before yesterday. Whatever else that meant, it definitely meant that she was worried about him.

'No, I'm not sleeping much. But I'll get through this, Sara.'

'Have you seen that counsellor again at all?'

'I'm seeing him on Thursday.'

There was silence on the line for a few moments. He could almost hear her searching for the words.

'I had an idea . . .'

'Yes?'

'I want you to come up here for a few days. Just you on your own – one weekend maybe?'

'I don't know . . .'

'It would do you good.'

'I have to think of the kids.'

She sighed. 'They'll be fine, Dad. They're almost grown-up.

You're the one who's been hit hardest, and I'd like to spend a weekend with you in Stockholm . . . We could go to the theatre. Or a film. Or just go for walks and have meals at some nice restaurants. Just the two of us. Talk . . . you know?'

'Yes, I know. It sounds good, Sara.'

'You mustn't just say it sounds good. We've got to make it happen, too. This coming weekend, what do you say to that?'

'It's a bit difficult this particular weekend. I've got to . . .'

'All right. Let's say the one after. That would suit me best, too, because my last exam will be out of the way by then. And we can come back to Kymlinge together afterwards.'

'I'll check whether that would work, Sara.'

'Promise?'

'All right. I promise.'

Silence for a few more seconds.

'They're not little children, you know, Dad. They need you, but not in that way. Not all the time, every day.'

'I know, I get it. Well, let's be in touch in a few days' time and we'll see.'

'Of course. And, Dad, you know you can ring me any time you want?'

'I'll remember that.'

'Good. So I'll hear from you as soon as you know when you're coming. Tomorrow at the latest.'

'Yes. Thanks for ringing, Sara.'

'I love you, Dad. You can sleep on my sofa, of course.'

'I love you, too. Good luck with your revision.'

Then they hung up. He was vividly aware of conflicting feelings of light and dark running riot inside him. Or perhaps rather a little streak of light trying to make its way through all the darkness. A few drops of milk in black, black coffee . . . what did they call that? Macchiato?

He drained his own cooling and milk-free coffee. Before getting back to Little Burma, he thought about Sara for a while.

She was an adult. There was no question of treating a twenty-four-year-old as anything else. She was also the one among the children who had had least contact with Marianne – because she had more or less moved out when Villa Pickford became a reality. She had lived with the family off and on for a few months at the start, to be sure, and after she broke up with her first real boyfriend, Jorge. But in more recent years, since her move up to Stockholm, she had been standing on her own two feet.

What an idiotic expression, he thought. *Standing on your own two feet.* What does that mean? Is it what I'm in the process of learning now? Learning the pain and accepting the fundamental terms? That we are born alone and die alone? On two feet.

He thought, too, about how he loved Sara more than any of the other children, if such comparisons were allowed. She had chosen to come and live with him after he and Helena got divorced; when she was growing up, virtually every single day, they had been near one another, and that left its mark. A benign and lifelong mark. But with the boys, he had been separated from them – apart from in the school summer break and on some of the big public holidays – for more than five years, and that left a different sort of mark. Maybe he had let them down; it was a recurring worry to him. He ought not to have relied on Helena being a good mother to them, but how could he know? He sometimes got the feeling, however – and especially after Marianne's first aneurysm – that Jenny was a kind of reprise of Sara. It wasn't something he ever said out loud, absolutely not, but he had found himself occasionally experiencing that familiar warming of the heart as they sat there talking about one thing and another. A plucked string with a unique and distinct note. And the fact that they felt able to give way to their raw grief together spoke volumes.

But a weekend in Stockholm? Just him and Sara? Why not?

He decided to give the idea serious thought and then re-immersed himself in his work.

In actual fact DI Backman stuck her head round DI Barbarotti's door twice on that slow-moving Wednesday. The second time, at about 3.15, he was oblivious to the visit because he was slumped back in his desk chair, fast asleep with his mouth wide open. His head on one side and a thin trickle of saliva running down his cheek and chin. Eva Backman gently closed the door again, knowing that was precisely what he needed.

For the moment, at any rate. What he might require in the longer term and on another level remained far from clear to her.

As did the role she would play herself. What was to be done? How could you look after a man like Barbarotti? She was sure there was no human being on the planet who knew him better than she did – now that Marianne was gone. They had been colleagues and good friends for twenty years, and she had been close to Marianne as well, so if Barbarotti was now drowning in sorrow, it could reasonably be seen as Backman's responsibility to pull him out.

I could do with a good sleep in *my* desk chair, too, thought

Eva, returning to her room where a slew of political speculations lay waiting for her. Or a nice little nap, at any rate.

The opportunity did not present itself, of course. It was just work, work and more work – until she noticed it was a quarter to six and high time to pull down the shutters.

8

It took Barbarotti until Thursday to make contact with Ellen Bjarnebo. She was at a small mountain guest house near Vilhelmina and the mobile-phone reception up there was pretty poor. He didn't ask what took her so far north and tried to conceal his reason for ringing, but he was naturally obliged to tell her he was from the Kymlinge police. Ellen Bjarnebo received the information with a simple, 'Ah, I see,' and said she would be back in Kymlinge the following week. Barbarotti asked if it would be all right to call her again then, but before she had time to answer they were cut off. Possibly she ended the call, and he understood her completely if that was the case.

He had four other people on his little list, and he made slightly better headway with those. But only slightly.

His conversation with Laura Westerbrook took five minutes. She was English by birth, but was still living in Sweden, now in Slite on the island of Gotland, and was married with three children. She worked part-time at a school and had very little to say about her misguided marriage to Morinder. She had only been twenty-four when they divorced and she described the whole thing as a youthful indiscretion. If Barbarotti was interested in digging around in such pointless history, he was naturally warmly welcome to come to Slite.

Yes, she had replied to a number of questions at the time of Morinder's disappearance, and she had nothing new to add on the subject now. She was certain of that; time passes and memory fades.

Barbarotti thanked her and rang off. His mind went for a moment to the house Marianne and her sister owned in Hogrän on the same magical island, but he pushed the thought away. He put in a call to Alfons Söderberg instead.

From the sound of him, Alfons Söderberg had been a smoker all his life. He was now retired, having owned and run the company Söderberg's Electrical for more than thirty years. One of his employees – for ten years, until they fell out – was Arnold Morinder. From 1975 to 1985, to put it in round numbers. Arnold Söderberg had also been what might charitably be described as Morinder's friend. For at least part of that period, anyway. He had, for example, been among the wedding guests when Morinder married that thin but rather attractive English girl, and he was one of the few people who had ever set foot – and even spent the night – in Fisherman's Cottage.

These were facts that Barbarotti already knew, and he listened to them again between the wheezy breaths and fits of coughing. And gobs of spit – it actually sounded as though Söderberg had a spittoon beside him. Barbarotti decided it might be worth taking a closer look at various things and arranged a visit for Friday morning. Since what he termed his fall from grace – June 2001, when he got divorced from his wife, a real harridan, now dead and buried – Söderberg had been a resident of Fabriksgatan in central Kymlinge.

The other two names on Barbarotti's list were linked not to Arnold Morinder but to Ellen Bjarnebo. The first was a woman called Lisbeth Mattson. Once upon a time she had shared the name of Bjarnebo, because she was married to Ellen's brother Gunder, six years her senior. At the time of the murder trial in 1989 they had both changed their names to Mattson, Lisbeth's maiden name. They had also taken pity on Billy Helgesson, who was only twelve at the time and very much needed to be in someone's official care, as his father had been butchered and his mother faced the prospect of at least ten years in Hinseberg prison.

Gunder and Lisbeth Mattson had no children of their own and they had stepped in without any fuss to look after Billy – the boy hadn't needed to change his name because Helgesson was not considered tainted, unlike Bjarnebo; for some reason the axe woman herself had reverted to her maiden name before the trial had even begun, so that was the name that had appeared in all the newspapers. Billy had shared a home with his new parents until 1999, when he was called up for military service and sent to Stockholm. Gunder Mattson had died about a year ago – a blood clot on the brain that ended his life in August 2011 – but Lisbeth was still living in the house on Kvarngatan in Hallsberg.

As for Billy Helgesson himself, he was the fifth and final person on the list and had an address, wife and child in the Södermalm district of Stockholm. When Barbarotti phoned it was Billy's wife who answered; she said he was at work but would be back that evening. Barbarotti thanked her for the information and said he would ring back.

His telephoning duties done, he took out a map and registered that Sweden, famously a long, narrow land, was not in fact all that narrow from one side to the other, either. He could speak to Söderberg and Ellen Bjarnebo in Kymlinge – hopefully tomorrow and next week respectively – but Hallsberg,

Stockholm and Slite would require longer journeys and probably overnight accommodation.

He scratched his head, thought for three seconds and crossed out Slite.

But if he timed his train departure from Gothenburg right, he could break his journey for a few hours in Hallsberg and then take another train to the royal capital. In said capital, he would find not only the Helgesson family in Blekingegatan in Söder, but also Sara. In Vikingagatan in the Vasastan district, to be exact, and that was what clinched it, without a doubt.

That's what I'll do, thought DI Barbarotti, closing his notepad. At the end of next week – if nothing unexpected comes up before then.

Genuine investigative work or occupational rehabilitation: that remained the question.

He checked the time. Ten past eleven. Thursday 24 May. The sun was beginning to break through the cloud in the sky outside his window.

Marianne! cried a voice inside him.

He guessed it must be his own.

9

'How's it going?'

The question was Backman's. They were having lunch at the King's Grill. Everything could have been just as usual, and he wondered what it really meant, that simple expression. *As usual.*

Was it something to aspire to or escape from?

That was an idiotic question. Of course. It depended on the circumstances and on what the usual actually comprised. It certainly wasn't anything to sit there brooding about and he could see that Eva Backman was regarding him with a worried frown. Was he losing control, was that what she could see?

'What? What did you say?'

'I asked how it was going. The Morinder case, that is.'

'Oh, I see. Well, I haven't really got very far. I'm seeing Söderberg tomorrow.'

'Who's Söderberg?'

'Somebody who knew him a bit. Well, I hope so, anyway.'

'And the axe woman?'

'At a guest house.'

'Guest house?'

'Yes. Up in Vilhelmina. She'll be back next week and then I'll be able to speak to her on the phone. How are you getting on with Fängström?'

'Poisoned,' said Eva Backman, cutting a meatball in half with her fork. 'It hasn't been confirmed yet, but everything points in that direction. What are you doing tonight?'

Barbarotti considered the matter. 'Making dinner. Seeing my therapist.'

'Is he any good? What's his name?'

'Rönn. His name's Rönn. Yes, he's pretty good. He's from Norrland.'

'Sounds reassuring.'

'Yes, he is . . . reassuring. I suppose that's what they're meant to be. So, he was poisoned?'

'Yes. We're working on that assumption.'

'Why haven't you had the results back yet?'

Eva Backman sighed. 'There was some mix-up at the lab. We've just got to wait.'

'But the suspicion remains that it was a criminal act?'

'For now.'

She hesitated for a moment. Then she rested her knife and fork on her plate and leant forward over the table. 'Why don't you want to talk to me, Gunnar? About Marianne, I mean.'

He offered no answer because he had none. She gave him a hard stare.

'We human beings do actually exist for each other,' she declared in a tone verging on the teacherly. 'I don't want to force you, of course, but I find it odd that you're so bloody buttoned up.'

'Buttoned up?'

'Yes. I know it's a male thing, and that you're going through a horribly hard time and everything, but even so . . .'

He stared for a while at his own meatballs and Eva Backman's.

'But we *have* talked. We've talked every day since she died, haven't we?'

She nodded. Took a deep breath and let her shoulders drop. 'Oh yes. Masses and masses of words. But maybe . . . ?'

'Yes?'

'What I mean is that I need to talk, too, Gunnar. It's hard for me, as well.'

'Mmm?'

'Marianne wasn't only yours. And you have to admit, don't you, that you're . . . you've deliberately avoided sitting down with me to talk about this? Why does it have to be so goddamned complicated? She was your wife, but she was my friend. I miss her too. Perhaps we could . . . be of some help to each other?'

'You don't need to tell me that. I'm not a complete idiot, Eva. Just give me a bit more time. I think—'

He broke off and knotted his brow in thought. Eva Backman leant her elbows on the table, clasped her hands and rested her chin on her knuckles. She said nothing.

'I don't think she likes to see us falling out over her.'

Eva Backman sighed. Or snorted. Perhaps there was a fleeting smile in the mix, too, and he felt that in that pitiful fraction of a moment he caught a glimpse of something.

Was it her?

Was that how it worked? Could it . . . ?

It surely couldn't be possible?

What sort of questions am I asking here? was his next thought. If I don't even understand the questions, how can I get anywhere near the answers?

'You're a long way away now, aren't you?' said Eva Backman.

'These meatballs are nothing to write home about,' said Gunnar Barbarotti.

'They're exactly the same as usual,' said Eva Backman.

Rönn had agreed to late-evening appointments, and as Barbarotti emerged into the street he saw that it was twenty past ten.

Over an hour then, as they had started on the dot of nine. He couldn't remember what they had talked about for the first half hour, but then Rönn had asked Barbarotti if he had any kind of faith. To be more precise, he had asked if he thought Marianne still existed in some way. Although it was their third session, they had not broached that topic before.

Which did seem – he thought in retrospect, as he walked through the gentle drizzle to Norra torg where he had parked the car – a little strange. Fancy there being so much scope for *general* conversation about death. On the other hand, death was an extremely general occurrence, undeniably, and maybe that was what this counselling aimed to achieve? To adapt to the client – no, rather, to adapt the client to the ubiquity – so naturally it had to be quite general to start with. But still?

Of course, he had replied. I have a faith and I believe Marianne still exists. The problem is, I haven't made contact with her yet.

And you count on being able to? Rönn wanted to know.

Well, I wouldn't exactly say count on, he answered. How do you stand on that yourself?

And Rönn responded with an *uh-huh, well yes, actually*, and Barbarotti wondered what the hell he meant. The whole believer thing was really all or nothing. But there were also diverse shades in between; like the Sami names for snow, or like feminism. Or like the many names for the Almighty, with only the camel knowing the hundredth and last: why not? Diverse and equivocal, anyway. A tangle of words and human meddling around with something that ought to be simple and clear.

Either you believed or you didn't.

Of course, he reiterated once Rönn had sat in silence for some time. She'll be in touch, I'm sure of it.

One has to be patient, was Rönn's advice on the matter, and then he had talked about the Norrland author Torgny Lindgren and the art of slowness. Lindgren had written that we should try to live at the same pace as the bearded lichen. Growing a millimetre or so per year. At most.

And then, finally, they did actually spend the last half hour talking about those things. Trust and hope and unnecessary haste, and Barbarotti found himself thinking that if he'd had a real father instead of a runaway Italian *papa*, he wouldn't have minded him being something like Rönn. Or an older brother, at least; he couldn't be much more than sixty.

Though it wasn't easy to say exactly what conclusions they had arrived at, and maybe it didn't matter. There was no need to nail everything down with proper words; there was valuable knowledge beyond language, too. Barbarotti climbed into his car on Norra torg, inserted another fado CD into the player and set off towards Kymmens udde.

He put his hand on the seat beside him and tried to imagine she was there.

And as he sat there like that, he heard her voice at last.

I've written you a letter, she said. *You'll get it in a few days' time.*

He was a hair's breadth from crashing into a lamp post.

10

2 June 1989

The moment she got off the bus she saw that her bike had a puncture. It was propped against the bus shelter, where she had left it that morning, and there was absolutely no doubt about it.

The back tyre. As flat as a pancake. A slow puncture, most likely, and she hadn't brought a pump with her. There were at least two at the farm, but that was a fat lot of use to her. There was nothing for it but to hook her bags over the handlebars and start walking; it was typical, in fact she had almost expected it, and she had no space inside her to fit any sense of surprise.

She jammed the bag from the off-licence into the basket on the parcel carrier. Six hundred metres of dirt track, a slight uphill slope, it wasn't the end of the world. Fine drizzle came blowing in across the fields, and that wasn't the end of the world, either.

Great Burma came first. The farm was in a beautiful elevated location on the left; it had a view out over the fields from the main farmhouse, over the long, wide valley that ran from south to north, stretching all the way from the main road to the forest beyond Little Burma. Their farm. Their home.

Little Burma was in a less attractive location. It had the

forest at its back, and there was nothing wrong with that, but its outlook was limited by the rise on which Great Burma stood. It left you in the shade, as it were. It was a more or less automatic thought – *the sunny side and the shady side* – and so appropriate for the situation generally, and for relations between the farms and between the cousins. Göran Helgesson was an only son and the sole heir to Great Burma; Harry Helgesson, the cousin four years his junior, was also an only son, and was likewise master of Little Burma. A freeholder and yeoman farmer, to be sure, but beyond that the contrast was glaring. Big Claus and Little Claus: she had heard people refer to them by those names more than once.

She could have gone up to the big farm and borrowed a pump, but she chose not to. It wouldn't have saved any time and she had no wish to see either Göran or Ingvor. Especially Göran, considering the agreement. No need to shine a light in dark corners. Better to leave them dark and undisturbed.

She didn't want to see the children, either. They were so annoyingly well behaved, all three of them. Clean, perfect and rosy. She made do with a quick glance up the well-raked gravel path to the flowering chestnuts and the arbour of lilacs, thinking how long it was since she had walked its challenging fifty metres. But that was how things stood now; there was nothing to do but suck it up. If things weren't right between the cousins, it followed that they weren't right between the cousins' families, either. Between the wives and children.

Envy or whatever. Bitterness.

She shrugged her shoulders at the familiar thoughts and carried on down the short slope between the cowshed and the machinery store, turning to cast a sideways glance at where building work was in progress behind the hedge; it was going to be a swimming pool, or so she had heard. Unusually the builders were still at work, even though it was six o'clock on a Friday evening. Two workmen's vans were parked beside the farm-vehicle store; presumably there was some detail that couldn't wait until after the weekend. Something that had to be isolated or covered before they could finish for the day. Yes, Göran knew how to handle people, she thought, when he wanted to. He could be persuasive when it was something really important, and it wasn't the first time the thought had occurred to her. To be honest.

Unless she cast herself in the role of a proud but defenceless woman, that was to say. Existence was an unyielding tangle of human needs and weaknesses, and her life was caught up in that tangle. She was trapped there, like some stupid blue-bottle in a spider's web, tensile and implacable.

Or something like that. If she forgot to close her eyes.

After the short downhill section the road climbed again and Little Burma came into view. It had such an unassuming look to it, and seemed almost to be cowering on the edge of the forest. As if it was ashamed of something; that thought was nothing new, either.

In fact she was suffering from a dire shortage of new ideas altogether. The same thoughts kept churning round and round until, for a couple of exhausted seconds, the inside of Ellen Helgesson's head went completely blank. Like a power cut or one of those mini strokes she had read about. Then her son popped up out of nowhere.

Billy.

Her Billy Boy. He would turn twelve in a fortnight, right on time for midsummer, as it were. That was the same as every other year, too, of course. Born at the high point of the year, and yet? She felt her chest tighten painfully, the moment he came into her mind. A sort of breathlessness. She swallowed hard and pushed away the thought of him.

I can't worry about Billy now. Can't let that anxiety bore its way right into me as well. The worst ingredient in the whole mess.

No, she didn't mean that. That really wasn't how it was.

She walked on.

As she covered the laborious last 200 metres she thought about what she had to offset it all: her job in town. Her breathing space.

She had been working for five years now; until Billy started school she had stayed at home. Not because she had wanted to, but because Harry had decided that was how it would be.

First she worked at the convenience store on Lilla Bergsgatan for a year, then in that leather shop, and since the autumn before last she had been on the checkout at Lindgren's hardware store. Five, six hours a day, four days a week. She had a day off on Wednesdays, or usually at any rate.

The 7.45 bus in the mornings, the same one as Billy took to school, so that was practical. The 3.30 or 4.30 bus back in the afternoon.

It wouldn't have worked if they had still had animals on the farm, but Harry had sold the whole stock when things reached crisis point, five years before. Now it was only Great Burma that had animals: cows and sheep. Plus two horses for Ingvor and the girl. And a couple of dozen hens, of course. Little Burma now concentrated on cereals. Various different crops, but mainly the traditional wheat. Things were as they were, and the crooked little cowshed to the right, on the forest margin, was unmistakably the building cowering the most in the driving rain. It had lost its justification for existing. If Little Burma was a cancer, then the cowshed was the site of the first tumour; it was a description that had occurred to her a couple of years ago and it became no less apt as time passed. It really didn't. *The heart of darkness.* What was that? A film she had never seen?

But back to Lindgren's. To be entirely honest she was not particularly happy at the hardware store. But she could put up with it, and that was all she asked. She needed no more than that; a breathing space was still a breathing space.

She could put up with the customers and with her colleagues, Mona, Gun and Torsten. Even if she didn't talk to any of them very much and couldn't claim she actually knew them. Nor they her.

And Lindgren himself, the boss with the wandering hands, well, there were ways of managing him, too. There was no serious intent in the straying hands; he was happily married with five children, and from the word go her two women colleagues had told her she should take no notice and he meant nothing by it. What was more, his wife Sofia helped out in the shop, too. Sometimes on Saturday mornings or at other times when there were a lot of customers.

So yes, work was her salvation; she had realized as much after only a few weeks at the convenience store, and the feeling had stayed with her. It was home where the bad things happened. The swamp in which she was slowly sinking and drowning. Home and weekends and holidays.

As she parked her useless bike in the rack and lifted the bags off the handlebars she felt again that her description was exactly right. A swamp of cancer in the heart of darkness. Where did all those images come from? All those disconsolate words? She quailed, there was no other way of putting it; she quailed at the prospect of a whole Friday evening. A whole Saturday and a whole Sunday at Little Burma.

With Harry and with Billy. Just the three of them. Just the family.

Yet again. Yet another interminable weekend.

And the fear. That wretched, constant, gnawing fear.

If I'd obeyed the Mutti voice, she thought. If I hadn't got off the bus. What would have happened then? *Drive straight past Burmavägen!*

She noticed Harry sitting in the dusky light on the veranda with a can of beer in his hand and a newly lit cigarette.

'You took your time,' he said.

11

Barbarotti parked outside Alfons Söderberg's address in Fabriksgatan and noted he was ten minutes early. He yawned, unfastened his safety belt and reclined the back of his seat as far as it would go.

I'm a robot, he thought. I sit or walk or lie down. Talk, eat, try to sleep and complete simple tasks. I work. I am a police officer. In a few minutes I shall go in through that hideous liver-coloured entrance, up two flights of stairs and ring at the door of a fellow human being called Alfons Söderberg, who may well have one or more spittoons in his two-roomed flat and whose asthma makes him wheeze like a bulldog. To be fair, I don't know if it's a two-roomed flat or not, but it makes no difference in the world. Nothing makes a single jot of difference in the world – that's all over now.

I shall sit at his kitchen table and drink coffee and question him about a certain Arnold Morinder, who went missing five years ago and with whom Söderberg was on friendly terms for a time, about twenty-five years before that, and it won't lead any bloody where. I'm not really working on a case; this robotic routine is nothing but therapy dreamt up by Asunander to keep me occupied so that I don't just droop around, thinking about my wife, who's died and left me in this black limbo where I . . . where I, very soon, from one day to the next, one minute to the next, will simply fall apart. That's how it is. The whole thing is completely pointless, life is a macabre joke; I am the incarnation of melancholia and might as well spare Söderberg the bother of seeing me. He can have his coffee on his own and munch his way through those dry almond cakes that he bought at the convenience store on the corner, and smoke his disgusting cigarettes and set himself on course for a premature death of his very own. He'll sit there wondering why that weird policeman never turned up, but after due consideration he'll decide not to ring Kymlinge police station and enquire. Morinder is missing, after all, very likely dead, and to show too much interest could look suspicious. Better to sit there and smoke, munch his way through the dry almond cakes and shut up. That policeman, incidentally, is coming to the end of his first week back at work since his wife died and left him in a state of panic and robotism and pointlessness – see, we're back there again, he's repeating himself, I'm repeating myself, my thoughts are going round in circles and extend no further than to the lowest common denominator, my mind is idling like a teenager's, but that's the inevitable way of things for superannuated robots and there's . . . there's really no need to get out of the car, enter through that liver-coloured portal, ascend those smelly stairs and ring at that damn door. No need at all; you can sit there at your miserable kitchen table, Alfons Söderberg, and spit into your spittoon and feel the days slipping away and death starting to breathe down your neck, ha-ha-ha, that's fucking well it.

This train of thought complete, Barbarotti got out of the car and cut across the street to number 16B.

★

Söderberg hadn't been out to buy almond cakes, but he asked whether the constable would like a beer.

The constable politely declined and they took a seat on either side of a coffee table with a computer and six chessboards on it.

'A hobby,' explained Söderberg and coughed. 'Keeps the brain active. I was a junior master once. Do you play?'

'No,' said Barbarotti. 'Not for a long time.'

'It was in Ljusdal,' said Söderberg.

'Excuse me?' said Barbarotti.

'That I became a junior master. But it wasn't yesterday.'

'I realize that,' said Barbarotti.

'Do you want a cigarette?'

'I've given up,' said Barbarotti.

'I'm thinking of doing the same,' said Söderberg. 'On the day I die.'

'Seems sensible,' said Barbarotti. 'To everything there is a season.'

Söderberg lit himself a cigarette and blew the smoke over the computer.

'I play via computer, but I need the boards to get an overview,' he said, indicating the various games with a sweep of his hand. 'Computers are all well and good, but they can't compete with reality. Three dimensions.'

Barbarotti wondered fleetingly how many dimensions his own reality currently contained. Not much more than one was the way it felt. Sloping downwards. He fumbled about in his jacket pockets and realized he had forgotten to bring his notebook.

'You looking for snus?' asked Söderberg.

'No,' said Barbarotti. 'I don't use snus, either.'

Söderberg took a drag on his cigarette and coughed. 'No beer. No fags. No snus. Hope you have a wife, at least.'

'Did have,' said Barbarotti. 'But she's dead.'

'Same here,' said Söderberg. 'Mine wasn't much to write home about, but it would only have been fair if she'd had a few more years.'

'You mentioned it yesterday,' said Barbarotti. 'On the phone.'

'Did I?' said Söderberg. 'Well, I talk a load of bullshit, as the vicar said. So why am I being honoured with a visit? You said something about Morinder, right?'

'Arnold Morinder, yes,' said Barbarotti. 'What can you tell me about him?'

'Why are you asking?' said Söderberg.

'There are a few loose ends,' said Barbarotti.

'Have you got a lead?'

'Not exactly,' said Barbarotti. 'We just want to check a few things.'

'So he hasn't turned up?'

'No. He hasn't turned up.'

'Aren't you going to take any notes?'

Barbarotti shook his head.

'Or record what I say?'

'It isn't necessary. Not at this stage, at any rate.'

'Oh. All right then,' said Alfons Söderberg and cleared his throat noisily. 'You know what, I've no bloody idea. Morinder was the way he was anyway, that's one thing for sure.'

'I read what you said about him five years ago,' Barbarotti told him.

'And what did I say then?'

'Don't you remember?'

'No.'

Barbarotti thought for a minute. Then he threw all the rules of interrogation overboard; this was only a waste of breath between two people who were a waste of space.

'You said he was introverted and shy and not that easy to get on with.'

'Did I? Yeah, well, that's about right. Pig-headed, too, if you want the full picture.'

'What do you think happened to him?' asked Barbarotti.

Söderberg took a drag, scratched his neck and looked thoughtful. 'I don't think anyone asked me that, last time.'

'Is that so?' said Barbarotti. 'Well, I'm asking you now. What do you think has happened to Arnold Morinder?'

'Dead,' said Söderberg. 'It's pretty damn obvious the bloke's dead.'

'How?' said Barbarotti.

'Eh?'

'How did he die, in your view?'

'It's not my bloody job to find that out,' said Söderberg. 'Is it you or me who's the policeman here?'

'Fair point,' said Barbarotti. 'But I only asked if you had an opinion. You don't need to justify it, and if you haven't got one, by all means say nothing.'

Söderberg smoked, coughed and took some time clearing his throat.

'It was her, I expect,' he eventually said.

'What do you mean?' asked Barbarotti.

'Her. The axe woman,' said Söderberg.

'Mmm?' said Barbarotti.

'I mean, she'd done it before. If you're stupid enough to take up with a woman like that, you've only got yourself to blame, right?'

'That's one view,' said Barbarotti. 'And was Morinder that stupid, the way you see it?'

Söderberg stubbed out his cigarette and thought about it.

'Well, I wouldn't say stupid exactly,' he said. 'I don't know. He was one of those types you can never get under the skin of. I didn't really keep company with him, either, but then nor did anyone else.'

'You stayed the night at his fishing hut,' said Barbarotti. 'You're pretty much the only one who ever did, as far as we know.'

'Except for the axe woman,' said Söderberg.

'Except for her, yes. But you were out there fishing, back in the eighties, weren't you?'

'Yes, I was,' said Söderberg. 'But only the once. Not a single bite, though we sat out there in that leaky old tub of his for hours. We had food and drink with us, too, and we got plastered. That was it. He was no more talkative when he was drunk. Most people are, but not Morinder.'

'I see,' said Barbarotti. 'What happened to end the friendship between the two of you?'

'Friendship?' said Söderberg.

'Call it what you like,' said Barbarotti.

'Hmm, well,' said Söderberg. 'He left the company and it petered out then, of course.'

'Why did he leave?'

Söderberg lit another cigarette and blew yet more smoke at his computer.

'It was an incident at one of the construction sites. He messed up and wouldn't take responsibility.'

Barbarotti waited.

'The bloody sauna burnt to the ground, and he was the one who did the wiring. It was as plain as a pikestaff.'

'But he denied it?'

'Lied through his teeth. So he had to go.'

'Did he make any trouble?'

'No. He just left. We gave him a couple of weeks' pay; he knew he was guilty, but he never conceded it.'

'Didn't you find that strange?'

'Yes, everybody did. But we knew he was odd.'

Barbarotti contemplated the smoky ceiling as he digested this.

'His wife?' he said. 'That Englishwoman. You were at the wedding, weren't you?'

Söderberg nodded. 'Yep. At the town-hall ceremony and at the meal afterwards. There were only about six of us.'

'Who were the others?'

'The bride and groom were there, if I remember rightly.'

Barbarotti gazed out of the window.

'There was some family member of his, too – a cousin or something. Big bloke with a protruding jaw, tongue-tied, I think his name was Bertil. And two female friends of the bride.'

'Not a big party then?'

'Not a big party,' said Söderberg. 'And I reckon it lasted about a year. She was a fair bit younger than him, and I got the impression she was regretting it by the time we were having the wedding breakfast. She was good-looking, too – way too good-looking for somebody like Morinder. A bit on the skinny side maybe . . .'

Barbarotti yawned.

'Jesus Christ. Am I boring you?'

'Sorry,' said Barbarotti. 'I didn't get much sleep last night.'

'You're not recording this, you're not taking notes, and

you're yawning your head off while I give you vital information. What kind of bloody useless cop are you?'

'I apologize. It's a bit stuffy in here, isn't it?'

'Stuffy?'

'Not a lot of oxygen,' clarified Barbarotti. 'That's what makes you yawn. When you haven't got enough oxygen in your bloodstream.'

Söderberg took another drag, inhaling deeply, and glared at him.

'Are there any more questions you want to ask me? I haven't got all day.'

'One more,' said Barbarotti. 'Ellen Bjarnebo, Morinder's partner, have you ever met her?'

'The axe woman?'

'Yes.'

'Only seen her,' said Söderberg. 'She lives in this town, so of course you see her now and then. She worked at the Post Office for a while, too.'

'Spoken to her?'

'Never,' said Söderberg. 'I take care not to.'

'Ah. Right then,' said Barbarotti, getting to his feet. 'Thanks for the chat.'

'You could let me know if you find him,' said Söderberg. 'Dead or alive, as they say. But you'd better give up yawning when you're interviewing people.'

'This wasn't an interview,' said Barbarotti. 'It was just a conversation.'

'You'd better stop the bloody yawning, even so.'

'All right,' said Barbarotti. 'I'll remember that.'

'Time you went,' said Söderberg. 'I've got to make a chess move within an hour. You can see yourself out?'

'Certainly,' said Barbarotti, shook Söderberg's hand and stifled another yawn.

Back in the car, he realized he was feeling tearful.

I want to hear your voice Marianne, he thought. There has to be a sign from you soon or I shall fall apart. You said yesterday that you'd written to me, or did I hear wrong? I'm on the verge of a breakdown here.

It wasn't easy to say exactly what form such a breakdown was likely to take, but it would come from below and from within, and that screen of normality and self-control and whatever was keeping a lid on everything felt dangerously flimsy. A spider's web trying to stop a buffalo, or something.

Or at any rate there were patches – certain situations – when for a few pale seconds at moments frozen in time that was exactly how it felt.

Like now, for example, after twenty-five minutes' conversation at 16B Fabriksgatan with a junior master in chess from Ljusdal. It was all bound up with what Rönn had called the petrifaction of grief; maybe it was simply a variant of that, because it was at those moments – or just before them – that it was hardest of all. When you couldn't even find the strength to give in and turn to stone. Water that couldn't bring itself to freeze, although the temperature had sunk several degrees below the zero mark. If he . . . it meant that if he didn't start the car and get under way within four or five seconds, it could very well be too late. Entirely too late and very sudden.

He started the car.

He put it into first gear.

He fastened his seat belt and pulled away.

I did it, he thought. What shall I do now? I'm at the wheel of my car, but where shall I go?

12

Instead of driving to the police station he headed out of town, turned left at the Rocksta roundabout and proceeded westwards on the 272. It was easier to be driving than sitting still, for some reason, and if he really was a working police officer now, it wasn't particularly hard to find a justifiable destination for a trip. It went without saying.

Fisherman's Cottage. It was just over twenty kilometres along the 272 from Kymlinge, along the tapering western arm of Lake Kymmen. It took him about twenty minutes to get there. He turned off along a narrow dirt road indicated by an old yellow sign: *Gertrudsholm*. After a hundred metres he caught sight of the lake between the pine trees; the road continued to curve left, but Morinder's place lay a short distance in the other direction. A bumpy forest track took him to a turning place in the middle of the trees, where he stopped. There was an abandoned pile of timber, and beside it a path that led down to a dark little building right at the edge of the lake. He saw it as soon as he got out of the car, and it had a distinct *Amityville Horror* look. That was the name of the old film, wasn't it?

He covered the remaining fifty metres of the path. It looked little used and there seemed no doubt that Fisherman's Cottage had now played out its historic role, whatever that had been. The hut was perhaps five metres by six and surrounded by a metre-high tangle of brushy shoots, but there was a little veranda looking out over the lake. The hut had a tin roof and the veranda was topped with a sheet of rigid plastic. No electricity, no water, by the looks of it. The hut's wooden panels had darkened and possibly started to rot under the assault from the wind and weather. Barbarotti picked his way round the hut and found sagging wooden shutters covering the three windows; there was nothing to indicate any human being had set foot there for several years. A tattered tarpaulin round the back covered a stack of wood in the same greyish-black hue as the hut. Two rusting, upended metal buckets and a pair of what had once been wellington boots. A plastic water container with holes chewed by mice. A privy, set slightly apart from the hut.

Perhaps no one had been here since August 2007. Or since the police lost interest in the case that autumn at any rate. Barbarotti made another circuit – in the other direction – and pondered. It was now almost five years since Morinder's disappearance, but he still hadn't been declared dead. If there were no compelling reasons to act otherwise, five years was the time generally allowed before the matter was raised again, and presumably there was no one in a hurry to inherit his estate. No one had requested that he be declared dead, so in official records he was still alive. Wasn't he? No children, no siblings; if there was any kind of heir at all, it must presumably be his partner.

And whatever things of value had he possessed, apart from this shack and a few bits of personal property in the housing co-operative flat in Rocksta – they could not be much to aspire to.

Such were DI Barbarotti's judgemental thoughts as he fought his way down to the lake through more coppiced shoots and over slippery tree roots. A rowing boat, rotted through, was pulled up between two alders; it was probably the very one Alfons Söderberg had gone fishing in, back in the early eighties. The shore was overgrown and barely accessible, and the bottom of the lake was in all likelihood muddy and uneven, but if you had tall wellies and the right spirit, it would be perfectly feasible to embark on a fishing trip from a place like this.

And five years ago it had presumably not been in quite such a state. But it was still hard to see how you could persuade a woman to come out here with you – Barbarotti continued the line of reasoning from which he knew his prejudices disqualified him. Nothing had emerged to indicate that Morinder had been a charmer of the opposite sex; what had made Ellen Bjarnebo fall for him? The only thing Barbarotti could find to recommend the place was that there didn't seem to be any neighbours. None that he could see or hear, anyway.

Which in its turn made this the ideal setting if you wanted to kill somebody. Chop him into several pieces and bury him, undisturbed.

And when it came to love and partners and suchlike, if you were a former axe woman you probably couldn't afford to be that choosy? You had to cut your coat according to your cloth, thought Barbarotti with a sigh.

He came to a stop with his hands in his trouser pockets and stared out across the smooth black water, lost in thought. It certainly didn't seem to have been much of an investigation that the Kymlinge police had mounted in those autumn months of 2007. It was the autumn in which he and Eva Backman had been so tied up with Mousterlin Man, an epistolary murderer and a case down in Brittany, and he most definitely hadn't had time to keep up with what his colleagues were doing. Moreover he had been suspended for a few days, but that was another story – and it was the autumn before the winter that he and Marianne moved in together.

But such thoughts served no useful purpose in these dismal surroundings beside a black lake, none at all; he picked up a small, flat stone from the ground and tried his hand at skimming instead. The stone cut straight through the surface of the water without a single bounce, and he dragged his thoughts back to the Morinder case.

Fusspot Månsson had been in charge of the preliminary investigation, of course, and the casework initially fell on Sorrysen's shoulders, but he too was soon caught up in the Brittany affair and responsibility passed to DI Gunvaldsson.

He remembered Gunvaldsson, though he had not retained any particularly distinct impressions of him. A tall, bulky, genial chap from Gävle. In Gävle, however, his wife left him in rather sensational circumstances. He put in for a transfer and ended up in Kymlinge. If Barbarotti remembered rightly, he had arrived in May and left them in December. Barbarotti had never discovered what the sensational circumstances were, and he did not know where Gunvaldsson had gone afterwards – but Eva Backman had once described him as an extremely effective chief investigator as long as the train stayed on the track.

Barbarotti didn't know how well founded this interpretation was, but by the time he had been through all the documentation, he thought he could see Backman's point.

It was all about Ellen Bjarnebo. Full stop. If there was any criminal act at all behind the introverted electrician's disappearance, then there could be only one – repeat, one – suspected perpetrator: the woman he lived with, once and forever known as the Axe Woman of Little Burma. The cases were virtually identical, after all. On both occasions, the aforementioned axe woman had reported to the police that she hadn't seen her husband/partner for a number of days. In 1989 they began to find the missing man after a couple of months, and as soon as it became obvious that he had been murdered and butchered, she had confessed. Eighteen years later, they never found any body parts, and therefore she hadn't been obliged to confess.

That was Gunvaldsson's reasoning, and perhaps you couldn't hold it against him. If Morinder really had been bumped off, then of course the main line of enquiry must involve his partner. She was close to him and, just as that heavyweight criminologist on TV used to say, in nine out of ten cases of murder, someone close to the victim was responsible.

What was more, she was already in the swing, so to speak.

The trouble was, however, that the investigation ground to a halt. They never found a dead body, only a dead moped. There was no circumstantial evidence to point to anything, and Ellen Bjarnebo did not break down under interrogation and confess.

Barbarotti had read all the interview transcripts and it was pretty obvious what the tactic had been, the sole tactic: to keep on interrogating her, repeatedly, until she made a slip, inadvertently revealed something or – their preferred outcome – broke down and admitted she had done it again.

But this had not happened. In fact Ellen Bjarnebo withstood their onslaught with no apparent difficulty. Her answers, if you could deduce anything from them, revealed only that she remained calm and collected throughout. She told them what had happened, over and over again: the fact that Morinder had set off on his moped and had not returned, after which she had waited a couple of days and then contacted the police.

It was not a particularly complicated account to stick to, of course, especially not if it happened to be true. Barbarotti left the lakeside and started his trudge back to the car. He continued to brood on why the devil Asunander had assigned him to this case, and once again reached the conclusion that it must be occupational therapy. Something to keep him busy and stop him doing any damage.

Or could it conceivably be something else? Something more? Asunander was a wily old fox on the verge of retirement and his inscrutability had not diminished with age. It was high time to talk to him about it, at any rate. Make it next week. Ask him what on earth the point was, and hope for some kind of honest answer. Then spell out that he was ready for real work.

Assuming that he was.

Or was it the old Burma case that really interested the chief inspector?

Barbarotti had all that case material on his desk, too, but hadn't yet made a thorough study of it. It was not as voluminous as one might have expected – but Ellen Helgesson-Bjarnebo had confessed straight away, so no protracted police work had been called for.

And the trial had been a formality, even though her barrister had gone through the motions of citing a number of extenuating circumstances.

And that was it, concluded Barbarotti, casting a final glance over his shoulder at the abandoned shack. You're in a sorry state, he thought. Somebody ought to make it their business to burn you down.

It was 1.30 p.m. by the time he was back on the 272; he remembered that it was Friday afternoon and that a weekend with the children stretched ahead. A family without a mother. A band of people that had lost its anchor. His tearful feeling returned, threatening to blanket him in its soggy embrace, and it was probably as an antidote to this bottomless despair that he decided to drop into the police station to pick up the Burma files. It couldn't hurt, in any event. The work of grieving? That wasn't how the term was normally understood – working instead of grieving – but he would grasp at anything to take his mind off the pain.

Robot life.

And it was just as he was formulating that sinister phrase in his head that he found himself passing another narrow road running down to the lake. The thought hadn't struck him on his way out – for some strange reason, because it should have – but now he saw it.

Axel Wallman.

His rootless old friend, his comrade from upper secondary. Steppenwolf, linguistic genius, dog owner and many other things besides. The dog was called Saarikoski, after the Finnish poet and polyglot, and ever since Wallman was thrown on the academic scrapheap and pensioned off early, the pair had inhabited another hut in the forest on the northern shores of Lake Kymmen. Or they had done the last time Barbarotti went to visit; when he came to think of it, five years had passed since then, too; in other words, it was the same summer, 2007, and naturally it was reasonable to wonder why he had simply stopped thinking about Axel Wallman altogether. For Wallman himself to take the initiative and get in touch would be unthinkable.

But as it had also been his first summer with Marianne, perhaps it wasn't that surprising and he could be forgiven. He'd had a heck of a lot on. People crop up and then fade away again.

Fade away? What kind of self-centred rubbish was that? He braked and pulled into a lay-by. Turned the car and drove back the way he had come. He took the rough track down to Wallman's den, very similar to the one he had just seen at Morinder's.

The track, that was. Wallman's cabin, fortunately, looked a bit more respectable than the fishing hut. Though not by much, Barbarotti noted once he was out of the car. A little larger certainly, but dilapidated, overgrown and without a trace of human life.

Axel Wallman did at least have a mailbox. A light-grey metal affair hanging lopsidedly on a pole, tied up with rope and bearing a laminated sign on the lid that said:

> *Arne! Gone away for a while.*
> *Please keep my post until you hear from me.*
> In fidem. *AW*

Arne? Must be the postman. One of those proper country posties you could develop a relationship of trust with, he assumed. The sort who could bend the Post Office's unaccommodating rules, if required. Barbarotti was about to get back into the car, his ill-defined mission unaccomplished, when his eye fell on the little name tag on the mailbox:

> *Wallman-Braun.*

Braun?

What did it signify? Could . . . ?

Barbarotti shook his head and registered a fleeting inward smile. Could Wallman have got together with a woman? It seemed an absurd idea, to put it mildly. The last time they met, Wallman had asserted that he was still a virgin, as single as a heavenly body, and that woman was a mystery he had long since given up any hope of solving. The figure he cut – his genius and his loud, opinionated way of expressing it, his habit of reading out long, impenetrable poems in his own translation or the original Old Bulgarian – together with the general griminess he chose to live in must surely . . . must surely constitute an insurmountable obstacle to any form of coupling, thought Barbarotti, starting the car. Wallman spoke twenty-one languages, it was true, but he was a crazy recluse.

So who was Braun? The question lingered in an obscure corner of his consciousness for the rest of Friday. As he fetched the Burma material from police HQ, in the course of his tender and tentative socializing with the children that evening – and as he lay there still sleepless after midnight, in the big bed where his wife had died and left him alone, almost a month before.

Wallman-Braun? A mystery.

13

Eva Backman woke at around seven-thirty on Saturday morning from a most unpleasant dream. She'd had a flaming row with her ex-husband, which had ended with the pair of them telling each other to go to hell.

As she rubbed the sleep out of her eyes and stumbled to the bathroom, she remembered it was no dream. It had actually happened. They had yelled down the phone at each other last night; just before she went to bed, to be precise, and she, for one, had furiously banished him to infernal regions. She was unsure whether he had reciprocated or not, but if he had held himself back, it was only because he had been brought up to be a coward and his new wife could hear.

She was called Blanche – the name alone spoke volumes – and was the most false and venal creature Eva Backman had ever run into. As tight-fisted as they come.

It was about the house again, the house in the Haga district of town where she had lived with Ville and their three sons for almost twenty years and where Ville now lived with Blanche and Kalle, the only one of the sons who wasn't yet old enough to leave. Plus Blanche's daughter, a cowed little girl of nine who went by the name of Ellinor.

Strictly speaking, it was about money and disputed obligations. Six months before, Eva Backman had released herself from the property, which she and Ville had owned jointly since their purchase of it in the late 1980s. Or she thought she had released herself, bought herself out, until Blanche started messing with things and finding hidden faults in need of attention: floors that would have to come up, rusted ventilation systems and Lord knows what else – correction work that should rightfully be paid for by both the former marital partners, as Blanche well-meaningly explained, with no hint of aggravation in her voice – because the faults had developed while the two of them were still joint owners of the place. That was the fact of the matter, and while of course they didn't want to cause Eva any bother or get into any kind of conflict, right was right and they were all adults, weren't they? A hundred and fifty thousand should cover it, and it was pretty easy to get loans at the moment, wasn't it? Don't let's fall out over this.

And more in that vein. The worst thing was that Blanche was so manipulative and smarmy. Superficially so polite, obliging and inoffensive – but boy, could she talk, and she put Backman in mind of a mamba slathered in high-factor sun protection. Yet Ville was so bloody dense that he fell for it.

And she turned the boys, or Kalle at any rate, against their own mother. As Eva Backman brushed her teeth, so hard that she made the gums bleed, she could feel herself coming to the boil. Again. Why, for Christ's sake, had Ville married such a stupid bitch? It somehow tainted her, too; this was her uncomfortable but accurate conclusion. If he had chosen to marry an airhead, then somehow his first wife must have been an airhead as well? Or was it as simple as the fact that Blanche was eleven years younger, used to be a dancer and had recently had a boob job? In that case it was Ville who was the airhead, but that still didn't help much with keeping the dark clouds at bay.

And how would it affect Kalle? Imagine if he took Blanche's side? Just to keep in with his father? How would the breakfast-table conversation go on a morning like this? It's old Mum, trying to cheat Dad and new Mum out of money? All wrapped up in layers of insidious psychological hogwash, not easy for an eighteen-year-old to see through?

I've got to stop thinking about it, concluded Eva Backman. I'll ring a solicitor on Monday.

With that decision taken, she put on her gear and went out for a run. She normally needed a light breakfast first, but adrenalin was presumably as good a fuel as anything else.

By noon she had returned from her run, taken a shower and made a terse call to her ex-husband to inform him that all future bullshit would have to come via her solicitor. Satisfied with that bit of straight talking – and with the fact that she restrained herself from answering when he called back – she prepared a generous breakfast tray, took the newspapers and went out to sit under the sunshade on her balcony.

The early phase of summer had arrived in earnest. The chestnut down in the garden was coming into flower, the lilacs were in full bloom and there was a general sense of the whole world being about seventeen again.

For her own part, she was forty-nine, and as her brain reminded her of that distinctly unwelcome fact she put aside the papers and turned her thoughts to the friend who had only reached forty-seven.

And to the friend's husband, whom she knew for sure to be fifty-one, but who seemed to have one foot in the grave himself.

What is it about us human beings? thought Eva Backman. We don't seem equipped for this world. We're forever falling apart – it's what we seem to devote our lives to.

Falling apart, falling out and failing to understand each other. Then we die.

Too early or too late.

Marianne's funeral was not the only one she had attended that year, although it still had more than half its course left to run. In January, Eva Backman's father had finally come to the end of his days and she really had been left wondering what his last two or three years had been worth to him. Until the autumn of 2009 he had lived with Eva's brother and sister-in-law at their smallholding outside Kymlinge, but the point came when the arrangement could no longer be sustained. His Alzheimer's worsened dramatically, he was moved to the Herta clinic out in Valbo and he no longer, not on a single one of her visits, had any idea who she was.

Too late, in other words. In all essential aspects, Rune Backman was dead long before he died.

But with Marianne it was exactly the opposite. Too early. She was dead and buried, but it was kind of impossible to acknowledge the fact. To acknowledge, to comprehend, to take in.

And if it was beyond her – Eva Backman, who had been no more than a best friend – how on earth could one expect the children and Barbarotti to manage it? To comprehend it and somehow move on.

Although Barbarotti did have a faith of some sort.

That was what he claimed, though they had never seriously discussed the subject.

What have we ever seriously discussed? thought Eva

Backman, sipping her tea. Even though we know each other so well after twenty years in the same madhouse.

It was a good but uncomfortable question. Good because it had to be asked, uncomfortable because of where the answer might lead.

So have we really never talked seriously about anything? she thought. What am I getting at here? If I've never seriously discussed anything with Barbarotti, then who?

Ville, to whom she had been married for twenty-one years? Scarcely, looking back over them and thinking about the way things stood now. What had all her words added up to? Pearls cast before swine? Water off a duck's back? And, conversely, a man who chose a woman like Blanche basically didn't deserve to be taken seriously.

The boys? Hopefully prospects were a bit brighter there, but only time would tell and the decision lay in their hands.

Marianne? Well, yes, it was undeniable. They had talked to each other about the things you needed to talk about. Life, death, love. Motivation and self-knowledge. Male folly, female folly and the dross that accumulates in the soul.

But there was no Marianne any more, that was how reality was constructed now, and as it abruptly came home to Eva Backman that she was as poorly equipped for this world as everyone else, the tears came.

It isn't the dead we grieve for, she thought, it's ourselves. Not death. Life.

A few hours later, the lilac and chestnut were still blooming. She had brought some paperwork home with her to read over the weekend – predominantly the Fängström affair, where they were simply marking time. Despite extensive efforts, they had not been able to identify and apprehend the individual who had visited the Sweden Democrat on the night in question, and the media reporting had started to take on that familiar note of scorn.

But it's only Saturday, thought Eva Backman, and I can't concentrate on this today. Sunday was bound to be rainy and more conducive to work; she pushed away the work material and decided on a long walk.

Even though she already had an eight-kilometre run behind her, maybe the Blanche adrenalin was still pumping away inside her somehow. Or maybe her brain was too active with thoughts of Marianne and Barbarotti, and all the rest, to tolerate her sitting still.

Or was it merely that the world outside was still only seventeen years old and hard to ignore?

Her destination was initially unclear, but once she had covered some ground, she realized she was heading for the cemetery. Her parents' grave and Marianne's were no more than a hundred metres apart; now that she seemed to be going that way, she would happily spend a while with each of them. On a day like today.

She began with her parents, dealt with the withered flower heads, watered the plants and collected up a bucketful of dead leaves and other debris, and was moving towards the newer part of the cemetery when she caught sight of Barbarotti.

Of course. What more natural way for him to spend a free Saturday afternoon than on a visit to his beloved wife?

She stopped at a slight distance and observed him. He was standing with his back to her, facing the grave where no stone had yet been put up, only the provisional wooden cross. His shoulders were hunched, as if he was freezing cold, even in the bright sunshine; his head was lowered and still, so perhaps he was praying. Perhaps he was trying to make some kind of contact. Backman thought it looked like a painting, an old oil painting by some early nineteenth-century artist: *At the Grave.*

Half a minute passed, then he turned round and saw her. He raised a hand in greeting and came over.

'Sorry, I didn't mean to disturb you.'

He shook his head. 'No, you're not disturbing me. I've been here with her for a good while.'

'I looked in on my parents' grave and thought I'd come and see Marianne, too.'

'Naturally.'

'It's a lovely day.'

'Yes.'

She hesitated. 'Would you like me to leave you in peace?'

He attempted a smile. 'Heavens, no. Sorry, Eva, no, we can talk for a while if you want. Let's sit on that bench. The kids will be here soon.'

'The kids?'

'The children, yes. Three of them anyway, Johan's got work. I wanted a bit of time to myself first, that's all.'

'Yes, of course.'

They sat down on a bench in the sun, a little way from Marianne's grave. It struck Eva Backman that she had honestly never felt embarrassed in Barbarotti's presence before, but she did now.

'I really don't know what to say, Gunnar.'

He shrugged his shoulders. 'We can perfectly well just sit here, that's fine, too.'

She nodded.

'Or we can have a little talk about Ellen Bjarnebo. I'd appreciate hearing your view, to be honest.'

'So you're putting in some work on that?'

'Yes, as best I can. But I don't understand why Asunander's dug it all up . . . unless it's simply a question of keeping me occupied, that is.'

'You never know, with Asunander.'

'You certainly don't. Anyway I've started looking at that older case, too . . . the Burma business. It isn't particularly complicated, but one does wonder about her.'

Eva Backman swallowed. 'Ellen Bjarnebo?'

'Yes.'

'And what do you wonder?'

Barbarotti thought for a minute. 'Various things, but one above all. Why on earth did she move back here when she came out of prison?'

'Perhaps she had nowhere else to go?'

He nodded. 'The same thought occurred to me, but it still seems odd.'

'Why's that?'

'Well, the way I see it is this: if you've murdered someone and served more than ten years in jail for it, you have to start all over again when they let you out, in any case. There's nothing to go back to. And if there's one place where she can guarantee she'll be recognized as a murderous axe woman, it's here in Kymlinge, isn't it? So why would she come back here?'

'I don't know,' said Eva Backman. 'I've never served a ten-year prison sentence and I don't know how axe women think.'

'Now you're being perverse,' said Barbarotti. 'You could at least agree that it's odd, eh?'

'All right,' said Backman. 'It *is* odd. But it worked out, after all. She got a job and somewhere to live. And eventually she found a man and . . .'

'And then he went missing, too. And what does Ellen Bjarnebo do then? Well, she stays on in her flat, doesn't leave town . . .'

'But she isn't working any more, is she?'

Barbarotti nodded. 'No, she's not. Just imagine, after the Morinder case she retired early. At only fifty-four. How did that come about, do you think? Well, what do you know, the Swedish Cashier Service suddenly decided she was surplus to requirements, at the same time as a company doctor happened to discover that she had some kind of work-related back injury, and within a month she was off their books. Smart work, eh?'

'Very smart,' Eva Backman conceded. 'Do you think her colleagues refused to work with her or what?'

'Maybe not them,' said Barbarotti. 'But the bosses. I had a ten-minute conversation with one of them this morning, which was more than enough to confirm it. And yet . . .'

'Yet she still stayed here.'

'She did,' said Barbarotti. 'And that's exactly what I'd like you to explain to me. Like I said.'

Eva Backman thought about it for a few seconds. 'But you haven't spoken to her? She's the one with the answer, not me.'

'I'm seeing her next week,' said Barbarotti, with a glance at his watch. 'She's at a guest house up in Norrland at the moment, didn't I say?'

Eva Backman nodded. 'Ah, I see.'

'And you're right, of course. A word with her definitely ought to shed light on a few things. But thanks for listening. I'm expecting the children about now.'

And just as he said it, she saw them approaching. Lars,

Martin and Jenny. Jenny was in the middle, with an arm round each of the boys. Eva Backman felt a lump in her throat and realized it was a picture by the same artist as that other painting she had visualized. This one was *On the Way to the Grave*.

When they arrived, she hugged all three of them. It felt slightly awkward for the boys, as it usually did. It was easier with Jenny, though she did start to cry as she went up to the grave. After some uncertainty, they all stood in a row and linked hands. For a few moments they all stood there in front of the simple cross. The silence was not remotely discomfiting; a little bird flew down and perched on the cross for a moment before it flew away again, and it wasn't hard to imagine Marianne could see them. Or that *she* was the bird, for that matter.

Not hard at all. To Eva Backman, it felt like a moment of – dignity? Eternity?

Before they parted, Jenny gave her another hug.

'Say hi to Kalle from me.'

She and Kalle were in the same year at upper secondary and part of the same extended group of friends, and Eva Backman suddenly felt touched by this simple fact. They had a friendship, Jenny and Kalle, that was entirely their own, independent of their parents – of herself, of Ville, of Barbarotti and Marianne – and there was suddenly something hugely reassuring about the fact.

As if it gave her permission to ease off a bit. A portion of responsibility slid from her shoulders, a new generation was taking over and she could see more clearly that the pea-brained Blanche simply wasn't worth wasting energy on.

'See you on Monday,' she said to Barbarotti.

'You don't want to come for a meal with us?'
'No, thank you. Another time.'
'OK, that's fine.'
And they parted.

14

2 June 1989

As she stood at the stove, peeling potatoes, he came past and gave her bottom a squeeze. He had a smell of beer and cigarette smoke with a hint of sweat, and without her brain thinking anything in particular, her fingers tightened their grip on the knife in her hand.

Like some macabre automatic response, some kind of preliminary move; that thought presented itself, at any rate, and tried to take hold – she would recall it later, afterwards, when everything had already happened – and then he asked her where the bloody boy was.

'I don't know,' Ellen answered truthfully. 'He's probably in his room.'

He muttered something and left her. She heard him take a handful of crisps from the bowl on the living-room table and thump down onto the settee. Crunch the crisps, neck some beer, belch.

She didn't know if Billy really was in his room, but where else would he be? He was presumably sitting at his desk, playing with his tin soldiers. Setting them out in rows facing each other, in various formations, silently and single-mindedly. He owned more than 150 of them; she had no idea what went on in his head when he was busy with his soldiers, but he could sit there with them for hours.

But then what went on in the boy's head the rest of the time was a mystery to her, too. Or very largely so, as he did not speak.

Well, he could say 'yes' and 'no', and on rare occasions a 'hungry' or a 'thirsty', but that was all. The teacher in the class he shared with eight other challenged pupils claimed that he occasionally said things like 'I can do it' or 'I don't understand'. Her name was Eivor, and Ellen knew that Billy loved her. There was a rumour of her possibly not coming back in the autumn and Ellen dreaded the prospect. Teachers who had attempted to teach Billy before she came on the scene had got nowhere with the boy, and there had been talk of sending him to a special school. He was currently attending mainstream school, in the special needs group as it was officially known, and with Eivor's gentle guidance it had at least become clear that he was not an idiot. Now, at just turned twelve, he could read, write and do his sums.

But his timidity and introversion were something else; Ellen wondered sometimes how much of herself had gone into his sullenness and averted eyes. If there was one part of her life that she did not want back, it was her early teens. Or her school years generally, for that matter.

Was there anything she would want back? Another question she avoided asking herself.

And Billy was big and strong, that was undeniable. There was no doubt that he would be able to defend himself, if the thought occurred to him. He was already half a head taller than his mother, and broad across the shoulders. She knew he had a nickname – Piggy – and presumably it was his bristly, almost-white hair that had prompted the comparison. Twenty years before, she had been called Mousey; some things were passed down to the next generation whether you wanted it or not.

She didn't know which animal would be most appropriate for Harry, but she had once heard someone call him *You fucking hyena*, and whether or not it quite fitted the bill, it had lodged in her mind.

The pig, the mouse and the hyena. Welcome to the Helgesson family at Little Burma.

Though the hyena was getting a bit too fat and heavy for a hyena. She dotted the potatoes and meat with butter and slid the baking dish into the oven. Sailor's beef, or a variation on it, one of her four or five staple weekend dishes. She looked at the clock. A quarter past seven, so at least they would be sitting down to eat before eight. She took off her apron and crept out of the kitchen to check Billy really was in his room and to take a quick shower.

She could hear that Harry had switched on the television in the sitting room. An American comedy, by the sound of it. Bright voices and canned laughter. She remembered she ought to water the house plants, but pushed the thought into the future. Better to lock herself in the bathroom for half an hour and pretend not to hear when he banged on the door and wanted to give her a squeeze.

Not before dinner. Not while the boy was awake – that was a boundary she did in fact manage to preserve.

She opened the door a little way and saw Billy sitting there. The washed-out green T-shirt and a bare strip of flab above the waistband of his jeans. Leaning heavily over the desk, he looked, well, cumbersome and ungainly, she couldn't help thinking. He was unaware of her presence and was making a soft sound, no words, just an inarticulate sound, something almost animal, but not at all aggressive. More like a female gorilla rocking her young.

What a strange image. He was a pig, wasn't he, not a gorilla? She closed the door and went upstairs to the bathroom. What was it the Mutti voice had said when she was on the bus?

Don't stop.

She had a glass of wine too many with the sailor's beef. Two, even.

It was neither deliberate nor unconscious. She didn't want to do it, but sometimes she gave in when he pressed her and poured her another glass. And it was easier to put up with him when she was a bit drunk. The alcohol in her bloodstream dulled her, she could switch off and let him get on with it; sometimes she could even pretend that she was enjoying it. That she liked him and the way he was behaving. She didn't know if he could see through her or not; maybe he would have done if he'd been sober, but he wasn't.

He seldom was these days. And definitely never at the weekend; Friday and Saturday evenings were for drinking away – what the hell else had they been made for? In the week he stuck to beer, a couple of cans in the evening after a day's toil. It made him sleepy and that gave no cause for concern. He never touched her on those days anyway.

They shared two bottles of wine while they were sitting at the table and Billy was still with them. Billy drank Fanta, as usual, it was his favourite drink in any category. Once the boy had gone to his room to bed or to carry on playing with his tin soldiers, Harry opened a third bottle of wine in front of the television. But he soon switched off the set and put on the stereo instead. Not Creedence tonight but an old Ulf Lundell album. She assumed he thought it was romantic; they drank more wine, he smoked cigarette after cigarette and sang along with all the songs. From time to time his hand casually groped its way up between her thighs, but not yet with serious intent. She took another mouthful of wine, rested her head against the back of the settee and closed her eyes. It was a Friday evening like any other at Little Burma.

It was hard to say when the impulse to resist came over her. And why. And how.

But it came, and once it had taken hold, it would not let go. Maybe it was something to do with the wine, which was a new kind, from Chile, and instead of making her weak and inert, it seemed to fill her with new strength. But how could that be possible? What grapes could possess such magical powers? Or was it because of Ulf Lundell?

Sixty-seven, sixty-seven, what happened to the year that felt like very heaven? She had been fourteen years old in 1967. Yes, you really could ask yourself where it had all gone.

She pushed away Harry's hand and stood up. Staggered slightly, which was what sometimes happened when she was drunk and got up too quickly.

'What's up with you?'

She ran her hands through her hair and felt it turning into some kind of gesture of independence. It made her straighten her back and expand her lungs; an illusion of freedom and energy swept through her and, for a second, she felt that everything was possible. That she could, for example, pack a light bag, put on her coat or jacket and go. Leave the pig and the hyena to their fate and set off into the world.

One second, maybe two. Then she was back in reality. Back at Little Burma. But not quite, not properly; the urge to resist – whatever it was and wherever it came from – still lingered in her. Unflinching, she looked him straight in the eyes as he lounged there on the sofa with a newly lit cigarette.

'Need the toilet,' she said, noting that her words came out slightly fuzzily. 'Back in a minute.'

'Take your knickers off while you've got them down.'

He smirked at his own ingenuity and took a drag on his cigarette. Put his hand to his crotch and winked.

You bastard, she thought. You're nothing but a disgusting bastard, Harry Helgesson.

It took a good while for him to come and bang on the door. Twenty minutes? Maybe even half an hour? She was sitting on the floor, resting against the bathtub, and had almost dozed off.

'What the hell are you playing at?'

She gave a start and hit her head on the edge of the bath. 'I'm just coming . . .'

'You've been in there all bloody night.'

She struggled to her feet and glanced at her watch. Half past ten. She looked at her face in the mirror above the wash-basin. Her eyes looked red, as if she had been crying, though she couldn't remember having done so. Maybe it was merely the wine, affecting her that way. Her lips and teeth were a blueish colour. He must be out of his mind to want to screw someone like me, she thought.

Screw? It almost reduced her to tears to find herself using such an expression.

'What the hell are you doing?'

She turned on the tap.

'I'm coming. Just give me a minute.'

'Christ All-fucking-Mighty!'

And as she splashed cold water on her face, she heard him cross the landing and go down to Billy's room. Heard the door open and the boy give an indistinct wail. No doubt Harry had flung the door wide and scared him.

Then there was more swearing, followed by a couple of loud thuds. It was all too easy for her to visualize the scene. The boy hunched over his desk with his arms protecting his head, and his father hitting him. She had heard it before, and she had seen it. She had no idea what had caused Harry to lose his temper this time. It could be simply the fact that the boy was still not in bed, despite it being late. Or maybe he had broken something in his room, or was picking his nose.

It never took much, and in fact it could well be her who had triggered it this time, by taking too long in the bathroom. She turned off the tap and heard a further three or four blows land before Harry slammed the boy's door with a final 'Goddamned freak!'

Then he was back outside the bathroom, yanking at the door handle.

'That's fucking well it, now! Open up or I'll knock the fucking door down!'

He must have downed a few more glasses in the time she'd been propped against the bath. He sounded the way he did when he was on the verge of losing control altogether, and for a moment she considered simply not letting him in. But perhaps he would then do precisely as he had threatened and break down the door. Or return to the boy and dish out some more violence. She gave a shiver and drew back the bolt.

He came tumbling in and almost overbalanced. Grabbed hold of the towel rail and managed to stay on his feet.

'Got to piss, for Chrissake. Move!'

She squeezed past him and out of the door and took a swift decision to give him everything he wanted. As long as he didn't hit her.

Anything but that. The resistance that had briefly revealed itself within her, an hour or so before, was not so much as a memory. When he came back to the living room, she was sitting on the sofa with her skirt pulled halfway up her thigh and her knickers stuffed under one of the cushions.

It was the only way. There was no voice inside her to give her any other instructions.

15

Late on Sunday night – when he had said goodnight to the whole bunch and closed his bedroom door – he finally took out the Bible. First he read the verses in Hebrews to which he had been directed; they were mostly about enduring torment and remaining strong in the faith, and didn't exactly cut through to him. But several days had elapsed since the suggestion was first made, and it was often a matter of seizing the moment and not delaying, so he had learnt.

Then he hesitated for a moment before opting for Paul's First Epistle to the Corinthians. Chapter 13 – might as well get straight to the heart of the matter.

I'll learn it off by heart, and then I shall have a chat with Our Lord, he thought, adjusting the pillows propped behind him.

It took a while. Midnight came and went, and so did half past, but soon after that he was able to recite the text three times with his eyes closed, without mistakes, and the last time it didn't even feel like something he had practised . . . *and the greatest of these is love*. As if another voice was talking inside him and the words were made flesh. He liked to imagine that anyway, and he jumped two chapters ahead:

For this corruptible must put on incorruption, and this mortal must put on immortality.

So when this corruptible shall have put on incorruption, and this mortal shall have put on immortality, then shall be brought to pass the saying that is written, Death is swallowed up in victory.

O death, where is thy sting? O grave, where is thy victory?

Then he switched off the lamp and stared out through the dark rectangle of window. The jagged forest silhouetted against the deep heavens beyond. What does it mean? he asked. Does it mean You really do have her with You, or what am I supposed to think, dear Lord? Is death's sting now neutralized?

It took a few seconds for the answer to come. But come it did, and he was immediately clear that it genuinely was Our Lord on the other end of the conversation. It wasn't his own voice doubling up in both roles; it was strange how easy it was to determine that fact. Not always, but sometimes.

What exactly is it you are enquiring about? asked Our Lord.

Is she really still there? said Barbarotti. Has she really gone home, as she used to say? I've had no sign from her.

So, you demand signs before you are prepared to believe? said Our Lord.

Hmm, well, said Barbarotti. I did hear her voice once, of course, but perhaps I misheard. She said I would get a letter. But I haven't had anything yet.

You've got it all the wrong way round, said Our Lord.

How do you mean? asked Barbarotti.

Our Lord sighed and adopted a slightly sterner tone. You want proof before you believe. What sort of faith is so feeble that it sets demands? Your faith is supposed to hold out for forty years in a wilderness. I refer you to that book in your hands. Once you truly believe, you'll find what you are seeking. But only through faith. Read that passage I gave you a bit more thoroughly. Through faith comes mercy, remember that. Not through feats or actions or bargaining. Give me a sign! What sort of nonsense is that? Believe first, then you'll get your signs!

Forgive me, said Barbarotti. It's just that it's so hard.

Of course it's hard! retorted Our Lord. What the devil were you expecting? Milk and honey all day long? But you are loved, don't forget that. The greatest of these is love, as you noted just now.

Quite right, said Barbarotti.

If you can only sustain the faith and hope, you will be able to see Marianne again. Throw away that doubt you are carrying round with you.

I went to school in the seventies, said Barbarotti. In those days they taught you to doubt everything.

I thought you had left school behind you? said Our Lord.

Basically, yes, said Barbarotti. But you're absolutely right, of course. Even so, I—?

What is it now? interjected Our Lord with a touch of irritation in his voice.

That letter, said Barbarotti.

Paul's letter to the Hebrews? asked Our Lord.

No, Marianne's letter, clarified Barbarotti. When I heard her voice, she said she had written to me. But I haven't had a letter, Lord, and if I'm to quash all these doubts, then presumably there ought to . . . ?

Oh, that, said Our Lord. Be with you on Thursday.

What? said Barbarotti.

Thursday. As long as she – the person supposed to be posting it – gets it in the box by 6 p.m. on Wednesday, that is. But I'll see to it. Anything else playing on your mind?

I don't think so, said Barbarotti. Thank you, Dear God, I promise to be firmer in the faith.

Promising is one thing, doing is another, Our Lord wound up. But you are loved and my patience is infinite. Goodnight to you.

Goodnight, said Gunnar Barbarotti, turning on his side and starting to doze off.

On Thursday?

Monday served up rain in Kymlinge and its environs. He had dropped off two teenagers at two different schools (the third one had a later start) and was on his way to the police station, but found it hard to imagine that it would soon be summer. Friday would be the first of June, and admittedly nature was blooming largely on cue, but the overcast skies all around him on this particular morning and the insistent patter of rain on the car roof seemed to belong more in November or February.

He noticed himself feeling a degree of gratitude for the fact. Early summer was a time of unguarded optimism, and if there was anything he felt out of sympathy with right now, it was unguarded optimism.

Simply stay firm in the faith, then. No sudden swings in any direction; the children needed a rock to stand on, not a quagmire. How did that Fröding poem about granite go? *Stay grey, stay grey, stay grey . . . ?*

He parked as close to shelter as he could and dashed through the rain to the entrance. Waved to Sippan and Jörgensson at the front desk and took the stairs up to the second floor.

Now I shall shut myself into my room and devote three hours to Morinder-Bjarnebo, he decided. Nothing else. No distractions, no self-pity, no brooding. Red alert, black coffee.

He began by ringing Ellen Bjarnebo's mobile. No answer.

The same when he rang her home number.

Oh well, he thought. She would be back sometime in the week; she hadn't specified which day.

What she could be doing in a Lapland guest house in May was a good question, of course. It would barely even be spring up there by now, surely? thought Barbarotti, who had only once in his life ventured north of Östersund.

Despite his best intentions, he had found little time for either of the cases over the weekend, and perhaps that was a good sign. He had some interviews to go through, among them two with Ellen Bjarnebo and one with Sofia Lindgren-Pallin, a fellow employee at the hardware store where Ellen had worked until the summer of 1989.

The summer it happened.

He was a good way through the transcript of the first interview when one of the questions and its answer pulled him up short. Most of the interviews had been conducted by a DI Kartén. Barbarotti had a vague recollection of a lanky, conscientious gentleman with brown-tinted spectacles and stomach problems; he had retired in the spring of 1990, just six months after the axe-woman case, and Barbarotti never got to know him.

Kartén: But the sledgehammer struck your husband in the back of the head. Yet you still say you acted in anger and on impulse. Why didn't he react?

Ellen Bjarnebo: I suppose I had a few seconds to think. It didn't essentially change anything, though.

Barbarotti leafed back through the transcript. The question and answer did not entirely match, but that happened sometimes. The crucial point was what had motivated the crime. Ellen Bjarnebo claimed that her husband insulted her in a most offensive manner, calling her something she refused to divulge, and that was the final straw. He had hit her the night before and he had hit her son. This had been happening repeatedly for some time, but it escalated that spring. Now she was standing behind him in some kind of workroom installed at one end of the barn; it was Saturday evening; he was sitting at a desk with his back to her, busy with something. Why they were there was not explained. Her husband had said something deeply offensive without turning round, her eye fell on a sledgehammer on a bench and she lost control.

That was the way she had described the whole episode, both in the interview he was currently reading and in several earlier ones.

But she *had a few seconds to think*.

And that moment's reflection *didn't essentially change anything*.

Barbarotti pondered. Once the brief pause for thought was over, Ellen Bjarnebo had landed one on her husband with the sledgehammer – which was of medium size and relatively easy to handle, even for a person with no great physical strength, according to the technical report – after which she had spent that evening and night, the night between 3 and 4 June, to be precise, chopping up her victim, putting the parts in black bin bags and dragging them to various places in the forest behind the farm. She had attempted to bury them, but had to make do with concealing them under debris on the forest floor. The reason for the butchering operation was simple: she would not have been able to carry him all in one piece. When he was alive, Harry Helgesson had weighed at least ninety kilos, and it is a well-known fact that bodies don't get any lighter when they are dead. Not immediately, at any rate.

After disposing of her husband in this way, Ellen Bjarnebo had waited several days before she reported him missing. If her neighbours, the family at Great Burma, had not started asking questions, she could have waited longer, she said. She did not miss her husband, dead or alive.

The crime-scene investigation, which was therefore conducted more than two months after the act was committed, supported Ellen Bjarnebo's version of events, insofar as that was possible. There were traces of Harry Helgesson's blood in the room in question, on the desk chair and floor, but that was basically it. It was impossible either to prove or disprove whether he had been killed in the way described. But there had naturally been no reason to doubt Ellen Bjarnebo's story.

Over the summer the police had pursued their investigations somewhat half- heartedly, Barbarotti could see. There had been no particularly compelling reason to think Harry Helgesson was in fact dead, still less that he had been killed. Neither his wife nor his relations at Great Burma farm found it implausible that he had simply gone off somewhere. His general unreliability was well documented, and some of his few friends in town, with whom he was in the habit of socializing over some beers and a game of cards, put forward the idea that he had won on the pools or the horses, taken the money and shoved off. To Denmark or Germany, or God knows where. The minor detail of him having taken no clothes or personal belongings with him – not even his passport – well, maybe it was a bit surprising, but nothing to get hung up on. As long as you had money, the rest could always be arranged – clothes, booze, a bit of skirt and anything else you might need – according to one Ziggy Pärsson, who claimed to be speaking from experience and whose name was not unknown to DI Barbarotti and his colleagues of the Kymlinge police.

No longer of this world, however. Choked on his own vomit at a campsite in Dalarna on Midsummer's Eve 2008.

The first bundle – definitively ruling out the theory that he had gone off on a spree – was found by someone out picking bilberries at the start of August. It comprised the former Harry Helgesson's head and arms in a black bin bag; he was quickly identified, and suspicion almost immediately fell on his wife. She confessed, at her second interview, the day after the grisly discovery. She also willingly gave directions to where the other parts of her husband were to be found. Two more bin bags, one for his legs, another for his torso.

Barbarotti looked out onto the rain and tried to visualize the scene in the workroom. No open quarrel. Man and wife, married with a promise to love each other, for better or worse. Equally repugnant in one another's eyes presumably. Maybe a few seconds' stillness and silence before the breaking point. With a few badly chosen words, Harry Helgesson had signed his own death warrant. He hadn't even turned round.

Because if he had, if he had turned his head even slightly, he would naturally have seen his wife with a raised sledgehammer, ready to club him in the head.

And he would have defended himself. Successfully or not. Put up his arms, at the very least. Wouldn't he?

But the blow had landed squarely on the back of his head. Fractured his skull with full force and penetrated his brain to some depth. Death must have been instantaneous.

Ellen Bjarnebo had disposed of the sledgehammer, but rather carelessly. The police had followed her instructions and found it in a sea of stinging nettles about twenty metres behind the barn. With her fingerprints on it and everything.

Why didn't you hide the murder weapon better, considering the trouble you took to conceal the body parts in the forest? Kartén had wanted to know.

It didn't occur to me, Bjarnebo had declared. It didn't seem important.

Barbarotti leafed on through the papers and found the report of the court proceedings. He leant back in his chair and read. The account given in court of the course of events was more or less identical to the police interview. Ellen Bjarnebo stuck to her story of thinking for a few moments before she dealt the fatal bow, and you really had to wonder why. She could have got away with manslaughter otherwise, surely? The fact that she had taken those seconds must have led automatically to the crime being classified as murder.

So why? Why those seconds that *didn't essentially change anything*?

Gunnar Barbarotti, finding no answer to that question, gave a shrug and moved on to the interview with Sofia Lindgren-Pallin. There was something familiar about the name, and eventually it came to him.

Hadn't her name come up in the other investigation as well? The Morinder case.

He leafed on through the file and found the place.

And yes, he was right. Although now, well into the 2000s, she only called herself Pallin. And Gunvaldsson had made nothing of the connection; in fact it was unclear if he had even been aware of it. In any event, in 1989 Sofia Lindgren-Pallin was married to one Torsten Lindgren, owner of Lindgren's Hardware Ltd on Södra torg, the shop where Ellen Bjarnebo worked part-time for the two years before the murder. Sofia Lindgren-Pallin occasionally had to help out in the shop; she also did the bookkeeping off and on and naturally knew all the employees. In her short statement as a character witness, she stated that she had no criticisms of how the suspect did her job. Perhaps she could have been a bit more sociable, but the customers of a hardware store were not the type to be impressed with chatty assistants, so it wasn't really worth mentioning.

The reason Sofia Pallin cropped up in the later investigation, the one involving Arnold Morinder, was simply that she again happened to work at the same place as Bjarnebo, this time the Swedish Cashier Service. The police conducted a short interview with her – just as with all the other members of staff – and she said nothing on that occasion about her previous acquaintance with the axe woman.

And Gunvaldsson had missed it.

Or at any rate there was nothing in the paperwork to indicate otherwise.

This was probably of no significance whatsoever, Barbarotti decided after a minute's reflection. But as he had been set the task of looking into these old cases of sudden violent death and human failings – and with every indication that the interview subject of primary interest was still somewhere up near Vilhelmina – he decided it was worth trying to contact the former hardware-store employee.

A minute or two later, he had her on the line. He explained the reason for his call and asked if Sofia Pallin might possibly have time for a brief meeting.

She explained in her turn that, as someone who had retired just over a year before but wasn't interested in golf or in day trips to Sweden's famous glassworks, she had all the time in the world. He was welcome to drop round for a cup of coffee in half an hour or so. Did he have the address?

Barbarotti asked if he was right in thinking it was Tulpanvägen 12, and she said it was.

Before he left the police station he tried Ellen Bjarnebo's mobile again. No answer. No voicemail option. He sent a text message asking her to get in touch as soon as she had time.

I almost feel as if I'm working, he thought as he pulled out of the car park. And the rain continued to pour down.

Stay grey.

16

It was in a row of low, generously proportioned sixties houses on the edge of the town's forest. Barbarotti did not think he had set foot in Tulpanvägen since the late 1970s. Not number twelve that time, but he suddenly remembered the occasion with surprising clarity: a fancy-dress party at the house of a tall, blonde girl with soulful eyes . . . it was number fifteen, wasn't it, that cherry-blossomed place with the freshly painted fence, a bit further along on the other side?

She was in his form at upper secondary and was indeed named Blondie. Or known as Blondie anyway, but people didn't christen their little girls Blondie back in 1960 or so. Barbarotti had elected to go as a pirate, the party theme being The Sea. He spent most of the evening engaged in some heavy petting with another classmate called Åsa. Or possibly Anna; she was dressed as a jellyfish, and the operation had not been without its complications.

Sofia Pallin was not dressed as anything but herself when she let him in: a tall, rather elegant woman in a red tunic and black jeans. Barbarotti knew she was sixty-seven, but she had invested considerable effort in looking younger. And not without success.

A dog came up to say hello. Big, brown and short-haired, it looked as distinguished as its mistress and only spared him a few seconds' inspection before returning to a sheepskin in front of an aquarium.

'Do have a seat,' said Sofia Pallin. 'Tea or coffee?'

'Coffee, please,' said Barbarotti, sitting down in the Bruno Mathsson armchair she showed him to.

The refreshments were already set out. Sofia Pallin sat down opposite him in another Bruno Mathsson-designed chair and looked at her watch. Adjusted her platinum hair with a simple turn of the neck. 'I wasn't strictly truthful on the phone,' she said. 'I've only got an hour, in actual fact. So let's start straight away. You wanted to ask me about the Axe Woman of Little Burma?'

'An hour will do me,' Barbarotti assured her. 'Yes, that became her stage name, so to speak. And is that how you think of her, too?'

'Not at all,' said Sofia Pallin. 'It was just a joke. I thought that was how the police saw her.'

She leant forward and poured coffee from a brushed-aluminium pot. Indicated a plate of chocolate-coloured biscuits that looked to Barbarotti like little mice without legs.

'First let me ask why you are interested in her again. I thought both those cases had been shelved.'

'And they have, in a way,' said Barbarotti. 'But anything left unresolved is always an irritant.'

'You mean Morinder?'

'Yes.'

She raised one eyebrow and looked mildly sceptical. 'You know what – your people didn't handle that business very well. Perhaps you weren't involved yourself, but she was put under a lot of unnecessary pressure.'

'I'm sorry about that,' said Barbarotti. 'No, I didn't have

anything to do with the investigation personally, you're right. But that isn't the point. It's regrettable when things are handled badly. So can you tell me how you saw it? And how you saw Ellen Bjarnebo?'

Bloody Gunvaldsson, he thought. Though his hostess clearly took a dim view of the police force as a whole.

'Of course,' she said and sipped her coffee, ignoring the dead mice as she settled back into Bruno Mathsson. 'Providing you'll allow me to apply a gender perspective.'

'Fine by me. You can apply whatever perspective you think most appropriate.'

'Thank you,' said Sofia Pallin. 'Then I will. Ellen Bjarnebo certainly did kill her husband, but she had her reasons for it.'

Barbarotti gave a neutral nod.

'There were a few of us who knew things were far from right at home. Harry Helgesson didn't treat his wife well, and that's putting it mildly. I assume he mistreated his son the same way. I'm only sorry we were too passive; we ought to have intervened somehow, but I wasn't the person then that I am now.'

'Who do you mean when you say *we*?' asked Barbarotti.

'I mean myself, Mona Ivarsson and Gun Biermann,' replied Sofia Pallin. 'We all worked with her at the hardware shop. We chose to pretend nothing was happening. It was cowardly and I feel ashamed when I think back on it.'

'How could the three of you know what was going on?' said Barbarotti. 'Between her and Harry Helgesson?'

'Well, it wasn't that she said anything,' observed Sofia Pallin with a slight shrug. 'But we noticed things and we put two and two together. Afterwards, at any rate. Someone saw them together in town, too. Saw him behaving like a bastard. No, there can be no doubt that he was hitting her. He exploited his male advantages, the way the patriarchy always has, through the ages. Nothing unusual in that, as far as it went.'

Barbarotti thought for a moment.

'And Morinder? What's your view on him?'

'In this particular context?'

'Let's say yes.'

'I have no view,' said Sofia Pallin. 'I don't know anything about Arnold Morinder. Arnold, that was his first name, wasn't it?'

Barbarotti nodded.

'Well, that's all I can tell you. As far as I know, there's no evidence of history having repeated itself there. She wasn't entirely stupid.'

'Did you get to know her well, over the years? I mean—'

She interrupted him with a determined shake of the head. 'Absolutely not. Ellen Bjarnebo and I happened to share a place of work for two separate periods. I never socialized with her, not at the shop or at the Swedish Cashier Service.'

'Staff parties?'

'There were none of those at either place. No, when I say I have respect for her, I'm not basing it on personal acquaintance. But she was – is – a woman who got nothing in life for free. I think she did what she felt she had to, out there at Burma, don't misunderstand me on that, and she took her punishment. What's more, she came back to Kymlinge once she'd served her sentence. Everyone knew who she was, but she started a new life with . . . well, with her head held high. What has she herself got to say about the police starting to root around in this again?'

'I haven't talked to her yet,' said Barbarotti.

'Why not?'

'She's away at the moment. What happened about her job after Morinder went missing, by the way?'

Sofia Pallin appeared to wrestle with herself for a moment before she answered. She stretched out a hand towards the dead mice, but then withdrew it again.

'She took early retirement in 2007, on grounds of poor health.'

'Yes, I'm aware of that,' said Barbarotti. 'It's in the case files. But I get the impression it was tied up with Morinder's disappearance, don't you?'

Sofia Pallin gave a shrug. 'Quite possibly. But I think she was happy to take it. She'd been having some problems with her back and . . . you know, maybe she'd simply had enough. Don't forget she was very much under suspicion, in the police's eyes and everyone else's. Especially everyone else's.'

'But not yours?'

'I didn't have an opinion. I still don't.'

'I see,' said Barbarotti. 'So the general mood against her just got too much, you think?'

'That's about it,' said Sofia Pallin. 'It wouldn't have been acceptable to let her stay in the job. What surprises me is that she didn't move away. I believe her son lives in Stockholm, but it may well be that she doesn't have much contact with him. He was taken into the care of other people after what happened at Burma, wasn't he?'

'Correct,' said Barbarotti. 'Do you know anything about him?'

'No.'

Barbarotti drank coffee and gathered up a bit of silence. Then he asked, 'Did you ever talk to her about this? About her husband and what happened out there . . . when you found yourselves working together again?'

Sofia Pallin again took a few moments to consider. 'Not really. I got the sense she didn't want to drag it all up, so I left it. I regret not having tried to approach her, but it was a very individual kind of job. We sat in our little booths and served our customers, and that was about it. No communal breaks or anything like that. But I regret that I was a bit of a coward.'

'So you're saying you were still too cowardly when you came across her again?'

Sofia Pallin said nothing for a few moments.

'Yes, perhaps I'm saying that. On the other hand, it was pretty clear that she didn't want to talk about what had happened. She had a lot of integrity, Ellen Bjarnebo . . . and still does, I presume. That was a precondition for moving on with her life, I imagine. It comes back to me now that I did actually try to talk to her then, when the Morinder business came up, but she said she didn't feel like discussing it.'

'Didn't you think that was odd?'

'Not at all. And I only brought it up the once. She was only at work for two or three more days after the story came out, and everybody knew, you see. If I'm not mistaken, she was just back from her holidays and after that . . . well, they gave her leave of absence virtually right away.'

'Leave of absence?'

'That was what they called it.'

'I see. To go back a little, how did you hear that her partner had gone missing, do you recall?'

Sofia Pallin furrowed her brow. 'I don't really remember. Somebody must have mentioned it. I didn't hear it from her, at any rate. I was aware of it before I spoke to her at work.'

'Do you know whether Ellen Bjarnebo had any female friends? Anybody she could have opened up to?'

Sofia Pallin shook her head. 'No idea. But if you want me to hazard a guess, I'd say no. Ellen Bjarnebo gave the impression of being a very solitary woman. Very solitary. The victim of a real shit of a man, but not a defenceless victim.'

Barbarotti nodded and changed tack. 'What happened to your husband, the ironmonger? Did the two of you get divorced?'

'I left Torsten,' she corrected him, breaking a dead mouse in half. 'I'd made up my mind about it a long time before, I was simply waiting for the children to leave home.'

'How many do you have?'

'Five. No, I've had enough of men, I'm afraid. But now you've got to give me something in return. Why on earth are you digging about in all this? Morinder hasn't turned up out of thin air, has he?'

Barbarotti shook his head. 'No, no. We're just trying to tie up a few loose ends, that's all.'

Sofia Pallin's lip curled disdainfully for a second. 'That's no answer, Inspector. But let me give you some advice. If you people are intending to stir things up for Ellen Bjarnebo yet again, you'd better be prepared for some rough going.'

As he drove out of Tulpanvägen her comment still hung in his mind. *You'd better be prepared for some rough going.*

He had left Sofia Pallin with no reply. He had not revealed to her that he was not remotely prepared for rough going, but was simply being kept occupied with this futile task because his wife had died a month ago and his boss thought him incapable of proper work.

But in noting this for the umpteenth time, he also realized

it was time to break out of the absurd situation. High time to go in to Asunander and tell him to lay his cards on the table. If he had any.

What reasonable grounds could there be for clumping around in the wreckage of a five-year-old case? What was the point of reading all these dreary transcripts and reports and harassing this succession of unsuspecting people? Why not merely see to getting Arnold Morinder declared dead and move on to newer, more solvable problems instead?

Good questions.

But Asunander was not there. He was on leave – a personal matter – and would be back on Thursday, so Sippan at the reception desk informed Barbarotti, and before moving on to his phone call to Gunvaldsson he decided to have a word with Eva Backman. There was never any harm in that.

'Have you got a minute?'

She looked up from a pile of papers and shook her head.

'No. But have a seat.'

He moved three folders from a chair and sat down.

'Fängström?'

'Yes,' said Backman. 'But don't talk about the wretched thing. How are you?'

'Fine,' said Barbarotti. 'Though there is one thing I wonder.'

'Oh?' She rested her chin in her hand and contemplated him. He thought she looked slightly cross-eyed, which he was sure she didn't normally.

'Yes. You know when you spoke to Asunander?'

'Mmm?'

'About this mess he's got me swimming around in, that is . . . what did he actually say?'

'How do you mean?'

'He must have explained why he was keen to dust off this old case?'

Eva Backman leant back and thought for a few seconds. At least that was what she appeared to be doing, but perhaps she was just pretending.

Why am I imagining it? he asked himself. That she's pretending? Why would she . . . ?

He abandoned his train of thought as she cleared her throat and answered, 'I've honestly no idea, as I think I told you. I asked, of course, but you know how he can be.'

'He must have let something slip? Think hard.'

'Why is it so important all of a sudden?' said Backman. 'Go and ask him yourself.'

'Can't. He's away on business of some sort, back on Wednesday evening.'

'Oh. Drat. No, I'm pretty sure he didn't even drop a hint. But there must be a reason. Although . . .'

'Although?'

'Although it can hardly be called the most important task in hand here, at present. Obviously he thought you needed something not too taxing, to ease yourself back in, but I don't think he would have picked something entirely at random.'

'That's what I'm hoping, too,' said Barbarotti.

'You could always ring him?' suggested Backman. 'They do say that even he has a mobile.'

'I'll do that,' said Barbarotti.

'But you haven't spoken to the main character yet? Bjarnebo, I mean.'

Barbarotti shook his head.

Eva Backman frowned. 'So what exactly *are* you doing then?'

Barbarotti sighed. 'I've read all the files, both cases. Talked to various people on the periphery. The engine's running, but I'm not really going anywhere, you could say. I can't face driving round to see all these odds and sods who . . . you know, who happened to have some little walk-on role. It feels pretty pointless, frankly. Apart, of course, from . . .'

'From what?' asked Backman as Barbarotti got up and started moving the files back to the chair. 'Oh, don't bother with that.'

'Apart from the fact that I'm starting to wonder what the hell did happen to Morinder,' said Barbarotti. 'And exactly what it is that makes Ellen Bjarnebo tick. Ah well, I'll just have to wait until I can see her, I suppose.'

'Nothing beats sitting down face-to-face with someone,' said Backman. 'On that note, when are you coming round to dinner at my place? You've got a standing invitation, you know that.'

'Next week perhaps,' said Barbarotti. 'I'm going up to Stockholm for the weekend.'

'Stockholm?'

'Interviewing a couple of people . . . and then seeing Sara.'

'Good,' said Backman. 'It's good that you're going to be with Sara for a bit.'

Barbarotti nodded and retreated to his room.

17

Inspector Gunvaldsson sounded as if he had a cold.

'Hay fever,' he explained. 'It's always the same at this time of the year.'

'Don't you take antihistamines?' asked Barbarotti. 'Have I got the name right?'

'They don't always help,' said Gunvaldsson. 'A trip to Morocco would do a better job.'

'I see,' said Barbarotti. 'But, for now, you're at a desk in Karlstad?'

'Correct,' said Gunvaldsson. 'Somebody has to do it. What can I help you with?'

Barbarotti cleared his throat. 'It's an old case you were involved in when you were working down here. I don't know how well you'll remember it, but I'm going back over it at the moment.'

'Ah?' said Gunvaldsson.

'Arnold Morinder. The chap who went missing, and who lived with a woman they called the Axe Woman of Little—'

'Oh, that,' Gunvaldsson interrupted and sneezed. 'Yes, well, it went the way it went.'

'It did,' agreed Barbarotti. 'Bless you, by the way. What's your take?'

'On Morinder?'

'Yes.'

'Why are you working on that?' asked Gunvaldsson.

'Orders,' said Barbarotti. 'Don't know if you remember Asunander? The boss.'

'Hard to forget him,' said Gunvaldsson. 'Has something new emerged then?'

'Not exactly,' said Barbarotti.

'You haven't found Morinder?'

'I'm afraid not.'

'Well, that's what it all hinges on,' he said. 'Without a body it isn't easy to nail a murderer.'

'What's your view?' said Barbarotti.

'My view?' said Gunvaldsson. 'I don't really know any more, but when I was working on it, I thought it was her, I suppose. I still don't get why you're ferreting around in it all over again, though. Isn't there anything more important needing attention down there? Thought I heard something about a poisoned politician?'

'Not my pigeon,' explained Barbarotti. 'I'm working on a little one-man investigation, that's all. Asunander's retiring in a month's time, and it seems he doesn't want to leave any loose ends. So he's looking over a few things before he leaves.'

'Ah, I see,' said Gunvaldsson. 'Yes, cold cases are very popular nowadays. But there's very little I can offer you. I assume you've been through all the material?'

'I'm in the process,' said Barbarotti.

'I remember thinking it was a tricky case,' said Gunvaldsson with a sigh. Or possibly he was just breathing out through his mouth because the other route was blocked. 'It was virtually the only thing I got to work on while I was down there with you lot, as well. Turned out to be only a few months, and then

I ended up here. Well, it could have been worse, but I shall never forget the moped dumped in the middle of that bloody bog. Those infernal mosquitoes. What was it doing there?'

'Good question,' said Barbarotti.

'It certainly is. If she – or anyone else for that matter – had wanted to get rid of it, she could have driven it into the lake or anywhere she chose. If you can get rid of a body, disposing of a moped can't be any problem, can it?'

'Exactly,' said Barbarotti. 'So what conclusions did you draw from that, then?'

'How do you mean?'

'The fact that the moped was found.'

Gunvaldsson sneezed again. 'Conclusions? I don't know. How do you see it yourself?'

'Bless you,' said Barbarotti and admitted that he had no opinion on the matter.

'A suggestion was put forward, you know,' said Gunvaldsson. 'But it came from her, so we didn't give it much credence.'

'And what was it?'

'She reckoned – Bjarnebo – that he might have gone off to Norway.'

'Yes, I saw she'd said that,' said Barbarotti. 'What was he supposed to be doing there, if so? I don't think it was made clear.'

'Visiting an old mate,' came the short reply. 'He apparently had an old friend in Drammen. Or maybe it was Hamar, I don't remember. Bjarne, I do remember that, because it sounded like her name. Could equally well have been her own invention, of course.'

'Did the police try to get hold of him?'

'We put out a feeler, but it didn't lead us anywhere. We

hadn't got the surname, after all. And why would Morinder have set off for Norway on a moped, just like that? Over two hundred kilometres – it sounds insane. According to her, the moped broke down and he started hitching. Doesn't sound particularly plausible, does it?'

Barbarotti had no opinion on that, either. He changed tack and asked, 'What about Ellen Bjarnebo? What impression did she make on you? You must have spent quite a few hours with her.'

'Have you read the interviews?' asked Gunvaldsson.

'Yes.'

'Did you get anything out of them?'

'Not much.'

'Nor me, and that was the problem. But you're right, I must have spent more than twenty-four hours talking to her, all told. I thought she was bound to throw in the towel at some point, but no, she didn't. Have you met her?'

'Not yet,' said Barbarotti. 'But I will. She's away at the moment.'

'Good luck,' said Gunvaldsson.

'If you could cast your mind back,' Barbarotti went on. 'Did your team have any other theories . . . apart from her guilt, and apart from the Norway idea? From what I can gather, the detectives didn't cast their net all that wide, so to speak?'

Gunvaldsson excused himself, was gone for a few seconds and then came back on the line.

'Sorry. Just had to close a window. The pollen's on the march. Didn't cast the net wide, you said? I wouldn't entirely agree. We followed all the usual procedures, but there was no getting round the fact that we had a very clear focus from the very start. That was pretty natural, wouldn't you say? She'd murdered and butchered a man once before, for God's sake, so what the hell else were we to think?'

'How much did you go back and look at the old case?' asked Barbarotti. 'The murder that led to her conviction?'

'Not all that much,' admitted Gunvaldsson. 'It was an open-and-shut case, as I remember it. Confession, forensic evidence, the full works.'

'I'm not convinced about the forensic evidence,' said Barbarotti. 'But yes, I suppose in a way it was open and shut.'

'That was the problem with the Morinder case,' observed Gunvaldsson through his sniffles. 'It seemed equally open and shut the second time. The only difference really was that she didn't admit to it. Plus the absence of a body, of course.'

'Quite a big difference,' observed Barbarotti.

'I grant you that,' said Gunvaldsson.

Barbarotti thought for a moment. 'I'm still getting the sense that you've changed your mind,' he said. 'Or have I got that wrong?'

Gunvaldsson sounded doubtful. 'Depends what you mean,' he said. 'It's just that you start feeling less certain. When you've had the answer from the very start, and then can't get everything to add up . . . well, of course you start to have your doubts.'

'It happens,' said Barbarotti. 'But you never had suspicions elsewhere?'

'You mean a different perpetrator?' asked Gunvaldsson.

'Maybe, yes.'

'No, I didn't, as it happens,' said Gunvaldsson after a short pause. 'He honestly was a solitary type, that Morinder. Hardly an acquaintance on the map. We never really believed in that Bjarne. And his ex-wife hadn't seen him for twenty years, she said. So who would we have suspected? He had no friends, and no enemies, either.'

'Could have been robbed?' suggested Barbarotti.

'It's possible,' said Gunvaldsson. 'He apparently had nearly a hundred kronor in his pocket when he left.'

'And then the robber took the moped and drove on until the fuel ran out.'

'That would have taken a long time. The tank was almost full; he'd just been to fill up.'

'Yes, you're right,' said Barbarotti. 'Sorry to keep going on about this, but when you were interviewing Ellen Bjarnebo, what was your gut instinct? Did you get the feeling she could have done it?'

Gunvaldsson thought about it before he answered. 'I really don't know,' he said. 'Initially I definitely did. But she stuck to her story, and what was I supposed to do?'

'Not a particularly complicated story to stick to?'

'No. He took his moped, went to fill up and never came back. A seven-year-old could remember it. If only we'd had a body, it would have been quite a different matter.'

'Of course,' said Barbarotti. 'Incidentally, I read something about a disagreement at a restaurant.'

Gunvaldsson sighed again. 'She never told me what it had been about. Just said it was private and had nothing to do with him going missing.'

'And you accepted that?'

'When you've had the same answer thirty times, you accept it.'

Barbarotti said he agreed with that, asked if it would be all right to call again if anything else came up, and wished Gunvaldsson some relief from his allergic symptoms.

'Death to all bloody pollen,' said DI Gunvaldsson. 'Well, as I say, the best of luck. And by all means get back in touch if you need to.'

Barbarotti promised that he would and hung up.

18

Rönn had a plaster on his neck, just under his right ear.

'My cat,' he explained when Barbarotti asked, but there was something in his tone hinting at alternative explanations.

One, anyway. Barbarotti wondered why his grieving brain was having such daft thoughts. Or was the one giving rise to the other? Did its state of grief make it excessively receptive to anything that his senses happened to light upon? Wallman-Braun. A hopeless old murder case. The plaster on a sixty-year-old bereavement counsellor's neck.

Though the murder had nothing to do with his own washed-up state. Maybe not with those other things, either.

'That's what they always say,' he said, putting his right leg over his left.

'Eh?' said Rönn. 'Who says what?'

'Victims of crime,' said Barbarotti. 'When they don't want to reveal what really happened. Women who walked into doors, people who fell down the stairs or were attacked by their canaries . . . or cats.'

Rönn inserted a finger at the neck of his shirt, not on the same side as the plaster, and regarded him over the top of his spectacles.

'I prefer to stick to my story,' he said in English. 'It was the cat.'

Barbarotti gave a shrug. 'OK. We'll call it that. And some people even tell the truth.'

Rönn opened his black notebook without taking his eyes off Barbarotti. 'I get the impression you're on edge.'

'Is that a question?' said Barbarotti.

'If you like,' said Rönn.

Barbarotti considered. 'I don't know I'd call it on edge,' he said. 'But it feels as if something's gone wrong with my brain's sorting capacity. I can't focus. Or my focus is distorted. All kinds of idiotic things catch my attention and I find myself asking questions that . . .'

'What?' asked Rönn curiously.

' . . . that I must have first asked myself when I was around ten years old. Why the water doesn't run out of the bottom of a lake, for example. Whether all the migrating birds have to know the way or can rely on the leader. But I don't know, maybe it's a sign that I'm going mad and isn't worth worrying about. I . . .'

'Yes?'

'I'm finding life hard to cope with – that's the long and the short of it.'

'Hmm,' said Rönn, clasping his hands. 'Shall we perhaps try to bring the tempo down a little and find something to stand on?'

'We?' said Barbarotti.

'You,' said Rönn. 'To be precise.'

Barbarotti crossed the other leg and took a few deep breaths. 'You're right,' he said. 'It's just that I can't see any light.'

'Explain,' said Rönn.

Barbarotti thought about it and tried to assemble some kind of image. 'I'm a bird, plummeting to the ground. I'm flapping my wings frantically, but it . . . well, it isn't going to help for long. I know I'm going to crash anyway.'

Rönn nodded.

'It's not the months and the years that are the hard part,' Barbarotti went on with gloomy inspiration. 'It's the days and the hours. The minutes, even.' Something he had read, no doubt.

'Most people experience it that way,' said Rönn. 'But what about your faith, tell me about that?'

'My faith?'

'We talked last time about Marianne having gone home, and the fact that you'll be able to see her again when the time comes.'

'All the more reason to crash,' said Barbarotti.

Rönn removed his glasses. 'Now you're being cynical. You have five children who need you – you've got to get through this hard time. Your life doesn't only belong to you.'

'My life doesn't . . . ?'

'Correct,' said Rönn, 'doesn't only belong to you.'

'You're right,' said Barbarotti. 'And that makes me feel guilty.'

'Why?'

'Because I'm not looking after them properly. Because I haven't got what it takes.'

'Oh, I'm sure they understand,' said Rönn. 'Can you talk to them about it?'

'I don't know,' said Barbarotti. 'Perhaps. The boys are being a bit strong and silent about it . . . a male thing, I suppose.'

'But you have two daughters?'

'Yes. One at home, one in Stockholm.'

'It's a good idea not to give up on talking,' said Rönn. 'Silence isn't to be recommended, you know.'

'I realize that,' said Barbarotti. 'But it doesn't feel as if anything's getting easier. More like the opposite. I mean, it's been a month now.'

'What did you think would happen?' said Rönn.

'What did I think? I thought I would make contact with her . . . somehow.'

'And you haven't?'

Barbarotti hesitated, then shook his head.

'Has she come into your dreams?'

'If you don't sleep, you don't have dreams.'

'It surely isn't that bad?'

'Well, not entirely. But in any case, she hasn't shown herself there. Not that I remember anyway, and I'm pretty sure I would. The only thing . . .'

'Yes?'

'The only thing I know is that she's written to me and I shall get it on Thursday.'

Rönn pushed his spectacles up onto his head and looked nonplussed.

'Written to you?'

'Yes.'

'And how do you know that?'

'She popped up and said it.'

'After . . . ?'

'Yes, after. But only for a few seconds. I shall get it on Thursday.'

'So you have had contact after all?'

'Only for a moment. It was in the car, a few days ago. She was in the rear seat, behind my back. I never saw her.'

Rönn was silent.

'And I had it confirmed when I was talking to Our Lord.'

He looked at the therapist and realized he had crossed a line. Presumably it had dawned on Rönn that his client had lost control. That there was no longer any reason to take this drifting detective inspector seriously, and that an entirely different kind of therapy would be required from now on. Whatever kind that might be, Rönn seemed to be digging deep into his psychological cellar.

'It's so terribly hard,' Barbarotti said in the end. 'So terribly hard to imagine not being dead when you are.'

'I know,' said Rönn. 'I've been doing it for twenty-five years.'

'Twenty-five years? Why have you . . . ?'

Rönn took a deep breath and looked down at his clasped hands. 'I had a daughter who lost her life when she was twelve.'

Barbarotti swallowed. 'I'm sorry to hear that,' he said. 'I apologize for my moaning. Is that why you . . . ?'

'Why I do this job, yes. Or it's one of the reasons, anyway. I'm not saying I understand your pain, but I certainly recognize it.'

'Does it get any easier?' asked Barbarotti. 'I'm sorry I had my doubts about the cat earlier, by the way.'

'Some days, I find several hours can go by without my thinking about her,' said Rönn.

How do people manage to go on? he thought, after he had left Rönn. Or do they just learn to live with being turned to stone? *Modus vivendi*, isn't that the phrase? Another different state that you get accustomed to, whether you want to or not?

But why was it that he couldn't really take the idea of Heaven seriously? If he could only believe in that finer point, he would be home and dry.

And then there was this wallowing in self-pity, day after day.

He wasn't the one who was dead. Hanging onto self-pity's hand came its cousin, shame. A shame that expanded in the light of what others had suffered in the course of history and still gone on living. Found a direction to continue in, with some kind of dignity. Grieving but unbowed: concentration-camp prisoners, people whose families had been wiped out, who had seen their children killed, their wives and daughters raped, close relations tortured to death – the list was endless. Humanity's history was the history of its suffering, that was nothing new.

Those words from Hebrews that he had dismissed the other day came back into his mind:

They were stoned, they were sawn asunder, were tempted, were slain with the sword: they wandered about in sheepskins and goatskins; being destitute, afflicted, tormented; (Of whom the world was not worthy:) they wandered in deserts, and in mountains, and in dens and caves of the earth. And these all, having obtained a good report through faith, received not the promise.

I'm in good company, thought Barbarotti. I'm not the first in this seat, and those are the terms and conditions.

Once again he was in his car on the way out to Kymmens udde. Once again it was time to meet the children, take on the role of the unifying factor, their refuge and strength. *Received not the promise?* There certainly were some slightly odd translations in the Bible – his edition anyway – and they could do with some attention surely? But there he was again, under attack from yet more stale trivia. A completely pointless question, swimming around in the sea of gratuitous details that his conscious mind comprised. Received not the promise? Cat or fingernails? None of it mattered in the slightest.

Towards the end of their conversation, Rönn had brought up the question of depression. The option of taking a low dose of something to keep yourself airborne. But they had decided to leave it for future consideration. Better to be in pain than blunted, at least while Barbarotti was still just about on top of things.

'What are you working on?' Rönn had asked.

'An old case,' he had replied. 'A woman who murdered and butchered her husband. Possibly two husbands, it isn't clear.'

'Sounds macabre.'

'Yes, it is. But I don't know if I'm meant to be taking it seriously. My boss might only see it as keeping me in therapy. I'm sure I'm not going to get anywhere with it.'

'Hmm,' went Rönn and thought about it. Then he abandoned that train of thought and opted for the life beyond instead. 'I think you need to grab hold of your faith,' he suggested. 'Half a faith is no faith, and nor is two-thirds.'

'Go on,' said Barbarotti.

'You don't have to take this to heart if you don't want to. And this isn't what I'm really meant to talk to my clients about. But if you really are one of those people who can believe – and it isn't granted to us all, God knows – then you should just lie down and prostrate yourself beneath His mercy.'

'Prostrate myself beneath His mercy?'

'Yes. Have faith in a force stronger than you are – faith in that, and in mercy. But this is something between you and God.'

'You sound as if you know what you're talking about,' said Barbarotti after a while.

'Don't shoot the messenger,' Rönn replied in English, a language Barbarotti had already noted that he had rather a weakness for.

Yes, I know, muttered DI Barbarotti as he turned in between the slightly wonky gateposts of Villa Pickford. I know it as well as Rönn does. But the fact is, I was born a half measure, and it takes time to shift shape, and the handkerchief of reason can't mop up the tears of emotion.

He wondered where that last bit had come from. Something else he'd read, he supposed, a poem remembered from his receptive high-school years – why not? *The handkerchief of reason, the tears of emotion.*

Then he switched off the engine, raised his eyes and saw there was a light in every window of the house.

19

3 June 1989

A morning like any other.

She wanted to throw up.

Or stay in bed until it passed. It was eight o'clock, it was Saturday morning at Little Burma and she had been awake for a good half hour. Beside her, Harry was lying on his back, snoring open-mouthed. She thought that if she could just – for a brief moment – have weighed 300 kilos, she would have been able to put a pillow over his face and lie down on top of it. For a minute or two. Put an end to the snoring, and to him.

She had a sore place below one of her eyes. He had lashed out at her, she couldn't remember why. If there had been a reason, of course; it never took much, and it had only been the once. Billy had come off worse, not that she had been in to check, but he would have had plenty to endure in his room last night, she was sure of that.

Before she had parted her legs and let Harry take her on the sofa. The only way.

Though even the sex was a kind of fight, too. Sometimes anyway. There was an anger in Harry that she couldn't entirely understand, and in the middle of the act of love he had hit her. As if he thought it was part of it, somehow. As if he couldn't come unless he got that anger out of him first.

Act of love? A phrase that belonged somewhere else. Not at Little Burma.

When it was finally over, when she had received his sacred seed, he had drunk another glass of wine, smoked a cigarette and fallen asleep. Not a word to her. Ulf Lundell again. She had left him there on the sofa and made her way upstairs to bed, and sometime during the night he had done the same. Plainly. Because there he lay, snoring, with a dribble of saliva hanging like a miniature condom from one corner of his mouth.

This can't go on, she thought. It's got to end.

The thought was far from new.

Two hours later he took the car and went into town. He needed to get something from the farmers' co-operative. Or so he said, but perhaps he simply wanted to get away.

She stood at the kitchen window, saw the old Volvo passing Great Burma and wondered whether the phone would ring or not. She hadn't thrown up, but she still didn't feel well. She had put some ice in a plastic bag and applied it to the sore place under her eye.

There had still been no sound from Billy's room, but the boy always slept late at weekends. Until lunchtime, or even longer unless someone woke him.

I don't want to go in and check, she thought. I can't face it right now.

And I don't want the phone to ring.

*

But it did. About five minutes had passed since she lost the car from view, as usual.

Her first thought was not to answer it, but that wouldn't do. He knew that she was at home, after all. And that Harry was out. That was the clever part. He had once said: we've got this very nicely arranged, haven't we?

He didn't generally say much, either.

So she answered the phone. And he came over. It took half an hour, which was also just as usual, and after he left her, she made the same excuse to herself that she always made.

If I can give myself to Harry, then I can give myself to him, as well. I can give myself to anyone – it really doesn't matter any more.

Because Harry's always going to be the worst.

And the boy slept on.

It had started about six months ago. The week between the first two Sundays in advent, and she was at the sink, peeling potatoes. Harry was out, it was early evening and suddenly he was there, sitting at the kitchen table. This was not unusual in itself, but it took her by surprise nonetheless. She hadn't heard him coming, he must have sneaked in really quietly. Although the radio was on of course; she remembered switching it off when she caught sight of him.

She asked if he wanted coffee and he shook his head.

'It isn't coffee I want.'

She thought his voice sounded strange. She didn't entirely recognize it. As if he was nervous about something, which he generally never was. Not in the slightest.

So she realized right away that something unusual was happening.

'That loan,' he said.

She didn't reply. She felt the uneasiness taking hold of her.

'The repayment's due now, before Christmas.'

'You'll have to talk to Harry about that.'

'Do you really think that's a good idea?'

'What do you mean?'

There was an ambiguity in the situation – something she could not interpret – but she went on peeling, her back turned to him. It felt safest that way. It wasn't the first time he had demanded his money back; she didn't know how much they owed, but it was no doubt quite a sum. Harry didn't run the farm as well as he ought to, they were always short of money and his cousin at Great Burma was always the one they turned to. Someone like Harry didn't find it easy to swallow his pride and go cap in hand, anyone could see that; every time he was forced to, it added to his bitterness and anger. And he didn't discuss it with her, of course not. Beyond saying that life was an arsehole. A gigantic, fucking unfair arsehole – if they put that on his gravestone he would have no objection, none at all.

He gave no immediate reply to her question. He sat there at the kitchen table fiddling with something, possibly a couple of spoons, she still remembered the faint metallic sound of them in the seconds before he said it – before she understood; remembered it as well as if it had happened just now, not six months ago.

The silence. Only the tick of the kitchen clock and the chinking of the spoons. The action of the peeler in her hand. Yes, it felt like yesterday.

'We could arrange it another way.'

'What?'

'You and I could make another arrangement.'

She stopped peeling. His voice gave it away before he even said the actual words. It was thick and scared at the same time. Scared by his own presumption.

'You're a beautiful woman, Ellen.'

The clock ticked. He cleared his throat and mustered his courage.

'Pity to have money worries in the run-up to Christmas.'

She put the peeler down on the draining board. Slowly turned to face him, drying her hands on her apron.

'It'd be a real pity if—'

He broke off. For a second, something weighed itself up in her head, and that, too, was a moment she remembered with utter clarity, long afterwards. The fact that she could just as easily have told him to go to hell. That she virtually had it on her tongue; but when she saw his shamefaced look, his helplessly horny state, she took the other option.

Gave in.

Simply that.

Was that really how things had gone? Despite her very clear memory of the strained conversation in the kitchen, looking back it was hard to believe in . . . in the casualness of it all. That first time she hadn't even needed to take all her clothes off. She had just taken off her knickers and pulled up her skirt. They did it out in the laundry room, and it was all over in five minutes.

They were partway into January before it happened again. The same stumbling conversation, the same allusion to how much money they owed, but the bedroom instead. More or less naked, and almost fifteen minutes that time.

They never talked about it. Not even while they were doing

it. It was a sort of tacit agreement; no words were called for and she was glad of it. She thought of them as fucking like dumb animals. Once, it was in the middle of March, she had experienced something almost like arousal while they were at it.

But only that once. The feeling had never come back. The only coming back was done by him, over and over again.

And anyway, if she had enjoyed it, what sort of agreement would that have been?

She stood at the window and watched him stroll back up to his farm. That idea of comparing people to animals came back into her mind. What sort of animal was Göran? The hyena, the pig, the mouse and . . . ? She had known for a long time that Ingvor was a cow, more dairy than beef, but her husband was harder to place. Despite what he was getting up to, he was no bull, absolutely not. There wasn't any other association that came readily to mind, either; his outline was too blurred. His character somehow indistinct. Even though she had by now seen almost every bit of him, it was hard to visualize him naked. He was always smartly dressed, even on workdays – despite living so far out in the country and working with the animals and in the fields, where you were pretty much bound to get dirty. And if there was any common denominator for animals, it was surely that they had no clothes?

Merely human then, she thought, watching him pass out of sight beyond the hedge of fir trees. Nothing more, because in his case it was most definitely reductive. He was taking a route back over the fields, the way he generally did; it meant he would arrive home from another direction. If anybody – his cow or his kids (calves?) – wondered where he had been for the past hour, he could say he'd been out on the estate. Fixing a fence, looking for a sheep or something. It naturally wouldn't have done to say he had been at Little Burma with Harry's Ellen. Having sex, the way they did from time to time. Because she wouldn't care to think what might happen at Great Burma then.

She sometimes imagined that she held the advantage. Whatever happened in life, however badly things went, at least one day she would be able to sit down at the other side of the table up there in Great Burma's gleaming kitchen with its wealth of burnished copper, fix frigid Ingvor with a look and tell her that her precious kingpin farmer wasn't above traipsing down to pathetic Little Burma to fuck the pathetic little woman next door.

Because he wasn't allowed to do it with his oh-so-refined wife any more. So she had heard.

Well, yes, that would have been some kind of revenge. Short-lived and joyless, undoubtedly, and as for how things would play out for her afterwards, it didn't bear thinking about. In view of what Harry was capable of on a daily basis, in normal circumstances, let alone when things went awry.

She went to the bathroom and took a shower. She let the water cascade over her tired body like some undeserved act of mercy, washing away the semen of two cousins.

Then she finally went in to the boy. It was fifteen minutes before noon. She still felt queasy.

20

Tuesday and Wednesday saw numerous fruitless attempts on Barbarotti's part to make contact with Ellen Bjarnebo. He rang her mobile once an hour, and her landline in Rocksta at roughly the same intervals; there was no answer from either of them, and no way of leaving messages. He sent two more texts, but both went as unacknowledged as the one he had sent the week before.

He also took a trip to Valdemar Kuskos gata, but there was nothing there to indicate that the former axe woman had returned from her guest house in Norrland. He spoke to two neighbours, but neither of them had seen hide nor hair of her for several weeks. No, they didn't know her, but oh yes, they knew who she was. Everybody in the neighbourhood did.

On Wednesday morning he tracked down the details of the relevant guest house in Vilhelmina and in the afternoon he put through a call. It turned out to be named Ragnhild's, after the present owner's mother. The owner herself was called Mona Frisk, and she told him that the establishment was very popular and had been open for more than sixty years, and confirmed that they had had a guest by the name of Ellen Bjarnebo staying in Room 12 for the past two weeks – but said that she had left, as planned, on Sunday morning.

Left? Barbarotti had queried.

Yes, on the bus from the bus station down in town, Mona Frisk had explained. Lycksele and Umeå, then the train south. You could fly from Vilhelmina Airport, of course, and reach Stockholm Arlanda in an hour, speedy as you liked, but Bjarnebo did not like flying, if she had understood correctly. What was the reason for his call?

Barbarotti had avoided answering. He had thanked her, hung up and sat at his desk absorbed in thought for a good while.

Train from Umeå? How was the service on that route nowadays? The tracks were used by a number of different rail operators; it was not like the old days when Swedish Railways had the monopoly, but that shouldn't make much difference, should it? If you set out from Umeå on a Sunday evening, you ought to be in Kymlinge within twenty-four hours, even so.

Tuesday morning at the absolute latest. Today was Wednesday. It was half past two. He tried again. No reply from either her mobile phone or her landline.

The mobile might not be working, that was one possibility; he certainly found himself obliged to buy a new one every couple of years. Ellen Bjarnebo's had worked for a few seconds when he spoke to her last week, but it could have given out on her since then. Or the delay could simply be because she had decided to break her journey on the way back. To see her son in Stockholm, say? Why not?

He rang that number and the call was answered by the same woman as before. His wife. Billy was at work this time, too; hadn't they arranged to meet at the weekend? Her tone was a little sharper than he remembered it from the previous call.

Yes, they had, confirmed Barbarotti. The reason he was ringing now was that he wanted to get hold of Billy's mum. Did she – he realized he had never found out her name, or had forgotten it – did she have any idea where her mother-in-law might be? Was she, in fact, currently visiting them?

Most definitely not. They saw very little of Billy's mother. There were reasons for that and, if Mrs Billy remembered rightly, they hadn't heard from her since Easter time. Although possibly her mother-in-law and her husband had spoken on the phone, she did not know for sure.

And that was all she could offer. Barbarotti thanked her and hung up.

'Next week?' he thought. Ellen Bjarnebo had promised she would be back next week – in other words, this week – but she had not specified the day. They had spoken for no more than eighteen seconds, according to his mobile, but that much had been clear.

It was entirely conceivable that she would turn up sometime on Thursday or Friday, having stayed the night with some friend, male or female, along the way. Gävle, Stockholm or Katrineholm, why not? Why should she be in any hurry to get back to Valdemar Kuskos gata in the Rocksta district of Kymlinge – and to a melancholy detective inspector who showed every sign of wanting to drag up that old story again? There was no reason to.

The question was why he didn't buy this simple explanation. And it was a very pertinent question. Why did he feel, more clearly with every passing day and hour, that there was some-thing wrong? That Ellen Bjarnebo was not going to turn up in Kymlinge, either later that week or at any other point.

But because Gunnar Barbarotti had always felt ambivalent – to put it mildly – about intuition, he pushed his questions and doubts aside that afternoon.

That beautiful May afternoon, to be precise. The weather

had finally turned and something a bit more like early summer had arrived. If he had still had a wife in the land of the living, he would very likely – and with joy in his heart – have called her at work and suggested dinner at one of the town's outdoor restaurants.

But he no longer had a wife – that was the way things had gone.

Thursday exceeded even Wednesday, where the weather was concerned. He woke early, to the sun shining in a familiar stripe across the bedroom floor and the loud twitter of the birds in the garden outside. It was half past five.

Today I'm going to get her letter, he thought. It's today.

The thought jolted him wide awake. After ten minutes it was clear that there would be no more sleep for him that night, so he got up, went for a shower and pondered how he was going to handle the day.

Should he stay at home and wait for the postman or go into work? Something – though not intuition – told him there would be no point just sitting there waiting for the letter. That would be tempting fate, mercy and conscience; no, Marianne's words would have to wait until the evening, it was as simple as that. Or at least until after lunch. And the question of how you could possibly write letters and get them posted when you were dead . . . well, he looked forward to some clarification of that conundrum. He made a provisional plan to pop home and check his mailbox in the early afternoon; that was a reasonable compromise. After all, nobody was monitoring his comings and goings.

*

But things did not turn out that way. Thursday was the day of Asunander's return from his leave of absence; Barbarotti did not need to ask for an audience, as he had anticipated, because the chief inspector had left a note on his desk asking him to come to his room at two o'clock.

Which also thwarted his plan for a quick trip home to Kymmens udde. Or was at any rate a clear disincentive for attempting it.

He spent the morning reading, making phone calls and thinking. Ellen Bjarnebo still wasn't answering on either of her numbers and there was no response to his text message, either. He had four different photographs of her, all of them taken more than twenty years ago – two before the murder of her husband, two after – and for want of any more sensible activity, he spent a while seeing if he could read anything from her features. A slight, rather beautiful woman, he thought. Pure lines, high cheek-bones. Roughly the same, dark-brown hair colour in all the photos, perhaps an indication that she didn't dye it; the file told him they had been taken over a period of about eight months. He had no later picture of her to go on; there had been no reason to take her photograph in connection with Morinder's disappearance. But surely there was something he could glean from them, even though several decades had gone by?

A candid gaze and the hint of a smile. A slight fragility, he thought, at least in three of the pictures. Number four was in profile and did not reveal much, but as for the other three, it was hard to imagine this was a woman capable of killing her husband with a sledgehammer and butchering him afterwards. With that unguarded look?

Exactly how a woman of that stamp *ought* to look was hard to say, of course. Murderers rarely displayed black eye patches, broken noses and cauliflower ears these days, and Gunnar Barbarotti needed no convincing that the so-called science of criminal physiognomies was only fit for the scrapheap of criminal history.

But murderers who butchered their victims were unusual, even if it was no harder from a purely technical point of view to joint a human being than a pig. And Ellen Bjarnebo had worked at the Meat Man abattoir in Gothenburg, so perhaps it didn't seem all that remarkable to her, when it came to it? She had described it in all the interviews as a practical matter. He husband had simply been too heavy, and she hadn't wanted to leave him too close to the house.

He put away the photographs and took out another of Gunvaldsson's interviews. The interviewee in this one was a Lisa Koskinen, who had been a neighbour of Arnold Morinder long before he got involved with Ellen Bjarnebo and moved to Rocksta. He had read the transcript a few days earlier, late in the evening; he had decided to come back to it in the clear light of day and was now putting that plan into action. Not least because it contained testimony about the missing woman's character. Or did it?

Gunvaldsson: How many years did you and he live in the same block of flats?

Koskinen: God, ages, must have been getting on for ten years. The whole time I was at that address in fact, from 1976 to 1986, roughly speaking.

Gunvaldsson: Did you get to know him well?

Koskinen: I'd hardly say that.

Gunvaldsson: What do you mean?

Koskinen: He was a bit weird.

Gunvaldsson: Go on.

Koskinen: He was one of those, you know, lone wolves. He'd say hello, but that was about it. He made me feel uncomfortable really.

Gunvaldsson: Uncomfortable?

Koskinen: Yes, I think that's how I'd put it. He had that look in his eyes. Like certain kinds of men do. You know what I mean?

Gunvaldsson: Perhaps. Was there anything else? To make you feel uneasy, that is?

Koskinen: I don't know.

Gunvaldsson: You sound as if you're unsure.

Koskinen: I don't know if I'm right. I mean, nothing ever came of it.

Gunvaldsson: Of what?

Koskinen: [After some hesitation] There was this other neighbour. A young girl on the ground floor.

Gunvaldsson: Yes?

Koskinen: He was a peeping Tom.

Gunvaldsson: A peeping Tom?

Koskinen: Yes, you know. He hung around and spied on

her. She lived on the ground floor so, you know. And . . . well, anyway, she reported him.

Gunvaldsson: You're telling me that this neighbour made an official complaint? On what grounds?

Koskinen: God, I don't know. Harassment, I suppose. But nothing came of it, and she moved away.

Gunvaldsson: What was her name? Are you still in contact with her?

Koskinen: No, I'm not in contact with her. Her name was Linda something . . . Bengtsson, I think. It ended in -son anyway. I think she got together with an American and moved abroad. Well, to the US, I dare say.

Gunvaldsson: When was this?

Koskinen: Which part do you mean?

Gunvaldsson: When she reported Morinder.

Koskinen: Must have been around 1980. Maybe a bit later . . . yes, '81 or '82, I think.

Gunvaldsson: Did you ever discuss this with her?

Koskinen: No. Like I told you, I didn't know her. We bumped into each other in the laundry room now and again, that's all, and that was where she mentioned it. She'd seen him lurking about outside her window at bedtime, she said. On a couple of occasions. That must have been horrible – thinking he was trying to spy on her when she got undressed. Probably wanking while he was at it.

Gunvaldsson: And he wasn't married at that stage?

Koskinen: Married? Morinder? No, I can't imagine that. There was this woman living with him for a while, later on, but it didn't last. She moved out pretty soon. I didn't see her many times.

Gunvaldsson: Do you know what her name was?

Koskinen: I only remember that her Swedish wasn't very good. She could have been English or something.

Gunvaldsson: I see. Is there anything else you can add about Morinder?

There wasn't, and Barbarotti asked himself if Lisa Koskinen's testimony had been all that enlightening after all, even if you read between the lines. He had looked for an official complaint lodged against Morinder, but found no record. Perhaps the ground-floor neighbour had thought better of it, or perhaps Lisa Koskinen had got the wrong end of the stick. Unfortunately this proved impossible to verify, Lisa Koskinen having died in a diving accident in Australia. Three days before the end of the old millennium, to be precise: 28 December 1999, on the Great Barrier Reef.

And a Linda in the USA? He assumed there were quite a few of those. Of course one could go on and ferret out other neighbours of the 1980s, but Barbarotti knew he was lacking the necessary drive. What did it really matter that Morinder was a peeping Tom? Perhaps that young woman had merely imagined it? It was thirty years ago, and Morinder would not be doing any more peeping. Or at any rate, all the signs were that he wouldn't.

It would be simpler just to ring up his ex-wife in Slite again –
if he wanted to go deeper into Morinder's character – but even
that seemed a bit pointless.

He knew that someone like Eva Backman, for example,
would not have accepted such evasions, but this was a one-man
investigation and he had no intention of debating it with her.
There was no plausible reason for thinking that Arnold
Morinder's possible antisocial behaviour at Norra Kyrkogatan
had any connection with his disappearance twenty-five years
later, surely?

No, concluded Barbarotti and slammed the file shut.

This afternoon I shall tell Asunander I'm closing down this
case, he decided.

'Have a seat,' said Asunander. 'Right, where do we stand?'

It was roughly the same question he had used to open every
discussion for the past fifteen years. Barbarotti sat down.
Asunander leant forward, which was his way of showing that
he was all ears.

'Off you go.'

'I have a couple of questions,' said Barbarotti.

'Oh?'

'I've been working on this for nearly two weeks now. I can't
claim to have got particularly far. But I would like to know
why.'

'Why what?' said Asunander.

'Why I'm re-examining this old case at all,' said Barbarotti.
'There must be some reason.'

'There is,' said Asunander.

Barbarotti waited, but nothing followed.

'Would it be asking too much to know what that reason is?'

Asunander pulled at one of his earlobes and then let go. He opened a desk drawer and closed it again. Clasped his hands and looked out of the window.

'For the time being, I have to answer yes. It would be asking too much.'

But it was obvious there was more to come and Barbarotti had the presence of mind to keep quiet.

'I have exactly one month left in this seat.'

You don't say? thought Barbarotti. 'Yes, I know,' he said.

'There are various bits of unfinished business hanging around and annoying me.'

'I can well imagine that,' said Barbarotti.

'Like this dratted Morinder.'

'Ah?' said Barbarotti. 'And why is that?'

'There you go again, asking for reasons,' said Asunander.

'I apologize,' said Barbarotti. 'But you don't happen to want to keep me in some kind of sheltered workshop because I've lost my wife?'

Asunander gave him a hard stare. 'Not at all,' he declared. 'If that were the case, I would have put you on bike thefts. No, I want to find out what happened to Morinder and whether there could be any link to that old business at Little Burma.'

'I get the feeling you're implying something there,' said Barbarotti.

'And I am,' said Asunander irritably. 'Have you spoken to her?'

'Ellen Bjarnebo?'

'Who else?'

Barbarotti sighed. 'No, I haven't spoken to her.'

'Why the hell not?'

'I haven't been able to get hold of her. She's up in Lapland, at a guest house.'

'Lapland? Well, get her down here then. Or go up there. It can't be that damn difficult.'

'Only she isn't there any longer,' Barbarotti corrected himself.

'Isn't there? Where is she then?'

'I don't know.'

Asunander uttered a sound that lay somewhere between a cough and a growl. 'What's that?' he managed to articulate. 'Haven't you even talked to her on the phone?'

'For eighteen seconds,' said Barbarotti.

'Christ almighty,' said Asunander. 'I should have consigned you to the bike thefts. Have you been spending your days on crosswords, by any chance?'

'It might look that way,' said Barbarotti. 'And you're welcome to take me off this case. Bike thefts sound like sweet music to my ears.'

Asunander opened his mouth, but said nothing. Perhaps there was a flash of blackly humorous amusement in his cloudy eyes, but it was hard to say.

'There'll be no bikes for you.'

'I was afraid of that.'

'What are your plans?'

'I'm off to Stockholm for a word with her son tomorrow,' said Barbarotti.

'Her son, eh?' said Asunander with renewed interest. 'Glad to hear it.'

'Plus an interview in Hallsberg.'

'Interview?' said Asunander.

'Conversation,' said Barbarotti.

'In Hallsberg.'

'Yes.'

'And Bjarnebo?'

'I'll make sure I get hold of her,' Barbarotti assured him.

'So shall we say you'll report back on Tuesday?' suggested Asunander with a glance at his watch.

'I assume I shall be better informed by then,' said Barbarotti. 'About the reason I'm doing this, I mean.'

To his surprise, Asunander appeared to be giving this demand some consideration. He furrowed his brow anyway.

'I shall think about it,' he said. 'It's a bit personal, actually. Right, off with you now, I've got two gentlemen from the Security Service cooling their heels outside.'

'The Security Service?' said Barbarotti. Personal? he thought.

'Our friend Fängström,' said Asunander and pulled a face. 'Our poisoned Sweden Democrat. Same time on Tuesday.'

'Same time,' confirmed Barbarotti.

21

A letter just like any other.

A white A5 envelope, handwritten name and address, nothing to indicate who the sender was.

Unfamiliar handwriting, certainly not Marianne's.

He waited to open it until he was alone. Dinner, conversation about how their day had been, someone's overdue assignment on writer Aksel Sandemose, a quiet moment with Jenny. The last of these had become a sort of routine, and as they sat there he wondered if he ought to tell her about the letter, but decided against it. Better to read it first; it might be intended only for him.

He lay in bed and opened the envelope. It was half past eleven.

Inside it a smaller envelope, pale yellow: 'To my darling Gunnar'. Unmistakably Marianne's handwriting. A little card, too, from Elisabeth, Marianne's sister, and he started with that:

Dear Gunnar,

I don't know if I am doing the right thing here, but Marianne gave me this letter about six months ago. She said she wanted me to make sure it reached you if she died. It was almost as if she had some kind of premonition. I was to wait a month, she said, and as it is now that long since she left us, I am

*carrying out her instructions. I have no idea what the letter
says, but I hope it will bring you some kind of comfort.*

*Feel free to ring me whenever you like. We are thinking of
you, and the children.*

Love

Elisabeth

PS Warm wishes from Bosse and the kids too, of course.

It was as simple as that. She had written the letter in advance,
just in case.

It was no stranger than that. He felt a slight wave of disap-
pointment rising in him, even as he wondered what he had
been expecting. When it came right down to it.

Had he actually imagined Marianne would have written to
him from the other side? A letter from the Land of Shadows,
from Philip Larkin's *sure extinction that we travel to and shall be
lost in always* – or from the alternative, which felt so inconceiv-
able and dizzying that all words were thrown off-track. Heaven?
Paradise?

On the other hand . . . on the other hand, she really
had come to him from the back seat of the car and told him
about . . . about this very letter, which he now held in a hand
that was shaking because he didn't really know what was going
on and scarcely dared to open it.

Yes, certainly she had spoken to him about it after her death,
only once, but plainly enough. *I've written you a letter.* And Our
Lord had confirmed it and promised to keep a watchful eye
on the postal service. That was how it was. That was the reality
of it.

Why am I in doubt? thought Gunnar Barbarotti. Why do I
always feel this compulsion to nail down existence at all four

corners? It's so cheerless and miserable. Why is my faith so feeble?

Prostrate beneath His mercy, that's where you should be, Rönn had told him.

He took a deep breath, pulled open the envelope and read:

Dearest Gunnar,

By the time you read this I will have been called home. I'm sorry about that, not because I've ever been afraid of death, as you know, but sorry for your sake. For your sake and the children's – I needed a few more years, I feel that very much, but we have no control over life and death. We've talked about that since my little accident, haven't we, and I know you've been prepared, to some extent.

But I also know how tough it is for you right now. I can imagine that you lie awake at nights, that you worry about not being adequate for the children, that you are trying to contact me in various ways and that you are filled with gloom and despair when it doesn't work.

Because, as I write this, I don't know if it will work. Perhaps we'll find we can meet in your dreams, or I shall be able to come and pester you in some situations, but even though my faith is stronger than yours, I have no idea what is waiting for me on the other side. I only know that I'm not afraid of it. I feel a sense of trust and I want you to feel that, too. The time we live in is just the blink of an eye in eternity, and if we can't have the kind of contact that we hope for in that blink of an eye, well, we shall get it later. All in good time and then forever – try to take that in.

But now I'd like to be a bit practical, if you'll forgive me, my beloved friend. I absolutely hope that you'll grieve for me for a while – I'm worth it – but you have to call a halt in the end. Grief isn't a state anyone should stay in for too long. Please, Gunnar, don't do it! I don't want you to be permanently sad and passive and unhappy; it's no good for either you or the children, and it simply doesn't help. Pay a bit of attention to my grave, a few fresh flowers once a month, at least for the first year, but that's all I ask. No carnations, though, remember that: I can't abide them! And you're very welcome to talk out loud to me if you happen to linger for a while and there aren't too many people around. Perhaps I'll be able to hear you, even if you can't hear me. But you mustn't bury yourself in loneliness and brooding or I shall be disappointed in you. I think you need a woman at your side – in the years we have been together you've always seemed to struggle rather when you were by yourself. But then that's true of most men with a softer side. Now I don't want to force you out into the marriage market right away, but I want to be sure you know what I think. And if it were true that you can sit up in Heaven and pull strings, as some people think but neither you nor I believe, I would honestly try to pull you and Eva Backman a bit closer to each other. Now don't be shocked or read too much into what I say, but she is one of the best people I've ever met, and I reckon the pair of you would be crazy not to give it a little try. Though mainly you, Gunnar, and you are the only one getting a letter like this. If I'm dead, then both of you are free, you know. Unless she happens to have found a man recently, that is. In that case, I withdraw my suggestion.

Well, this is maybe not quite the letter I saw myself writing, or the letter you were expecting, but if I can't think of anything better, I shall just have to leave it like this. I'm going to ask my sister to help and I'm sure she'll do as I ask. I want you to *know two things: firstly, I love you, Gunnar, and feel immensely grateful for the years we had together; and secondly, I will wait for you and keep an eye on you. A loving eye, of course.*

I think it would be best for you not to tell the children what I've written here, especially not the part about Eva – young people can be so sensitive. But you must do as you see fit. In any case, I know that you will take good care of all five of them. And that they will take good care of you. They're grown-up enough now for it to work both ways. Johan will soon be ready to fly the nest, but you must make sure to keep hold of Jenny, and if her dad has other ideas, you can tell him from me to get lost. I know that you and Jenny get on really well and that she certainly doesn't want to live with Tommy and his poor goose of a new wife. If it comes to a battle, then you must fight. Or you'll have me to answer to, when we see each other. Remember I shall be watching you, ha-ha.

Those are the most important things. I may have a few more to add as time goes by – we'll see. I don't even know if you'll ever be able to read this, but perhaps you will.

Kisses from Heaven,

M.

He wept.

He wept and he laughed. Read it again. Slowly, word by word, virtually letter by letter. Then he put his arm around her pillow and gave it a hug. Thank you, my darling, he thought. That was most definitely what I needed.

But . . . but a big nudge from his dead wife to be bold and step out into the love market? Most peculiar, thought Gunnar Barbarotti. And Eva Backman?

Sometimes Marianne didn't know what she was talking

about; he had noticed that even when she was still alive, and the fact that she was now on the other side did not seem to have improved matters.

But he found himself smiling. And he was damned if he could hold that smile in check.

He scrabbled around for the Bible and went straight to Lamentations. The old wall clock down in the living room struck twelve and it was June.

THREE

June 2012

June 1989

22

There was something not quite right about Lisbeth Mattson.

He reached that conclusion on about ten seconds' acquaintance. She was around seventy, perhaps a little younger, a thin, slightly crooked-looking woman with small, nervous movements and a voice an octave higher than it should have been.

It wasn't her voice that made him wonder, however, but her facial tics. Admittedly she looked him in the eye as they shook hands, but instantly looked away. She found it very hard to stop her gaze from flitting restlessly, and the corners of her mouth turned continually up and down, as if she were trying out a smile but realized every time that it wasn't working.

Nerves, thought Barbarotti, following her into an over-furnished living room. An anxious old squirrel woman. I need to slow things right down here.

He had walked from the railway station. It was only about a kilometre, and the town did not seem to have changed very much since his last visit. He had been hunting the Mousterlin Man on that occasion; this time he had no real idea what he was after.

He had passed the watch and clock shop where he remembered having bought the worst wristwatch he had ever owned, but he did not go in and complain. Time did not seem to play all that large a role in his life any more and the shop could have changed owner. Five years had elapsed, after all.

The detached house where Lisbeth Mattson lived was right by the railway line, as were many other things in Hallsberg, and he knew that her husband, who was Ellen Bjarnebo's elder brother, had been a Swedish Railways' employee. He also knew that the man had died a little under a year before, and once his widow had come to rest in the green armchair opposite him, he began to understand that her nerviness was linked to the shock of her loss. Or that was one factor, at the very least.

'It feels so empty with Gunder gone,' she began. 'I don't know how I'm going to get through this.'

'Was it unexpected?' asked Barbarotti.

'Yes, a bolt from the blue,' declared Lisbeth Mattson. 'Nobody should be allowed to die like that.'

'You're right,' said Barbarotti and swallowed. For a few moments he fixed his eyes on a stuffed bird perched above the TV set and tried to compose himself. This was not a topic of conversation he wanted to get caught up in.

'It's awful,' said Lisbeth Mattson. She smiled but instantly regretted it. Made a vague gesture towards the plate of biscuits, folded her hands, but then changed her mind. Started to rearrange her facial muscles, but thought the better of it and put on a pair of glasses. They had pale blue frames and would have looked perfect on a twelve-year-old. Barbarotti cleared his throat.

'I've come to talk to you about Ellen Bjarnebo,' he said. 'And Billy.'

This did nothing to calm her. 'Why? What on earth would be the point of raking up that old story? I mean . . . I think—'

She broke off. He had already explained his business over

the phone, after all, so it probably struck her that the time for surprise was past. For his part, Barbarotti wondered whether there was any better response than the same old meaningless excuse of tying up a few loose ends, but failed to come up with one.

'We're working on a few loose ends,' he said.

'Ends?' said Lisbeth Mattson, as if she had never heard the phrase before.

'It's important to get to the bottom of things,' clarified Barbarotti. 'And there's a second case as well, in which your sister-in-law may possibly have been involved . . . a case that we weren't able to clear up. Perhaps you know about it?'

'Please don't call her my sister-in-law,' said Lisbeth Mattson. 'All right, I know we were . . . but we've never related to each other in that way.'

'Is that so?' said Barbarotti. 'But you took care of her son – you and your husband?'

'We certainly did.'

'How did that come about?'

'How did it come to be arranged, do you mean?'

'Yes.'

Lisbeth Mattson gave a little jerk of the head and took off her glasses. 'It was for the boy's sake. Not for hers.'

Barbarotti was on the verge of saying that he understood, but held his tongue and asked her to give him a bit more detail.

'Detail?' she asked. 'What sort of detail do you want? There's nothing more to say about these things, and if Gunder was still alive, he'd . . .'

She trailed off. A series of small twitches distorted her face and Barbarotti was aware of wishing that he had Eva Backman at his side. He said nothing and tried to look like a benevolent father confessor.

'Sorry,' she said after a while. 'I haven't really been myself, and thinking back to that old story opens up all the raw wounds in my heart again.'

She blinked at him a couple of times, evidently content with this poetic form of words. Barbarotti blinked back and gave a cautious nod.

'You're quite right that we took care of Billy,' she went on without any prompting. 'What would have become of him otherwise, poor boy? We made our minds up on the spot, as soon as it had happened, Gunder and I. We had no children of our own, after all, and we . . . well, we've always thought of Billy as our own son.'

'How old was he when he came to you?' asked Barbarotti, although he knew the answer.

'Twelve,' said Lisbeth Mattson and gave a deep sigh. 'Just to think, he was already twelve and he could barely talk.'

This was news to Barbarotti, up to a point. He had read that Billy Helgesson had been an introverted and slightly problematic boy, but there had been no mention of him not speaking.

'I didn't know that,' he said. 'What lay behind it?'

'It was his home life,' came Lisbeth Mattson's instant response. 'His parents, of course. Ellen and Harry were really the worst mother and father you could think of. Billy was scared, it was as simple as that. Scared of the scoldings and beatings for the least little thing.'

'But when he came to you, his speech improved?'

'It did,' Lisbeth Mattson agreed eagerly. 'It improved pretty quickly. At school, too. He made friends . . . he'd never had any before.'

'Did you and your husband see much of the family?' asked Barbarotti. 'I mean, before you took the boy on?'

She shook her head. 'No, we saw barely anything of them. But we still knew how things were. We went there just once that summer and Gunder actually said – once it had happened, a few weeks after our visit, that is . . . I'm muddling things up here, but . . .'

She hesitated and eyed him uneasily.

'What did Gunder say?'

'He said he wasn't surprised.'

'Really?'

'Yes. It was exactly what he'd been expecting, for one of them to eventually kill the other. That was what he said – *exactly what he'd been expecting.*'

'Your husband didn't exactly get on with his sister, then?'

'No,' said Lisbeth Mattson, 'they didn't get on at all. There was . . . well, there was something not right about her. Even before . . . before things went the way they did.'

But this was said with no aggression, noted Barbarotti. It was more as if she was repeating something that had been a refrain and a sad fact for many long years. Mrs Mattson's late husband had undoubtedly been the one who ruled the roost at their home in Kvarngatan in Hallsberg; he would have been the one to write those refrains, and Barbarotti decided to try to move the historical narrative on a little.

'What sort of contact was there between Ellen and the boy while she was in prison?' he asked.

'What?' said Lisbeth Mattson, as if she did not really understand the question.

'Contact between Billy and his mother?' he repeated.

She did not reply at once. Her mouth worked a little and

he could see she was struggling with reluctant words. He waited.

'Billy calls me Mum,' she said. 'That's the way it is.'

'I see,' said Barbarotti. 'Well, he lived with the pair of you for a long time, so it's probably natural. How long was it, all told?'

'Nearly twelve years,' she said.

He knew it could only have been nine or ten, but chose not to query it. 'And after that?' he asked.

'After he finished his military service, he met Juliana and they moved to Stockholm.'

Yet another source of conflict, if he was not much mistaken. As she pronounced the woman's name, Barbarotti somehow found a picture of a vegetarian in his mind's eye – a vegetarian who had put a meatball in her mouth by mistake and was desperate to get it out as fast as she could. The image was as unexpected as it was telling, but he was not sitting in this uncomfortable armchair in the role of poet or therapist, and he supposed it was time to pin her down. To try, at any rate.

'I realize there are strong emotions in play here,' he said. 'But I'm really only after the answers to a few simple questions. So how often did Billy go to visit his mother while she was serving her sentence?'

'Once,' replied Lisbeth Mattson.

'Once?'

'Yes.'

'You're telling me the boy only visited his mother once in eleven years?'

But Lisbeth Mattson clearly did not see anything odd in this. 'A pastoral care adviser at his school arranged it,' she explained.

'We thought it was a stupid idea, and Billy was upset after-wards.'

'When was this?' asked Barbarotti.

'When she'd been there for a couple of years,' said Lisbeth Mattson with a shrug. 'Billy and the pastoral adviser did the round trip in a day.'

'Hinseberg prison isn't particularly far from here, is it?'

'I think it took them about an hour by car,' said Lisbeth Mattson. 'Less, even. Billy was back home by the evening. But he was in a state. It was a misjudgement, but we didn't make a fuss. That adviser left the post quite soon afterwards.'

The sun had rounded a corner and was starting to find its way into the room where they sat. She got up, went over to the window and adjusted the blinds so the table was once again in shadow. She tried another of her abortive smiles before she sat down again.

'There's too much sunshine nowadays.'

'Just so,' said Barbarotti.

'And so many dreadful things. You read in the paper—'

She broke off and began polishing her glasses. Barbarotti's sense of discomfort intensified and he wished he could end the conversation there and then, head straight back to the railway station and make his escape. He gulped a mouthful of coffee, but it had a funny taste, like face powder left uncovered overnight. Another of those weird sensory experiences, but that was the way of things with him at the moment. It was what he had tried to describe to Rönn. This is a conversation that could just as well be taking place in some corner of the madhouse, he thought.

'Didn't she ever get day release?' he asked, in a bid to get back onto his agenda. 'So she could come and see Billy.'

'Once,' she repeated flatly. 'She was here once.'

'And?' asked Barbarotti.

'There was no point to that, either. She made the boy nervous.'

'And when she was released?'

'Billy was on military service by then. And he moved away afterwards.'

'To Juliana and Stockholm?'

'Yes.'

Barely audibly.

'When did you last see her?'

'Ellen?'

'Yes.'

'It was that time. When she came here.'

'Which year was that?'

'1993. They let her out for the day. It was the year after Billy went to see her.'

'In Hinseberg?'

'Yes.'

'Didn't she come to her brother's funeral?'

'No.'

'Why not?'

'I asked her not to. I didn't want her there in the church with all those people.'

This silenced Barbarotti for a moment. The thought in his head was that if Lisbeth Mattson asked to borrow twenty kronor from him, he would say no.

'Did Billy talk about his mother very often?'

'He never talked about his mother.'

'Never?'

'No. When he came to us, he didn't talk at all. I told you that.'

Barbarotti raised his coffee cup and put it down again.

'And as for Billy, what sort of contact do you and he have these days?'

He might just as well have kneed her in the solar plexus. She bent over as if he actually had. Then slowly straightened up again.

'Sorry. It's my stomach ulcer. What did you say?'

He noted that she had switched to using the formal pronoun for addressing him.

'I asked how contact is between you nowadays – you and Billy.'

'It's good.'

'Do you see each other very often?'

'Not especially. We speak on the phone sometimes.'

'What line of work is he in?'

'He's a builder. He always has a lot on.'

'When did you last see him?'

'It was a while ago.'

'A while?'

'Yes.'

'They have children, don't they? He and Juliana?'

'A girl, yes. Julia.'

'I'm seeing Billy tomorrow. Would you like me to give him your regards?'

She gave a start. 'Yes . . . no, there's no need. I may give him a ring this evening.'

Right, that's it, thought Inspector Barbarotti and got to his feet. I'm calling a halt here. If I carry on, I shall find myself in that corner of the madhouse along with her.

'Thank you for letting me talk to you for a while,' he said. 'I'll leave you in peace now.'

'Thank you very much,' said Lisbeth Mattson.

She put on her spectacles, took them off again and showed him to the door.

Just over an hour later he was on the train again. Trying to remember if he had ever in his life been part of such a dismal conversation, but he could not come up with one offhand. He was also pretty sure that if Lisbeth Matsson had not happened to live right on the route between Kymlinge and Stockholm, he would not have bothered to seek her out at all. Which would undoubtedly have been best for both parties.

He was not looking forward to the encounter with Billy Helgesson and his Juliana, of course not, but at least Stockholm also meant Sara. Perhaps he would not have bothered with Billy, either, if Sara had not happened to live there. It was as well to be honest about his own motivation.

There was really only one protagonist whom it was vital for him to talk to, and that was naturally the leading character herself: Ellen Bjarnebo.

He had called and texted her from the train that morning, but again to no avail. It certainly was starting to seem a little strange. It was Friday, she had said she would be back in Kymlinge in the course of the week, and she had left Vilhelmina five days ago.

What the heck is the woman up to? thought Barbarotti. Is she keeping out of the way deliberately, or what?

And what the heck was he himself up to? That was a burning question in its own right. Thinking back to his meeting with Asunander, he could only note that it had clarified nothing. Except, well, possibly, that there was some vague reason behind it all.

A reason for him to be sitting on this – currently stationary – X2000 express train in the rather lovely setting of a forest in early summer, somewhere in the borderlands between the two provinces of Närke and Södermanland, on the hunt for an old truth or two that had not yet revealed so much as the letter they started with.

The truth of the Arnold Morinder case.

The truth of the Ellen Bjarnebo case.

Oh well, thought Barbarotti at the very moment the train eased forward again, there are clearings in the forest that you can only find when you're lost. Perhaps it was the same with truths? Why not?

That line about clearings was in something Marianne had read out to him. Tranströmer, presumably, a poet whose work had always been in the pile of books on her bedside table.

No, not *had been*, because the pile was still there. God forbid that he should touch them. God forbid that he should erase any traces prematurely. He retrieved her letter from his bag, leant back and started reading.

23

3 June 1989

He looked so vulnerable. That was the word that came to her when she saw him sitting on his bed with a comic. Vulnerable. Despite his size; he was the tallest and heaviest eleven-year-old in his school, but it made no difference. He wouldn't hurt a fly, she thought as she went over to him and stroked his hair. He peered at her from under his scruffy white fringe, and when she looked at his face, at least she could detect no sign of a fist having struck it.

Why am I letting this happen? she thought. Why is this allowed to carry on?

Why can't we summon the strength to revolt, the boy and I?

But, as usual, the questions made no serious impact. The weight of shame in the other scale-pan was too great and, with shame weighing down the other side, you were helpless. That was how it worked, her mouse childhood and mouse upbringing had taught her as much. You could think – all manner of things – but actual action was out of the question.

'Did you sleep well?'

He looked at her and gave a vague nod. His mouth, with its full, pouting lips, was an inverted *u*. She expected no proper

answer and, as the years passed, it grew more and more difficult to talk with him. To talk *to* him, because that was all it
ever amounted to. She wondered about the progress that his
teacher had referred to; perhaps it was just the sort of thing
they said to comfort parents?

But he could read, write and count, that was undeniable.
And she still felt that tenderness for him. It came and went in
waves and right now, as he sat there on his unmade bed with
his Disney comic on his knee – he had got out of his pyjamas,
at any rate, put on his jeans and green T-shirt, the same things
as he'd worn yesterday, he only ever put fresh clothes on if
she told him to – in that moment of vulnerability then, she
would have liked to fold him in her arms. Just hold him like
that, rock him if he would let her, and try to convey some
sense of security to him. Confidence and hope, and that sort
of thing.

But he didn't like being hugged. He always went rigid and
heavy – heavier than ever, if you tried, she didn't know why,
but there was no mistaking the fact that he found it unpleasant.
As if he were hostile to his own body in some sad way, and
therefore hostile to everyone else's as well.

Then it struck her that it was Saturday.

Harry was in town, but it was hardly likely he would bother
with anything beyond his own needs. Hung-over and irritable,
as usual. She thought for a moment.

'Shall we go for a walk?' she said. 'To the petrol station. And
get some Saturday pick'n'mix?'

He raised his eyes and his whole face brightened.

'Ohh . . .'

*

The Shell petrol station was merely 500 metres along the road from Burmavägen, at Hamrakorset, so it was only about two kilometres there and back. It was a well-worn stretch. If they needed anything, the petrol station was the closest shop. Milk, cigarettes or a newspaper. Harry always took the car, while she and Billy normally cycled. But she had a puncture, of course, and she wouldn't trust herself on Harry's rickety men's bicycle.

And Billy seemed to have no objection to going on foot. The weather was good, too, a day that was a real prelude to summer, with blue skies and a few drifting clouds, and as she looked out over the green fields around the two farms she found herself thinking that days like this were made for being happy. Happy merely to exist.

It was another of those notions that were nothing more than dust-collecting constructions in her head. Happiness? Joy? There wasn't the remotest hope of cinematic confections like that ever coming within their reach. The good things of the world didn't belong to them and it was ridiculous to imagine they might. She would have liked to hold her son's hand, but the same thing applied there. Nothing but a fleeting thought.

As they approached Great Burma she could see that the builders' vans were there today as well. There was clearly a deadline for the pool job; it had to be ready for the summer of course. Maybe for the end-of-school celebrations next Friday? Would Tomas and Erik be inviting their classmates round? Or Inger? An invitation to swim in a blue pool to mark the start of the summer holidays? Swanky as you like – yes, that must be it.

She imagined what it must cost to have the builders there on a Saturday, but there was never any shortage of money at the big farm. That was a simple fact. And that recurring self-indulgence of his, down at Little Burma, didn't cost a thing, did it? Beyond the delayed repayment of a little loan that was presumably neither here nor there to them.

She let her mind slide over to the cousins and the farms, a familiar succession of thoughts in the same old rut.

The way it had all been staked out in advance, somehow, when Harry and Göran's fathers, the Helgesson brothers, came to this place to settle fifty years ago. Back then there was nothing here but two smallholdings, the sort allocated to returning soldiers, and not even a proper road to reach them; that was why they had had to build the Burma Road. It was a reference to some famous road project far away in Asia that was going on at the same time, but she didn't know the details. In any event, each of the brothers had built his own new farmhouse, brought more land under the plough and established himself in the district; they had money with them from a farm they had inherited down in Halland, and, as far as Ellen knew, neither had had more than the other. But maybe they had, after all? Maybe Sven, the elder brother and Göran's father, had had more money in his suitcase right from the start than Arvid, Harry's father? She didn't know, and it was never talked about, but a difference had soon emerged, she did know that. The very names, Great Burma and Little Burma, gave away their relative strengths. And the locations: Sven's farmhouse on the hill, with a prospect over everything, Arvid's crouching on the edge of the forest.

They were gone now, and had left their farms to their respective sons. Harry was an only child; Göran had a younger sister, who had made an early marriage to a dentist and was out of the picture from then on. She lived in Trondheim in

Norway, and although Ellen had by this time been at Little Burma for fourteen years, she had only met her three times. Two of those occasions had been funerals: Sven's in 1977 and Arvid's two years later.

And the women at the farms, her train of thought continued, they didn't really count, did they? Harry never spoke of his mother, who had died of some kind of lung condition in the late 1950s. And she knew virtually nothing about Göran's mother. She was in residential care and had been there ever since Ellen came to Burma. She must be about ninety by now. She was called Louise, a name she shared with the late Queen of Sweden.

So Harry had only been ten or eleven when his mother died, and she thought about how that had left its mark. Just as her own mother's death had done. She also thought about phrases like that – how little they really meant. It leaves its mark. It was as obvious as it was empty. Everything left its mark. Could Harry's mother's death explain why he hit his wife thirty years later then?

Had Arvid been as bitter as his son? That was another question for mulling over. Was it passed down without resistance? Had Harry's father spent his life at Little Burma in rancour and rage, exactly as Harry was doing now? He had certainly shown no pleasure at the arrival of a grandson, she remembered. Billy had been barely two when his grandfather died, and it was hard to know whether the boy had any memory of the old man.

Life and death. Generation after generation. The same old song?

*

As for her, she had come to Little Burma because she was pregnant. It was as simple as that. They lost their first baby, a little girl, two months before she was due, but it was too late by then. They were already married, she and Harry.

She thought about her own family a bit as well, as they toiled along the little road between the fields – there was no avoiding the topic. Her mother, who had had a screw loose and had ended up taking her own life. Her brother and father, two silent men. They knew how to talk, they weren't like Billy, but they almost invariably chose not to. When Ellen was eighteen and had completed the two-year upper-secondary course for less outstanding young people, she was offered a job at the Meat Man processing plant in Gothenburg. The offer came via one of her teachers, who had taken to her for some reason. The teacher's husband was some kind of foreman there.

It's probably just as well, her father had said. You go. Gunder had already gone, several years before. He was living in Katrineholm, working for the railway.

And it was in Gothenburg that she met Harry, at a dinner-and-dance place. After only a couple of months. They had both got wasted and randy, and he'd come back with her to her dismal little bedsit in Majorna. Initially she had described it in different terms, but the urge to embellish had faded over time.

Wasted and randy – no need to mince words. And she fell pregnant, that was the whole story.

And took the consequences.

Yes, that really is the whole story, she thought. And now I'm being screwed by two cousins. I'm the wife of one and the whore of the other.

Two men's woman.

I ought to be Billy's and no one else's.

They had left Great Burma behind them, but just as they came down to the long straight stretch to the main road, as they passed the patch of lilacs running wild on the right, the Mutti voice made itself heard. Plain and clear, as always. And this time it was not addressing a new bus driver.

There is someone watching you, it said.

She immediately felt that it was true. That there was someone standing close by, observing them.

She paused mid-step and looked around. She could see nothing; that was to say, she could see no other person, but the lilac foliage was rustling and shifting, wasn't it? She stood stock still for five seconds and Billy stopped, too, a few metres ahead, but seemed as oblivious to his surroundings as ever.

Nothing. No movement in the lilacs. Or anywhere else. Except for the birds in the air, singing in the June sky. Larks, if she wasn't mistaken.

Watching me? she thought. Ingvor, is it? If not her, then who?

Don't be stupid. Piggy and Mousey on their way to buy sweets at the Shell garage at Hamrakorset. Who would lift a finger to keep watch on those two?

Who on earth would bother?

24

He met Sara at the Kryp-In pub on Prästgatan in the Old Town, as arranged. It was just after seven, her final exam of the term had ended less than three hours before, and he could see from the way she looked that it had gone well. They got seats at an outside table in the narrow lane and he had a sudden sense of her radiating something. Youth, belief in the future, that sort of thing. Beauty and intelligence, too, and much more besides, of course; it made him feel proud and old in equal measure and he was pretty happy with that. What more could he wish for in his current situation? The observer's gaze, passive, yet always alert. Ready when required, but only then. He wondered whether there would be an opportunity to meet that boyfriend over the weekend; she had hinted that there would, and whoever he was, Gunnar Barbarotti thought he deserved congratulating. You could scarcely imagine a better catch than Sara.

My God, he thought, why am I using a phrase like that?

But she turned the radiance down a few notches as soon as they were seated at their table. Became a daughter rather than a woman.

'How are you, Dad?'

'You've got to stop asking me how I am, Sara. It takes time, that's all.'

'It's good manners to ask someone how they are when you see them.'

He blinked at her. 'Not in that tone. You sounded as if you were talking to a patient. Or to someone who's just been run over by a steamroller.'

'And haven't you?'

'Of course I have,' he admitted. 'But that was a while ago. I'm more normal than you think.'

'Good,' said Sara. 'We'll talk about everything properly, but let's eat first. I'm starving.'

'I can see that the exam went well.'

'You know what, I think it did.'

'So now it's your summer holidays? More or less?'

She laughed. 'Dad, I'm twenty-four. Summer holidays like that are a thing of the past, you know that.'

'Yes, I suppose so.'

'I shall come down on Sunday evening and stay for a week. Then I've got a seven-week placement at a legal firm.'

'Do you really need seven weeks?' asked Gunnar Barbarotti, who for his part had worked for about half that time at a similar establishment down in Lund. But that was back in the dawn of time.

'What would you like to drink?' asked the waitress, who looked about the same age as Sara, but not fully as radiant.

'Red wine?' asked Barbarotti, looking at his daughter.

'Red wine,' said Sara, nodding to the waitress. 'A really good bottle. I reckon it's him over there who's paying.'

Barbarotti put up his hands and smiled. *Him over there.*

It was a warm evening and they stayed at their table in picturesque Prästgatan for several hours. And they genuinely did talk about everything, it seemed to him: about life and death, bereavement and grief. About the boys, about work and the future, Marianne, and Sara's boyfriend Max, whom he would meet the following evening – and once he had paid the bill, they strolled through a Stockholm so beautiful that it made him wonder why he lived in Kymlinge. Five years from now, he thought, five years from now, all the kids will have gone their own ways. Then I shall move here.

He didn't say it out loud, but he realized it was a sign that he was still alive. If you're planning five years ahead, you're not dead. Not quite.

'What have you got to do here in town then? asked Sara when they were back at her small flat in Vikingagatan. It was a sublet – or possibly a sub-sublet – but he knew that was the way the accommodation market worked in Sweden's royal capital. Notwithstanding that, it was an attractive old apartment, with traditional parquet flooring and high ceilings. A view over an inner courtyard where the trees were in blossom. He contemplated the fact that something just like this could be his in five years' time.

'Hmm, well,' he said. 'I don't entirely know. I'm working on an old case. Tomorrow I'm seeing someone who was slightly involved, to try to form some kind of impression . . .'

She poured green tea into his cup and pulled a face at him.

'That's the woolliest answer I've ever heard. But never mind, if you can't talk about it, that's OK . . . Or don't want to, perhaps I should say?'

He considered the matter for a second or two, then told her the whole story in broad outline. The murder and dismemberment at Burma. Morinder and his blue moped. Asunander. And the elusive leading player – and even the dismal interview in Hallsberg, which he had almost managed to repress for the evening.

'How very peculiar,' was Sara's verdict when he had finished. 'I heard about that murder . . . but what I mean is, it's a really tricky one, isn't it?'

'I'm starting to think so, yes.'

She frowned and poured more tea. 'How strange some people are. And sad. Though I have to admit I find it fascinating, too. I can't help thinking I shall end up as some kind of judge, you know. This company law I've got to slog away at all summer . . . no, it isn't really what interests me.'

'Nor me,' admitted Barbarotti. 'If I'd carried on, I'm in no doubt it would have been the judiciary for me. But I didn't really have the right qualities.'

'You mean you didn't study hard enough?'

'Those were different times,' said Barbarotti.

'You came out of it as a pretty smart police officer anyway,' said Sara.

'Now that's where you're wrong,' said Barbarotti.

'Hmm,' said Sara. 'All right, you can come to visit me when I'm a judge at the Supreme Court. Ridiculously palatial premises, in case you didn't know. On Riddarholmen island, with a stunning view over the water. Yes, I can see myself working there.'

Her mouth formed itself into a self-mocking smile, but she was soon serious again. 'So tell me about this Billy. What do you think about him? He must have had a horrendous time of it, growing up . . . How old is he now?'

'Thirty-five,' said Barbarotti, glancing at his watch. 'No, it's never ideal for a child's development to have one parent kill the other.'

'Sometimes you pull it off, you know,' said Sara.

'Even a blind chicken finds a grain of corn once in a while,' Barbarotti reminded her modestly. 'You're right that it can't have been nice for the boy. But as I'm seeing him first thing tomorrow, I'd better get a bit of sleep. This sofa, is it vacant or am I supposed to doss down here at the kitchen table?'

'Well,' said Sara, 'seeing as it's you, you can have the sofa.'

It was not Billy Helgesson who opened the door at 76 Blekingegatan the next day. The woman at the door did not appear particularly thrilled to be opening it, either, but once she had looked him up and down she took a step back and let him in. She was eating a carrot; he wondered whether he had ever been received by a carrot-chewing woman before and came to the conclusion that she was unique, at least in that respect.

'Juliana Peters,' she said when she had swallowed her mouthful of carrot. 'Yes, we were expecting you.'

She was about 185cm tall. Dark and strong-looking, and Barbarotti instantly guessed that she did not have her roots in Knivsta or on the Västgöta Plains. He wondered whether it was biased of him to draw that sort of conclusion and decided it was not. There was something impressive about her, at any rate – she had the look of an Olympic javelin-thrower from, say, Romania.

And in that capacity she obviously had to consume carrots by the kilo every day to stay on top form. Who on earth is letting observations like that into my brain? thought Barbarotti irritably. Be gone, you load of drivel! She had dark eyes anyway, and dark hair with a few streaks of grey creeping in. She must be older than her husband, he thought. By at least five years, possibly more. A hint of an accent, but no more than a hint. German, perhaps?

'Thank you for seeing me,' he said. 'This is easier than having to go to a police station.'

Just as well to emphasize where the power lay, he thought. And he could see that the comment surprised her, but she let it pass unremarked.

'Of course,' was all she said. 'Billy's through there. I thought I'd sit in, if it's all right with you?'

'I have to talk to Billy on his own,' explained Barbarotti. 'I could have a few words with you afterwards perhaps, although it may not be necessary.'

They were still standing in the narrow hallway. She held up the stub of carrot that she had been hiding behind her back. As if she was trying to penetrate its inner mysteries, somehow – or compare it to the police officer she had reluctantly allowed into her home. There was a faint sound of music, playing elsewhere in the apartment, but Billy had yet to make an appearance.

'Julia and I will go and get the shopping then,' concluded Juliana, now the trial of strength was over, and she called out to her husband, 'Billy, that cop's here!'

Five minutes later he was sitting opposite Billy Helgesson across an oval glass table covered in ornaments, mostly little animals, which were also made of glass and arranged on diminutive crocheted mats. There was barely room for their coffee cups. Juliana and Julia – a tall, thin girl of around twelve who had come in to say a polite hello – were off to the shops, with a promise to be back soon. In case the cop wanted a word, as he had indicated.

He wasn't sure she was using the term 'cop' in a derogatory sense. It didn't feel that way.

Billy Helgesson more than matched his wife for size and strength. Outwardly at least, but inner strength was quite likely another matter. That was Barbarotti's immediate impression anyway. There was something pliant and submissive about the big man slumped on the leather sofa; he looked uncomfortable, both in the room and in his own body – and in Barbarotti's company. The coffee cup was like a thimble in his large fist. The only thing he had said so far was a cautious 'Hello'. To say he was diffident didn't begin to cover it, and Barbarotti was reminded of a character in a John Steinbeck book he had read a long time ago, but couldn't remember the name of.

'Right then,' he said as he heard the front door close. 'I'm glad you had time for a little talk with me.'

'Yeah, OK,' said Billy Helgesson.

'As I said,' said Barbarotti, 'I'm here because there are a few things we're trying to clear up. Mainly to do with Arnold Morinder, who your mother lived with for several years. I assume you met him?'

'Yes,' said Billy Helgesson. 'Once.'

'Only once?'

'Yes. I went there.'

'You mean you went to visit them in Kymlinge?'

'Yes.'

'Where did they live?'

'I can't remember the street. In, er, it's Rocksta, isn't it?'

'So you never got to know Arnold Morinder?'

'No.'

He sat there in silence, looking at his big hands. This was what it must be like to interview a skier from Abisko, thought

Barbarotti. One who had broken his ski poles and come last in the race; why should anyone feel compelled to interview a person like that? There I go, showing my prejudices again, he noted. A skier and a javelin-thrower? No, Billy Helgesson was far too bulky for a skier. He quickly closed his eyes and tried to pick up some kind of thread.

'When was this? When you went to see your mum and Arnold Morinder?'

Billy Helgesson thought about it. 'Can't remember,' he said. 'Five or six years ago, maybe. Before he went missing.'

I realize you couldn't have met him *after* he went missing, thought Barbarotti. 'What was he like?' he asked.

'He was quite small,' answered Billy Helgesson.

'And you only met him that one time?'

'Yes,' said Billy Helgesson.

'What did you think of him?'

'Good,' said Billy Helgesson.

'OK,' said Barbarotti. 'How much do you see of your mother?'

'Not much.'

'What does that mean?'

'Eh?' said Billy Helgesson.

'I'm wondering how often you see each other. If you talk to each other a lot, and that kind of thing.'

'Why do you wonder that?'

'Maybe because I need your help,' suggested Barbarotti.

Billy hesitated. Shifted position on the sofa and cleared his throat.

'We don't see each other very much,' he said. 'She rings sometimes. Well, not all that often.'

'I was in Hallsberg yesterday,' explained Barbarotti. 'I had a chat with Lisbeth Mattson. But maybe you don't have all that much contact with her, either?'

Billy Helgesson crossed his arms over his chest. 'I've got my own family,' he said.

'Juliana and Julia?'

'Yes.'

'What was it like growing up in Hallsberg? With Lisbeth and Gunder?'

'It was good,' said Billy Helgesson.

'In what way?'

'They looked after me. They were great.'

Barbarotti paused and sipped his coffee. He hoped Billy might volunteer more information, but nothing came. But those arms firmly crossed on his broad chest seemed to have boosted his self-confidence a touch, so it seemed. I've got my own family.

'When Arnold Morinder disappeared,' Barbarotti went on optimistically, 'you must have spoken to your mum a few times then?'

'No,' said Billy Helgesson. 'Not really.'

'So you never discussed with her what could have happened to him?'

'No.'

'But you knew about it?'

'Yes.'

'How?'

'I think she rang me. It was in the newspapers. But she didn't have anything to do with it.'

'How can you know that?'

'I just know. She told me.'

'Did you ever go out to that fishing hut?'

'What fishing hut?'

'Don't you know that your mum and Morinder had a summer place?'

He hesitated. 'Yes, maybe . . . was that where he left from, on his moped?'

'Yes,' said Barbarotti. 'That's the general opinion, at any rate. So you don't know any more than this?'

'No,' said Billy Helgesson with a careful shake of his large head. 'I don't.'

'All right,' said Barbarotti. 'We'll leave it. When did you last speak to your mother? Does she come and visit you here?'

That was two questions instead of one, and Billy Helgesson thought for a good while before he answered.

'We do Christmas,' he said. 'Sometimes, and she comes then. Juliana's cousin comes, too. Yeah, they were both here last Christmas.'

'Juliana's cousin and your mother?'

'Yes.'

'And when did you last see her?'

'It was then.'

'Last Christmas?'

'Yes.'

'But you've spoken to her on the phone since then?'

'Oh yes,' was Billy Helgesson's emphatic answer. 'Of course.'

'Do you remember when the last time was?'

He thought again.

'It was a few weeks ago. She was going to Lapland.'

'Yes, that's right,' said Barbarotti. 'She's been somewhere up near Vilhelmina, I understand?'

'Yes,' said Billy. 'That's where she generally goes.'

'Oh?' said Barbarotti. 'Always to the same place?'

'I think so. It's run by someone she knows, I'm pretty sure.'

'What else did the two of you talk about when she rang?'

'Nothing special. She just asked how we were and that kind of thing.'

'Did she say how long she would be up in Norrland?'

'No. A week, I think. It could have been a fortnight.'

'Do you know where she is now?'

'My mum?'

Who else, thought Barbarotti. 'Yes, your mum,' he said. 'You don't happen to know where she is at the moment?'

Billy Helgesson lowered his arms from his chest and shrugged his large shoulders. 'Isn't she at home?'

'No, said Barbarotti.

'Or in Lapland?'

'No, she's left there.'

'Then I don't know.'

Excellent, thought Barbarotti. So that's that. How shall we continue this inspiring conversation then?

'Can you think of anyone your mum knows who she might have gone to visit?' he asked. 'I don't mean the guest house. She isn't up there any more. I need to talk to her, and I don't know how I can get hold of her.'

Billy scratched the back of his neck before he answered. 'She doesn't know that many people. No, I can't think of anyone.'

Barbarotti changed tack. 'How did you come to move to Stockholm? After all, you grew up in Kymlinge and Hallsberg.'

'I was on military service,' said Billy. 'And then I met Juliana.'

'You did your military service here in Stockholm?'

'Yes. In the Life Guards.'

Barbarotti wondered whether he wanted to hear Billy

Helgesson's conscription reminiscences and decided he could live without them.

'It must have been terrible for you – what happened at Little Burma?' he said instead. He didn't really know what made him plunge into that question; he had more or less decided to avoid the topic. Billy had been twelve when it happened, and Barbarotti knew the police had made some attempt to engage with him but had been unable to get anything out of him. There were no interview transcripts, only the bare report that they had talked to him. Tried to talk to him – and if Lisbeth Mattson's claim that he was more or less mute at the time was actually true, it was hardly surprising.

'Yes,' was his answer on this occasion. 'But I don't want to talk about it.'

'I can understand that,' said Barbarotti. 'It was an awful thing to happen. Did you get any help in dealing with it?'

'Lisbeth and Gunder looked after me,' said Billy Helgesson.

'I know that,' said Barbarotti. 'And your actual dad, what do you remember about him?'

That was another question he hadn't been intending to ask, but now he had done it, and Billy Helgesson went quiet for some time and resumed staring at his hands, now clasped on his lap.

'He was a bastard,' he said finally. 'I didn't like him.'

'But you like your mum?'

'Yes,' said Billy Helgesson. 'But I've got my own family now.'

Barbarotti decided to leave it at that.

He had a chance to exchange a few words with Juliana Peters, too, before he left Blekingegatan. She and her daughter came back, each carrying a plastic bag of groceries, just as he was in the hall saying goodbye to Billy Helgesson.

They went into the kitchen and closed the door before they started; she was the one who insisted on it, not him.

'There's something I want to explain to you,' she said. 'I married Billy because I needed a husband who would stand up for me and make me feel safe. There were some things that happened to me before we met, but I don't want to go into any detail. I had a difficult time growing up and a difficult life before I met Billy. I know he is like he is, but he's a good father and a good husband. He'll never let me down. I just wanted you to know that.'

'Thank you,' said Barbarotti. 'I think I understand.'

Then he asked whether she could suggest any way for him to make contact with Ellen Bjarnebo, but on that point Juliana Peters had as little information as her husband.

When Gunnar Barbarotti emerged from the front entrance of the flats at 76 Blekingegatan it was a quarter past twelve and, with regard to the so-called investigation he was engaged in, he distinctly felt he had reached the end of the road.

25

Eva Backman was annoyed.

She was annoyed with almost everyone. With Assistant Detective Wennergren-Olofsson, with whom she had been stuck in pointless forensic deliberations until six the previous evening. With her former husband, to whom she had been on the phone that morning. With his silly, stuck-up wife, and with a lawyer called Wilkerson, who had urged the former man and wife to talk to each other. Also on the list: a journalist at the GT newspaper who had called her eleven times in the past two days; Raymond Fängström, for being an idiot and a racist for as long as he lived and then having the bad taste to let himself be bumped off by a poisoner or poisoners unknown; Gunnar Barbarotti, for going to Stockholm so that he wasn't there to grumble at; and Almighty God, for letting Marianne die.

And more in the same vein. To top it all, she would be starting her period in two days' time and it was Saturday.

It was incompatible with Eva Backman's outlook on life to have to work on Saturdays, but when a democratically elected Sweden Democrat dies in suspicious circumstances you simply have to pull out all the stops.

That had been Asunander's phrase at the well-attended press conference the day before and as she was already engaged in listing all the sources of her annoyance, she quickly slotted the chief inspector into one of the medal-winning positions.

She was in her office, waiting. Sitting at her unsightly, wobbly old desk where there was a computer bulging with unanswered emails and a litter of poorly written reports that she still had not found time to read. Outside the window it was the start of summer. Lill-Marlene Fängström had promised to be there at ten. It was now quarter past.

Lill-Marlene? thought Eva Backman. What sort of a name is that?

She was wearing heavy make-up and looked more or less as she did in the newspaper pictures. And as she had done on their previous encounters. A woman of sixty trying to play the part of a twenty-eight-year-old. Lill-Marlene Fängström had made a great song and dance about the death of her son, the elected representative. She voiced her opinions in every conceivable form of media, social and traditional. On her newly started blog she had collected names and voices and supportive comments from a range of dubious sources; some had even expressed the view that she should be allowed take the late Raymond's place on the council.

She had not expressed this opinion herself, however. She had no such ambitions and was not, as far as Eva Backman knew, particularly interested in politics. But it was no secret that she shared her son's general view. In her tweets and her blogs, and in her statements to news-starved journalists, she basically maintained two things: firstly, that the police must be sure to catch the treacherous, untrustworthy foreigners who had killed her son; and when that was done and they (he? she?) were under lock and key, then the rest of them could be sent packing from Kymlinge, too. The other traitors, she meant. Those of foreign extraction, she meant. Or whatever the phrase was. So that honest folk could go about their business at night.

Secondly, she wanted her own police protection. She didn't feel safe in the streets and squares, and of course those murderers would be after her, too.

So that was how things stood. Eva Backman had spoken to her twice before, and it was at Lill-Marlene Fängström's own request that they were having yet another meeting. Late on Friday afternoon (towards the end of that dire session with Wennergren-Olofsson) she had called the police station to say that she had some vital information for them – so vital that she wasn't prepared to give it directly, over the phone.

Later that evening was out of the question, because she would be busy then.

'So it isn't important enough for you to prioritize it, then?' Eva Backman had asked. 'Whatever it is you want to tell us.'

'Pri . . . what?' Lill-Marlene had answered. 'You're talking rubbish. I'm coming in tomorrow morning.'

And here she was finally, sweeping in. Newly tinted hair and high heels.

'Sit down,' said Eva Backman. 'You're twenty minutes late.'

It took a while to establish what the vital piece of information was.

The bereaved mother began with a tearful spell, as she had at the start of both their previous encounters. She apologized, wailed and sobbed for several minutes, and was then obliged to spend quite a while repairing her make-up, while telling DI Backman for the third time about all her son's – her only son's – many unique qualities and good points. His patriotism.

His pride. His unmatched knowledge of Swedish history, his bravery and his passion for justice.

Not forgetting his short but glittering career as a Scout leader and his political talent.

Genius, even. Political genius, that was it. Backman shut her ears as best she could and let the woman run on. Why can't I feel sorry for her? she thought. It's dreadful.

She had done to start with. Of course. A mother whose only son has been killed – the fact that it was a case of poisoning had been established a few days before, but they didn't yet know what kind of poison or how it had been administered; there seemed to be some kind of hitch at the National Forensic Lab – you could barely imagine anything more pitiful and heartbreaking, could you?

But there was something about Lill-Marlene Fängström's performance that proved too much as the days went by. Simply that. Backman had done her best to retain her empathy, but on a day like this – a working Saturday, with all its annoyances – her efforts were pretty much doomed.

'You see, I'd noticed them the day before yesterday,' declared Lill-Marlene Fängström at long last, and paused for effect.

Backman realized she had been lost in thought and straightened up in her chair.

'Sorry. Who had you noticed the day before yesterday?'

'Those men,' said Lill-Marlene Fängström. 'Like I just said.'

'Tell me about them,' requested Backman.

'That's what I am doing, if you hadn't noticed,' said Fängström, swinging one of her high-heeled shoes. It was pale green, clearly several sizes too tight, and hanging from the big toe of the foot she had crossed over the other. 'I'm telling you, I only got a proper look at them yesterday, but it was the day before – Thursday – that I saw them for the first time. There were two of them, and they had no reason to be hanging about just there. Why should they? You get me?'

'Where?' asked Backman. 'Where did you see them?'

'Outside where he lives, of course,' said Fängström. 'I went round to clean the place up. And I went through his things. It's got to be done, hasn't it?'

'Of course,' said Backman.

That was indeed the case. The flat where Raymond Fängström had lived and later been found dead was no longer classified as a crime scene. The forensics team had spent several days making a meticulous search of its sixty-two square metres, taken 250 photographs and laid claim to anything that could conceivably constitute a clue. Fingerprints had been secured. Rubbish bags, strands of hair, a computer and some nail clippings had been removed for analysis. Naturally the victim's mother could go round and do some cleaning if she wanted.

'I saw them from the kitchen window, you see,' went on Fängström. 'Two men sitting on that bench in the courtyard, pretending to talk. But they weren't. They were keeping watch.'

'Keeping watch?' said Backman.

'Keeping watch on the flat,' elaborated Fängström. 'That's what I'm saying. They sat there the whole time I was in the flat. For nearly an hour from when I first spotted them. They had newspapers, but they weren't reading. And they didn't follow me. I called Kjell-Arne and he came to pick me up in the car, so they wouldn't get the chance.'

Kjell-Arne was none other than Lill-Marlene Fängström's current boyfriend. They did not live under the same roof, but they had been together for more than a year, so nothing was impossible. This information had emerged in the course of the two previous interviews. As for the rest of Lill-Marlene's family, there was a daughter named Belinda, now living in Florida. She had been asked the names of the fathers of Raymond and his sister, but had opted not to answer the question. They were entirely irrelevant, in any case.

Eva Backman had written *irrelevant* in the interview transcript without seeking confirmation that this was actually the word intended.

'I'm sorry,' she said, 'there has to be more to go on. Two men sitting on a bench in this nice weather . . . it could very well be a perfectly innocent way of passing the time.'

'Now listen to me: they weren't innocent. I'm going to write about it in my blog this afternoon.'

'That's nothing to do with me,' said Backman. 'But you say that you saw them again yesterday?'

'Yes, I did,' said Lill-Marlene Fängström, her pale-green shoe bobbing up and down even more irascibly. Backman noted that the price label was still stuck to the sole. 'When I was there yesterday, they were sitting in the same place again. Not to start with, but they turned up after a while. The same men, the same bench. They were looking up at the window, too.'

'Did they do anything else?' asked Backman.

'No, they just sat there keeping watch.'

'What did you do?' asked Backman.

'I rang here,' said Fängström. 'As you may recall. Don't you want to catch my son's murderer? I sometimes wonder, I have to say.'

'Of course we aim to catch whoever did it,' said Backman. 'How long did they stay there?'

'At least half an hour.'

'And then?'

'Then they went.'

Backman pondered and made a few illegible squiggles in her notebook to win time. To give herself a few extra seconds in deciding how to handle the information that this semi-hysterical woman was imparting.

'Would you recognize them?' she asked. 'Do you think you could give me a good description of them?'

'I think so,' said Lill-Marlene Fängström. 'One of them, at least. He looked just like that goddamned Morinder.'

'Morinder?' queried Backman.

'Arnold Morinder, yes,' said Fängström. 'I know he's been missing for a few years, but he looked exactly like him.'

Eva Backman closed her eyes for a moment while her synapses caught up with each other.

'You mean Arnold Morinder, the electrician who disappeared five years ago?' she asked.

'Him, yes,' said Lill-Marlene Fängström. 'There can't be that many people with that name in this town, can there?'

'Did you know him?' asked Backman.

'Well, I wouldn't call it that. But we were in the same form at school for nine years.'

'Aha?' said Backman for want of anything better.

'I didn't really know him, though. He was a strange customer. He got together with that Ellen in the end.'

Backman leant over her desk. 'Wait a minute. You're referring to Ellen Bjarnebo, I take it?'

'The axe woman, yes,' said Fängström, turning up her nose. 'Can't exactly be an unfamiliar name to you lot.'

'What do you mean by *in the end*?' asked Backman.

'Is that what I said?' said Fängström.

'Yes,' said Backman. 'You said he got together with her *in the end*.'

'OK. I suppose I said it because he'd been after her ever since we were at school.'

'What?' said Backman.

'He fancied her even then, I remember that. Fucking odd couple – pardon the expression, but that was exactly what they were. I think he was some kind of Gypsy, by the way, that Morinder . . . or *traveller*, they called it, but that sounds way too posh for people like him. Is it because they travel around a lot, do you reckon?'

Can you simply keep quiet for a second, so I can get my thoughts in order, thought Backman.

'She was only in our form for a year, but he was totally infatuated with her,' Lill-Marlene Fängström babbled on. 'And I think she let him once, as well – I mean, not the whole way, only necking. Though she was just as weird herself, such a shrinking violet. She didn't have any friends, that's for sure. Then she changed schools and it was just as well.'

'And when was this?' asked Backman.

Lill-Marlene Fängström put her finger in her mouth and thought for a few moments.

'In Year Eight,' she said. 'Yes, it was in the spring of Year Eight. That was when I saw them necking. It was at a school dance, as we called it in those days.'

'Hang on a minute,' said Backman. 'You're claiming that Arnold Morinder and Ellen Bjarnebo were in the same form in Year Eight, and that they may have . . . got it together, to some extent?'

'What's this got to do with anything?' countered Lill-Marlene Fängström and managed to ram her foot back into her shoe.

'All I said was that one of those guys on the bench looked like Morinder. I'm not saying it actually *was* him. You wanted a description, didn't you?'

Eva Backman leant back in her chair and briefly considered the matter.

'Yes, of course,' she said. 'Well done. And this other man, what did he look like?'

'He looked younger,' said Fängström. 'Long hair dangling down over his face. Hard to get a proper look at him, behind all that. He was dark-haired of course, like the other one. But I couldn't stand there staring at them, could I? I mean, how did I know they weren't armed?'

'Can you tell me what they were wearing?' asked Backman.

At the same time she started her recorder, which she had not felt any need to deploy until now. The mother of the deceased Sweden Democrat took five more minutes to describe the couple on the bench, while Eva let the recorder whirr away and her own thoughts stray in entirely different directions.

Does this mean anything? she asked herself.

And if so, what? Was it significant that Bjarnebo and Morinder had known each other back when they were teenagers? Not a bit, in all likelihood, but the one thing she did know was that this was new information.

Get out of my hair now, you bitch, she thought. I've got an important call to make.

But it was another twenty minutes before Lill-Marlene Fängström was ready to leave Kymlinge police station – and by the time she did so, Eva Backman had instructed her in no uncertain terms to return to the station at 9 a.m. on Monday morning. At that time she would be expected to sit down opposite Assistant Detective Wennergren-Olofsson and repeat to him exactly what she had said in the course of the past hour.

Yes, that was standard procedure in cases of this kind, she explained. They took everything very seriously and left nothing to chance. Particularly when elected representatives were involved. Anything else would be unthinkable.

Alone in her room at last, she rang Wennergren-Olofsson and passed on the observations that had just come her way. She said nothing about Morinder and Bjarnebo, however. Wennergren-Olofsson made a swift assessment of the situation and declared that they were very probably on the verge of a breakthrough. Why wait for Monday morning?

Because it's nice weather, said Backman. Don't get carried away.

She hung up before he had time to protest.

She rang Barbarotti's mobile number. He did not answer, except to tell her that she could leave a message after the beep.

She did so, without revealing what was on her mind. She kept it short and sweet and merely asked him to pull his finger out and call her immediately.

Once this little detail was dealt with, she noticed that most of her annoyance had drained away.

26

3 June 1989

She had meant to set an upper limit, but found herself yielding.

She had meant to say he could spend twenty kronor, but seeing his imploring eyes and sad bottom lip, she gave in. As usual. They bought bootlaces and rainbow strips, little boxes of pastilles and loose pick'n'mix, the whole lot adding up to more than thirty-five kronor, and as they walked back from the petrol station she could see he was happy.

As happy as he could be, anyway. He didn't say anything, of course not, but he walked close beside her, chewing and growling, the way he did when he was feeling good.

As good as he could feel. A sort of vibrating Ur-tone emerging from his throat; she wasn't sure he was aware of it himself. My piggy, she thought, how are you going to cope with life?

As they passed Great Burma on their way back they bumped into Ingvor and Erik, who were just getting into the car to go into town for something, and it struck her that to an outsider it must look like a meeting of two worlds. Erik and Billy were almost the same age, but they had stopped playing with each other by the time they reached seven, they were simply too different. Now they didn't so much as look at each other. Erik

was wearing tight black jeans and a red shirt under a pale-
yellow V-necked pullover; not a single item of his clothing
looked more than a week old, and the same thing applied to
his mother's outfit. It really was like a scene from an old English
film: the master and mistress coming across two of the servants
in front of the house.

'Hello. We're in a bit of a rush.'

'Don't let us detain you,' said Ellen.

I was fucking your husband a couple of hours ago, she could
have added. It would have served no useful purpose, but it
would have been amusing to see their reactions. The son's and
the deceived wife's.

'How's the pool coming on?' she asked instead.

'Very well, thanks,' said Ingvor, making an effort to keep
the smile on her face. For a few seconds she presumably considered whether she was under any obligation to invite them over
for a swim, to try it out, but her more matter-of-fact side
persuaded her against.

'We're in a bit of a rush,' she said again. 'See you.'

'See you,' said Ellen, and Billy gave a growl.

Erik said nothing. He allowed himself a vacant nod, deli-
cately plucked a hair from his pullover and got into the front
passenger seat.

We've one thing in common, at any rate, Harry and I,
thought Ellen as she watched them drive away. We both have
the same opinion of our neighbours.

He took his time getting back.

She had nothing against that, but as the afternoon wore on,
anxiety started to gnaw at her nonetheless. When Harry stayed
on in town, it usually meant he had met up with his old friends.

Not that there were many of those. At a guess, just two: Staffan and Börje – possibly an unpleasant, greasy individual called Ziggy, too – but that would very likely lead to them playing cards. Poker and beer. If Harry lost, he would be in his foulest mood when he got back. And he generally did lose.

What was more, he had the car. They occasionally had discussions about drink-driving. The last one had ended with him giving her a split lip.

She decided to get the Danish pork fillet ready anyway. If Harry was very late, she and Billy could share it, and if there was any left, she would save it for warming up in the oven. She couldn't be certain he would be hungry when he got in, either – he might have had pizza with his mates, like he sometimes did.

A thought that had kept recurring to her lately surfaced again as she sat at the kitchen table chopping mushrooms: it wouldn't make a blind bit of difference if he never came back. If he had a fatal crash when he was driving in a drunken haze, she wouldn't be remotely sorry. Except for the sake of appearances, of course. It was dreadful to be thinking like that, and as usual she pushed the thought away into a poorly lit corner of her consciousness.

It was just a thought, after all, and made no difference to anything. There were quite a few of them tucked in that dark corner.

It was just after half past six when she heard the car arrive and pull up in front of the house. They still hadn't had dinner, so there would presumably be three at table, after all. She went over to the kitchen window and looked out.

She clapped her hand to her mouth, but couldn't help letting out a stifled cry. Billy was in his room, however, behind a closed door, so there was no one to hear her.

It was worse than she had feared. Harry pretty much *poured* himself out of the car.

He had parked it at an angle with one wheel up in the flowerbed and as the driver's door opened, he rolled out of the car and landed on all fours. He shook his head and started crawling towards the kitchen door, but thought better of it after a couple of metres and staggered to his feet.

He stood there swaying for a while, rubbing his hand across his face. He wiped it on his trousers and she could see that he had thrown up. His light-blue shirt was spattered with vomit, his trousers too. They could be splashes of something else, of course, but it seemed unlikely. She took a step back from the window to stop him seeing her. She felt an impulse to run away. Just leave everything, take the boy and get away forever from all this . . . this exhausting, slowly darkening and contracting hopelessness that . . . was the life given to her. To her and Billy.

But the impulse died away. There was nowhere to go. No friends to take them in, no family to return to. No safety net and no way out. She simply stood there instead, watching her husband.

This can't go on, she thought.

27

Gunnar Barbarotti walked right along Götgatan, all the way
down to the waterfront. At Slussen. His conversation with Billy
Helgesson came with him like a lump in the stomach.

And it wasn't just Billy, he realized as he tried to scrutinize
the lump, but this whole business. The woman killing her
husband because she can't bear it any more – and who accepts
the consequences. Because that was what it came down to,
wasn't it? Everything he had heard about Harry Helgesson
pointed in the same clear direction. He had been a swine, a
tormentor of his own family, a *bastard*, as Billy had said of his
own father. Barbarotti was not entirely unreceptive to the idea
that the boy's muteness was the result of his father's bullying
behaviour. That he had felt so inhibited and scared throughout
childhood that he had not dared to speak. Was it possible? Had
Lisbeth Mattson been wholly correct in her judgement, after
all? Hard to know, but in any event Billy and his mother had
had a hard time of it at Little Burma – how could it have been
otherwise? So hard that one day she had taken the only way
out she could find: had rid herself of the tyrant and taken her
punishment.

The fact that she had also butchered him and hidden him
in the forest was, well, something that Barbarotti felt inclined
to overlook. At least on a sunny day such as this, in retrospect,

and she had in fact served a sentence of more than a decade in Hinseberg.

Or was that a completely misleading picture? Were there other circumstances pointing in different directions that had never come to light? But in any case she seemed to have lost the boy into the bargain. Didn't she? Contact between Ellen Bjarnebo and her son basically seemed to have stopped when she was sent to prison. Billy had been taken into the charge of his uncle and aunt without further ado. He had left his home and been expected to settle in with the childless couple in Hallsberg. New parents who saw no value in allowing mother and son to continue seeing one another. A single visit in the company of a pastoral care adviser. One visit in return. In eleven years.

Although perhaps it was understandable, thought Barbarotti. Seeing it from the outside and from a certain point of view. Billy's dad had been murdered; his mum was a murderer. Not particularly nice baggage to bring with you to your new life. Especially if you happened to be mute, of limited mental capacity and inhibited in every way.

Could it not have been handled better? With a bit more consideration? You couldn't help thinking so, with the benefit of hindsight. What had social services been doing all that time?

Or had it all been for the best? Perhaps the boy's relationship with his mother had been as toxic as the one with his father? Perhaps Gunder and Lisbeth Mattson had done exactly the right thing by uprooting Billy from his difficult past and planting him in new soil on the fertile plains of Närke?

How could one know? thought Barbarotti, stopping between two pushchairs at the red light of the pedestrian crossing. Billy Helgesson had eventually enjoyed the benefit of a dignified life. Of some sort, at least: *I've got my own family.* It was very clearly Juliana Peters who wore the trousers at Blekingegatan, but Billy had been used to some other person being in charge at home, all his life. He had learnt to speak passably well in his teenage years in Hallsberg, but the fact that he had so readily moved away told its own story, didn't it? You could suspect some kind of tug of war between Gunder Mattson and Juliana, but it was all too easy to stray into the boggy territory of speculation. Yet he had no such doubts about his observations at Lisbeth Mattson's the day before: she had displayed all the signs of being unhappy and fearful, and he wondered whether she had been any different ten or twenty years earlier.

The crossing symbol changed to green. Yet another of his biased lines of argument – he was the first to admit it. If anyone asked you to put two and two together, surely you didn't need to prevaricate and pretend you didn't have the answer?

But in any case, this was – and always would be – primarily about Ellen Bjarnebo. Perhaps she had, after all, kept some sort of contact going with her son once he left Hallsberg? Even if they didn't often meet face-to-face. She came for Christmas now and then, Billy had said. Or at any rate she had done so at least once. And Billy had been aware of her trip up to Norrland. So maybe it wasn't as bad as Barbarotti had first imagined. Maybe there was a bond between them.

Barbarotti very much doubted whether Billy's step-parents had been in the habit of visiting Blekingegatan. And it seemed equally unlikely that Juliana Peters would have regularly got off the train in Hallsberg.

Another crossing, another red light. What about Arnold Morinder then? How on earth did he fit into the picture? It was his disappearance that was of primary interest, wasn't it, not the sparse contacts between the disparate parts of the Bjarnebo-Helgesson family? The main focus had to be the task that Asunander had set him.

And what was that exactly?

End of the road, thought DI Barbarotti, avoiding a collision with a delivery bike by about five centimetres as the light turned green again. That was the conclusion I came to earlier, wasn't it?

Back to square one. The metaphors were legion.

He came to a narrow parallel street sloping up to a higher level – Puckeln, he had an idea it was called – and then caught sight of Söder Bookshop, which brought him to a stop. He decided to abandon all his dismal thoughts and go in to buy a present for Sara instead. At the end of a conscientiously completed term, with the summer ahead, as a thank-you for being able to stay over on her sofa, and simply for being precisely who she was.

He found a nice-looking edition of the collected poems of Gunnar Ekelöf, had them gift-wrap it and paid his bill. A good antidote to all that legal slog, he thought. There has to be some balance in life. I hope she likes it. He himself had read Ekelöf as a law student at Lund. More Ekelöf and other things of that ilk than law, to be honest, which was no doubt why his results were nothing to write home about.

By the time he got down to Slussen he had pushed the Helgesson-Bjarnebo family to the back of his mind and was again thinking about how unfeasibly beautiful Stockholm was. Especially on an early summer's day like this one, when everything in this densely packed city of stone – all its heavy buildings, its cliffs and rock faces, streets and squares, parks and trees and people and cars – appeared to be floating on the water. Suspended above it, almost. The Old Town, Riddarholmen and Kungsholmen, the green oasis of Djurgården away to the right. All the church towers and spires reaching up to blue sky and puffy white clouds. It's almost too much, thought Barbarotti, coming to a stop just below the Hilton hotel and trying to draw it all in, in deep breaths. To inhale and absorb it: taking in the capital city through your nose. He let his eyes follow a single, unknown spire up into the blue. Was it the German Church?

Is that where you are, Marianne? he asked – a question he delivered into mid-air, and it struck him that he might be drawing undue attention to himself. But nobody turned a hair. Well, fine, it makes no odds to me, he thought. People talk on their mobiles all day long, after all, and anybody who feels like it can listen in. Talking to the dead, to people you were grieving for, was nothing to be ashamed of. Hello, my darling, can you see me down here?

He resisted the impulse to wave nonetheless, and detected no clear response – except perhaps for a slight twinge, deep in his heart, but perhaps that was enough. What more could a person ask? He went on in the direction of the Old Town, cut through the hordes of tourists on the square at Järntorget and started along Österlånggatan; he ambled northwards as he considered how he was going to spend the afternoon. He had a rendezvous with Sara and Max in Humlegården Park by the Royal Library at five o'clock; it was only a quarter to one, and although he had been entrusted with the key to the Vikingagatan flat and liked the place, he didn't want to sit indoors on a day like this. Djurgården perhaps? Or a park? Stretched out on the grass, gazing up at the fresh new leaves of an elm or chestnut? That would be a place where he could unobtrusively carry on his talk with Marianne. Why not?

He opted for one of the outdoor cafes in Kungsträdgården Park, the cafe nearest the water – at least as a starting point, and afterwards he would ask himself if there were stronger powers up in that seductive summer sky than he had imagined when he was standing at Slussen a short time before, invoking Marianne.

'Hello! It's you, isn't it?'

A young woman. Sara's age, around twenty-five? Jeans, a red T-shirt with a laughing clown's face. An uncertain smile on her own.

'Er, I don't quite know . . . ?'

'Anna,' she said. 'Yes, it's you . . . Barbarotti, isn't it?'

'Yes,' he said. 'That's right.'

'Sorry. Anna Gambowska. What was it, your first name?'

'Gunnar.'

'Ah yes, of course. How funny that I should run into you, today of all days. But you don't remember me, do you?'

'No, I don't think . . . but wait a minute . . .'

Her smile widened. 'OK. Let's put police memory to a little test. If you need a bit of help, it was . . . well, four years ago in fact. Nearly four years.'

'What did you say your name was?'

'Anna. Anna Gambowska.'

'Ah?' said Barbarotti 'Oh yes, now I remember. But is it honestly you? You've really . . . I mean . . .'

'Changed?'

'Yes. When I saw you down there in . . . where was it?

Maardam? You weren't in the best of states – if you'll pardon me saying so.'

She laughed. 'No, I know. Is it all right if I sit down?'

'Of course. Sorry . . .'

She sat down. 'Yes, it's been a few years. And things are different now, you could say. Er, you're sure I'm not disturbing you?'

'Not at all. We could have a coffee?'

She shook her head and looked at her watch. 'No, I won't have time, though it would be nice. I'm meeting somebody soon . . . but if you can spare a few minutes?'

'Yes, of course.'

'It really is the strangest thing that I should happen across you . . . today of all days, I mean.'

'Oh? Why's that?'

She thrust one hand into her black cloth bag, then hesitated. 'No, maybe it's not right.'

Barbarotti turned up the palms of his hands. 'Anna, I don't have a clue what you're talking about.'

Her expression grew serious. She was frowning and her lips were tight. 'No, of course you don't. But I need to think this through. I honestly didn't think I'd bump into you. You're still a police officer, are you?'

'A detective inspector. Just as I was then.'

'But on the other hand . . .'

'On the other hand?'

'If I don't show it to you, who else *can* I show it to?'

He could see she was wrestling with something. She was clearly torn between two options.

'Sorry,' he said. 'I still have no idea what you're talking about. But take whatever time you need, I'm in no hurry.

What are you up to these days? Have things turned out well for you?'

She nodded and took her hand out of her bag. 'Yes, incredibly well. I've said goodbye to all that wretched mess – thanks mainly to that money I came into. I've really sorted myself out. Even my mum agrees. I think you met her, didn't you?'

'Yes, I did.'

'No more taking drugs or being stoned, or any of that shit. I caught up with school at adult education classes and now I've got a place to study medicine. My course started last autumn. I bet you wouldn't have thought it last time you saw me, in the hospital, right?'

She laughed. Barbarotti could not help agreeing with her.

'No, to be honest, I would have had trouble imagining it.'

When he became aware of Anna Gambowska four years previously, she was on the run from rehab – in a car being driven across Europe by a sixty-year-old man. Barbarotti had no problem remembering the circumstances. He and Eva Backman had found the girl in a pitiful state at a hospital in Maardam. Her sixty-year-old companion had vanished, leaving a suicide note. Now what was his name?

Green . . . ? No, Roos, that was it. Ante Valdemar Roos – how could he forget a name like that? The car the two of them had been travelling in was found abandoned in a forest just outside Maardam. If Barbarotti wasn't mistaken, Roos had been declared dead, two or three years later. At the request of his wife, the one who in a sense had started the whole business . . . or given the police a trail to follow anyway. Oh yes, he remembered it all very well now.

'Oh God, what shall I do?' said Anna Gambowska, but then she appeared to reach a decision. She took out an iPhone, rang a number and explained to someone that she would be ten minutes late. 'OK,' she said after that. 'Maybe I've misunderstood the whole thing, and it probably isn't anything worth bothering with, but I can't help myself.'

Barbarotti nodded. His cheese sandwich and coffee arrived.

'Are you sure you don't want anything?'

'I'm sure. I just hope you won't set any wheels in motion. Because in that case . . .'

Barbarotti took a bite so he wouldn't have to say anything. Anna Gambowska ran her hand through her short hair.

'Can I swear you to secrecy?'

He laughed. 'That depends on what this is all about.'

But for some unfathomable reason he began to sense where this was leading. I think I know what's coming, he thought. Or maybe it was simply a stab in the dark.

'This is about Valdemar, isn't it?' he ventured.

She stared at him, looking little short of terrified.

'What makes you think that?'

'Tell me all about it,' he said. 'Admittedly I'm a police inspector, but I'm a human being, too. And I understood more about that death than you may realize. The death of your former boyfriend, I mean.'

That put her on the defensive. He could see that she was sorry she had come over and introduced herself to him. They eyed one another for three silent seconds.

'Anna,' he said. 'You don't have to tell me what you'd decided to tell me. You can go on your way and meet whoever it is, and we'll forget the whole thing. Or . . .'

'Or what?'

'Or we can make a deal.'

'A deal? What do you mean?'

'How about we say something like this,' said Barbarotti. 'You tell me what you'd thought of telling me, and I'll forget it.'

She looked at him in surprise. Then she burst out laughing. 'All right. Human being instead of police officer, you mean?'

'I don't know what you're talking about,' said Barbarotti. 'Well?'

She bit her lower lip. It struck him that she was almost as pretty as Sara, which was a completely irrelevant thought that only crept in because she was taking her time. Then she fished an envelope out of her bag. A standard white envelope, twelve centimetres by fifteen. He glimpsed her name on the front of it. She took out a photograph and passed it to him.

It was a picture of a man and a penguin. It looked as if it had been taken at a fairground; there was part of a carousel in shot on the right-hand side. The penguin and the man were the same height, and the penguin appeared to be a giant cuddly toy. He assumed there was a person inside the costume. The man had his arm round the bird's neck and sloping shoulders and was smiling broadly into the camera.

And that was it.

'Turn it over,' she instructed him.

He did so, and read:

Take care of yourself. V.

He looked at her.

'It came yesterday. In the post.'

She pushed the envelope across the table towards him. Spanish stamps. Her name and address: Vintergatan in Solna, just north of Stockholm. The postmark was barely legible, but it started with *Ma-*. Malaga, he thought.

'Is it him?' He handed back the envelope and photograph. 'I don't recognize him. I never met him, you know.'

She put the card and envelope away in her bag. Clasped her hands on the edge of the table and looked at him for a long time. He looked back without moving a muscle. Finally her mouth formed itself into a smile.

'No,' she said. 'It must be someone else. It can't possibly be him, can it?'

'It would certainly be very strange,' agreed Barbarotti, 'if it was him. But it was so nice to see you again. I'm sure you'll make an excellent doctor. Take care of yourself, like the man said.'

She stood up, hugged him and walked quickly away towards the Opera House.

28

An hour later he claimed an elm all for himself behind the Royal Library.

He stretched out on the grass beneath it, rolled his sweater into a pillow to put under his neck and stared up into the mass of foliage. There's something about mighty trees and their dignity, he thought, they have a grasp of life that we humans can come nowhere near emulating, something utterly fundamental and natural – but before he could let his thoughts stray too far in that obscure direction, he remembered that his phone had been on silent since he left Blekingegatan and it was high time he checked it. Sara might need to get hold of him, for example. Or the youngsters down in Kymlinge. Or even Ellen Bjarnebo?

But there was only one message. From Eva Backman, as it happened, asking him to give her a ring when he had the time.

He looked around him and registered that he did have. He called her number and waited. He was about to give up when he heard her breathless answer.

'Hello?'

'Barbarotti here. Were you doing press-ups?'

'No, I've just come up from the laundry room. You got my message?'

'Yes, that's why I rang. I'm lying in a park in Stockholm.'

'Lying?'

'Yes.'

'Are you pissed?'

'Not as far as I can tell. But it's lovely weather and I've got a couple of hours to spare. What did you want?'

'I expect it's nothing,' said Eva Backman at a slightly more collected pace. 'Merely Just a snippet of information that I wanted to share with a colleague, to show willing.'

'Classy,' said Barbarotti. 'Go on.'

'Well, I was talking to Fängström's mother this morning.'

'The Sweden Democrat?'

'Yes, him. How are you, by the way?'

'Stop asking me how I am. What did Fängström's mother have to say?'

'It was about Morinder. And Bjarnebo.'

'Morinder and Bjarnebo? What's *she* got to do with them?'

'Nothing. But she was in the same school form as them for a while.'

'The same form?'

'Yes, apparently. That was all. Oh, and she had the impression that Morinder fancied Bjarnebo even back then.'

'What?' said Barbarotti.

'I said she had the impression that Morinder fancied—'

'I heard you. When was this then?'

'Oh, about forty-five years ago,' said Backman. 'They were in Year Eight.'

Barbarotti said nothing for a while.

'Hello?'

'I'm still here.'

'It doesn't signify anything of course, but I thought you ought to know.'

'That Bjarnebo and Morinder knew each other from way back, you mean?'

'That sort of thing.'

'Right, I see,' said Barbarotti. 'I suppose that made it easier for him to pick her up at the pub later. But I don't see how it helps me, beyond that.'

'Nor do I,' said Eva Backman. 'And they were only in that form together for a year. Anyway, that was what I wanted to get off my chest today. How's the weather in Stockholm? It's not bad here.'

'It's glorious,' said Barbarotti.

'And you're on your way to solving the case?'

'I am,' said Barbarotti. 'It's only a matter of time.'

'Well, don't let me detain you any longer,' said Eva Backman. 'Kiss-kiss, and give my love to Sara.'

'Will do,' promised Barbarotti and ended the call.

Kiss-kiss? he thought. Did she usually say that?

Once he had his hands clasped on his chest and was gazing up into the lush green leaves again, he attempted to gather his thoughts; they were proliferating and straying in too many different directions. He started with his colleague's phone call. Morinder and Bjarnebo in the same form at school? What did that mean? Very likely nothing at all – except what he had just suggested to Backman. When they came across each other in Kymlinge in the early 2000s, they were already acquainted. That naturally made things easier if you wanted to embark on a relationship – especially if you were a bit shy and socially awkward, as many had observed Morinder to be.

It was naturally a failure on the part of the 2007 investigators that this connection had not come to light. But he already knew that; the police had done a poor job, that was the simple truth, and it was one possible reason why Asunander had asked him to take another look at the case.

The next question, thought Barbarotti – as an elderly sausage dog came up and sniffed him, found him pretty boring and snuffled on its way – what did I learn at Blekingegatan then? And in Hallsberg, if you weighed the two of them together? What did it actually amount to?

Hard to say. Nothing, as far as Morinder's disappearance was concerned; perhaps a little, when it came to Ellen Bjarnebo. Something about relationships and loneliness and taking your punishment. Truly taking your punishment. Naturally one could draw a few conclusions – or, at any rate, reasonably speculate about – where Billy Helgesson's personality and fate were concerned, but was any of that relevant to the investigation?

What investigation? he thought. Is what I'm engaging in even worthy of the name?

He sighed and stared up into the green canopy for a while. He had been wandering up and down these culs-de-sac for two weeks now. The same blind alleys, the same dingy lighting, ever since his return to work. The only sensible move that remained – the only sensible course that had existed, from the word go – was somehow to engineer an interview with the prima donna herself: Ellen Bjarnebo.

It suddenly struck him that he hadn't tried her since the day before. He took out his mobile and rang her number. First her mobile number. Then her home number in Valdemar Kuskos gata in Kymlinge.

No answer from either.

He called home to the children instead.

It was Jenny who answered. She assured him they were managing fine without him, said she hoped he would have a nice time in Stockholm with Sara, and promised to cook a delicious and hearty dinner for them both when they got home on Sunday evening.

But she was about to jump in the shower. Was he ringing about anything in particular?

The moment they hung up, the grief came washing over him.

He had no defences and wondered how it could happen so fast. The old elm with all its experience of life was just the same, the grass where he was lying was just the same. The Royal Library stood where it stood, and he could still see the sausage dog, nosing about in the distance. The world went on.

Yet here he was, falling headlong.

Dear God, he thought. Marianne, help me. How can everything give way in an instant like that?

I'm not responsible for my actions any more.

But it was possible to lie absolutely still and simply let it come. And perhaps there was no alternative.

Meet it, go down to rock bottom and endure it.

Grief opened a door between body and soul, making the experience a wholly physical one. He had learnt that it was so – could be so – after Marianne's death. That he could actually be paralysed, incapable of changing the position, the conditions, in which he found himself. In a state of petrification. Because every movement, every action and every thought was utterly meaningless. Because you were knocked flat by the sheer weight and pressure of grief. It was hard to breathe, your chest contracting rather than expanding. Maybe it was a case of what they called panic disorder? He didn't know. You could only wait for it to stop, maybe ease off a little; the only thing he felt capable of was praying – wordlessly, because there were no words – in some kind of vaguely heroic effort to focus his mind.

On her. On the hope that she was still living, in some sense. On whether there was any kind of meaning at all.

Blind faith, that was what he had discussed with Our Lord the other day.

This was something Rönn had talked about, he remembered. *When grief strikes you, one solution is simply to let it strike fully. You can't run away from it, however hard you try.*

So that was what he did. Prostrate beneath grief, prostrate beneath mercy.

A period of time passed. Wordless thoughts swirled incomprehensibly in his head, the leaves rustled faintly, happy laughter came from somewhere further off – and then, after a while, the thought of the letter, which he still had in his inside pocket and by now knew by heart: *I don't want you to be permanently sad and passive and unhappy; it's no good for either you or the children, and it simply doesn't help.*

He sighed. He stayed where he was for a bit longer, lying there with his hands folded on his chest. Then he got to his feet and made his way out of Humlegården Park in the direction of Karlavägen.

29

3 June 1989

She stood there looking out at her husband.

He appeared to cough up something and then spit in the gravel. To the right, to the left, and wiped his mouth again. Staggered a few steps, but instead of going in at the door, he made for the bike stand. He stopped again, his back turned to her, and it took a second for her to realize what he was doing.

Unzipping his flies to take a leak.

Without thinking she dashed outside. 'Harry!'

'Huh?'

He didn't turn because he already had his willy out and had started. He directed the flow of urine at her punctured back wheel.

'What the hell are you playing at?'

Where did that sudden, bold anger come from? She felt it rising almost like a stream of lava from her diaphragm and for a few moments, as she ran towards him, as she planted herself two metres away from him and put her hands on her hips, it gave her a power and a strength that could not be her own.

He paid little attention to her, or appeared not to. He took his time and, when he had finally finished, he stood there swaying as he put his willy away and rezipped his flies. He turned round, almost fell over and tried to fix her with a look as he pulled his mouth into a sneer.

'What did you say?'

'I asked what the hell you were playing at.'

It sounded lame, despite the oath. The strength and anger had only been borrowed and were already draining away, leaving her in the lurch. Fear and hopelessness filled the vacuum as if it was the most natural thing in the world. Oh shit, she thought. Help me, somebody, please help me!

He took two steps forward and hit her.

It was a feeble blow that she parried with her forearms and he almost toppled over.

'You've had a skinful, Harry.'

It was scarcely an accusation; she could hear that herself. It came out sounding more as if she pitied him. He tried to land another blow, but missed. He clasped his stomach, then put his hands on his knees and groaned. She turned on her heel and went back indoors, leaving the door open so as not to provoke him more than she already had.

She heard him throwing up outside.

He had lost 800 kronor.

That was more or less what she earnt in two days, before tax. There was something about his voice as he said it. As if he took pride in it. As if he wanted to rub it in, to etch it into her slow-witted brain. The fact that he had casually lost a load of money they really needed for other things – there were so many holes to fix at Little Burma – and not just that: the fact that he had got drunk and driven his car when he was so far over the limit, that he had hit her and pissed on her bike . . . and that he was fully within his rights to do so. Fully. Within. His. Rights.

'Eight hundred kronor! You hear that?'

They were sitting round the kitchen table. He had changed his shirt, but not his trousers. Billy looked scared. He was waiting for a clip round the ear or a reprimand, twitching like a dog that expected a beating. She had served Harry a big portion of pork fillet, but he wasn't eating; he sat there smoking, keeping them on tenterhooks. His elbows on the table as his eyes flitted erratically between his wife and his son, looking for their weak spots. No, not weak spots – little hints of treachery were what he was after, tiny signs of disobedience and opposition that gave him the right to react. The right, and the duty. Spare the rod and spoil the child. He was still extremely drunk and she had no problem reading his thoughts.

To the extent that the contents of a drunken hyena's head could be called thoughts. If only I weren't so scared of him, she thought. If only we weren't such timid baby hares, Billy and I. Mousey and Piggy, just baby hares? If only . . .

'Isn't that so?'

She had no idea what he had said or what she was expected to answer. But then neither was the question directed at her; it was Billy who was the target.

'I said ISN'T THAT RIGHT?'

Billy cowered away from him and stared down at the table.

'Harry, please,' she said lamely, 'surely you could at least—'

'Shut it! I'm talking to my son!'

'But surely we can—?'

'You stupid . . . fat . . . idiot . . . misfit of a son!'

He was speaking affectedly slowly, maybe because his thoughts wouldn't go any faster, maybe so that he wouldn't slur his words.

'Who can't . . . use the . . . tongue . . . in his bloody . . .

head . . . to give his father . . . a civil answer . . . WHEN HE'S ASKED!'

He took a swing at Billy across the table, but missed again, exactly as he had done in the yard. But Billy fell backwards, dragging his chair with him and crashing to the floor, to his father's fleeting amusement.

'Ha-ha-ha! You fucking . . . abortion! Get out. Leave us . . . in peace!'

Not stopping to say thank you for his dinner, Billy rushed off to his room. Harry stubbed out his cigarette and lit another.

'I might as well clear the table,' said Ellen.

But the critical point did not come until half an hour later. She had finished the washing up and was wondering where to go to avoid Harry. He was sitting on the sofa in the living room, watching TV; that was where she had seen him ten minutes earlier, at any rate, and the TV set was still on. Perhaps he had fallen asleep, in which case she could take a long shower and then go to bed, hoping he would spend all night on the sofa. And thus another day in her wasted life would be gone forever.

Before she could make up her mind, however, she heard Billy. A long-drawn-out wail that could have come from . . . from a wounded animal. These constant animal associations, they were starting to get on her nerves, but that was how it was and how it felt. She went straight to his room – seeing from the corner of her eye that Harry was no longer parked in front of the TV; maybe he had gone out to the cowshed, he had a kind of office out there, where he liked to sit – and pushed Billy's door open. It was ajar, which was not at all usual.

He was lying on his bed, curled into a foetal position. Legs drawn up, hands between his knees. His whimpers were coming in waves; it sounded like nothing she had ever heard before and she dreaded to think what had been done to him. Billy had taken a thrashing before, many times, but this felt different. On a whole different scale. Despair, she thought. Bottomless despair, black as night.

'Billy, how are you?'

She sank to her knees and stroked his hair. His face was wet with tears and he wasn't opening his eyes.

'What happened, Billy boy?'

He gave a couple of sobs. Tried to wipe away the snot and tears with the back of his hand, rubbed his eyes until he could open them and pointed to his desk.

She saw instantly and understood everything.

His toy soldiers.

They were gone. Not a single little tin figure left. Not anywhere in the room. She took hold of Billy's hand and squeezed it. There was no response, but cold shivers of horror were running up and down her spine.

30

Gunnar Barbarotti had brought one more name with him to Stockholm.

One other person he could potentially contact for a chat, if the situation called for it.

If the situation called for it? What did that mean? It was a quarter past four and his panic attack had abated. He still had forty-five minutes before he was due to meet Sara and Max in Humlegården Park. He was sitting at a cafe in Brahegatan, had finished his coffee and his cinnamon bun and was on the horns of a dilemma.

What use would it be?

But then what use would *not* making contact be?

If all this was basically intended as limbering up for a return to real work – a notion that he was finding harder and harder to dismiss – then surely it was better for him to work than not? Lying idly on his back under an elm tree had not provided the harmonious balm for the soul that he had hoped for.

It was an address in the suburbs, in Midsommarkransen; he had checked it and written it in his notebook before he left Kymlinge. And now the notebook was open in front of him on the black-lacquered cafe table:

Inger Berglund. Erikslundsgatan 12.

There was a telephone number, too, and after hesitating for so long that he almost changed his mind, he rang it.

It rang twice before Inger Berglund picked up.

He tried to explain why he was ringing and she said that personally she could see no real point to it, but she agreed to meet him the following day.

Sunday morning at a coffee place out in Midsommarkransen. A Pantry, eleven o'clock. Would that do?

A pantry? queried Barbarotti.

That's what it's called, Inger Berglund explained. Two minutes from the underground station.

That'll do very well, said Barbarotti, and they wished one another a nice Saturday evening.

And it *was* a nice Saturday evening. For Barbarotti anyway. He never got round to enquiring how Inger Berglund's had been, but it was of negligible importance in the wider scheme of things.

Max Andersson turned out to be a surprisingly agreeable acquaintance. Sara had had a number of boyfriends over the years and he was the fourth – or possibly fifth, it depended how you counted. They had been together for nearly six months, quite casually at the beginning, but in an increasingly steady way, so it seemed to be serious. Barbarotti had always felt a bit uncomfortable in the presence of the young men in Sara's orbit, with the possible exception of the one called Jorge, whom she had lived with at home in Kymlinge for nearly a year. He knew it was his own fault for being an over-protective and anxious parent, and perhaps he had gradually learnt to hold that back over the years. Faced with this Max, he at least felt no spontaneous hostility, and in fact found him to be a rather quiet and modest young man, good-looking (as far as Barbarotti could judge, but he felt more confident where the opposite sex was concerned) and studying law a term ahead of Sara. He was also a fan of diving and many other kinds of water sport. Healthy, talented and easy to warm to, in other words – the only negative being that he could rather too readily be viewed as every mother-in-law's dream. But as the likeliest potential mother-in-law had died a month ago, it was an unconvincing argument. What was more, this was a thought that passed so fleetingly through Barbarotti's mind that it caused him almost no pain at all. Thank goodness, at least that was something.

For many years Gunnar Barbarotti had also found it difficult to have dealings with people who were successful – in one way or another – but this seemed not to apply to prospective sons-in-law. They took their time over a delicious dinner at a restaurant at the top of Drottninggatan, the conversation kept turning to law and Barbarotti found, to his surprise, that he hadn't forgotten quite everything in the half lifetime that had elapsed since he was sitting there with his nose in his books. Though admittedly a few new laws had been passed in more recent times. Several hundred a year, to be frank.

Afterwards they said their goodbyes in the street outside. Max took the underground home to Enskede, and Sara and Barbarotti strolled back to Vikingagatan.

They drank more tea, talked for another hour and then, for the second night in a row, he fell asleep on her capacious red sofa.

He had a dream about a giant penguin who worked as a diving instructor, and woke up shortly before seven on Sunday morning.

Sara was still fast asleep and he watched her for a moment through the slightly open bedroom door. He made some coffee and installed himself on the lounger on the tiny balcony overlooking the courtyard, where the sun had just risen above the ridge of the roof to the south.

He sat there for almost an hour in the pleasant morning warmth and tried once more to fathom out what he was actually doing. In the line of professional duty, that was to say. He went back in for his notebook and pen and eventually came up with six questions, which seemed to him to encapsulate the whole mess quite well:

1. Why am I working on this case (these cases) in the first place?
2. Why can't I contact Ellen Bjarnebo?
3. What really happened to Arnold Morinder?
4. Could he possibly still be alive?
5. Have I missed anything from the interviews I have conducted so far?
6. What further steps should I take?

Each and every one of these naturally generated supplementary questions, but there seemed little point in writing them down. He realized that Question 4 had been prompted by his unexpected encounter with Anna Gambowska. If someone like Ante Valdemar Roos (possibly against all the odds) could be alive and kicking, then of course Arnold Morinder (possibly against all the odds) could be, too. A moped in a bog proved nothing. Or no more than a car in a forest outside Maardam, certainly.

As for his failure to get hold of Ellen Bjarnebo, it felt more and more frustrating with every passing day. Frustrating and downright odd, he thought. The idea that she was deliberately keeping out of the way (for motives that he did not understand, but there must surely be some reason?) was growing correspondingly more insistent. Or was it simply that she was tired of the police? That she was just ignoring him and couldn't care less? In view of the pressure they had put on her when Morinder disappeared, it would hardly be surprising. Barbarotti was more than ready to subscribe to that view.

And that brought him to the answer to Question 6. The only thing that was really left for him to do was to find Ellen Bjarnebo. Sit down with her face-to-face and listen to what she had to say. Everything else – including all that he had accomplished so far – seemed pretty irrelevant by comparison.

He had already spent enough time racking his brains over Question 1: why he had been set to work on the web of unsolved Bjarnebo/Morinder problems. Asunander had conceded that there was a reason, and Barbarotti assumed that when they met again in two days' time, he would find out what it was. If not, well then, he would feel free to tell the detective chief inspector that it was time to close the case and set it aside. Not that it had ever really been opened properly.

That left Question 5: the extent to which he might have missed anything crucial in his interviews so far. At home in Kymlinge and its environs. With Lisbeth Mattson in Hallsberg and with Billy Helgesson in Blekingegatan.

Naturally he could also have missed things in the reports he had read, he willingly admitted that, but he couldn't help feeling that his recent interviews had in some way contained something new.

What do I mean by that? wondered Barbarotti, looking out

over the purple lilacs in full bloom in the courtyard. Something new?

Rubbish. Or not rubbish? He sank back into the chair a little, closed his eyes against the agreeably warming morning sun and tried to get his short-term memory to return to the topics he had covered, with Billy and with Billy's stepmother. Or the other way round, to take things in their correct order. Was there anything either of them had said that could be considered significant? Anything he had noted or barely noted that could open the door a crack?

He realized there was every risk of him falling asleep before he got anywhere near that mental door, but nonetheless it was just there, in the cloudy borderland between waking and sleep, that something Billy Helgesson had said came back to him. A comment Barbarotti had omitted – *almost omitted* – to pay proper attention to.

Something about his mother up in Norrland.

Something about . . . some acquaintances of hers up there.

But what had he said?

After even that fraction of insight, warm sleep enfolded him and he did not wake in the comfortable lounger until his daughter put a hand on his shoulder and asked if he wanted any more coffee.

31

Inger Berglund was Billy Helgesson's second cousin, but there wasn't much of a physical resemblance. None at all, in fact; she was in her early thirties, dark-haired and slim, and clearly kept herself in trim. Above all, she was considerably more talkative than her reticent relation.

A Pantry was too bustling and noisy and full of pushchairs to make a suitable setting for their conversation, so they took their mugs of coffee with them to a bench with a view over one of Stockholm's many stretches of water. He wasn't sure which, but it must surely be one of the branches of Lake Mälaren?

'I've been thinking about it since you rang,' Inger began without waiting for his prompt. 'It is rather strange that I've never been asked about this by a police officer before.'

'How old were you when it happened?' asked Barbarotti.

'Nine,' she said. 'That's twenty-three years ago. But I suppose it was only natural that they didn't question me at the time. It wasn't particularly complicated . . . I presume.'

There was a whole world hidden in those two last words and for the first time since being presented with these old cases, he felt a chord was being struck inside him. It was that faint note that told him something was on its way. And that it was time to listen really hard.

Or he was simply imagining it; there were sometimes false notes, too.

'Go on,' he said.

She hesitated for a few moments, took out a cigarette and lit it. This surprised him, because she seemed so fit and sporty.

'Sorry,' she said. 'I only smoke twice a year. New Year's Eve and whenever something particular comes up.'

'I see,' said Barbarotti. Clearly what she had to say would emerge of its own accord, without the help of any leading or misleading questions.

'Yes, I've been thinking about it since you rang,' she repeated, 'and I've decided I want to tell you about it. Maybe it doesn't mean anything and I don't really know where you're hoping to go with this, but I don't see why I shouldn't.'

She stopped and took a drag on her cigarette. He nodded, cautiously encouraging.

'There were three of us, growing up at Great Burma,' she said. 'But I'm sure you already know that. And then there was Little Burma, where Harry, Ellen and Billy lived. It was . . . well, they were family, of course, Dad and Harry were cousins, but we had hardly anything to do with them. Especially not with Billy. Not Tomas or Erik, and not me, either. Erik and Billy were exactly the same age, but Billy was so weird that it . . . it didn't work, it was as simple as that. He, kind of, *couldn't* play. Have you met him?'

Barbarotti acknowledged that he had.

'Then you know,' she said. 'He lives here in Stockholm actually. I bumped into him and exchanged a few words with him. You can do that, nowadays.'

'He didn't speak when he lived at Little Burma?' asked Barbarotti.

'No. He was such a loner. He's been diagnosed with some form of autism, I think, but that's not what I want to tell you about. It isn't about Billy, it's about something else.'

Barbarotti nodded. Inger Berglund cleared her throat.

'My mum and dad got divorced two years after Harry was killed. We children never really understood why; well, I didn't, anyway. But a few years later Tomas, my elder brother, explained it to me.'

'Oh yes?' said Barbarotti.

'Our dad – Göran Helgesson, that is – was in a relationship with Ellen Bjarnebo.'

'Ouch,' said Barbarotti, for want of anything better.

Inger Berglund took another drag at her cigarette. 'Exactly. It's funny that I think of her as Bjarnebo, isn't it, and not Helgesson. But who cares? They'd been at it for several years apparently, and if I've understood correctly, it carried on that summer too . . . when Harry was only missing, I mean. Before they found him.'

'How were relations between your mum and dad?' asked Barbarotti.

'I don't know. They were as they were, I suppose, but it came as a shock that they were getting divorced. The farm and everything . . . Ordinary people can split up, but if you run a farm it's an entirely different matter. I was eleven when she moved out; Dad sold the place three years later. You didn't know all this?'

'No,' said Barbarotti. 'I didn't. How did it come out, about your dad and Ellen Bjarnebo? I'm sorry to have to ask, but if I've got this right, they decided to get divorced . . . what did you say? A year and a half after Ellen went into Hinseberg? The relationship can hardly have carried on while—'

'Somebody told Mum,' Inger Berglund interrupted.

'Somebody?' said Barbarotti.

'I think it was her . . . Ellen, that is. As some kind of revenge maybe, I don't know. She must have sent a letter or phoned from jail, but I could be wrong. Anyway, Mum found out about it. After the divorce I moved to Gothenburg with her, but Erik and Tomas stayed with Dad. I suppose the idea was that they would all help each other with the farm, but it didn't work. Neither of my brothers was really interested in farming, and Dad realized that eventually. They wanted to go to university, not do messy work with sheep and cows. Perhaps Dad was tired of it all, as well. At any rate, the whole family split apart. And that's the way it still is. Dad died two years ago, down in Spain. His drinking got entirely out of hand, to tell the truth. Tomas is a computer geek and works in California, and Erik . . . well, Erik has property interests, does deals all over the place, mainly down in Malmö. He's got himself into tight corners more than once. We don't see each other, not even at Christmas. Tomas and Erik never meet up, either.'

'It doesn't sound as if you miss them?' said Barbarotti.

'No,' said Inger Berglund, dropping her half-smoked cigarette on the ground and grinding it with her shoe. 'You're right, I don't, and that's the sad thing, I suppose.'

'What is?' asked Barbarotti.

She looked out over the water for a few seconds. 'We were still a family when I was little. We held together, had some solidarity, or that was what I imagined anyway. But then I was just a child. Mum has cast me off, by the way. How can I put it? Distanced herself. Officially.' She laughed and went on. 'It's my sexual orientation, you see. I live with another woman, and it was too much for her in the end. I think Tomas and Erik are about as enlightened as she is on that score, too.'

'How do you come to have the name Berglund?' Barbarotti remembered to ask.

'I wasn't always entirely clear about that orientation,' said Inger Berglund with a shrug. 'I was married to a man called Berglund for a couple of years – poor guy, it didn't work. And since my partner's called Lundberg, we thought it was rather fun. Berglund and Lundberg. The world turned upside down, you know . . .'

She laughed again.

'So now I've told you about that wretched old business, anyway. Goodness knows if it's any use to you, but I must ask you: what made you contact me at all? Is it that other case, the one they never solved, or . . . ?'

Barbarotti sighed. 'It's a long story,' he said. 'But am I reading this right when I sense that you . . . that you're suggesting something about Harry Helgesson's murder?'

Her eyes followed a sailing boat as it came gliding by, thirty metres below them. Three tanned young men in shorts and baseball caps, their chests bare. Barbarotti observed the progress of the same vessel and waited.

'No,' she said finally. 'Not really. It's just the fact that so much never came out. It was all kind of instantly obvious, as soon as they started finding him. She confessed right away. And then . . . well, then she came under suspicion again, didn't she?'

'Yes,' said Barbarotti, 'she did.'

'And when was that?'

'About five years ago.'

'But that time it wasn't her?'

'There was nothing to prove it, certainly.'

'The way I remember it, they never found a body, right? That second time, I mean.'

'That's right,' said Barbarotti.

'I've heard that's the way to do it,' said Inger Berglund, starting to smile but thinking the better of it. 'If you've killed somebody, you have to make sure the body is never found. It gives you a much better chance of getting away with it.'

'That's a good rule of thumb, yes,' admitted Barbarotti, deciding it was time to wind things up. 'Thanks for taking the time,' he said. 'Is it all right if I get in touch again if there's anything else?'

'Of course,' said Inger Berglund. 'And do let me know if . . . if you hit on anything.'

'I'm not so sure I shall hit on anything, I'm afraid,' said Barbarotti.

He took the Tube back to the centre of town. It was still only half past twelve; it was four hours until he and Sara would be sitting on the train going south, and he thought he might just as well find an outdoor cafe and have some lunch. There were a few things Sara needed to see to, she had told him, and they had agreed to leave Vikingagatan at around 4 p.m.

A bite to eat and a bit of brainwork then. The chord that had been struck in Midsommarkransen was still vibrating.

And one thing was growing increasingly clear to him. It wasn't one incompetent police investigation that Asunander had put in his hands, but *two*.

32

3 June 1989

He still wasn't on the sofa.

The TV was playing to itself, an American cop show, to judge by the sounds and the bluish flicker. She turned it off. An empty beer can on the table. She automatically picked it up and took it to the bin bag in the kitchen. She emptied the ashtray and rinsed it under the tap. Wiped down the cooker.

Ordinary, everyday actions, and yet not. She was in the grip of a kind of intoxication, even though she hadn't touched a drop. As if she didn't really know what she was doing; it was something about her perception, something new and strange. She was waiting to hear the Mutti voice again – maybe that was what this portended. Or would whatever it portended suddenly become clear? But the voice remained silent. And she was thrown by the very nature of these questions that she was asking herself. Portend was scarcely a word she was in the habit of using, not even to herself.

It was the disappearance of the tin soldiers that set it off. It stayed in her, demanding that steps be taken: that must be how it worked. *How it worked? Steps?* What sort of steps? Perhaps it was something akin to the deceptive sense of power that had come to her earlier in the day, but then deserted her.

Or it could be something else. Reality had taken a hard knock and it wasn't easy to know where that would lead. But she couldn't shake off the conviction that she was waiting for something, waiting and wondering.

She had left Billy on his bed, after hunting round his bedroom for a while to try to find the soldiers. She looked in the wardrobe, the chest of drawers, the cupboard just outside this room – although she knew there was no point. Billy had undoubtedly looked in the same places. That was why he was lying there. Because the soldiers were gone. That was why he was in deeper despair than she had ever seen him.

Bottomless, without hope. She had tried to get through to him, but there was no contact to be made. There was no sign that he even registered her sitting there with him. The boy was an impenetrable stone of silence and suffering.

She wondered what Harry had done with them. It wasn't at all easy to destroy a set of tin soldiers. Maybe he had just thrown them out into the forest?

She wondered what he had done with himself, too. He wasn't in the room at the end of the cowshed, either, she had been out to check. It was where he liked to lurk; it had been conceived as some kind of office – when the place was still a proper, working farm – with shelves along one wall for files and so on, and a big American desk. It was a family heirloom, battered and worn. A matching leather chair, too, and a pretentious wall clock that was also a product of the 1930s, the pioneering days of the farm. It stood at ten to twelve, as always. The workroom ought naturally to have been in the main house, but there somehow wasn't the space. No space for it then, for some reason, and no space for it now.

In any case, it was where he liked to sit. Pretending to do

his paperwork and accounts while he drank beer and smoked. Poring over his men's magazines, which he kept in one of the desk drawers; she had discovered them there a few years ago, but had decided it was not worth saying anything. At least there were no scantily clad pin-ups on the walls, only the calendars from the agricultural supplier and Kymlinge car showrooms.

But this evening there was no sign of him there. No Harry Helgesson and no tin soldiers; she spent a few minutes hunting for the latter. The car was still out the front where he had left it, with one front wheel in the flowerbed, so he had not gone back into town at any rate. The idea of Harry ever taking the bus was ludicrous.

She stopped in the yard between the cowshed and the house. Hovering between possible options, she looked at her watch; it was a quarter to nine, but still broad daylight. The sun hung an inch above the edge of the forest in the north-west, casting an almost transcendent glow over the fields. Only two weeks to midsummer, she thought; this was the loveliest time of year and she was experiencing it with all the intensity of a worm under a stone in a ditch.

But *something had happened*. She could not be rid of the thought. It had attached itself to her like a leech and refused to let go. Matters had reached a point, a boundary that made it impossible to carry straight on. *Matters?*

She shook her head and decided on a walk round Leonora's Path. It had got its name from a Leonora who had gone out and frozen to death one winter's night, more than a hundred years ago. The wife of one of the first soldiers given their own smallholdings when they returned from war, if she remembered rightly. History did not reveal the reason for Leonora's misadventure in the forest. Perhaps she had a child in her belly, a child that should not have been there, like in all those folk songs. The well-trodden path – parts of it a track for tractors pulling trailers of timber, although that sort of thing had not happened for many years – wound its way through the forest, twice crossing a purling stream; it was by the second simple wooden bridge that they had found Leonora. It took about half an hour to go the whole way round, and it was better to be in motion than sitting still. Ellen had been along this path quite a few times before; it forked at various points of course, but she could still have done it blindfold.

Maybe she had hoped to reach some kind of conclusion, and that her walk in the quiet murmur of the forest would somehow help her with the task, but it proved not to be the case. Thirty minutes later she was back in the farmyard, still full of the urge to decide and empty of decisions. The sun had gone down and dusk was descending fast, helped by a bank of dark cloud that came sweeping in from the north-east. She wondered whether Harry was back. Assuming that he had gone anywhere in the first place; while she was walking and cogitating, he could easily have been flat out and snoring in the bedroom. She hadn't checked before she left and it was as plausible an alternative as any other. The step from aggressive inebriation to drunken stupor was usually a very short one.

But as she was going towards the house, her eye was caught by a movement on the road up to Great Burma, and when she turned her head that way, she saw two figures standing there in conversation. She assumed they were conversing anyway, for what else would they be doing? They were almost a hundred metres away, under the huge chestnut tree just below the other farm, and in the shadows of its wide crown. They could be anybody, she thought, but she somehow had a feeling one of them was Harry.

In which case, who could the other one be, if not cousin Göran? The High and Mighty Farmer of Splendid Great Burma. Her whoremaster.

Her husband and her whoremaster.

But even though she screwed up her eyes and tried hard to focus, she couldn't make them out. She wasn't even sure that it was two male figures. She shrugged, left them to their fate and went indoors to check on Billy.

She had expected to find him still lying on his bed, but he wasn't there. The room was empty and the lights were off. She called his name a few times, but there was no reply.

It was the same with Harry, too, though she didn't bother calling him. But he wasn't in the bedroom. So it probably *was* him, up by the road, she thought.

And Billy did sometimes hide, especially when he was upset. He never went far, often simply to some secluded corner of the cowshed or a little way into the forest. To the big glacial boulder or what was left of the wooden hut that Göran had put together for him and Erik many years ago; it must have been before he started school, when they could still play with each other. In any case, wherever Billy took refuge, he would always come slinking back before it got really dark.

A sudden weariness came over her, and she thought that this was basically like any other evening at Little Burma. A hopeless day, reaching its end among a dreary succession of other hopeless days. A couple of bats came flitting across the yard, reminding her of a book she had read as a child, in which bats were bringers of knowledge, if she remembered rightly, like messengers from the next day. That was then, she thought, when there were still forks in the road and illusions.

But then she remembered the tin soldiers, clenched her fists and tried to summon back that courage, that impulse to act.

Something must have happened.

Something must be happening right now.

Afterwards – over the summer and winter and all the long years that followed – she would repeatedly recall those stubborn thoughts and try to understand where they had come from.

33

It came to him just as the bill arrived.

That thing Billy had said, which he should have been able to fix in his mind when he was on the balcony that morning, when he fell asleep instead.

Someone she knew up there?

Billy had said that his mother had an acquaintance up in Norrland, and that was why she often went there.

It wasn't a particularly remarkable piece of information, of course, but it was the first time Barbarotti had heard speak of this axe woman having any kind of social circle at all. Apart from Arnold Morinder, but that was a separate story.

Even before he left his outdoor table at the Vasagatan cafe, he had Billy on the line. First Juliana, who handed over to Billy.

'Yes?'

'Sorry to bother you again,' said Barbarotti. 'It's just something I've been wondering about. You said your mum knew somebody at that guest house up in Vilhelmina, and that was why she kept going back. Have I got that right?'

'Yes,' said Billy. 'I think so.'

'Is it somebody I could get in touch with?'

'I don't know,' said Billy.

'Do you know who it is?' hazarded Barbarotti. 'Have you

got a name or a phone number, say? I could do with speaking to someone who—'

'It's her, the woman who runs it.'

'Sorry?' said Barbarotti.

'She owns the place. I don't know her name.'

It doesn't matter, thought Barbarotti. Because I do.

'So, have she and your mum known each other a long time?'

'I think so.'

'All right,' said Barbarotti. 'Sorry to trouble you. Give Juliana and Julia my best.'

'OK,' said Billy Helgesson.

He left the cafe and started walking up towards Vikingagatan. He was trying to decide whether this was of any significance at all – but was more focused on remembering the name of the guest house. And the name of the owner, to whom he had spoken a few days before. He had both of these things written on a sheet of paper in his room at Kymlinge police HQ, but he hadn't bothered to bring them with him to Stockholm. Careless of me, thought Barbarotti. I'm a buffoon, not a policeman. The number was stored somewhere in his mobile, of course, but he would need to know exactly when it was that he had rung.

Luckily for him, there was a shortcut.

'I see it's you,' responded Backman.

'What do you mean by that?' asked Barbarotti.

'Nothing,' replied Backman. 'But I assume you need help. Since you're on the line.'

'Thanks for offering,' said Barbarotti, and suddenly recalled the nugget of information that she had passed on to him the previous day. The fact that Ellen Bjarnebo and Arnold Morinder were in the same form at school, a hundred years ago. But he shelved it for future reference. It wasn't the reason for his call.

'You did well, coming up with that connection between Morinder and Bjarnebo,' he said. 'But this is about something else. You don't happen to have a computer handy?'

Eva Backman admitted that she did, as it was raining in Kymlinge and she was indoors. 'You'll get it in Stockholm tonight.'

'What?' said Barbarotti.

'The rain. So, what was it you wanted?'

'By then I'll be leaving,' Barbarotti informed her. 'But now I need a guest house outside Vilhelmina.'

'Are things that bad?'

'No, it's not for me. It's that place where my axe woman generally stays. I can't remember what it's called, that's all – or the name of the woman who runs it. If you could just google it for me, there can't be that many to choose from, I did it myself last week, but . . .'

'Guest houses in Vilhelmina?'

'And the surrounding area.'

'Why not get yourself a less antique mobile phone?' asked Backman. 'Then you could do this sort of thing for yourself.'

'Sorry, I didn't quite catch that,' said Barbarotti.

Eva Backman sighed and started googling. It only took half a minute; Barbarotti, meanwhile, tried to whistle the theme tune of *The Bridge* without really knowing why he was doing it.

'Ragnhild's Mountain Guest House, how about that?' said Backman. 'The owner's called . . . hang on a minute . . . Mona Frisk.'

'That's it,' said Barbarotti. 'She's the one I spoke to. Thanks.'

That was most definitely it. But he realized he needed a bit of time to think, so he asked Backman to text him the number.

'Anything else?' asked Backman.

'Not for the moment,' said Barbarotti. 'Thank you.'

'Can I leave my computer? Is it OK if I go out?'

'I thought it was raining,' said Barbarotti.

We're starting to sound like we always used to, he thought after they had hung up. For a second, that absurd suggestion Marianne had made in her letter floated into his mind.

But he pushed it away, like so much else.

When he got back to the Vikingagatan flat, Sara was still out, doing whatever it was she had to do. It was only about two o'clock, which left two and a half hours until the train was due to leave; might as well try to make efficient use of the time while he was in form. In form? he thought. Wasn't that the expression Rönn had used? Well, why not – everything was relative. He rang the number.

'Ragnhild's Mountain Guest House. Good afternoon.'

He explained who he was and outlined the reason for his call. He checked that it was Mona Frisk he was speaking to.

'My understanding is that the two of you know each other, you and Ellen Bjarnebo?'

'Who told you that?'

'Her son.'

The line went silent. Barbarotti thought how remarkable it was that so much information could be conveyed by a few seconds of nothing.

Or how much he had time to imagine, at any rate. But

when she cleared her throat and finally spoke, it was pretty clear that he had not imagined it.

'That's right,' she said. 'We're old friends.'

'She comes to visit you.'

'Right again.'

'Often?'

'Now and then.'

Gruff and abrupt. Mona Frisk sounded as if she could be in her sixties, but it was best not to make assumptions. She certainly wasn't much of a talker, whether that was to do with her Norrland roots or had some other explanation.

'Do you know where she is at the moment?'

'Why are you asking?'

'I thought I'd explained that,' said Barbarotti. 'I need to have a quick word with her. I'm taking another look at a couple of old investigations that still have a few loose ends . . . cold cases, if you're familiar with the expression?'

'A quick word?'

'Yes.'

'Cold cases? Was that what you said?'

'More or less, yes,' said Barbarotti. 'So, do you know where I can get hold of your friend?'

Another pause.

'Can I ring you back in a few minutes?'

'Er . . . yes,' said Barbarotti. 'Yes, of course.'

It was more like fifteen, and he put them to good use. He had time for another word with Backman, who luckily had not ventured out into the rain after all. He asked her to run a quick check on Mona Frisk, and it only took her a minute to confirm that he had hit the mark.

Pretty much a bull's eye, in fact: Mona Frisk had spent nine of her sixty-one years in the Hinseberg women's prison in Bergslagen. From 1988 to 1997, to be precise.

'How do you come up with this stuff?' asked Backman. 'I'm verging on impressed, but please note: only *verging on*.'

'It was something about her voice,' Barbarotti explained. 'It wasn't the first time she'd spoken to a police officer. But we'd better get off the line now, she'll be ringing back any minute.'

'Your wish is my command,' said Eva Backman. 'Good luck, and see you tomorrow.'

'Yes, you will,' said Barbarotti. 'Incidentally, before we hang up, what was she inside for? Did you happen to see?'

'Murder,' said Eva Backman.

Of course it wasn't the first time Mona Frisk had dealings with a police officer, he thought with an exaggerated jab of self-criticism. She spoke to me only last week.

But Backman hadn't picked up on it, and anyway it didn't matter. It was the terse and practised replies that had aroused a suspicion in him; not that Mona Frisk had murdered anybody, but that she had fallen foul of the law at some point. Nor did she beat about the bush with it when they resumed their conversation on the phone.

'So this is how it is,' she declared. 'Ellen Bjarnebo and I have known each other for more than twenty years. I assume you know about our backgrounds. But I don't know what you're after, and I suggest you leave her in peace.'

'If I could just sit down with her and talk to her for a little while, that's exactly what I intend to do,' countered Barbarotti. 'So what you're driving at, if I'm not mistaken, is that you know where she is?'

'I don't know about *driving*. It's mainly skis and snow-scooters up here.'

'Don't mess me about,' said Barbarotti. 'Well?'

'She's here,' said Mona Frisk after a short pause.

'Last time we spoke, you claimed she'd caught the bus to Umeå.'

'Maybe I did,' said Mona Frisk. 'She's had enough to contend with in her life from the police.'

'You lied to me,' said Barbarotti. 'In my experience, people only lie to the police if they've something to hide.'

'Rubbish,' retorted Mina Frisk. 'There are a thousand good reasons for keeping the police at arm's length. Especially for honest, hard-working people, but there's no way someone like you can appreciate that. Anyway I'm giving you the facts now, aren't I? Ellen Bjarnebo is here at my guest house.'

'She didn't take the bus on Sunday?'

'No.'

'And she's a frequent guest?'

'Not a guest. She helps me out here on a fairly regular basis.'

'She works for you?'

'If you like.'

'Can you get her to the phone for me?'

'I'm afraid not,' replied Mona Frisk, and he could hear that she was starting to enjoy the call. 'I've just explained the situation to her, and she says that if you want anything from her, you'll have to be so good as to get yourself here.'

'To Vilhelmina?'

'It's beautiful up here. Our guests come year after year. I'm sure I can squeeze you in for a night if you want to see for yourself what it's like in these parts.'

Barbarotti sat there in silence.

'If I understand you correctly,' Mona Frisk went on, 'you aren't actually calling her in for a formal interview. So what *are* you doing?'

'I don't have to explain that to you.'

'Oh? Well, that old case involving her partner must have been dead and buried for a few years now. I'm talking about the case, not the man. Cold cases are just some crap idea they've dreamt up for TV series.'

'All right,' said Barbarotti. 'I'll come up.'

'Really?' replied Mona Frisk, sounding grimly amused. 'You'll be most welcome.'

'But if she isn't there, it will put things in a very different light. I hope you understand that.'

This produced a laugh from her, brief and not exactly cordial. 'I understand far more than you realize, Mr Inspector,' she said. 'Shall I *drive* ahead on the assumption you'll be showing up tomorrow then?'

'I'll let you know,' said Barbarotti and ended the call.

Damn and blast, he thought, and at that moment, Sara came through the door.

She was the one who persuaded him.

If he had to go to Norrland, he might as well get it out of the way as soon as possible. It only took Sara a few seconds to reach that conclusion. She would take charge of the teenagers in Kymlinge. She was going to be at Villa Pickford for the coming week anyway, wasn't she? That was how they had planned it. If he flew up to that guest house in Lapland on Monday morning and flew back on Tuesday, he would be home on Tuesday evening. Or Wednesday morning at the very latest. What was the problem?

'The problem,' said Barbarotti after a few moments' thought, 'is that I know my place is here with the family. Not at some guest house north of the Arctic Circle.'

'Vilhelmina is a long way south of the Arctic Circle, if I'm not mistaken,' Sara informed him. 'And whether it is or not, it only takes about an hour on the plane. An hour back. I actually think it would be good for you to be away from home for a while.'

'I was looking forward to thrashing you at German whist on the train,' said Barbarotti. 'Just like I used to.'

'You've never beaten me at German whist,' objected his daughter. 'You're starting to get old, Dad. Your memory's going.'

Barbarotti reflected. 'OK,' he said. 'I'll leave you in peace with your misconceptions. And thrash you at home in Kymlinge on Wednesday instead.'

'I'll give you the chance to try, at any rate,' promised Sara, and so it was decided.

He went with her to the station to wave her off. As he walked back to Vikingagatan, his thoughts returned to the idea of moving to Stockholm. In a few years, that was, once the kids had left home. Assuming he managed to stay alive that long. He couldn't rattle around on his own in a house of more than 300 square metres, and there was something very attractive about walking these well-populated streets. It was easy to imagine yourself part of a greater whole. What do you reckon, Marianne? he asked. If one's going to be alone, it's better to live in Stockholm than in Kymlinge, isn't it?

He got no answer. Oh well, he thought, there's no hurry. The future will get here when it gets here. Once he had crossed the park at Norra Bantorget and passed the turreted facade of the Trades Union Confederation, he sensed his grief closing in again and walked faster, reminding himself that it was all about filling up the time. Not just sitting there, turning to stone. Or lying under an elm tree, with all your defences down.

An hour's chat with Marianne and Our Lord, he decided, followed by an hour's analysis of the current state of play. That's a good plan.

Then I'll go out for a simple dinner.

Then I'll go to bed. He had good reason for making an early night of it: the plane to Vilhelmina left from Arlanda at 9.40 the next morning, and he was still hazy about how long it would take him to get out to the airport from the streets of Vasastan.

He stuck to his blueprint for the evening. The lines of communication to Our Lord and to Marianne – or perhaps they were one and the same, in actual fact – were a bit rusted up, but he decided not to let that put him off. His analysis of the temporal dimension somehow didn't come up to expectations, either, but the same thing applied there; he would have plenty of time to scrutinize it the following day. That feeling of having reached the end of the road no longer seemed to apply, but what was the real value of the snippets of information that had floated his way in recent hours: sad Lisbeth Mattson in Hallsberg; Billy Helgesson's unforthcoming attitude at Blekingegatan; the situation at the guest house in Vilhelmina; Inger Berglund's account of family relations at Great and Little Burma; and Backman's tip-off about the earlier link between Bjarnebo and Morinder? It all felt like a soup with rather too many ingredients. But he hoped it would acquire a more distinctive taste once he was finally able to sit down with Ellen Bjarnebo and hear what she had to say.

Soup ingredients? he thought. What on earth will I come up with next?

Still, perhaps at long last, at Ragnhild's Mountain Guest House, a short but unknown distance south of the Arctic Circle, he would get the answer to the question of why he was bothering with these old stories at all. Cold cases? Maybe it was just that Asunander had been watching a lot of TV recently and his interest had been piqued. So he started obsessing on festering leftovers. I bet that's it, thought Barbarotti.

He took himself out to a basic little Chinese restaurant a couple of blocks away, devoted twenty minutes to an uninspiring rice dish and, when he got back, rang home to see how the children were faring. Sara had just arrived and all was contentment. Jenny and Martin were both keen to emphasize the fact, and he had no reason to question what they said.

They're coping fine without me, he thought when he had rung off. He suppressed the sense of ambivalence that this simple fact produced in him and went to take a shower.

Sara had insisted that he sleep in her bed, but he opted for the sofa again. He had spent two nights on it already and he could very well make it three. He put out the light and was asleep before midnight, and within what must have been minutes he had Marianne standing in front of him with her hands on her hips.

34

It was odd for her to be standing like that.

As if she had a bone to pick with him.

Or wanted to warn him about something. She said nothing, merely stood there motionless, but her slight frown conveyed her thoughts to him. Somehow.

Watch out, Gunnar, they said. *Life isn't a game.*

What? he thought. Why do I need to watch out? What does she mean by saying life isn't—

You must concentrate, she went on, before he could finish formulating his thoughts. *It won't do to blame everything on your bereavement – you must think clearly! Maybe you think this investigation is merely a way of killing time, but it isn't. You're in danger, Gunnar, do you understand what I'm telling you?*

Well . . . er . . . yes, I think so, muttered Barbarotti. Despite being to all intents and purposes asleep on the sofa, he was aware of articulating the words; his lips moved, so presumably he was suspended somewhere just below the surface of consciousness. Can't you come a bit closer, Marianne, so I can touch you? he tried to say.

But she did not move. She stayed in something that looked like a doorway; behind her it was broad daylight and evidently summer, and looked rather like her family's place at Hogrän on Gotland, but he could only really see her as a dark silhouette; he couldn't make out that creased brow any longer, but she was still plainly very concerned.

Gunnar, I want you to be careful, she said, and now she really was addressing him directly. Almost like the mother of a naughty, defiant child. *I don't want anything to happen to you.*

It seemed a shame that, now she was finally appearing to him, it was to admonish him . . . and that he couldn't see her properly; the silhouette was expanding, growing bigger and darker until finally it blocked the whole doorway. Or perhaps she was moving towards him, after all, and that was what had cut out the light; he held out both his hands to be sure not to miss her, but before she reached him and before he could be clear what was going on, he was thrown upwards and out of his dream with such force that he almost fell to the floor.

He sat up. His heart was beating like a tilt-hammer in his chest. Whatever a tilt-hammer was. Had he even got the name right? And what was the point of wondering about it? He went to Sara's kitchen, drank a glass of water and returned to the sofa. He lay there for a long time with his arms crossed on his chest, trying to recapture the dream and Marianne's presence. Nothing came back, absolutely nothing, but he had no difficulty remembering what she had said.

Watch out.

You must think clearly.

Don't want anything to happen to you.

It was so strange. And the strangest thing of all was not for her to turn up like this, but for her to talk to him about his work.

About these old cases and Ellen Bjarnebo.

Because that was surely what she had been doing? How else could he interpret it? And what did it signify?

When he woke up five and a half hours later he still had exactly the same questions in his head.

'Who did she murder?'

'Eh?' said Eva Backman. 'What's the time?'

'Half past six,' Barbarotti enlightened her. 'But I'm off to Arlanda shortly. I just thought it would be useful to know who it was . . . that Mona Frisk battered to death, I mean.'

'Oh, you thought that, did you?' objected Backman, and gave a yawn that could be heard all the way to Stockholm. 'So now you're ringing me at half six in the morning to get me to find out for you?'

'Er . . . yes,' said Barbarotti. 'But only when you've got the time. Maybe you could give me a call later in the day?'

'No need,' said Backman. 'I already know the answer. Mona Frisk murdered her husband. His name was Eugen Markström, but she didn't batter him to death. She shot him with his elk-hunting rifle.'

'I see,' said Barbarotti. 'Drastic measures.'

'Quite so,' said Eva Backman. 'Two shots: one to the heart, one to the head. I needn't bother ringing you later, then?'

'No. I'll be in touch.'

'Can I grab another half hour's sleep, as I'd originally intended?'

'Be my guest,' said Barbarotti. 'Thank you. We'll speak later.'

After breakfast and a brief analysis of the possibilities he decided a taxi to Arlanda would be the best option, and he got to Terminal 4 by a quarter to nine, just under an hour before the flight to Vilhelmina was due to take off.

According to the schedule, at any rate. In real life the aircraft in question was still on the ground with a technical problem at an airport in Värmland, and its revised departure time from Stockholm was estimated as eleven thirty.

That's great, thought Barbarotti as he purchased a cup of coffee, a cinnamon bun and three morning papers. How come people don't like flying?

An hour later he had read all the news three times, spoken on the phone to two of his children, drunk another cup of coffee and grown so bored that he was seriously considering leaving the terminal, taking a taxi back to the royal capital and hopping onto the next train home to Kymlinge. Throwing the whole venture overboard, in other words – seeing as he was already on the subject of modes of transport – and leaving the two murderesses in peace up in Lapland.

Why not? he thought. Why not draw a big black line under it all and tell Asunander it was uninvestigable and he was ready to get back to real work. And make no bones about it.

But that was when Axel Wallman made his entry.

Like Strindberg's protagonist Carlsson, he came in like a storm on an April morning, and he was dressed in a suit of mustard-yellow corduroy. What was more, he was sporting a straw hat, a walking stick and green-tinted glasses, and if he hadn't stopped by the table and snorted with delight, Barbarotti would never have recognized him.

'Gunnar, dear fellow!'

There was no mistaking the voice. Or the physical bulk; the last time Barbarotti had seen his former fellow student, he had weighed around 120 kilos, and he did not appear to have shed any of it.

His hair and beard, however, were neatly trimmed. Now

that Wallman was standing a metre and a half from him, arms spread wide for a bear hug, Barbarotti thought he looked like a cross between Luciano Pavarotti and Orson Welles.

'Axel, old friend,' said Barbarotti, getting to his feet and receiving the hug despite the obvious risk of rib damage.

'*Iiken ii teda mi uz päiv ili pagenu emähändikaz i`'ces kerdale tob*,' declaimed Wallman, before claiming the spare chair at the table and sinking down on it like a grizzly bear on a golf tee. 'It's Vepsian, and it means, "Nobody knows what a new day and a missing she-wolf have in their bellies." Freely translated, of course, but we're free beings, are we not?'

'I think so,' said Barbarotti. 'You've changed. What's happened?'

'Everything and nothing,' replied Wallman. 'What are you doing here, my friend? Waiting for a crashed aeroplane?'

'I don't know whether it's crashed,' said Barbarotti. 'But it's certainly delayed.'

'Same here,' observed Wallman and waved to the girl at the counter. 'I'm off to the southern provinces on business, but I find myself stranded here like a starving seal.'

'I think you have to order at the counter,' said Barbarotti.

'I think not,' said Wallman. 'Look, here she comes. Perseverance pays.'

He ordered coffee and three almond tarts, and Barbarotti took the opportunity of asking for another coffee, now that table service was on offer.

They continued to exchange hearty but politely hollow phrases until the girl brought their order and then Barbarotti demanded answers.

'Excuse me saying this, Axel, but you look like an actor in a children's theatre show. Please be so good as to update me.'

Axel Wallman looked at his watch.

'All right. I've got forty minutes until my flight goes, so we've time enough. But if you reveal a single word of what I'm about to say, I shall kill you.'

'Fair deal,' said Barbarotti. 'I thought something must have happened. I came past your place the other day. Wallman-Braun?'

'Shhh! Not so loud!' Wallman leant heavily across the table. 'Terminals have a thousand ears. Maybe we should move over to that corner instead?'

He indicated a more secluded table that was just being vacated by a young couple. They took their coffee and the pastries and moved over.

'There, that's better,' said Wallman. 'All right, here goes. You've noticed that I'm in clover, I assume?'

'I did detect that,' said Barbarotti. 'Most definitely.'

'Ha,' said Wallman. 'Not a day too soon, either. To be honest, I'm tired of being an unappreciated genius. That was why I decided on a new career. I think it was Saarikoski's death that gave me the impetus.'

'Saarikoski's dead? I'm so sorry.'

'An animal of great wisdom,' declared Wallman. 'And dignified to the last. He passed away without fear or suffering. Fourteen going on fifteen – that's quite an age for a big dog. But we have to remember that most of our four-footed—'

'Your new career,' Barbarotti reminded him.

'I'm coming to that,' said Wallman emolliently and took a large bite of almond tart. 'Mm, mm, well, that's tribute enough to Saarikoski, may he rest in peace. But remember what I said. Not a word about this; you're the first person to hear anything about it.'

'The first?' queried Barbarotti.

'Apart from my publisher, of course. But he's a veritable clam.'

'A book,' said Barbarotti. 'You've written a book.'

'You must have been top of the class at police training college,' grunted Wallman contentedly, brushing the cake crumbs from his beard. 'I say "publisher", and you say "book"! Brilliant, Holmes, sharp as a knife! I'm impressed.'

'Thanks,' said Barbarotti. 'Please go on. What is it you've written? A new history of language?'

'Not at all,' declared Wallman, and tossed the other half of the tart into his open mouth with an awkward backhand. 'I've put linguistics behind me, at least temporarily. It isn't enough to live on. What I have produced is a so-called blockbuster.'

'A blockbuster?'

'Precisely. A bestseller. It's already sold to thirteen countries and my publisher, who by the way is a very cautious general, as well as a veritable clam, as I said, calculates that it'll sell between thirty and forty million copies, all told. Not to mention what the film rights will bring in. What do you say to that, Holmes?'

'Stop calling me Holmes,' said Barbarotti. 'Axel, you don't happen to have had a screw come loose and are on the run from . . . what shall I call it, some kind of institution?'

'In this attire? Who do you take me for, old chap? My role demands a modicum of extravagance, that's the fact of it. If I were on the run, I'd be at pains to blend in with the crowd, wouldn't I?'

Which wouldn't be easy in any circumstances, in your case, thought Barbarotti. 'But what is it you've written then?' he asked impatiently. 'I thought the market was more or less swamped? As far as Swedes go, at any rate.'

'Now just you listen,' said Wallman, leaning so far over the table that its thin metal legs gave a creak of protest. 'I'm only going to take you through it once. You'll soon be able to read about this marvel in every single newspaper. Here and in the rest of the world. You mark my words. *Imperatorem stantem mori oportet.*'

Barbarotti didn't bother asking him to translate that last bit. 'Go on then,' he said and took a gulp of coffee. 'What's it about?'

Wallman coughed and there was a slight twitch of his facial muscles. He removed his green glasses. 'The truth about Adolf Hitler,' he said modestly.

Barbarotti nodded.

'Written by his grandchild.'

'What?' said Barbarotti.

'Exactly,' said Wallman. 'This is how it fits together. Are you ready?'

'I'm ready,' confirmed Barbarotti.

Wallman cleared his throat at some length, tapped the floor with his cane and pushed his straw hat to the back of his head. 'So, it's like this, my friend,' he intoned earnestly. 'There has been speculation about Hitler's last days ever since the end of the war – that can't have escaped anybody. A deluge of unsubstantiated theories. But what I present is the genuine picture, you see. The final solution, one might say, if it didn't sound so terrible in the context. My line is that the crazed Adolf Hitler didn't die in that notorious bunker at the end of April 1945 – nor did Eva Braun. In actual fact they removed themselves to a place of safety in the January of that year; their roles in the last phase of the war, those dreadful final months, were played by two doubles, it was as simple as that. Two actors, who had in actual fact already performed the roles on various earlier occasions. They were insane, too, no doubt about it, and they – the replacements – were the ones who died in the bunker. Adolf and Eva had long since got safely beyond the borders of Germany.'

'Aha?' said Barbarotti. 'But I think I've heard some variant a bit like that before. Maybe not with the doubles, but otherwise . . . if you'll forgive me saying so.'

'Forgiven and forgotten,' said Wallman, tipping his hat forward to show he was on the offensive. 'But it's not history I'm writing here, it's a fictional blockbuster, just keep that in mind. What I do is to prove – pretend to prove, I should say – that Hitler and Braun in actual fact calmly survived the end of the war. And not somewhere in South America, *nota bene,* which is the usual misconception, but in Sweden.'

'In Sweden?' said Barbarotti. 'Why? I mean, how credible is . . . ?'

'Forget about credibility, I said,' stressed Wallman again, and wolfed down another half an almond tart. 'What actually happened was that they lived on until the late 1950s at a house in the countryside of Skåne. New appearances, a cosmetic procedure or two, off with the moustache, and a hell of a lot of discretion, of course, but that was what they did. There were plenty of Nazis in this country even after the war ended, but I probably don't need to tell you that. Especially at our more southerly latitudes. But never mind all that, the real sensation – the bit that's made my book sell to thirteen countries, with another twenty or so in the queue – is the fact that Adolf and Eva had a baby, back in December 1945. A little girl they christened Brynhilde. To cut a long story short, as my aeroplane will be taking off shortly, this Brynhilde went on to have a daughter of her own, in the late 1970s. We're still deep in the rich earth of Skåne at this point, and it's this Bettina who has written the book. She's my pseudonym: that's the genius of it. Bettina Braun. Hitler's own granddaughter! What do you say to that? And large parts of the sensational story are built on Hitler's own diary. From the 1920s, the Beer Hall Putsch and so on, right through to . . . well, right through to his death at the house in Skåne in the autumn of 1958. In the Sjöbo area, to be more precise. I see you blanching, Comrade Upright?'

Barbarotti gave this a moment's thought. 'I'm speechless,' he exclaimed. 'What's it called?'

'*Hitler's Third Rebus*,' supplied Wallman.

'*Hitler's Third Rebus?*'

'*Exactement*. Simple but striking. A well-known name in the possessive, an ordinal number, that's the way to construct a blockbuster title. Plus a mild mystification . . . cipher, enigma, code – whatever you prefer. But of course it's the author herself who's the real draw in this case. Are you with me?'

Barbarotti nodded.

'Good. Well, so Bettina Braun is now about thirty-five and living under an assumed name in one of our Nordic countries. She is without doubt a linguistic genius, and in her day-to-day life works as a lecturer at an unspecified university: Copenhagen, Åbo, Lund, who knows? Just consider that she has single-handedly translated this magnum opus of hers into no fewer than nine other languages. That's entirely without precedent in the literary world, I'll have you know.'

'You mean that you . . . ?'

'Exactly, Holmes,' declared Wallman with becoming humility. 'The fact is that I wrote the whole pile of rubbish in parallel in all ten languages, which was what lent spice to the whole

creative process. It came out at six hundred pages in the end –
times ten, that is – and it took a couple of years. But with the
project now successfully completed, I feel I can say without
exaggeration that the Second World War is going to be seen in
rather a new light. We launched the book at the London Book
Fair this spring and, if I may put it coarsely, the publishers were
up on their hind legs like randy dogs. Bettina Braun and her
rebus are going to make waves, I can promise you that,
Constable!'

Barbarotti reflected in silence while Wallman polished off
his last almond tart and washed it down with half a mug of
coffee.

'But what about you, though?' asked Barbarotti. 'What are
you meant to look like in that . . . get-up?'

Wallman smiled and ran his hand smugly down his blood-red
tie. 'Agent,' he said. 'I'm her literary agent. I handle the rights
deals with all the publishers. And all the press contacts. Don't
forget that Bettina Braun is a very shy individual. She shuns
publicity and she absolutely doesn't want to appear in public
as the granddaughter of the worst mass murderer in history.
That's only natural, surely? I'm her sole link to the outside
world.'

'*Hitler's Third Rebus*?' said Barbarotti. 'Does it actually work?
I mean, are people really that gullible nowadays?'

Wallman threw out his hands. 'It isn't my job to raise the
general consciousness level. I got tired of sitting on the
academic scrapheap, as I've explained. While the hoi polloi got
rich on cat shit. What's wrong with prostituting one's talents
a bit?'

'OK,' said Barbarotti. 'I get it. But perhaps you could let me
have a signed copy when it comes out?'

'With pleasure,' said Wallman. 'Just let me know which tongue you'd like it in. There are going to be exactly a hundred signed copies in each language. Hitler's granddaughter's signature in the first edition of her sensational debut novel . . . well, I don't need to tell you what price they're likely to command? I dare say they'll be sold to collectors via internet auctions. But you'll get yours free of charge, of course, for old times' sake.'

Barbarotti speculated again whether his old friend really could be on the loose from some mental-health establishment, but there was no time to voice his suspicion, because Wallman looked at his watch and declared the audience over. 'I can't afford to miss my aeroplane,' he said. 'I've an important rendezvous with some German journalists down in Malmö tonight. Look after yourself, my friend, stay in touch, and we'll see if I can squeeze in one of our beer evenings sometime.'

'Why not?' said Barbarotti, exhausted.

'Don't forget now: defend my secret with your virtue,' Wallman reminded him. 'I shall kill you if you breathe a word.'

'You have my promise,' said Barbarotti. 'Of course.'

'Good,' said Wallman. 'Peace be with you, Constable Holmes!'

He got to his feet, patted his old comrade kindly on the head and shambled off in the direction of gate forty-two.

Did I really wake up this morning? thought Gunnar Barbarotti once the mustard-yellow back was out of sight. Was I talking to someone? Am I sitting here?

But if he really was – and if he really had been, then he could at least be glad that one question mark had been straightened out. *Wallman-Braun?*

That simply left all the rest.

*

Ninety minutes later he was in the air at last. The number of passengers came to a grand total of four, and Barbarotti assumed a dozen or so had tired of waiting and decided to go somewhere else instead. Or to take the bus.

But the flight only lasted just over an hour, and as he emerged from the tiny terminal at Vilhelmina airfield, there was indeed a young man waiting with his name on a sign, exactly as Mona Frisk had promised when he spoke to her on the phone that morning.

The heart of the matter, thought Barbarotti, inserting himself into the back seat of a grey Toyota. About time, too.

And then Marianne reappeared in the doorway.

FOUR

June 2012

June–August 1989

35

That summer.

It was the strangest time she had ever experienced; the fact began to dawn on her after just a few days. On Sunday she had slept until half past twelve, a deep, dreamless sleep, and had woken to find Billy standing at her bedside, looking at her. That had definitely never happened before. Neither the sleeping so late nor being woken by the boy.

It was understandable, of course, because she had not got to bed until five in the morning, shattered after all the urgent activity. She studied Billy, who was rocking slightly from side to side as he stood there; he undoubtedly wanted to say something to her, but the words were too deeply buried on a day like this. Even more deeply than usual, and it struck her that for once it was an advantage to have Billy as he was. What would they have said to each other? The sun was shining in through the window behind him and his virtually white hair filtered the light in the most extraordinary way, so that it almost looked like a halo round his head. She lay motionless on her side, watching him gravely for a few moments, and he did not look away as he usually did. He held her gaze, and she sensed it was in this moment that something decisive happened between them. Of course the really crucial thing had already happened the previous evening, but what passed between them now was a kind of . . . what was it called? A confirmation? A pact?

She couldn't say. Not then, and not now, twenty-three years later almost to the day, up in the silent expanses of Norrland.

But she can summon up that image of the bedroom, without the least resistance. Everything else is still there, too, but in a different way; nothing else appears in such sharp detail, so vulnerable and exposed, as Billy standing there against the light, looking at her. The moment they are reflected in one another and remember what has happened, and that . . . nothing will ever be the same again after this. The future lies before them, as open and unfathomable as an unknown ocean, and the pact between them is sealed.

Yes, she thinks, that's the word: *sealed*.

And now this detective inspector, after all those years. After Hinseberg. After her return. After Arnold.

What did he want? Why was he so eager to talk to her?

He's coming today. This afternoon, Mona has told her; the flight from Stockholm is badly delayed. But it was impossible to put him off any longer – Mona told her that, too. Not if one wishes to avoid arousing suspicion. And one does.

She mulls over these thoughts as she goes for her usual morning walk: the path that runs across the bog to the stream, the knotty old dwarf birches, the low, windswept scrub. The snow has not long melted; on the north-facing slopes a few streaks are still visible, and the ground is very waterlogged. The spring flood period is still not over. But summer seems to be waving from just around the corner. That's how it is in these regions; spring comes on so fast and lasts only a week or so, graciously allowed to shoehorn itself in between winter and summer. The long, long winter and the wistfully short summer.

The light, however, has already adjusted itself for the summer ahead; the nights have long been white and shimmering, and it is only a fortnight until the year turns. She has taught herself to sleep without the blinds down, and it was Mona who told her it was only a matter of training. She pointed it out several years ago now, but it takes time to get used to. After all the darkness, it pays to make the most of every gleam of light up here at our latitudes, that's Mona's view. It's part of the terms, our unwritten agreement with nature. The body must have its allocated share and store the light away inside, so it can cope with the darkness that is almost as long. Roller blinds? Venetian blinds? Nonsense.

And yet they are provided in every room and at every window; you have to bow to the guests' demands. But Ellen isn't a guest. She has worked out that she is up here for the thirteenth time. If you tally it all up, she has spent over a year at the guest house. Other sisters sometimes turn up as well, for a few days or a week or two, but she is definitely the most frequent of them. There is a tie between her and Mona that strengthens with every passing year. With every visit, every phone call; she has even tried to tempt Mona back to Kymlinge with her, but that has proved a step too far.

Those years in Hinseberg were quite enough for me, says Mona. My years in the south – that's how she refers to them. She's going to end her days up here where she belongs, and as she doesn't know which day will be her last, she has no plans to leave the place. And that's that.

But *storing the light*? Ellen likes the phrase, and the idea. It covers more than Mona presumably intended, because it's all too easy to store up the darkness. It happens whether we want it to or not, and it takes great effort to stop it. And to save what's worth saving instead.

Ellen looks at her watch. It is almost ten, and she hastens her steps along the path over the bog. There are three more rooms to clean between eleven and two, and it would be good to grab a sandwich before she's due to meet that police inspector.

On the way back she thinks about Göran Helgesson. It happens occasionally, and especially more recently, now that she knows he is no longer alive. He died last winter, down in Spain, and he wasn't in a good state. A drinker, alone and miserable, if her information was correct, a far cry from the strong man he once was.

Or pretended to be. Or acted the part of. The master of Great Burma – well, yes, there was a lot of acting, in those years. Although acting and performance are two different things, of course.

Three days after Harry goes, Göran comes to her; it's the Tuesday evening, she and Billy are at the table having dinner. That's another image she can recall in vivid detail. Smoked sausage and mashed potato. Freshly chopped chives and a knob of butter in the mash. Billy always insists on that butter.

Where's Harry? he wants to know, and it's as if he can ask the question specifically because the boy is there in the kitchen, too. I haven't seen him.

It's as if he is addressing himself directly to Billy, in fact. Even though he knows the boy doesn't speak.

Or maybe for that very reason. Yes, of course that's it. He knows he won't get an answer, and that's why he can ask the question. It's a game.

So she doesn't answer, either. She asks instead if he would like coffee, but he says no. There's another unspoken question in his eyes and she knows he will be back. Maybe even that evening: the coast is clear, after all. The coast is clear for all time, but Göran Helgesson doesn't know that. Or does he? Does he?

Before he goes, he strokes Billy's hair. The boy stiffens; a touch like that has never happened before, and there's a general kindliness in Göran's manner. A wish to please, or something like it; it's plain to see. It isn't just the usual, but a sort of gentleness that surprises her and yet doesn't.

Because this is a new time, isn't it? Only three days have passed, yet everything has changed. Nobody knows what lies ahead. Not Göran, not Ellen, not Billy, but there's a hint of unspoken togetherness – yes, that's exactly it, *togetherness* – in the kitchen that beautiful June evening at Little Burma.

And then he came, naturally he did. Several times over the next few days. And then the next few weeks.

And for the rest of the summer, too, after Harry had officially been declared missing. All is as usual and yet entirely different. On one occasion she can't help letting herself go and taking pleasure in it. He notices and it makes him proud. But no words, no unnecessary gestures. Little Burma is a den of silence.

But there are different sorts of silence.

Ingvor comes over as well, which has not happened for many a year.

And Ingvor is a stranger to silence. On the contrary: words are important tools for her. What do you think? she wants to know, accepting both coffee and a slice of sponge cake. Where's he gone? Have you heard anything from him?

Over a week has gone by when she poses these questions. The summer holidays are about to begin, and it is after the coffee and cake that she invites Billy to come and try out the swimming pool. Ellen too, naturally.

But Ellen has no answers to give her, and Billy doesn't feel like taking a dip. It's to do with his body, of course, and the fact that he's a poor swimmer. Not at all like his second cousins, who are all as lithe as fish in the water.

A few days later, however, they go over there all the same. They swim a few lengths together, Piggy and Mousey in the pale-blue, highly chlorinated water. But they don't feel like Piggy and Mousey any more and it is only long afterwards, up here in the wilds many years later, that she remembers those animal names.

She comes up over the crest of the slight rise and the guest house is in sight, down the slope. It looks so lovely there, surrounded by magnificent, unspoiled countryside. The majestic mountains in the background; on a clear day like today they look incredibly close, their outlines as sharp as razor blades against the bright-blue sky. No wonder people come here, thinks Ellen, shading her eyes with her hand. No wonder I yearn to be here even though I already am.

But you can yearn for what you already have, she read that somewhere.

Certain other things, certain situations and sequences from that summer, can seem as sharp as that morning's outlines of the high mountains. Her first encounter with the police, for example.

At Ingvor and Gunnar's request, she has phoned them to report Harry's disappearance. She makes the call on the Wednesday evening, and they turn up on the Friday.

A quiet, older man who is obviously in charge, and a younger one with short-cropped red hair. Neither of them in uniform. The younger one jots things down in pencil in a black notebook as they make their slow and deliberate way round the farm and the inside of the house. The weather is good.

It is right after lunch. Billy has just returned home from the end-of-term festivities at school. She has taken a day off work at the hardware store for both reasons: the early finish for the end of term and the visit from the police. No objections were raised, especially when she explained to Lindgren that her husband has gone missing.

It is the older, rather more timid one who asks the questions and the redhead who notes down her answers, that is the pattern. All she says is written down in the little notebook, and the only times the younger one speaks is if he has to ask her to repeat something.

Is this an interrogation? she thinks. Is this what goes on at one of those?

But she doesn't ask. It's only natural for them to want to know various things if someone is missing, that goes without saying.

When did you last see him? the little grey-haired one wants to know.

Saturday evening, she says. But once we'd had dinner I lost track of where he got to.

Didn't he say anything? Anything about having plans to go somewhere, for example?

No.

Did you argue?

No.

How was he?

The same as normal.

And he never went to bed that night?

No.

What did you think?

I thought it was odd.

And what do you think now?

Odder still.

Why did you wait so long before calling us?

I don't know. I suppose I thought he'd gone off somewhere.

Who could he have gone to see?

Maybe some friends of his in town.

But his car was still there?

Yes, it's strange.

Have you checked with these friends?

Yes. He isn't there.

They are making their way slowly across the farm as they exchange these questions and answers. The policemen are walking one on either side of her, the redhead sticking close, so he won't miss any of what she says. Her explanations and her conjectures.

Eventually they go indoors, processing gradually from room to room. The little grey one often pauses, says nothing for a while and appears to be on the lookout for something. He is almost sniffing the air for a lead. He often says nothing for thirty seconds or so, but she doesn't find it unpleasant, it doesn't bother her. She senses that this is what he is aiming for. He wants her to feel uncomfortable and start to blab. He has presumably ordered his assistant to keep his mouth shut.

But she doesn't blab. She understands silence, and always has done.

What did he take with him?

Sorry?

Have you looked to see what's missing? His wallet, for example? A bag?

I don't think he took a bag. But I haven't seen his wallet, so I expect he's got that with him.

Passport?

I think his has expired. He was talking about renewing it.

Are the two of you in the habit of going abroad?

No.

She finds the passport in a drawer.

Clothes? A coat or jacket?

She says that as far as she can make out, the only clothes missing are the ones he was wearing on the Saturday evening. A pair of jeans, a shirt, a thin sweater.

Not even a jacket?

No, she doesn't think so.

They go through the wardrobes and she sticks to her view that he hasn't even got a jacket with him.

Well, the weather's fine and warm, says the little grey detective.

She asks them if they want coffee, but they politely decline.

And this is your lad?

They come across Billy in the kitchen. He is tucking into vanilla ice cream with strawberry jam, to mark the start of the holidays. The little grey man goes over to him, holds out a hand and says hello. Billy takes the hand and even gets to his feet. He also shakes the red-haired assistant's hand. Gives a bow.

So you've broken up for the summer holidays now?

Billy nods.

But you miss your dad?

Billy nods again. Thank goodness. She thinks about that moment in the bedroom. The sealing of their pact.

Where do you think he's gone?

Billy shakes his head.

She thinks it's a good job that he doesn't speak. The policemen no doubt interpret this taciturnity as a sign of unease. Think he is anxious about what has happened to his father.

They leave him in peace at the kitchen table almost at once. No point making it any worse for the boy. The little grey one even puts a hand on his shoulder for a moment. Like Göran's pat on the head a few days ago, more or less.

The visit lasts no more than twenty-five minutes, half an hour at most. They stand out in the yard and take their leave. The little grey one says they will do everything in their power to find Harry. It isn't unusual for people to disappear and then turn up safe and sound. Especially in the summertime.

Had he been drinking? is his final question. Was he intoxicated?

A bit, she admits. I wouldn't say he was sober.

The assistant notes this down, too.

Then they tell her they are going to have a word with the residents of Great Burma, as well. They are neighbours, after all, and they may have seen something.

Yes, why not? says Ellen. You never know.

She stands there and watches them drive away. Billy comes

out of the house and stands with her. Unusually close to her, and she feels almost as if she should take him by the hand. As if he wants her to.

But she doesn't. She just stands there until the black Saab has disappeared over the top of the rise, behind the lilac hedge.

And now, twenty-three years have gone by. She is in room number eight in Ragnhild's Mountain Guest House, changing the sheets. It's hard to grasp that she is the same person now as she was then. Hard to grasp the flow of time itself.

In a few hours' time that detective will be here. What on earth is that going to achieve? What does he want?

36

Barbarotti is in the back seat, but it is not a conscious choice.

The passenger seat in front is the preserve of a shaggy dog. It has a strange smell and seems very old and tired, and perhaps Henning has put it there so he can avoid having a conversation.

He certainly hasn't much to say. Beyond giving his name as Henning. And with Barbarotti having no wish to explain what brings him to Ragnhild's Mountain Guest House, very little is said altogether.

Despite the car journey taking almost two hours. He had not bargained for that, having imagined that the guest house would be on the edge of the settlement, but that naturally isn't the case. The mountain kingdom does not start just around the corner. They speed off through the wide, open landscapes of Norrland, after only a glimpse of the beating heart of civilization that is the town of Vilhelmina.

His thoughts are an unruly mess. But he doesn't want to let go of them, because without thoughts, that sense of being abandoned is lurking. Ominously close, especially in conditions like these, in such breathtaking surroundings, where he seems simply to be leaving everything behind him. Kilometre after kilometre, with no going back. No wife to ring, not a human soul to talk to, no sensible purpose at all . . . No, there is no point letting loose that sort of monster.

So he thinks about Axel Wallman. And Billy Helgesson. Inger Berglund, Lisbeth Mattson and those people he has never met, who populated two farms outside Kymlinge, twenty-five years ago. He is going to encounter one of them shortly, however. The leading lady, to be precise, the one who has gone down in history as the Axe Woman of Little Burma. Her and her alone; the others seem to be scattered to the winds of the world – unhappy, dead, misunderstood and Lord knows what. Like people generally, you might say.

He also tries to think about Arnold Morinder, and the potential significance of him and Ellen being school fellows back at the dawn of time, but the missing electrician is so fuzzy round the edges that his thoughts find no purchase. Rides off to buy an evening paper and then dumps a blue moped in a bog and leaves it behind him? What sort of idiotic prank is that? Norway? Was he really on his way to Norway, could there actually be something in that throwaway comment?

But if his thoughts slide too readily off Morinder, then their grip is all the stronger on the axe woman herself. The one he is about to see. To face across a table at last, with a chance of establishing how everything fits together.

Does he really think he is going to get to that point? Is there even a possibility? *Please could you tell me how everything fits together?*

No, he can't be serious. What he seriously believes is merely that he will manage to have a talk to her, and will then conclude that he has made no progress worth mentioning on this case. On these cases. But he has done everything he could. The fact that he is making a trip to Lapland and back is proof enough that he has done his best, surely? Asunander won't be able to deny it.

Or maybe he really will find something? It isn't entirely out of the question. There must be some reason why Ellen Bjarnebo had lied to him. Or for her friend to have done so – another person alleged to have done away with her husband once upon a time, and who had served many long years in Hinseberg for it. What sort of women are they, these two waiting up there in the wilds for him?

And it is somewhere here, in his freely flowing stream of thoughts, that Marianne reappears to poke her nose in. There she stands again, hands on hips, and urges him just like before: to watch out. Not to see this assignment as merely a way of killing time. To be careful. Just because he imagines Asunander has allocated him this business as a way of passing the days, it doesn't mean that he is on safe ground. *Stay alert*, says his dead wife. *Don't imagine this is merely a game.*

What does she mean by that? Should he really rely on her judgement? She also pretty much told him to try to get together with Eva Backman after all. Her words sound like mad ravings, and who is to say that the dead have better judgement and overview than the living?

'Malgomaj,' says Henning the driver unexpectedly, with an expansive sweep of his right arm. Barbarotti looks out of the side window, across the lake to which Henning has just referred; it winds its way through the landscape like a wide blue ribbon, or a scarf dropped by some young beauty on her way to meet her beloved. Henning is presumably trying to say that he finds it beautiful. That he is proud of living up here. That this is what it's all about.

Barbarotti can well understand him, if so. It is majestic,

stunning. What he finds impossible to get his head round, however, is that he is sitting here behind Henning and Henning's ancient dog, being whisked through this awe-inspiring landscape to meet two former murderesses. An axe woman and a . . . what had Backman said? Two shots with a hunting rifle? One in the head and one in the heart?

'Yes,' he says, in answer to the driver's unique attempt at conversation. 'I can understand people not wanting to leave this place.'

Yet that is exactly what he wants to do. He does not belong in this mighty setting, he is astray in every possible respect and, if he is not careful, he will find himself overwhelmed by that great surge of grief once more. The grief that paralyses and petrifies him, and he very much doubts that Henning and his canine consort are the right company for that kind of mental avalanche.

'How much further is it?' he therefore asks.

'About twenty minutes,' says Henning.

Then he looks as if he might be chewing over a question, but nothing comes. Barbarotti leans back and closes his eyes. He tries to establish some kind of contact with Our Lord, and after a while he starts to feel somehow enfolded. Neither of them says anything. Our Lord is as uncommunicative as Henning this afternoon, but it doesn't matter. He knows what the trouble is, of course He does. There is no need to put it through the sluggish mill of formulation in words.

For there is not a word in my tongue but, lo, O Lord, thou knowest it altogether.

And it's best that way, thinks Barbarotti. Then he takes Marianne's letter from his inside pocket and reads it again. He sees that it is already looking a bit worn, and the paper has softened on the folds, and he decides he will have to get it laminated somehow. Or perhaps make a photocopy and keep the original in a safe place.

But she gets him to smile, it can't be denied. Dead and buried, but still present in a sense that is all her own.

They pull up in front of the white wooden building at exactly half past three in the afternoon. The sun has gone in, dark clouds are massing over the mountains in the west and, as Barbarotti gets out of the car, he feels a cool gust of wind. A powerfully built woman in her sixties has come out onto the long, narrow veranda that runs along the front of the house. She exchanges a few words with Henning without acknowledging Barbarotti's presence; Henning slides back into the car and drives off, while the woman stands there on the bottom step, scrutinizing Barbarotti. There is little doubt that it is none other than Mona Frisk herself. She radiates authority and strength, both internal and external. Her steel-grey hair is tied back in a ponytail and she is wearing washed-out jeans and a checked flannel shirt; she has a red cotton scarf tied round her neck and black clogs that look exactly like the ones Barbarotti used to go around in when he was at high school in the seventies.

'It's going to rain,' she says.

No introduction. No handshake. No welcome.

'I've put you in number seven,' she says. 'That'll be best.'

Barbarotti has no idea what it will be best for, but he follows her into the building. On the ground floor there is a sort of reception area: a wooden counter set in a hole in the wall and some armchairs grouped round two tables. A wall-mounted television up near the ceiling. To the right, some double doors that presumably lead to the kitchen and dining room. A variety of dead creatures on the walls – whole or only parts of them – birds and furry animals. A collection of skis of various antique-looking vintages.

A wooden floor with rag rugs. An open hearth. All very snug, it couldn't be denied.

But Mona Frisk doesn't pause for any kind of check-in; she takes the curving stairs up to the first floor and goes ahead of him along the corridor. It runs the length of the guest house, with rooms on both sides. Number seven is at the far end of the building, and she opens the door and invites him to step in.

A bed, a small desk, a chair. A free-standing wardrobe and a picture on the wall of what he guesses to be a wolverine. A handbasin with only one tap. A rag rug in here, too. Through the window he should be able to see the mountains, but they are obscured at the moment by the advancing clouds.

'The bathroom's opposite,' she tells him.

Barbarotti nods and puts his bag down on the chair.

'You're a charmer and no mistake,' he says.

His intention had only been to think it, but for some reason the words slip out of his mouth. Perhaps it's just as well; there is a slight twitch in her face, which he interprets as an incipient smile. She stops it in time and mutters something to distract him as she goes over to the window and turns her back on him.

'When can I talk to her?' he asks. 'I haven't come up here to go hiking or take a bath.'

'I need her to help me with the dinner,' says Mona Frisk. 'We have six guests including you. The two of you will have to have your chat afterwards. We eat at seven, down in the dining room.'

Barbarotti checks his watch. That means he has three hours to wait, but perhaps there is no reason to kick up a fuss. He can't think of one, anyway. He isn't sure he could beat Mona Frisk at arm-wrestling and he is unarmed, as always.

'All right,' he says. 'How's your mobile coverage here?'

'Upstairs it generally works. Depends which service provider it is. If necessary, you can use the landline down in reception.'

'Thank you,' said Barbarotti. 'I'm planning to take the afternoon flight tomorrow. Can I prevail on Henning for that?'

'Him or his brother,' says Mona Frisk. 'Was there anything else?'

'I'd like a word with you, too,' hazards Barbarotti.

'Don't see what that would achieve,' says Mona Frisk. 'Tomorrow morning, then. After breakfast.'

'Excellent,' says Barbarotti, and then she leaves him, to continue her preparations for dinner.

The rain comes down five minutes after she has closed the door behind her. It beats on the window like a volley of bullets, and the thought at the front of his mind is that he ought to be a bus driver rather than a police officer.

Or a dentist or a furrier, or anything at all. In this pathetic room in this guest house of the Far North, without aim or purpose – he himself, that is; the guest house seems to have plenty of both – and as rudderless as a flat-bottomed rowing boat on the open sea, there is simply no end to the images infesting his mind.

He lies on his back on the bed, clasps his hands behind his head and looks up at the ceiling. It is white and devoid of content. He listens to the rain pounding on the windowpane and sill with rising and falling levels of intensity, and wonders what it means that he has reached this point in time and space in his fifty or so years' pilgrimage on this earth. Why is he lying here? Right here, right now?

It is not an uplifting thought; he wishes he was at least at home in Kymlinge, talking to his children, or to his bereavement counsellor – and then he remembers that he has a session booked for the next day, Tuesday, which he will obviously not be able to make. He gets out his mobile and finds Rönn's number, but when he looks at the display, he sees that he is beyond reach of any signal, which merely confirms the conclusion he has already come to.

Sorrow is better than laughter: for by the sadness of the countenance the heart is made better.

The heart of the wise is in the house of mourning; but the heart of fools is in the house of mirth.

That's exactly it, thinks Barbarotti. I don't feel good and it's meant to be that way. The worse, the better, to put it bluntly.

If he remembers rightly – though he still doesn't bother looking it up – it comes a bit later in the same chapter, the passage that says *anger resteth in the bosom of fools*. But nonetheless, and without taking it as a direct lesson, he knows that this is exactly the feeling now slowly igniting inside him. After self-pity comes strength, that's how it usually goes.

So Mona Frisk shot her husband with a hunting rifle, he thinks, and there's nothing I can do about that. But she's not bloody well going to run this all her own way. Black clogs from the seventies, that's the limit.

And for the next hour – as hunger starts its assault on him, presumably prompted by the clear and growing signals of food preparation that come seeping into the room from below – he devotes himself to devising a web of poisonous questions. A web that he has no intention of letting Ellen Bjarnebo escape from, once his stomach has been satisfied and he is finally able to talk to her.

And it really is no more than fair that she should have to cook him a good, substantial dinner first.

37

The days turn into weeks.

Harry is still missing. The police send out two men, who spend two days making a search of the immediate area.

But they find nothing. No Harry, no traces.

The little grey one comes to visit her again, this time with a different assistant, a young woman. They ask questions, some old and some new. She answers as far as she is able. They also try to talk to Billy, but Billy just successfully shakes his big head and looks sad. They soon leave him in peace.

At midsummer they are invited up to Great Burma. They sit out in the garden for the traditional herring and potato. Salmon and savoury tarts, and all sorts of other things too, of course. Schnapps, beer and wine. Strawberries and ice cream for dessert, and the weather is glorious. Ingvor's sister and brother-in-law are there, with their two children. Five adults, Ellen counts six children in all. The children bathe in the pool – not Billy, but the others. She drinks a shot of schnapps, a beer and a few mouthfuls of wine; not much, and she doesn't get inebriated. Göran and his brother-in-law, on the other hand, are drunk and loud, but not like Harry used to be. It makes them merry and a bit opinionated, that's all; there's a world of difference. Göran gives her a wink on the sly.

Yes, it is a remarkable summer. She starts her annual leave, too, a week after midsummer, and suddenly she is in constant contact with her neighbours at the big farm. It's inevitable, of course, the farm work has to be done, it will soon be harvest time and, with the master of Little Burma missing, of course his counterpart at Great Burma has to step in.

And he does. Göran sees to everything that needs doing on both farms, and when he comes to her in secret, it suddenly seems quite right. He has two farms and two women. One woman won't let him close, but he has no problem with the other. They don't discuss it, but she can tell he is thinking along the same lines.

She also knows that it can't last. The summer and the whole situation will have to come to an end sometime, perhaps both of them at the same time, there are signs to indicate as much. It's hard to put her finger on what they are, but the Mutti voice speaks to her a couple of times and reminds her.

That everything has its time. That somebody will find Harry sooner or later. Yet she doesn't go out into the forest to conceal him better; the idea occurs to her now and then, but every time it feels as if all the strength has been sucked out of her. This is the one thing she can't bring herself to do. Better to let fate take its course.

Now, looking back on it twenty-three years later from Ragnhild's Mountain Guest House – or Mona's Mountain Guest House, she prefers that name, having never even met Ragnhild – she thinks she should have got a grip on herself. As the days turned into weeks that summer, she should have taken a shovel out into the woods one night and made sure her husband was buried good and deep. Six feet under, didn't they say?

But it's easy to think things with hindsight and be wise after the event; it went as it did because it was necessary. Things had to be resolved, and when that day in August arrives, she feels no bitterness or regret. Since then she has sometimes found it hard to understand that, but that was how it was.

That is how it is. She and Billy are on holiday, they only have each other and it's amazing how simply and easily everything goes. Particularly with Göran, and even Ingvor, being so helpful. Yes, amazing is the word.

Her brother and sister-in-law come to visit. Gunder and Lisbeth; it is just after the Öland trip. It has never happened before, and they even stay the night. She talks mainly to Lisbeth; things have always been difficult with her brother. But they all have dinner together and share a bottle of wine. Billy is at the table with them, too. Lisbeth tries to talk to him a few times and also spends a little while on her own with Billy in his room.

A few months later, this suddenly appears in a more significant light.

As if she knew.

But of course she can't have done.

Six guests. But as she and Mona are eating, too, albeit in peace and quiet in the kitchen, there are really eight of them.

Game casserole with the almond potatoes of the region. It's a classic, and more or less what the guests will expect; the game in the stew can include a bit of anything. As long as they serve the customary lingonberry sauce, cornichons and little balsamic onions on the side.

She has said hello to the guests in advance, even Inspector Barbarotti. The other five are a young couple from Stockholm and a German family with a ten-year-old son. The family has been staying for nearly a week and will be moving on tomorrow. With no particular destination planned, perhaps the North Cape eventually – that was a route the German visitors tended to favour.

But now here she is, sitting in the kitchen with Mona, eating dinner. The detective she is about to speak to is seated at a table on his own out there. She doesn't feel particularly anxious, but it's still good to know that Mona will be on hand. Just in case anything goes wrong. She doesn't quite know what she means by that thought, but chooses not to scrutinize it any further. Instead she asks Mona if she thinks there are enough juniper berries in the stew.

Oh yes, plenty, says Mona, and gives her a wink. You're not nervous, are you, sweetie pie?

The hell I am, says Ellen, and they laugh together in that way that makes her feel utterly safe.

She has never told Mona that her laugh has that effect on her. Mona knows, even so. To be precise, Mona basically knows everything, and Ellen has sometimes thought the best idea would be to move up here permanently herself.

But it is important to be away from here, as well. Above all, perhaps, to be able to come back, and they have never really discussed the more radical solution seriously. The main thing is that she knows she will always be welcome.

And that she isn't a burden. She pulls her weight and Mona often says she doesn't know how she would cope without Ellen.

The thought keeps recurring to her that she gets more love in a minute from Mona than she got from both her husbands put together, in more than twenty years. A different sort of love, of course, and thank goodness for that – but to think that she had to go to Hinseberg jail and to Vilhelmina to find it. Life is not a walk along a straight path.

At the start of July that summer she and Billy go camping on the island of Öland for four days. Billy is happy, she can see that, but he still doesn't speak. She doesn't put any pressure on him; the pact they have sealed works best in silence, there's no doubt about it.

But they have never before been as close as they were on those days in Böda – and they never will be again. When everything comes to an end on that Monday in August, she knows that is how it will be, and Billy knows it just as well as she does. The whole time in Hinseberg, and ever since, she has felt grateful for that summer, and above all for the trip to Öland. She knows she is going to lose the boy and she knows it is this knowledge that makes the bond between them so strong.

Enjoy each day as it comes, enjoy it while you can, the Mutti voice tells her, but she doesn't really need reminding. She thinks, both then and now, that she has never been as worldly-wise as she was in that short interlude.

As for Arnold, she hardly ever thinks of him. It's a conscious decision; he pops into her head now and then, of course he does, but she always banishes him. He has nothing good to give her, nor ever did have, and the memory of him is little more than a burden. But she knows, of course, that he plays a crucial role, and that things wouldn't have gone the way they did if he hadn't existed. For better or worse, that's just the way it is, and maybe that's why she doesn't want to think about him.

For better or worse?

But right now, with the dessert course of curd cheesecake and warm cloudberry sauce almost finished, both in the dining room and here in the kitchen, she feels a sudden stab of apprehension. Now that she is facing her talk with the detective sitting out there, waiting for her; Mona can see it and puts a hand on her arm.

'There's nothing to be afraid of, Ellen,' she asserts in her deepest, most reassuring voice. 'You know what you're going to say – he can't hurt you, remember you're in the safest place on earth. Do you fancy a small brandy?'

They have a small glass each, and then they go out to clear the tables.

'Ten minutes,' she tells the detective. 'I'll be done in ten minutes.'

38

So there they are, finally.

The same table where he had dinner. A red-and-white checked tablecloth. Salt, pepper and HP Sauce. A knotty candlestick and a view over the mountains. The rain has stopped, but their outlines are still blurred by the low, scudding cloud. It is a few minutes past nine, they are alone; the other guests have retired and Monica Frisk is probably lurking in the kitchen.

They each have a cup of coffee. He puts his recording device on the table between them, she looks at it with surprise and he asks if she has any objection. She shakes her head.

She reminds him of a teacher he had at upper secondary school, he thinks. History and religious studies, if he remembers rightly, possibly social studies, too. Cool, correct, composed; her name was Miss Jonsson, wasn't it?

She is quite small, too, Ellen Bjarnebo. Especially compared to Mona Frisk; there must be a thirty-kilo difference in weight. But she isn't slight, he thinks, and she would certainly still have the strength in her body to deal a man a fatal blow with a sledgehammer, if the need arose. Her hair is short, dark and straight. Her eyes are calm and a greenish-grey, her facial features have a clean cut to them. He knows she is seven or eight years older than him, but it feels as if they are much the same age.

He has had time for these reflections as he was sitting over his meal. Some of them, anyway. They had exchanged greetings when he came down, and she has been back and forth between the kitchen and the dining room several times, to serve and to clear away. It feels very weird, he thinks, for this really to be her.

The Axe Woman of Little Burma.

And just as he has had time to observe her, so she has had time to observe him. Of course. He can't remember ever having been part of such a protracted build-up to an interview. Or an interrogation, or whatever this is.

'There are a few things I need to discuss with you,' he begins. 'Primarily about the disappearance of Arnold Morinder. We're going through a few old cases that are still unresolved, and we'd be grateful for your cooperation. But we're also still interested in the murder of your husband in 1989, for which you were convicted and served a prison sentence, because . . . well, because we think the two are linked.'

'I see,' said Ellen Bjarnebo. Her voice is calm and quite deep. Pleasing to the ear, thinks Barbarotti.

'First, I want to ask you why you have been deliberately keeping out of my way. Both you and Mona Frisk lied to me when I was trying to make contact with you.'

'That wasn't my intention,' answers Ellen Bjarnebo after a slight hesitation. 'But I am under no obligation to turn up to this interview, as I understand it. I have paid for the crime I committed, and I have nothing more on my conscience.'

'I can see your point of view,' says Barbarotti, 'but still.'

'But still?'

'Why such flagrant lying? All I want is to ask you a few questions. It makes me suspicious, you can see that, surely?'

'It was Mona's idea,' says Ellen Bjarnebo. 'But I agree with her. The police didn't treat me correctly after Arnold went missing. I'm tired of being interrogated.'

'We have to do our job,' said Barbarotti, 'and now I've come all this way to ask you to answer a few questions. Shall we start?'

'I'm here, aren't I?' says Ellen Bjarnebo.

'Thank you,' says Barbarotti, and glances at his recorder. He glances out at the veils of cloud, too, and thinks of a game of chess in which he has already made several bad moves. Alfons Söderberg crops up for a moment, as unwelcome as a cold sore. He ignores him, gives a little cough and launches in again. 'Right then. I've read everything you said in the interviews and at the trial, and there are a few points I wonder about. If we start with Arnold Morinder, I get the impression you weren't particularly surprised when he went missing. Is that right?'

Ellen Bjarnebo shakes her head. 'That isn't right at all. I was as surprised as everybody else. But you don't need to be a Nobel prizewinner to understand what the police were thinking. It's hard to be surprised when you're a suspect from the very first instant.'

'I can see that,' says Barbarotti. 'But *were* you surprised then?'

'Of course.'

'What were your spontaneous thoughts?'

'Sorry?'

'When he didn't come back that Sunday. What was the first thing that occurred to you?'

She gives it some thought, but only for a moment. 'That he must have gone back into town.'

'To the flat you both shared in Rocksta?'

'Yes.'

'And do you think he actually did?'

'No, I don't think so.'

'But if we assume that he did, can you see any reason why he might have?'

'I don't remember. What sort of thing do you mean?'

'Well, perhaps you'd quarrelled?'

'No, we hadn't quarrelled. But Arnold was an odd one. He didn't like talking. I didn't always know what he was planning.'

'But when he didn't get back by the evening, you must have started to wonder?'

'Maybe. Or when I didn't hear from him the next day, at any rate. But I had the car, so I was all right.'

'Did you try ringing him?'

'Yes, I did. But I got no answer. I assumed he'd forgotten to charge his mobile. He often did. And the charger was still there at the hut.'

'Did you have electricity out there?'

'He'd fixed up a cable running from a transformer. Illegally, I think, but he was an electrician, after all.'

'You say "was".'

'I don't suppose he's still an electrician, if he's alive.'

'And why's that?'

She shrugs, but says nothing.

'OK. But he had his mobile with him?'

'I assume so. It was never found, anyway.'

'Had it happened before? Him pushing off for a day, or longer?'

'Only ever for a day.'

'But you didn't go into town to check whether he was there?'

'Yes, I did.'

'When was that?'

'It was the Wednesday.'

'The day you called the police?'

'Yes. Once I realized he hadn't been back home, I called them. That must be in the interviews you read, surely?'

'Yes,' confirms Barbarotti, 'it is. I just want to make certain that I understand.'

'That you *understand*?'

'Yes.'

'And what is it you want to understand?'

And the sense of similarity with his old teacher abruptly intensifies. Her ostensibly simple question puts him on the spot – exactly as Miss Jonsson used to put him on the spot – and he feels he has been rumbled. Not completely exposed, but she has somehow shifted the balance to her advantage. He doesn't know *how*, only that she has contrived to do it, and with no visible effort. Because what is there actually to *understand*? He fortifies himself with some coffee before he responds.

'I want to understand what happened. That's why I'm sitting here.'

She makes no comment. Sips her own coffee and eyes him coolly.

'So you two were in the same form at school?'

Just as well to try to reset the positions right away, he thinks, and it is clear that he has caught her out.

'Y . . . yes, we were. How do you know that?'

'It doesn't matter how I know. But you never mentioned it to the police when they interviewed you?'

'Why should I have done? It's irrelevant, surely, that Arnold and I were at the same school for a while?'

Barbarotti shrugs his shoulders. 'You never know. So you two were well acquainted from before, when you met?'

'I wouldn't say that. I mean, it must have been . . . what, forty years since we'd seen each other. I remembered who he was, but that was all.'

'So it wasn't a factor in the pair of you embarking on your relationship?'

'No. And that's my private business. I'm not going to talk to you about my relationship with Arnold Morinder. It's got nothing whatsoever to do with his disappearance, I told them that a hundred times, five years ago.'

'All right,' says Barbarotti. 'I accept that.' But only because I'm actually more interested in the other case, he thinks.

'Can you see any link at all between what happened at Little Burma and the disappearance of Arnold Morinder?' he asks.

She shakes her head. 'No,' she says. 'Of course I can't, because there isn't one.'

'When Arnold left that petrol station in Kerranshede, do you know which way he went?'

She has no way of knowing this, since even the girl on the till had not been able to answer the question. She happened not to be looking as Morinder pop-popped on his way, according to numerous accounts Barbarotti had read. But before he starts delving deeper into the summer of 1989, he wants to explore the Norway lead as far as he can.

'No,' she says in surprise. 'Obviously I don't.'

'You threw out the idea that he may have decided to head for Norway. He knew somebody there, didn't he?'

Ellen Bjarnebo shrugged. 'I know that's what I said,' she concedes. 'But I don't really believe it. I didn't believe it then, either, but when they sit you down and make you answer questions all day long, you'll say just about anything in the end.'

'Just about anything?'

'Maybe not just about anything, but you get tired.'

'And does this feel equally oppressive?'

'Yes, it does. But keep on with your questions – let's get it out of the way.'

'Surely you can appreciate that we want to find Arnold?'

'Certainly, but it's nothing to do with me. I can't help you. I couldn't then and I can't now.'

'When you got back to the flat that Wednesday, was there anything at all to indicate that he had been there?'

'No, I'm pretty sure he hadn't been back.'

'How could you tell?'

'Newspapers and post on the hall rug. The blinds down. Everything.'

'Do you miss him?'

'What?'

'I'm asking whether you miss him.'

'Yes, of course I do.'

'Are you saying yes because you're expected to?'

She suddenly smiles. Only fleetingly, but it's enough for him to see how much charm she must have had in her younger days. Perhaps still does, but she definitely won't intend wasting it on a straying DI.

'I was never in love with Arnold,' she says. 'If you absolutely must know. But it can be nice to have someone, even so. Though as it turned out . . .'

'Yes?'

'As it turned out, it would have been better if we'd never got together.'

'You mean his disappearance?'

'Yes, that and everything that came after it. Five years have gone by and I'm still stuck here talking to the police.'

'Sorry.'

He wasn't intending to say sorry, but he finds he is starting to like her. He never liked Miss Jonsson, he's sure of that, but then *she* never smiled. Not for a single second in all those school terms – not that he can recall anyway – but maybe he's being unfair. It's all about power, he thinks, and when power smiles, its subjects don't always construe it as such. This is an irrelevant and distracting meditation and he resorts to more coffee to help him find his thread again. Marianne appears momentarily in his mind's eye once more. She seems to be moving her lips. *Stay alert, Gunnar,* she is presumably urging him as she melts away.

'I met Billy in Stockholm the other day,' he says.

'Oh yes?' she says, and now her smile has definitely been obliterated. For the first time he senses a hint of uncertainty. Or shame, or something.

'He asked me to pass on his regards.'

She nods.

'You don't see each other all that often these days?'

She takes a deep breath. Her shoulders rise and fall and she regards him gravely.

'No. We don't see each other all that often, that's true.'

'There's one question that was never really answered, where the murder of your husband was concerned.'

'Oh yes? Which was that?'

'It was about Billy's role. Did he know what was happening? Before it became obvious, that is.'

She shakes her head. Barbarotti indicates the recorder.

'He didn't know about it,' she says.

'No. That's what you claim in the interviews. But I don't believe it.'

She is silent for a while before she answers. She locks her hands together, rests them on the edge of the table and looks at him.

'Why don't you believe it?'

'Because it sounds absurd, to my ears,' says Barbarotti.

'Absurd?'

'Yes. The way you tell it, you kill your husband with a blow to the head, out in the office in the cowshed on the evening of 3 June. Then you joint him, package up the body in plastic sacks and drag them out into the forest. It's four in the morning by the time you're done. And Billy's at home, in the farmhouse, the whole time.'

'He was in his room,' says Ellen Bjarnebo.

'In his room?'

'In bed, asleep. He was a rather strange boy. And he liked being by himself.'

'Yes, I understand that,' says Barbarotti. 'But then the two of you are together all summer, for more than two months, and all that time Billy remains unaware of what's happened to his dad. The fact that you killed him, chopped him up and buried him. That seems completely absurd to me.'

Ellen Bjarnebo stares down at her clasped hands for a few moments.

'I don't know,' she says. 'I convinced myself that he never understood. But maybe I was wrong. Maybe he did realize something had happened. Or had a feeling . . .'

'A feeling?'

'How can we know? Billy was so unlike other people. That's

still true, and if you've met him, you must know that. He can speak nowadays, but he didn't, back then. No more than a few individual words.'

'I don't see what difference that makes,' persists Barbarotti. 'You're his mother, so of course you would have been able to tell whether or not he knew what you had done to his father. Regardless of whether he spoke or not.'

She turns her hands palms up, but it is an extremely tentative gesture. He has no idea what is going through her head now. Maybe she's just play-acting, he thinks. But it's not a difficult role, if so, and this isn't the first time she's found herself in this seat, after all. He looks out of the window, where the sun glints through the cloud for a few seconds. High in the sky, even at half past nine in the evening.

'Of course I ought to have been able to tell,' she says finally. 'But I couldn't ask him straight out. Or tell him. I was living in . . . well, in a kind of state of shock that summer.'

'Because you had killed your husband?'

'Yes. That's not so surprising, is it?'

'No,' says Barbarotti. 'No, perhaps not. But you must have talked about it since, you and Billy?'

'About what exactly?'

'Whether or not he knew.'

'No,' she says after some hesitation. 'Not in that way, I don't think so.'

'What do you mean?' says Barbarotti.

'I mean that I . . . that of course I tried to explain to him what had happened. Once they started finding Harry out in the forest. Before the police took me away. But I . . .'

He can't judge whether her doubt is genuine or feigned, and he lets her go on.

'I didn't manage it in time. And that wasn't really the most crucial thing, either.'

'What was the most crucial thing?' asks Barbarotti.

She swallows and seems to be gathering her strength.

'The most crucial thing wasn't whether he had noticed or not. For me, it was making sure he understood what had happened.'

'Why you'd done it?'

'Yes. I wanted him to understand.'

'Exactly what was there to understand?' He feels a flash of satisfaction at the way he has reintroduced that insidious word *understand* to such good effect.

'I don't know any more,' says Ellen Bjarnebo with a sigh. 'And it doesn't matter. I mean, I realized they were going to take him away from me. And that I very likely wouldn't get a chance to tell him and explain later on. And I thought that he . . .'

'Yes?'

'. . . that he would get it, somehow. Billy didn't like his dad. He was scared of Harry. I was scared, too – that was why it happened. That was why I did it. To . . . set us free.'

'But you hadn't planned it?'

'No,' she says and gives a resigned little shrug. 'I hadn't planned it.'

Barbarotti nods, trying to quell the surge of sympathy that is rising unbidden inside him. He well remembers his conversation with Sofia Pallin, ex-wife of the hardware-store owner. You shouldn't speak ill of people who have been dead for twenty years, he thinks, but Harry Helgesson was a bastard in his lifetime, and I'm happy to make an exception for him. The thought strikes him, too, that it is much easier to interview disagreeable people, and that most criminals are, thank goodness, pretty disagreeable. He says nothing for a moment, but turns the pages of his notebook and pretends to be considering what his next question will be.

'And your neighbours up at Great Burma,' he says, 'they didn't know the real state of affairs, either? They were in the dark all summer?'

'I think so.'

'Even Göran Helgesson?'

But she makes no reply to that. Instead she apologizes and says she needs to go to the toilet. She promises to be right back.

Barbarotti switches off the tape recorder. He feels just as grateful for the pause himself.

39

Back home on Wednesday evening after work, Eva Backman attempted a summary of her day. But only after she had eaten a thrown-together portion of pasta and started a long soak in a well-planned bath full of bubbles.

Whichever way you looked at it, a lot had happened.

To start with (and to end with), it had mostly been to do with Lill-Marlene Fängström, the fond mother of the dead Sweden Democrat. That morning Assistant Detective Wennergren-Olofsson had conducted a long interview with her, exactly as planned, with the emphasis on what she had observed and reported to Backman on Saturday: the two men she claimed were keeping watch on her dead son's flat.

The interview lasted almost two hours, because Wennergren-Olofsson did not want to leave any stone unturned – and afterwards, after Mrs Fängström had left the police station, Backman spoke to him briefly. He said he gave a lot of credence to her information and thought it worth taking seriously, but he wanted to listen to the whole recording carefully and write a thorough report before he could express himself with any certainty.

While Wennergren-Olofsson was talking to the grieving mother, Backman had been in a different room with another, rather younger woman. Her name was Frida Skare and the reason she had contacted the police was that she thought she might possibly know who Raymond Fängström had shared his last meal with.

But only *possibly*; throughout the forty minutes of their conversation she was at pains to stress that modality.

She had been just as specific about her insistence on anonymity. Having dinner with Raymond Fängström on a Saturday night wasn't exactly a feather in anybody's cap, and if Miss Skare was wrong and her friend found out who had tipped off the police, she would kill her.

This friend, whose name was Ellen Hökberg, had been very secretive about where she planned to spend – and, later on, where she had spent – the evening in question. Especially afterwards, and Frida Skare had pretty soon diagnosed the whole thing as an assignation that hadn't worked out. A date that Ellen had arranged online, the way you do, and had initially wanted to keep quiet about in case things went awry.

And afterwards because they had.

Well, something like that. Frida Skare explained that this was the way Ellen Hökberg operated; the same thing had happened twice before, and if she had gone and hooked up with some nerdy type or a complete bastard, she wouldn't want to talk about it. Not even to her best friend – a role that had been Frida's ever since they were at upper secondary together. For more than ten years now.

Turn the page and move on, that had been Ellen Hökberg's philosophy long before the King of Sweden took to doing the same thing.

And why would it have been specifically Raymond Fängström that she had met? DI Backman had wanted to know.

Well, Frida Skare had explained – in a virtual whisper by

this stage – another friend, whose name she simply could not give, because then she'd get killed all over again, thought she'd seen Ellen and Fängström together early on Saturday evening. In the ICA convenience store on Allégatan, to be precise, which was only half a block away from Fängström's flat.

And she had put two and two together.

Or added another two, you might say, seeing as Ellen Hökberg hadn't been herself these past couple of weeks. She'd had problems with her page-turning, basically. In Skare's opinion, it seemed to have been much more than merely an unsuccessful date. Ellen Hökberg had run into little underwater rocks like that before, but it was only to be expected and normally she could deal with it.

Well, that was it, in a nutshell. *Possibly*, as she had been at pains to point out.

Eva Backman had thanked her for the information, promised to keep Frida's name to herself as far as she could and taken a note of Ellen Hökberg's contact details.

It turned out that Ellen was in Särö, some distance south of Gothenburg, attending a two-day conference for work. Backman learnt this from her auto-response, and decided not to leave a message. If Miss Hökberg really was involved in Fängström's death, it would be best not to warn her in advance. She would be back in Kymlinge on Tuesday evening and, having waited sixteen days already, Backman decided one more would do no real harm.

After she had finished with Hökberg and her friend and had eaten a mediocre lunch at her desk – a sandwich, a banana and an out-of-date yogurt – she received a call from a woman at the National Forensic Lab in Linköping. It had taken them a fortnight to complete their analysis of the samples sent in from Kymlinge. She apologized for the delay, but someone – Backman got a distinct impression that it wasn't her personally, but a younger male colleague – had messed up slightly; such things happen even at the National Forensic Laboratory, and there was also a factor that had rather nonplussed them.

A factor, Backman had dutifully enquired, that nonplussed you?

Yes, indeed, the woman had continued – eight hours later in the bathtub, Backman simply could not bring her name to mind, but she was in the email contact list and the full report would ping in tomorrow, so it was of no consequence – and it had rather complicated matters, if DI Backman would excuse her saying so.

Backman continued posing the questions that were expected of her, and gradually the picture emerged.

The problem was the contents of the stomach versus the meat-and-tomato sauce. The vomit versus the bolognese, as it were. The analysis of the unfinished meal on Fängström's kitchen table on that fateful evening (the woman from the lab really had used the expression *that fateful evening*, and Backman quietly wondered whether she secretly nurtured a dream of writing scripts for TV drama) did not reveal even the tiniest trace of poison. Only the honest ingredients you would expect in a reasonably edible sauce of that kind: minced meat, of course, onions, carrots, stock, cream, tomato purée, chopped tomatoes, salt and pepper, plus four or five different herbs. A splash of red wine – the same variety that had later accompanied the meal, incidentally. A small amount of Parmesan, probably grated.

Backman had thanked her for this comprehensive recipe and

then they had got to the crux of the matter. Or, to be exact, the substance that had killed Raymond Fängström, elected local councillor for the Kymlinge Sweden Democrats.

The vomit and the stomach contents.

Or, rather, what had been found in these two quanta (the woman from the lab had clarified, following this with a short but well-placed theatrical pause). Here they had identified considerable amounts of two types of poison: amatoxin and orellanine. Both were well-known mushroom toxins and were present in all the poisonous species of fungi in the country, including the lethal ones. The death cap, the destroying angel, the deadly webcap, the funeral bell, and more besides. But Fängström must have ingested the poison before he sat down at the table with his mystery dinner guest and the bolognese sauce, as previously described. Not to forget the spaghetti, cheese, salad and wine – all equally harmless. It was possible to deduce this from the time, and the known characteristics of the toxins. Both amatoxin and orellanine take effect relatively slowly, with symptoms not manifesting themselves until at least eight hours later, Backman had been informed, but they can sometimes take up to twenty-four hours. The amatoxin usually progresses faster than the orellanine.

It was worth saying that if someone had only got Fängström to hospital that night, he would have had some prospect of surviving. Not a good one, but he would have been in with a chance.

Backman had expressed her thanks for this information, too, and asked if what this all amounted to was that Fängström had probably been poisoned over lunch, but had waited to die until dinnertime.

That, confirmed the woman from the lab, was precisely what it amounted to.

Within fifteen minutes of the call she received an email giving all the preliminary findings. And a few others, such as the fact that Fängström's stomach contents and vomit had contained not only the semi-digested remains of mushroom, bread and a number of pick'n'mix sweets, but also large quantities of egg – so much, in fact, that it seemed quite possible he had consumed an omelette on the day of his death.

Mushroom omelette, Backman had thought. That idiot ate a big lunch of omelette filled with death caps cooked in cream.

But where? That was the question. Where had he eaten the lethal dish? He had died on a Saturday. Was it conceivable that he had been served it at a restaurant or café?

Or had he been at home in his own kitchen then, too? Or at a friend's?

At Ellen Hökberg's?

Was it an accident or had someone prepared the omelette deliberately?

If the latter, then who?

Ellen Hökberg?

But why?

Because she was a political opponent?

Now slow down, Backman told herself, both in her office in the afternoon and much later, in the bathtub. We're not even sure that we're dealing with an omelette here.

Are we dealing with an omelette here? She was pretty sure that this was the very first time in twenty years and more with the police that she had had to wrestle with this particular problem, and she decided to remember it for her memoirs.

Unfortunately Fängström had emptied all his bins before his guest arrived on the Saturday evening – it was a real nuisance for the investigation, but they had known that from the start. For a moment Backman visualized a large police contingent hunting down the potential remains of a two-week-old omelette at the municipal dump out in Gräfsta. That would certainly have been an episode worthy of her memoirs, too, but on second thoughts she conceded that there must be a better way.

A number of ways, in fact, but opinion was divided on which would be most effective. She had just been talking through the options with DI Sorrysen and DI Toivonen when her mobile rang – and despite seeing that the call was from the continuing soap opera that was Lill-Marlene Fängström, she had answered.

'They're here again!'

'What?' asked Backman. '*Who* are *where*?'

'The terrorists,' hissed Lill-Marlene Fängström. 'I'm in his flat and they're out there on the bench again!'

Thirty minutes later they were in safe custody at the police station, the arrest having been painless. The terrorists' names were Abram and Kunder Harali. They were father and son, originally from Syria, but they had been Swedish citizens for more than ten years; they were immediately placed singly, in separate interview rooms, to prevent them communicating and conspiring.

Backman and Sorrysen had taken on Kunder, the son. Toivonen and Assistant Detective Tillgren had interviewed the father.

It was all over in less than an hour. The two suspects each told a story that was identical in every detail, and after a telephone call to Mrs Harali – Abram's wife, Kunder's mother – both interviewees were told they were free to leave.

The explanation revolved round Kunder's younger sister, Behara. On her twelfth birthday, about a month before, she had received as a present the violin she had been longing for. The girl thought she was very musical, her father explained with an ambivalent smile. Behara had also been given a series of lessons with one of the violin teachers in the town, and this tuition required her to practise at home for at least half an hour a day. The family lived on Rosengatan in a block very close to the home of the late Raymond Fängström. Theirs was quite a small, cramped flat where the walls were rather thin, and Behara's musicality and instrumental skills remained unappreciated by her father and brother, so they preferred to stay outdoors for the duration of her practice. It was early summer, after all, and both father and son quite liked to sit on a park bench in the sunshine, reading or chatting. Was that not permitted in this peculiar country that had been their home for more than a decade?

Oh yes, it very much was, DI Backman had assured them. The whole thing was a misunderstanding. Would they like a lift back to Rosengatan?

The Haralis had politely declined the offer, preferring to walk back to their flat, and said that if there was anything else with which they could help the police authorities, they would be happy to oblige.

Five minutes after they had left the police station, Assistant Detective Wennergren-Olofsson came into DI Backman's office with the report he had just completed, fifteen closely written pages, and as he disappeared out of the door, she threw it into her bin.

*

That was the broad outline of her day, thought Eva Backman, and pulled the plug out of the bath. In other words, nothing had emerged with any great clarity in the case of Raymond Fängström's death, but she still felt they were making good progress towards its resolution.

Now it all depended on a mushroom omelette. In all probability, anyway. She felt very grateful that no journalist had yet managed to sniff out this sensational, spectacular line of enquiry. In any event, she decided the case would be ready for filing away in the archives before Friday, and that she could then take her planned week's leave.

No trip away, just the simple pleasure of early summer in Sweden.

Emerging from the bathroom after she had dried herself, she saw that a message had come in on her mobile. It had come from another bathroom.

40

Gunnar Barbarotti was not back in his room at Ragnhild's Mountain Guest House until a quarter past eleven. The second part of his conversation with Ellen Bjarnebo had only taken about half an hour, but after that he had spent quite some time in the bathroom, the only place in the guest house where he could get his mobile phone to work.

He had had a word with Sara and Jenny, and told them he was planning to leave Vilhelmina the next day, and would in any case be home by Wednesday at the absolute latest. And then he would keep his promise to thrash the living daylights out of everybody who took up his challenge to a game of German whist. One after another.

After his conversation with the children, he considered his next move and eventually decided that a text message would be best for Eva Backman. It was already quite late and he hadn't forgotten a certain tartness in her voice, the last time they had spoken. He had asked her to answer his text by lunchtime the following day and wished her a good night's sleep.

Then he had sent a text to his bereavement counsellor Mr Rönn, regretting that he was not able to get to their session on Tuesday, and asking if he could be back in touch to make another appointment.

After all this communication, and a truncated shower – the hot water was running out – he went back across the corridor to his room. Pulled down the blind to block out some of the still-abundant daylight and got into the rather hard and narrow bed.

He switched on the bedside lamp and rewound his tape recorder to listen through his interview with Ellen Bjarnebo. Particularly the last part, after her trip to the toilet.

There's something, he thought. There's something in all this that's entirely back to front.

GB: So how were things with the neighbours at Great Burma? I gather you and Harry didn't really get on with them?

EB: I don't see how that's relevant to anything. You're here to look into what happened to Arnold, aren't you?

GB: Basically, yes. But as I say, I have a sense that there's a connection between the two cases.

EB: There's no connection. It's what the police thought, five years ago. They imagined that if I'd killed one man, I could easily kill another. But it's naive to think like that.

GB: Naive? Why?

EB: I had no reason to kill Arnold. But I had every reason to kill Harry. It had reached a point where we simply couldn't bear it any longer. Not Billy, not me. Harry tormented us, and it literally got worse and worse, until I could see no other way out.

GB: Does this mean you planned it?

EB: Of course not. If I'd planned anything, it would have been taking Billy with me and leaving him.

GB: But you killed him with a sledgehammer instead?

EB: It was the work of a moment.

GB: In the transcripts I've read, it says you gave yourself a few seconds to think.

EB: I don't know why you're interrogating me again. I answered all these questions long ago, and I spent eleven years in jail for killing Harry. I've largely lost contact with my son. Can't you accept that I . . . that I've paid the price?

GB: I apologize. Yes, you've paid the price. It's just that . . .

EB: That what?

GB: That I was sent here to ask these questions.

EB: Sent?

GB: Yes. Well, anyway, it makes no odds.

What threw me off-balance there? he thinks. What was it that meant I couldn't keep up my role any longer?

Because that was precisely what had happened. For a moment, just before he apologized, he had felt as if he was viewing the scene from outside, from some other position in the room: the pig-headed DI and the convicted woman, one on either side of the table in the otherwise empty dining room, and him harassing her with his insolent, insinuating questions.

And from that position – from the viewpoint of an outside observer – all sympathy rests with the woman. Indisputably. The policeman blatantly represents power and arrogance. His behaviour is intrusive, shameful. Without any consideration, he assumes he has the right to force his way into other people's lives. At any time, in any way, without even apologizing.

But he had apologized. He had said sorry. For that very reason.

EB: I don't really understand.

GB: [Gives a little laugh, false and grating] No, that wasn't the intention.

EB: What wasn't?

GB: Putting the blame on someone else. I suppose I was only trying to say that I'm here because I'm doing my job. Like most other people who are doing their job . . . I assume. You're allocated a task and then you try to complete it to the best of your ability. My boss told me to look into these two cases. Arnold Morinder's disappearance first and foremost, but also your husband's murder. That's the way things stand. [At least five seconds' silence on the tape]

EB: And just so you can do your job with a clear conscience, you expect me to answer all sorts of questions that I've answered a hundred times before?

GB: No, not at all. You naturally have a right to break off whenever you want. You'll have to excuse me. My wife died a month ago, and I'm finding it hard to concentrate.

Was it because of what she said about it being the work of a moment? he thought as he lay there in bed with his heart suddenly galloping wildly? Was that why I told her about Marianne? Was that why I didn't stop myself?

Work of a moment?

EB: I'm sorry to hear that. How did she die?

GB: An aneurysm. A small blood vessel in her brain burst . . . yes, that was it, basically.

EB: Maybe you shouldn't be at work at all?

GB: Probably not. In any case, it's not something I should be talking to you about.

EB: It doesn't matter. Anything's better than having to talk about all that old stuff.

GB: I can understand that. Do you think we could rustle up some more coffee? If you don't mind talking for a bit longer, that is?

EB: Would you like a small brandy as well?

GB: Brandy?

EB: Yes. You know what that is, right?

GB: Well, yes, I think I've heard of it. Why not?

[A short pause while Ellen Bjarnebo goes to get coffee and brandy, but for some reason he listens intently to the silence.]

EB: Here we are, Commissioner. *Skål!*

GB: I'm only an inspector.

EB: Well, *skål* all the same.

GB: *Skål.*

EB: All right then, feel free to go on.

GB: Thanks.

He would have to make sure to destroy the tape. Or perhaps he could try to sell it to the police training college as an example of how not to conduct an interview? Identify fifty-five mistakes. This is most definitely not the way to do your job.

But you can't hear everything on the tape, he thinks. Far from it, and it's often the parts you can't hear that are the most interesting. But as he lies there in that coffin-like room, eyes closed, and listens to their voices, he can also see all those other components: their relative positions at the table, their movements, their expressions, their interplay. Interplay? No, of course there was nothing like that. And he can't see his own movements and expressions, but there's something about the atmosphere in the room and her . . . presence?

Because she isn't finding this uninteresting. Somehow, every so often, she sends out a signal that belies her words. It isn't at all unpleasant for her to sit here and talk to him. Her attitude to him is positive, there's no mistaking it; in fact he would almost say that she likes him. And that she thinks what they are talking about is important. That she . . . that she actually has nothing against continuing the conversation, especially now they are each furnished with a second cup of coffee and a brandy. It is a light evening, there is nothing to indicate the presence of six other people in the house, though the timbers give an occasional click or groan, audible even on the tape. Perhaps some have gone to bed, and some have gone out for a walk; the cloud has lifted and the skies are clearing.

GB: Yes, it was your neighbours I was wondering about. Relations between the two farms were rather strained, weren't they?

EB: Yes, they were.

GB: Can you tell me about that?

EB: There was nothing special about it. Harry and Göran never got on. Harry was jealous of them. Great Burma was bigger, everything worked much better up at their farm, and he couldn't stand it.

GB: And they knew he didn't treat you and Billy well?

EB: They knew. But it wasn't their business and they didn't get involved.

GB: And once you'd done it, once Harry disappeared, they didn't suspect anything?

EB: I honestly don't think so. Göran helped me with the farm that summer.

GB: Until they found Harry?

EB: Yes. After that, everything was different.

GB: You could have got away with it – have you thought of that?

EB: Yes, of course. But I didn't.

GB: If they hadn't started finding the body parts, you would have got off scot-free. How do you think things would stand, if you had? Today, say?

EB: I try to avoid thinking along those lines.

GB: But you must have thought about it? That summer?

EB: Perhaps. But it's still . . .

GB: Yes?

EB: I think what happens will still happen. We can't influence anything.

GB: How do you mean?

EB: I killed Harry. I did it because I had to. But it was just as inevitable for me to take my punishment. Maybe I wouldn't have been able to live with the guilt . . . in the long run.

GB: I understand. But there was something else to feel guilty about, wasn't there?

[Five seconds' silence]

EB: You're talking about Göran Helgesson?

GB: Yes.

EB: How do you know this? There's nothing about it in any of the transcripts, is there?

GB: I spoke to Inger Berglund yesterday.

EB: Inger Berglund?

GB: Yes, I suppose she was Inger Helgesson in those days. The daughter at Great Burma.

EB: Oh, I see. And she told you?

GB: Yes, she told me. That you and her father had a relationship, and that it must have been you who gave the game away.

EB: [After some hesitation] Yes, it was me. Maybe it was wrong, I haven't given it much consideration since. But at the time I was convinced that I had to act that way.

GB: When was this, exactly?

EB: It was when I'd been in Hinseberg for about six months. It was important for me to do what was morally right. I had – well, in fact I've always had – this voice that kind of tells me how I ought to act. It may sound weird, or melodramatic, but I've sometimes felt it must be the voice of my conscience.

GB: I don't think it sounds particularly melodramatic.

EB: Thank you. Anyway, I was allowed out on special release for a last visit to the farm. Little Burma had already been sold by then to a couple escaping Stockholm for the good life in country, the land was leased out to Göran, and I told Ingvor the truth. I didn't even see Göran, but it seems to have completely shattered them.

GB: Was that your intention?

EB: Absolutely not. But it wasn't for me to carry Göran's burden of guilt. Maybe I even thought I was doing them a favour.

GB: But it turned out you weren't?

EB: It's not for me to judge. But there must be something wrong if he's going to the woman next door to get satisfaction. And I don't think I was the only one, incidentally. I reckon Göran Helgesson found himself someone else after I went to jail.

GB: But the two of you continued your affair that summer?

EB: Yes.

GB: Is it something you regret?

EB: Getting together with Göran?

GB: Yes.

[A few seconds' pause while the two of them sit in silence, finishing their brandy]

EB: At the beginning, he forced himself on me. We owed them money and he claimed me in lieu of payment. I never took the initiative and I never liked it.

GB: You didn't like it?

EB: No.

GB: And Harry never suspected anything?

EB: No. He would have reacted if he had.

GB: How, do you think?

EB: I don't know. Exploded with rage, I expect. Harry wasn't particularly good at bottling things up.

GB: And Billy?

EB: What about him?

GB: Could Billy have known that you and Göran were having an affair?

EB: No, I don't think so. We didn't see each other very often, and Göran was always very worried about being found out.

GB: Even by Billy?

EB: Well, no, perhaps not. But he was always careful to make sure Harry wasn't at home. That was easy enough, with the road going right past their place. When he saw Harry drive by, he knew the coast was clear.

GB: How long did it go on?

EB: Between me and Göran?

GB: Yes.

EB: Less than a year. Yes, that's right, it had started in the winter of that year.

GB: I see.

He turns off the tape for a moment. So what can I understand from this? he thinks. And of course that misused word is a lot more loaded now than it was before – at the beginning, when they were batting it to and fro between them in some kind of attempt to outmanoeuvre one another.

Can I divine anything from this stage of the conversation? he wonders. He sensed something as they sat there, and he senses the same thing now, in retrospect, lying there in the uncomfortable bed, his pulse rate still raised.

Is it something about her words, or her way of looking at him? That mild thoughtfulness that has come into her voice all of a sudden? As if she wants to tell him something, but can't. As if she's been carrying around something so heavy and hopeless for so long that what she wants more than anything is to unburden herself.

Imagination, he thinks. Over-interpretation.

He switches the tape back on. It starts with a short pause, and he remembers that this was the point when he heard someone turn a radio on, somewhere in the house, only to turn it off again almost immediately. But it isn't audible on the tape, for some reason. Instead he hears his own brutally open question:

GB: Billy? What really happened?

[As if he was asking her to put her cards on the table, finally; perhaps that is how she perceives it, too, but after a few seconds' thought she takes her answer in a different direction. And he's left not knowing what cards he had expected.]

EB: Yes, it's a great source of sorrow.

GB: Sorrow? At losing him? At losing contact with him, I mean.

EB: Yes, but you learn to live with the sorrow. I mean, I don't know how things would have gone at Little Burma if we'd carried on the way we were. Or rather, it couldn't have carried on . . . There was no solution to our lives, if you like.

GB: No solution to your lives?

EB: No, there really wasn't. Harry was a wicked person. Maybe not from the beginning, but he grew into one. His anger and bitterness consumed him. You know what: I've never regretted what I did. That's a sign, surely?

GB: A sign of what?

EB: That my actions were right. The things you do wrong, you regret all your life surely?

GB: I don't know. Perhaps you're right. That voice you mentioned earlier, was that what impelled you to kill Harry?

EB: No. No, I really don't think so.

GB: But when your brother and his wife came forward to look after Billy, did you think it was a good solution?

EB: I couldn't see any alternative.

GB: How did you get on with them? Gunder and Lisbeth?

EB: [Gives a laugh] Not well. To cut a long story short.

GB: But you raised no objections to them taking charge of Billy?

EB: What other option did I have? I was going to be in Hinseberg for up to fourteen years. They had no children of their own. And they did care about Billy, in their way. He . . .

GB: Yes?

EB: He was better off there than he had been with Harry and me.

GB: But why didn't you stay in contact with them?

EB: Because that was the way Gunder wanted it.

GB: And Lisbeth?

EB: Lisbeth's voice was never heard in that marriage.

GB: But you accepted it – the not having any contact?

EB: What choice did I have? I was a murderer, a butcher, don't forget. How would it have helped Billy if I'd been forever turning up in his new home? They kept it secret, where he came from, and that was only right.

GB: So you shouldered all the guilt and responsibility?

EB: Yes, you could say that.

GB: And you think that was fair?

EB: It wasn't about fairness. Can you see any better solution? With things the way they were?

GB: Perhaps not. But you haven't had much contact with Billy since you came out of prison, either, have you? And that was over ten years ago.

EB: It just turned out like that. I'm sad about it, but at least we see each other from time to time. And you've met Billy, you know what he's like. He finds other people difficult.

GB: Even his mother?

EB: Those years he spent at Hallsberg had an effect on him. No, we've never really found our way back to each other. But I'm pleased he's doing well. Juliana's a good person. And the main thing is . . .

GB: Yes? The main thing is?

EB: The main thing is that he's ended up with some dignity in his life. Not that things are perfect between him and me. Don't you agree? It would be self-centred of me to expect that. And I've even got a grandchild.

GB: You're not bitter?

EB: Do I seem bitter?

She had clasped her hands on the table in front of her and looked him straight in the eye as she said that. *Do I seem bitter?* He can clearly remember her look, entirely confident and at peace, and it strikes him that he has never encountered such calm before. What is it about this woman?

She is the only axe murderess he has ever met, and she isn't what he expected. He doesn't know what that was, but certainly not this. Sawing up another human being: what does that take? Several hours' suppressed panic and the required skills, perhaps. He remembers that Ellen Bjarnebo worked at the Meat Man factory. In the reports that he read, her jointing of Harry Helgesson is described as 'professional' or 'adequate'.

Adequate butchery?

He listens to the final minute of the tape, too, but there's nothing of note there. They agree to have a brief word with each other the next morning, if he feels it is necessary. Or she does. Then he thanks her, and she says she's sorry he was obliged to root around in all this old nonsense when he ought to be left in peace to grieve for his dead wife instead.

Did you love her? she wants to know, and that is the last thing said before he switches off the tape recorder.

Yes, he answers, *I loved her very much.*

Past midnight now. But sleep refuses to come, of course; he twists and turns under his thin cover and tries to shut off his brain. Failing to do so, he tries to dredge up a quotation from the Bible, maybe Ecclesiastes or Hebrews, and when he fails in that, too, he just lies flat on his back and attempts to remember Marianne's letter line by line, while summoning up her face in his mind's eye.

For a few quiet minutes he actually succeeds; he feels in some sense that he has her with him. But then Ellen Bjarnebo comes back. Their conversation, her calm, peaceful gaze, and the two of them sitting there at the table like two chess players with no pieces or board or intentions, and he suddenly hits on a question that he wishes he had asked her.

If I'd been your father confessor instead of a common-or-garden detective, you would have told me other things, wouldn't you?

Yes, indeed, he thinks, a few moments before sleep finally claims him, I shall ask her that question in the morning.

That question, word for word.

41

Past midnight. So hard to get to sleep.

It wasn't something she had ever experienced, that summer, and that must mean something. The fact that she didn't lie there agonizing over what had happened, that must have been a sign. A sign, and an acknowledgement that her guilt was slight, that she had only – in some deeper sense that didn't need to be pinned down – acted as she had been forced to act. And even if this was not the case, it is crucial to think it was, and has been, all these years.

The fact that she can't sleep on this particular night is something else. Something not very clear, but her conversation with the detective is still clinging on inside her, and she doesn't know if that's a good or a bad thing. She would have liked to exchange a few words with Mona afterwards, but Mona had already gone to bed by the time they finished in the dining room. Or at any rate she had closed her door, and there was no sound coming from her room as Ellen crept past.

And Mona always goes to bed early. But then she's up before six every morning. Summer and winter; really you should sleep longer in the dark season of the year, both she and Ellen realize that. Especially up in these parts, where it never gets properly light between November and February. But it doesn't work; the body and its vices are beyond our control, Mona is in the habit of saying. Better to listen to the signals and take them seriously.

But Ellen doesn't know what signals they might be that are keeping her awake on this particular night; they seem to be coming from her head, rather than her body. Perhaps she should pull down the blind, after all, but surely her head doesn't care whether it is light or dark? Not in that way; it is another kind of light and darkness that the various parts of her brain are wrangling over. Right and wrong essentially, things she couldn't talk to Mona about and has no intention of broaching with her. But it is as if her conversation with that kindly detective – kindly and a touch lost, she thinks, though with the death of his wife still so fresh, it was hardly surprising – their conversation, anyway, seems to have stirred something into life inside her. Something she has almost been waiting for, something she knew would come one day. Sooner or later, because she had clearly got off way too lightly five years ago? Hadn't she? They had harassed her, to be sure, the ever-persistent Gunvaldsson and several others, but it was still nothing like as bad as she had expected. When they suddenly let her walk away, just like that, she simply hadn't been able to believe it. Not really, not at first.

But there it was, she was no longer under suspicion for whatever it was they thought had happened to Arnold, and from the very first contact made by that DI Barbarotti – on the telephone a couple of weeks before – it had felt as if something was catching up with her. No, it isn't that she has been waiting for it all this time, she corrects her thoughts; not like that, but there's been something in the background all the same. Something unfinished, like a chapter still left unread in a book. A song with the late addition of a last verse.

And it all feels so clear and vivid now. All that time, those twenty-three years suddenly seem concentrated, compacted into a smaller, denser space. A few individual events, a few decisions and a set of long-term consequences.

Is that how life looks to everybody? she wonders. *Act in haste, repent at leisure* – did it have to be that way? She thinks she has read that proverb on an embroidered wall hanging, above a wooden sofa somewhere, but can't fathom where it could have been, if it actually is a genuine memory.

Not in her childhood home, at any rate. Not at Little Burma, either. There were no embroidered hangings in either of those places. But the question is a stupid one. She has long since stopped comparing her life with other people's. What use would it be?

Here she is anyway, lying awake, unable to get to sleep. That summer comes back to her. That final weekend, to be exact. She doesn't want it to, but still it comes.

Uninvited, like so much else in her life.

That Saturday and Sunday. The fifth and sixth of August. On the Monday, the seventh, blueberry picker Ernst Karlsson will find Harry's severed head and arms out in the forest, 300 metres behind Little Burma.

But she knows nothing of this when she wakes up on the Saturday morning, sees the sun shining and thinks of the two free days ahead of her. She has been back at work at the hardware store in recent weeks, but only on Thursdays and Fridays; it is still the holiday season, although on Monday Sweden will get back into gear again and she will be back to her usual hours.

But that's not the way it goes; there is no return to usual

hours, there are body parts and police officers and chaos and newspaper headlines instead, yet there is no need for her to worry about that now, on this almost-happy Saturday morning as she hurries to wake Billy and get his breakfast ready. This weekend Göran is going to harvest their wheat, or as much of it as he can, as long as it doesn't rain, and Billy will be joining him on the combine harvester. It is the first time her neighbour and lover has reached out a hand to the boy like that, and she can see it makes Billy happy. It takes a mother to detect it, but he is.

And he gets out of bed with no fuss, which certainly makes a change. But something has started happening to the boy over the summer. He is still mute, more or less, yet he seems content, in a way he never was before. His tin soldiers are back, all except three; they find them scattered behind the old earth cellar a few days after Harry disappeared – and they are not hard to find, really, which she tries to interpret as him slightly regretting what he'd done – but Billy isn't as fixated on them as he was before. He still plays with them occasionally, it's true, and still prefers to be by himself: *keeping himself busy* or whatever it is that twelve-year-olds do. But now and then he is up at Great Burma with his cousins. Not for very long, but it is definitely an improvement on how it was before. He feels at ease with moving more freely about the house, too, and is not as tied to his own room as he was the previous summer. For the first time in years she finds herself seeing some light when she thinks of him. Some kind of hope for the boy.

But then the thought always hits her that this is just a period of respite. Things are going to change.

Perhaps it is the Mutti voice telling her this; or at any rate, that was how she liked to look back on it afterwards.

Is she permitted to be just a little bit happy, while it still lasts? she asks the voice. Can I allow myself that?

And the answer comes in the words of a children's song: *Dance, my doll, while you are young.*

And she does. For two days more.

It is the same Saturday that she receives an unexpected visit. During the morning, an hour or two after Billy has set off to help on the harvester, an old Ford Mustang pulls up in the yard by the house. Two men get out and initially she can't identify them, not from her vantage point in the tumbledown greenhouse that Harry made the first summer she lived at the farm, in which she tries to grow tomato plants each year. There is never much of a crop, but she still enjoys pottering about in there and eating the sun-warmed tomatoes direct from the vine, which is exactly what she is doing when the visitors arrive. She brushes the soil from her hands and goes out to take a closer look.

Staffan Larsson and Börje Granat.

Harry's old friends. The ones he's known since childhood, the ones he – she suddenly realizes – spent time with, that Saturday in town. That last Saturday.

They'd played cards and knocked back the beer, and he'd lost 800 kronor; she hasn't seen them for years, except from a distance or when she passed them in the street, and the fact is that this isn't their first visit to Little Burma. They came over a few times in those early years. Staffan had a regular girlfriend back then, a shy Finnish girl called Riita, who would sing Karelian songs when she got drunk.

But that was more than ten years ago. Twelve, in fact; she can't remember having spoken to them since Billy was born.

Now they are clambering out of the car and looking about them, clearly unsure of themselves. Börje is clutching a plastic bag, Staffan a bunch of flowers. They remind her of two country bumpkins in an old Swedish slapstick film.

But then they see her and they pull back their shoulders. They greet her earnestly, with firm handshakes.

'It's too bloody bad about Harry,' says Börje. 'You haven't heard anything?'

She shakes her head. No, she hasn't heard anything. Staffan hands over the bunch of flowers. It is still encased in yellowish cellophane and she guesses he has bought it at some petrol station. 'We just thought we'd drop round, to see how things were,' he says.

She thanks them for the flowers.

'In case you want somebody to talk to,' Staffan goes on, 'or anything like that.'

She says she needs to get a vase, and invites them to take a seat at the outside table at the end of the house. When she comes out again, they each have a cigarette. She asks if they want coffee.

'No, thanks,' says Börje. 'You want a beer?'

He produces a six-pack from his plastic bag.

'Just thought we'd see how you were doing,' says Staffan.

'It's too damn bad,' says Börje, handing out cans of beer. Staffan opens his and takes a gulp, and Börje does the same. She hesitates, then opens hers, too, but doesn't drink it.

'You've got to wonder,' says Staffan.

'What the fuck has happened,' says Börje.

The story of Harry's disappearance has been in the papers, but not for several weeks now. Though Börje and Staffan would know the latest through the grapevine, she thinks.

'Yes, I'm completely at a loss,' she says. 'Have the police been to see you, too?'

'More than once,' says Börje. 'Especially at the beginning. It started to feel like we were suspects.'

'They've come up against a brick wall,' says Staffan, 'and I'm not surprised. Haven't got a clue where he's gone. Have you?'

'I've no idea,' she says. 'It's a mystery.'

'Exactly,' says Börje. 'A fucking mystery, that's what it is.'

'He was a bloody good bloke,' says Staffan. 'I hope nothing's happened to him.'

'That would be such a fucking shame,' says Börje.

They sit there for an hour, smoking cigarette after cigarette and polishing off their six-pack, and when she thinks back, it is the only hour of the whole summer that she spends feeling really wretched. Staffan Larsson and Börje Granat are the sum of all the people in the entire world who miss Harry; they come to see her with beer and flowers and she lies to their faces. It feels like a spike entering her heart. They are expressing – in their incoherent, oafish way – how much they like Harry, what a good mate he has always been and how desperate they are to see him back again. To find out what has happened and where on earth he has got to.

Desperate for everything to be back to normal. And they tell her how hard it must be for her and Billy, how much they must miss their husband and dad. They even promise to step up if she needs help with anything – *anything at all, just say the word* – and she is trapped there, unable to do anything but play along. Driving the spike even further into her heart so it can never, ever come loose.

Four days later they can read in the newspaper that she, the very person to whom they brought their flowers and beer and sympathy, was the one who killed Harry. Their mate Harry, his own wife. Who chopped up his dead body and hid it in the woods – and sat there with them, lying to their faces when they came to offer her help and brotherly feelings.

His own wife, for Christ's sake.

If there is anyone she'll no longer be able to look in the face, it is Staffan Larsson and Börje Granat.

And yet it happens. Not with Staffan, who has evidently left town by the time she gets out of Hinseberg, but she once had Börje in the queue when she worked at the Cashier Service. When he saw it was her, he turned on his heel and walked out empty-handed. Another time she rounded a street corner and almost walked straight into his arms. He eyed her for a second, then spat on the pavement and did an abrupt about-turn.

There is a lot she would like to explain to Börje Granat, but she knows she will never get the chance.

And in the late afternoon, that last fine Saturday when Billy helped with the harvest, they are invited to the poolside up at Great Burma. Home-made fruit cordial, freshly baked buns and a swim. They don't stay very long, but long enough for Göran to say that he'll be over later. Ingvor's going into town to see some friends, so there's no need to worry.

He comes as he has promised and it is the last time they are together. She neither enjoys it nor finds it particularly unpleasant.

On the Sunday Billy helps out on the combine harvester

again. There are two weeks until the start of the autumn term and he still has no inkling that he will be going to an entirely unfamiliar school in an entirely unfamiliar place.

It's hard, thinking back to that final weekend, and it doesn't get any easier with the passage of time.

But now that she has done it, sleep will be even more elusive – even though it is way past one o'clock. I must talk this through with Mona in the morning, she thinks. I simply must.

She sighs, gets out of bed and pulls down the blind.

42

He went for a walk before breakfast.

The mountains were hidden from view and there was little visibility anywhere. Low-growing trees and shrubs, water rippling over rocks. He followed a track that wound its way uphill for a long time and then descended. It felt as if it was only a few degrees above freezing and the overall sensation was of walking through a cold, vaguely hostile cloud. Back at the guest house half an hour later, he decided he would nonetheless refer to it as a mountain hike, a phenomenon he had often heard mentioned but never actually engaged with before.

In the absence of visibility and sweeping views, a line from Ecclesiastes had presented itself and kept him company:

That which is far off, and exceeding deep, who can find it out?

If I stayed here for a week, I would have time to learn Ecclesiastes off by heart, he thought, and wondered what the point of such a thought could be.

He wondered, too, what that solitary line could mean.

A breakfast buffet was laid out in the dining room. The German family had clearly already departed, presumably heading for more northerly adventures; the young couple were at one table, a map spread out between them. They each gave a friendly nod as he came in. He noted their sturdy boots and proper outdoor wear; they were no doubt intending to go on a mountain hike of their own. Probably rather longer than his own; perhaps they had worked out that the sun would soon burn off the frosty cloud cover.

When he had finished his second cup of coffee and was wondering how to make contact with Ellen Bjarnebo again, the owner of the guest house appeared and wished him a good morning. She asked him a little acerbically whether he had found everything to his satisfaction so far, pulled out a chair and sat down at his table. The same table as the night before, incidentally; humans are creatures of habit.

'Be my guest,' said Barbarotti. 'I could do with a quick word with Ellen. It won't take more than half an hour; perhaps we could do it this morning, so I'm ready to get off to the airport later.'

'As you wish, Inspector,' replied Mona Frisk. 'Henning or his brother can pick you up at about one. The flight leaves at four. That leaves you time for a little walk as well. The sun is definitely on its way.'

Barbarotti nodded and looked at his watch. Nine-thirty. The young couple had gone. Monica Frisk, her elbows on the table and her chin resting on her hands, was regarding him with an expression he found hard to read. As if she was weighing him up and trying to reach a decision, whatever that might be. He remembered that she had been known to shoot a man with a hunting rifle.

'It's a nice place you've got up here,' he said, 'but there aren't that many guests.'

'It's too early in the season,' explained Mona Frisk. 'We're fully booked from midsummer to mid-September. But you're not the type.'

'You may well be right,' said Barbarotti. 'A one o'clock pick-up will suit me fine, thanks. Have you any idea where I can find Ellen?'

'If you stay here, I'll ask her to come,' said Mona Frisk. 'But I want you to think carefully about what you talk to her about.'

'What do you mean by that?' asked Barbarotti.

'Exactly what I say,' said Mona Frisk, getting to her feet. 'Think about what you're saying.'

Barbarotti had various responses on the tip of his tongue, but decided not to rise to the bait. It felt as if the strapping proprietress had a whole arsenal of obscure insinuations stored away, and there was no reason to let her deploy them.

'I shall wait for her,' he said instead, and yawned. A surge of fatigue washed through him and as soon as Mona Frisk had gone, he helped himself to a third cup of coffee.

Why am I so tired? he thought.

And what's going on? What am I imagining?

She kept him waiting for fifteen minutes. He wondered whether to allow himself a fourth cup of coffee in the meantime, but decided against. There were no morning newspapers to read, so he had to make do with a booklet on mountain fauna, which did little to buck him up, although he had nothing against either lemmings or ptarmigan. He wondered if he was running a slight temperature.

Not that as well, he thought. It definitely wouldn't be advisable to get sick in a place like this, out in the middle of nowhere.

But if I can just talk to my axe woman for ten minutes I'll be able to fit in a nap afterwards, he decided. He had already ticked off his mountain hike, after all. Maybe he had simply taken in too much oxygen.

'Good morning,' said Ellen Bjarnebo. 'Mona says there are things you're still feeling nosy about.'

'Good morning,' said Barbarotti. 'Well, yes, but maybe that isn't the right word. For a police officer, nosiness is a virtue.'

She sat down without comment and he regretted this foolish remark. Once she was sitting in front of him with her hands clasped in her lap, he could see that she looked a little out of sorts. Much the same as him, in fact; he wondered if there was some kind of mountain fever running rampant. She merely shook her head when he offered her coffee, and she did not meet his eye, as she had done the previous evening. She hunched in her chair with the look of someone longing for it to be over, whatever it was, much like a patient in a dentist's waiting room.

'Sleep well?' he asked.

'No, I didn't,' she said. 'What was it you wanted? I've nothing to add to what I said yesterday. Just so that's clear.'

'Is that so?' said Barbarotti. 'Well, I enjoyed our conversation anyway.'

She gave him a tired glance. 'Enjoyed?'

'In comparison with a lot of the other things one has to do, yes.'

She shrugged. 'So what was it you wanted? I've got things to do.'

'All right,' said Barbarotti. 'I shan't detain you for long. It's mainly about this feeling I've got.'

'Oh, so the police have feelings?'

But she still wasn't looking at him. Her gaze was focused on the view out of the window, above his right shoulder. He stifled a yawn and tried to put his thoughts into words.

'If this conversation of ours . . . and the one we had yesterday,' he said, 'were to help us find out what became of Arnold Morinder, would you be happy about that?'

'Be happy?'

'Yes.'

'Maybe. It would depend on what actually happened to him.'

'How do you mean?'

'I don't know if I'd be happy if he turned out to be dead, for instance.'

'So you don't think he's dead?'

'You asked me more than enough about that yesterday.'

'Sorry. Well then, let's get straight to the point, since you seem so reluctant today.'

'Please do.'

'The thing is, I . . .' He cleared his throat and tried to find a few appropriate words to bring them somewhere near the heart of the matter, 'I get the feeling there's something that doesn't quite fit about what happened to your husband at Little Burma. There are some inconsistencies that I just can't get straight in my mind.'

He was aware of talking unusually slowly; it was presumably a result of the encroaching exhaustion and the fact that he was far from clear about what he was trying to say. As if he had to listen intently to the words as they tumbled out of his own mouth, so as not to miss their significance, and this felt distinctly odd.

'I don't know what inconsistencies you're referring to,' answered Ellen Bjarnebo after a short pause for thought. 'And I can't help what you get into your head, I hope you can understand that.'

'But you agree with what I'm saying?'

'In what respect, exactly?'

'That there's something you're not telling us,' he persisted. 'And it's been that way ever since it happened. For twenty-three years.'

What nonsense, he thinks. I have no control over what I'm saying.

'I've had enough of this now,' said Ellen Bjarnebo. 'I'm not going to carry on with this conversation.'

'You're telling me my suspicions are wrong?'

She finally turned her gaze on him. She looked him straight in the eyes as four or five seconds passed and quietly said, 'Completely wrong, Inspector.'

And since he was feeling as weary as she looked, he let out the question that he had formulated the night before, before he fell asleep. Might as well do it now, as they seemed to be in the process of breaking off communication anyway.

She was keeping her eyes on him again, this time with a hint of a smile.

'Father confessor?' she said. 'I've already done that.'

'When?' asked Barbarotti, without really understanding why.

'When?' she asked in surprise. 'Well, it wasn't to the prison chaplain at Hinseberg, that's for sure.'

'Later then?'

She shook her head, but it didn't seem like a denial, he thought. More like a confirmation that this Inspector Barbarotti could do with a couple of months' compassionate leave to get over the death of his wife, rather than . . . rather than conducting interviews in remote mountain guest houses that made a laughing stock of both himself and the entire police force.

Then she pushed back her chair and stood up. Barbarotti

stood up, too, took her outstretched hand, but all at once felt a wave of dizziness that forced him to sit down again. She looked at him with something that could possibly have been interpreted as pity or sympathy, then turned on her heel and left the dining room.

Barbarotti stayed where he was for a few minutes, trying to pull himself together. What's the matter with me? he thought. I feel completely shattered. I've got to get back to my room before I end up in a heap on the floor.

He got to his feet and staggered out to the lobby. There was not a soul to be seen, and he felt himself tracked by the glazed, watchful eyes of the vaguely menacing stuffed wildlife on the walls. He hauled himself up the stairs with both hands on the stair rails. Then along the corridor, which seemed to be rocking slightly, and into his room. When he was finally able to lie down flat on his back and close his eyes, he felt himself sucked downwards, whirling into bottomless darkness.

Marianne, he thought, I'm coming.

43

A sudden weariness came over her, and she thought that this was basically like any other evening at Little Burma. A hopeless day, reaching its end in a dreary succession of other hopeless days. A couple of bats came flitting across the yard, reminding her of a book she had read as a child, in which bats were bringers of knowledge, if she remembered rightly, like messengers from the next day. That was then, she thought, when there were still forks in the road and illusions.

But then she remembered the tin soldiers, clenched her fists and tried to summon back that courage, that impulse to act.

Has something happened?

Is something happening right now?

She went back out into the yard and came to a stop, caught between indecision and expectation. The figures under the chestnut tree up at Great Burma had gone, or were invisible now it was getting dark. She was still wondering who they were. Then she looked up into the menacing sky. The rain was sure to start any minute – there was that sort of ominous silence you get before a cloudburst, and a slight smell of burning in the air. Something electrical.

She doesn't know how much of this she has added subsequently; perhaps all these moments, all these brief but meaningful experiences, only take on their correct weight and significance once they are over. Once they have been filtered and weighed and appraised by the memory, but she has always clung to the idea that she had some kind of premonition. Maybe it was to do with the bats, a foreboding and a fore-knowledge of something normally unknowable. It had been there the whole afternoon and evening, a kind of prelude, a heightening that – like the bank of cloud growing ever darker and denser – would have to be discharged before the tension could be broken. Broken and dispersed.

The words have come later, she knows that; she could not possibly have clothed her thoughts and feelings in them as she stood there uncertainly, trying to sharpen her senses, and then took slow and hesitant steps towards the cowshed – but trying to articulate it is pointless, of course, nothing but vain formu-lations and thought patterns in which you can indulge for eleven long years of solitude, when sleep refuses to come.

She can see that the office light is on, inside the cowshed. Harry must be there after all. He has probably slept off the worst of the drink while she was out for her walk, woken up and come out to his desk for a smoke and a few more beers. Yes, that must be it. Maybe he's idly looking through his porn mags, too, and she realizes she doesn't want to see him. She simply can't face it.

And it is just as this becomes clear to her, as she is about to turn and go back to the house, and possibly just as a gust of cold wind blows in, heralding the first distant rumble of thunder and the opening salvo of raindrops – or that could have been one of her Hinseberg elaborations – at that moment, anyway, Billy comes out of the door with the sledgehammer in his hands.

He stops, two metres from her, and the two of them look

at each other. Neither of them moves a muscle, but the boy is breathing heavily through his open mouth, and his eyes express nothing but utter horror. She still doesn't know exactly what has happened, but that is revealed a moment later when she rushes past him, flings open the office door and sees Harry, slumped back in his desk chair with his arms hanging at his sides – his fingertips just reach the floor, she notes for some reason – and the blood dripping from a gaping dark-red wound in his head. The pool on the floor is the size of a regular pizza. She realizes that what looks like cheese must be brain matter.

She knows he is dead without needing to go any nearer, and at that instant the rain comes down, like some kind of celestial corroboration. *Harry Helgesson is dead.* Queasiness washes over her, and for a moment she thinks she is going to be physically sick, but she manages to hold it back. She stands absolutely still on the dirty floor, three metres behind her murdered husband, and listens to her pounding heart and the rain hammering on the metal roof.

She waits for her terror to abate. Waits for the waves of light-headedness and panic to ebb away and leave space for thoughts.

It must be a question of minutes, but even afterwards she has no way of telling how long she stood there. When she slowly backs out of the room, when she pushes open the outside door and looks around, the boy has vanished from sight. But the sledgehammer lies on the ground in the rain where he has simply dropped it, before making off.

She doesn't know where he has gone. Maybe to his room, maybe out into the forest.

It doesn't matter, anyway. Not now. She will have to deal with Billy later, once she finds him. It's Harry that matters now. And although she only has a few pitiful minutes in which to decide, she knows what she must do. There is only one way.

It takes all night, and the rain continues to pour down. She works in a kind of trance, calmly and methodically dismembering her dead husband on the floor of the office. She has spread out two old sheets, which she will burn the next night along with his clothes; there are some decent knives at Little Burma, she has to admit, and technically it presents no problem. She has cleavers, too, and she's had the knack since her time working at Meat Man; it's no harder to butcher a human than a pig. It occurs to her that it would have been useful if they'd had a proper manure heap, because she's heard that it is the very best place for getting rid of things. Such as bodies, which are said to disintegrate completely in just a few months. But there isn't one; they have neither livestock nor manure at Little Burma these days and the manure heap at Great Burma is too far away, too risky. She recalls that when they got married, Harry had weighed barely eighty kilos, but since then he has put on at least fifteen. Three plastic bin bags of the larger, sturdier type are still more than enough for him, and she feels confident that in portions of that size she can manage to get him a good long way into the forest. Remove him from the eyes of the world before morning comes and then . . . and then take things one at a time, as they present themselves. Sufficient unto the day, and all that.

Before she sets off into the trees, she hides away the sheets and clothes, and scrubs the floor and the desk chair reasonably well, and the whole time she is working she is in a state of subdued exhilaration. Subdued and yet frenetic. The three black plastic sacks lie waiting behind the cowshed. He won't be running off anywhere, she thinks. She still isn't worrying about Billy; she has to focus her strength on one thing at a time, and seeing the boy now would puncture her. It is two in the morning by the time she finishes her scrubbing and there isn't a single prick of light to be seen at Great Burma. Why should there be? She wheels the heavily loaded barrow along Leonora's Path and she knows there are no witnesses. Head, arms and legs on her first trip, and after that the torso. These are her second and third forest walks on this strange night, and she gets equally far each time. A few hundred metres into the forest, on the rise up to the sheer wall of rock, the path deteriorates; the barrow gets too heavy to push, just as she has expected, and she unloads the sacks there. Then, after her second trip when Harry has temporarily regrouped, she drags the three burdens in three different directions as far as she possibly can. The storm provides a constant accompaniment to her activities and in a way she is grateful for it; it provides exactly the right setting and she periodically tilts her face upwards to let the rain wash it clean. Her hands, too. From time to time she hears caretaker Mutti's voice, but it is only the one phrase, the same exhortation every time: *Go on!*

Go on! Go on!

And she does. She goes on until she has pumped the last ounce of strength from her body, and when it is finally all done, when all traces of farmer Helgesson of Little Burma have been expunged, she goes in to see Billy.

He is asleep in his bed.

On his side, with his knees drawn up and his face to the wall – yes, he is lying there under his quilt precisely as he always does. Peaceful, regular breathing, no detectable anxiety.

She stands in the doorway for a long time, watching him. Her body is trembling slightly after all its exertion. A cautious dawn is sifting in at the window, the rain is easing now and the light has put the darkness to flight.

He looks so vulnerable again. The same word and the same thought that had come to her fourteen hours earlier. *Vulnerable.* Mousey has to protect Piggy, she thinks; there is no scope for any other stance, no place for any other decision.

She strokes the back of his neck, leaves the room and goes to take a shower. She has put her clothes in the washing machine and set it going. It is rumbling quietly to itself in its usual reassuring way on the other side of the shower curtain, and the only thing that comes into her head is that stupid sticker that was so popular a few years before.

Tomorrow is the first day of the rest of your life.

She can't deny that it's true. Liberation, she thinks. Isn't it?

44

But he doesn't reach Marianne.

At the end of the dark, swirling tunnel he lands instead in the sunshine outside a church. There are various things to indicate that this is Kymlinge church, including the fact that he is there for a funeral. It is many years ago, he is still at police training college and he is waiting for somebody. It is a lovely autumn day and he has driven down from Stockholm. Actually he has been at home in Kymlinge for several days, because it is his mother who has died and whose funeral it is, and he is standing there waiting for his aunt. They constitute Maria Larsson's whole family in fact, a son and a sister.

And with no apparent transition he is suddenly inside the church, sombre organ music and an oppressive floral scent, for he and Aunt Anna are seated very close to the coffin, which is covered in a sea of flowers and wreaths. He cannot understand where this sea has come from, because the gathering of mourners is relatively small. Twenty at most, but perhaps there are larger numbers grieving from a distance.

One person who should most definitely be grieving from a distance is his father, but he presumably hasn't been informed. Assuming he is still alive, that is, but nobody knows anything on that score, because Gunnar's father removed himself from the scene even before the boy was born. Conceivably there is someone at large in the beautiful land of Italy by the name of Giuseppe Alessandro Barbarotti – he would be around sixty, if so, at the time of Maria Larsson's funeral, because she only reached fifty-nine – and perhaps one day, before he dies, his son will try to track him down. His mother did not encourage him in that enterprise, quite the opposite, but the thought has been there for a few years now, a slumbering, poorly tended seed at the back of his mind. Finding his father.

As he makes a real physical effort to focus his thoughts, he isn't sure it is actually his mother's funeral after all. Helena ought to be at his side, and pregnant, but she isn't. The people whispering and rustling in the pews are not the ones he would expect; he discovers significantly later arrivals dotted around – later arrivals in his own life, that is – and he is trying not to be disturbed by the fact that he can see all their faces, even though he is sitting in the front row with his back to them. Because that's how it always is with fictitious church tableaux, he thinks. As false as water. As dreams.

Chief Inspector Asunander is sitting there, sucking on his teeth just like in the old days. Eva Backman and her deplorable former husband, their three boys and his own two, plus Sara. Marianne's children, too, of whom he now has custody, but however hard he looks, he cannot see Marianne; perhaps the coffin is hers, but in that case he has no idea what someone like Axel Wallman is doing at her funeral. Dressed in the outlandish garb that is intended to signal his promotion to bestselling writer and literary agent. A yellow suit at a funeral. And that other figure, looking all the greyer by contrast: the sad individual he has never met, but has devoted a good deal of thought to. He seems to be half asleep in his pew and has no face, but is wearing a sign on his chest to make it clear who he is: Ante Valdemar Roos. But the girl at his side is instantly recognizable, Barbarotti met her only the other day after all, in the sunshine of the royal capital; and the same is true of the strapping guest-house landlady with the heavy rifle resting menacingly across her lap, though that was in more northerly latitudes of course – and her friend, who looks so sorrow-stricken and is somehow appealing for him to do something, though he has no idea what. The appeal is conveyed only by her remarkable calm, because talking in church is forbidden, especially if you happen to be a murderess – unless you happen to be the vicar, of course – yet that is exactly what the couple beside him start doing: talking to each other, and whether he wants to or not, he finds himself party to their rather intimate conversation.

'Ulf, I'm sure you've got me up the duff. You've got to buy better condoms next time.'

'I don't get why I need to buy condoms at all, if you're already up the duff.'

'That wasn't what I meant.'

'What did you mean then?'

'Why are you so cross with me?'

'I'm not cross with you. It wasn't my fault the damn thing split.'

'Oh no? Well, it certainly wasn't mine.'

'Come on, Cutie, it's nobody's fault. Shit happens without you or me having to be to blame. How many days have you gone over?'

'None. I'm due on Saturday, but I've just got this feeling.'

'You've had that feeling at least thirty times before.'

'I have *not*.'

'Oh yes, you have. If you'd been up the duff every time you

thought you might be, we'd have had a whole school class by
now.'

'That's not how it works, Ulf.'

'Eh? How do you mean?'

'In a school class they're all the same age. You can't have
thirty kids that are all the same age.'

'Shut up, Cutie, here comes the vicar.'

But no vicar appears. Instead it is Åke Rönn, the bereavement
councillor, who makes his entry, and suddenly they are alone
in the church. No vicar, no coffin, no rows of mourners in the
pews.

'Did you hear that?' he asks, presumably meaning the couple
with the split condom. But Rönn shakes his head. He hasn't
heard a word, and at that moment it comes back to Barbarotti
that the dialogue he has just been party to was in fact something he overheard on a train many years before and happened
to record on his tape player when he pressed the wrong button
by mistake. In the process he recorded over an interview of
some importance, an error that he would prefer not to
remember.

That last bit, *Shut up, Cutie, here comes the vicar*, sounded
highly implausible. It must have been a question of the ticket
collector, not a church dignitary.

'How are things with you?' asks Rönn.

'Not that great,' replies Barbarotti. 'I don't know where I am.'

'Are you talking about the internal or the external landscape?'
enquires Rönn.

'Both of them,' responds Barbarotti. 'Definitely both of
them.'

'I can't help you with the external one,' says Rönn, 'but then
that's less important anyway. It's what's inside you that we

need to set in order. That's where the grief is lodged.'

'It doesn't feel to me as if there's any order to anything,' he tries to clarify to Rönn. 'If I remember rightly, I went to lie down on a bed, up by the Arctic Circle, and then I woke up at my mother's funeral, but now the church is empty and you've come along. Am I dead, too, or what?'

'I shouldn't think so,' says Rönn. 'But I see you've cancelled your session. If you aren't dead, maybe you could give me a ring to book another appointment?'

He promises to do so. Then Rönn vanishes as well. It has grown much darker around him and he feels a sudden prick to his arm.

He opens his eyes and closes them again, the latter to counteract the bad nausea that sweeps right through him like a violent draught of cold air. But in the brief moment his eyes are open, he registers that it is pitch black in the room. Either that or he has gone blind.

He thinks it is the room at the guest house.

He thinks he is awake.

The place where something pricked his right forearm is still smarting. He seems incapable of moving his arms or legs.

Then he hears piano music, playing faintly, faintly. Then a voice, almost as faint.

Listen carefully.

The piano is still there. He is familiar with the piece, but is far too groggy to identify it. I wouldn't even be able to say the word 'identify', he thinks. What's happening to me? The voice grows a little louder. It is a woman speaking, a rather pleasant alto voice, but not one he recognizes. The sick feeling dances inside him. His body feels numb.

Listen carefully. Just lie still with your eyes closed and listen to what I've got to say.

He swallows and feels as if he's back in that tunnel again, despite everything. Or dead, as he told Rönn. Dead and blind? Can you really be blind if you're dead?

I'm going to tell you about The Sisters, and everything I say will be supposition.

Oh?

Nothing but supposition. Suppose, then, that there are a group of us who have had enough. Suppose there is a network.

A network, he thinks. A network?

Or perhaps he doesn't think it. Perhaps the voice is repeating it. Perhaps it is repeating everything to make sure he fully understands. The thick fog that has taken over the space normally occupied by his brain seems to need all the help it can get. He would like to put his hand into his skull to scoop it up and cast it out. But he can't move.

There is a network known as The Sisters. It has existed for many years and a lot of people have been glad of our support. Suppose there are about fifty of us, spread up and down the country.

Yes, I'm following, declares the fog.

We have our roots in Hinseberg and we are women who have grown tired of being abused by men. We have all had enough, and since society does nothing to help, we have to take matters into our own hands.

Oh yes?

Women should have done that long ago. There are men who hate women, but we are not women who hate men. We are just putting a stop to certain kinds of men. Suppose that we actually do this. Suppose that we have been doing it for a good number of years now. Suppose that we are more efficient at it than anyone might imagine.

Suppose that we are behind the termination of quite a few men by now.

What's that she's saying? wonders the fog. Am I in a film? But when he opens his eyes, all he can see is pitch darkness. I'm blind and sitting in a cinema, thinks the fog.

But he isn't sitting in a cinema. He isn't even sitting. He's lying flat on his back and can't move a muscle – not in his arms and legs anyway. You've gone mad, suggests the fog.

You? Why is the fog saying 'you' instead of 'I'?

Suppose this is a warning, the voice goes on. A lot of men have had similar warnings. We will use any means we can, but those who heed our warning are left in peace. You only get one warning, so suppose that those who lack the sense to listen are signing their own death warrant.

Suppose that The Sisters have existed for many years, yet are still practically unknown.

Suppose there are good reasons for that.

Suppose this is not a dream.

And then it's over. Another stab in his arm, a few seconds' deathly silence, then unconsciousness.

No sensations whatsoever.

45

On Tuesday afternoon Eva Backman interviewed Ellen Hökberg for two hours. To assist her she had DI Sorrysen, and when it was all over, she was extremely grateful it had not been Wennergren-Olofsson. It would have been total havoc.

Initially – for the first twenty minutes or so – Miss Hökberg flatly denied everything. She had never met Raymond Fängström. Never even seen him. And she had most certainly not had dinner at his place, and in no circumstances on the Saturday he died.

By the time they were onto the third or possibly fourth round of denials, Backman had had enough, and asked her if she would mind having her fingerprints taken. It would take no more than half an hour to establish whether she had set foot – or finger – in Fängström's kitchen or not.

Ellen Hökberg had assented to this request and promptly burst into tears. They had served her paper tissues, peppermint tea and a blueberry muffin, and after a while she had recovered sufficiently to start telling the truth.

This turned out to be that she had linked up with Raymond Fängström via an online dating site, exactly as her anonymous friend had guessed. They had spoken on the phone on Friday evening – the day before Fängström's death – and sent over a few pictures to show how cute and generally appetizing they were, eventually making a date to see each other at Fängström's on Saturday evening. Have a bite to eat, some wine and see where it led them.

The evening had started well enough, Ellen Hökberg said. They went to the supermarket together, made a bolognese sauce together, had a glass or two of wine together and things looked generally quite promising. But then Fängström got stomach ache. They were in the middle of the meal by then, or maybe they had just started; he tried stretching out on the living-room sofa for a while, but it didn't help. He drank half a litre of fizzy mineral water on Miss Hökberg's advice, but that didn't help, either. The stomach cramps had simply got worse and worse, and in the end he crawled – she tried to help him walk, she really did, but he insisted on crawling – to the bathroom and locked himself in.

She stood outside that bathroom for ten minutes, listening to him whimper and groan in agony. She tried to keep him talking, but got no real response; the only thing she got was cold feet, so she left.

Cold feet? Sorrysen had asked.

You left? Backman had asked.

This reduced Miss Hökberg to tears again. She hadn't realized it was so terribly serious. But he'd turned out to be one of those Sweden Democrats, hadn't he, though she hadn't realized until after a glass of two, and it was embarrassing to be associated with him. If she'd rung for a doctor, say, or something like that.

So if he'd been a Liberal, or just an ordinary Social Democrat, you wouldn't have left him there? Sorrysen had enquired.

At this point she dissolved into tears again, and the two

DIs reached an unspoken agreement to proceed a little more gently.

The gentler approach eventually produced a much fuller picture. Ellen Hökberg had heard about Fängström's death when she was at work on the Monday afternoon. That naturally put a really dreadful complexion on things; she had already been feeling a bit remorseful and uneasy about Saturday evening, she stressed, but now she was seized by total panic. Somehow she managed to hold it together and not tell anyone about her dinner with the dead man. When she had had time to think about it a bit more, by the Tuesday or Wednesday, she had decided that silence was the wisest course of action. To be linked to a Sweden Democrat was bad enough, but to be linked to a Sweden Democrat who had died in suspicious circumstances was a sheer disaster.

And did she now – looking back – think she had done the right thing?

Yes, that is, no, maybe not.

Once the tactfully conducted interview had been brought to a successful close and Sorrysen had gone to type it up, Backman tried to call Barbarotti. Mainly for an interpretation of the enigmatic message he had sent her the previous evening – but there was no answer.

He's probably on the plane, she thought.

Or in radio silence behind a mountain.

She sent back a text composed of three question marks and decided to wait until after lunch to try to comply with his request.

She had found the company in question and checked to see

if it still existed, but it was no longer in business. It had gone to the wall in the nineties, along with so many others. The question was whether she could get hold of anyone who knew anything.

The other question was why he was asking.

By half past two she still hadn't heard a peep out of DI Barbarotti, but she had located a potential interview subject.

His name was Hans Fridolin Hansson, and he was apparently now eighty-four and a resident of the Autumn Sun Retirement Home out at Kvarndammarna. She spoke to the nurse in charge of his section, who said he was in the early stages of dementia, but still had his more lucid days.

She remembered her own father and a lump came into her throat, but she swallowed it down and asked if it would be convenient to pay a visit in an hour or so. The nurse said that ought to be all right. Mr Hansson was having his physiotherapy at the moment, but he ought to be back in twenty minutes.

The room where they were sitting was pale blue, and she wondered who – if anyone – had made the conscious decision that these poor people should spend their final moment on this earth surrounded by such a ghastly shade. But perhaps it was meant to remind them of the colour of Heaven and help expedite the process; they were short of places in old people's homes.

'You can call me Hasse,' said the thin, slightly crooked old man in front of her. 'Or Double Hasse if you like. The Fridolin was my mum's idea. She liked those Karlfeldt poems.'

His voice was hoarse and slightly wheezy; he had a distinct tremor and she wondered if he had Parkinson's. He looked totally decrepit, she thought. His skin had the appearance of raw cod; his eyes were yellowish and watery and the sparse hairs on his lumpy, bald pate put her in mind of clear-felled forest or a badly plucked chicken.

He's just like Dad, she thought, and had to swallow hard to master what was welling up inside her. Though at least he seems a bit clearer in the head.

'Let's say Hasse,' she said. 'I'm Eva Backman. You can call me Eva.'

His face brightened.

'Eva? That was my wife's name.'

'Really?'

'Yes. But she's dead now. It's . . . I don't remember how many years now? It was around the Millennium, I know.'

'Twelve years,' Backman informed him. 'That makes it twelve years.'

'Yes,' said Hasse Fridolin Hansson, running a bony hand over his chin and cheeks, 'I expect you're right.'

'I understand that you've been a pensioner for a while now,' she said. 'But before that you ran your own company.'

'Lots,' said Hansson. 'I must have had about eight or ten of them, when I was still working. Went bust and started again. Going bust and starting again: that was the way life went . . . ha-ha, hmm.'

'You must have had a lot of employees over the years?'

'Hundreds.'

He tried to straighten his back, but it clearly hurt him and he changed position in his chair. Backman cleared her throat and wondered if this really was a feasible approach. She asked herself if it wouldn't be better for Barbarotti to take care of it himself once he was back; he would presumably have a slightly better grip on what this was all about.

'You do understand that I'm a police officer?' she asked.

'What did you say?'

'I said I was a police officer. I've come here because there's something we need to find out about.'

'From me? I haven't done anything . . . I mean, things sometimes happened . . . but that was all such a long time ago and . . .'

His sudden anxiety made his tremor worse. She wondered whether he actually did have any skeletons in the cupboard or if it was just that some of those bankruptcies hadn't exactly been on the level.

'Oh, but this isn't about you at all, Hasse,' she assured him. 'It's about this man who worked for you for a while. About twenty years ago in fact, most likely in the late eighties . . .'

'What was his name?'

'Morinder. His name was Arnold Morinder.'

He pursed his lips into a thin, slightly wavy line and squinted out of the window. She assumed this to be a sign that he was thinking. His mind going through his hundreds of employees perhaps, as he tried to recall whether any of them could have been called Morinder. Time passed.

'Maybe,' he said finally. 'That pain in the arse, his name was Morinder, I think. Though I can't rightly remember when it was.'

'You could do with a little bit of help, I bet,' suggested Backman.

'Betting – that was one of my lines of business too,' said Hans Fridolin Hansson.

*

And when she left that gentleman to his pale-blue fate, ten minutes later, she had found out something after all, something that could conceivably . . . *conceivably* be the answer to Barbarotti's question. Even Backman could discern a link there, but whether it had any wider application she had no idea.

What is it he's trying to get at? she thought. And why isn't he answering his phone?

She bumped into Asunander as she was leaving her room. It was almost as if he had been standing outside, waiting for her.

'I hear there's light at the end of the Fängström tunnel.'

'Quite right,' said Backman. 'I think we're going to find that there's nothing criminal behind it. But we're not entirely certain yet.'

'Good,' said Asunander. 'And Barbarotti, how's he doing? He's supposed to be coming to see me today, but I haven't seen him.'

'He's been up in Norrland,' said Backman. 'He may well be on his way home, but I haven't had any contact with him since yesterday.'

'Do you know if he's getting anywhere?'

'I'm not clear on that,' said Backman. 'You'll have to wait until he gets back.'

Asunander contented himself with that, and Backman eventually decided to do the same – after another half dozen failed attempts to get through to him.

She did not leave any messages. If he's seen that I've repeatedly tried to call him, yet still doesn't bother to call me back, he has only himself to blame, she thought. Unless he has good reason?

She found it hard to imagine what that reason could be, however, and a slight sense of irritation stayed with her for the rest of the afternoon.

46

She is standing in the kitchen, chopping onions. It is afternoon; in a few hours' time they are expecting a number of arrivals, and they are to be well catered for. They are booked in for five nights, and they are the kind of returning guests that Mona likes to take good care of. Ellen has encountered at least four of them before. Two senior military figures and their wives.

She still feels uneasy about the detective; she and Mona have had a long and detailed chat, but it hasn't really helped the way it usually does. There is something chafing away inside her. Maybe it was what he said about the father confessor. Maybe he seems to understand more than he's letting on.

But the fact that she is crying has nothing to do with the detective – it's all the onions' fault.

And for some reason she starts thinking about Dream Boy.

Damn, she mutters to herself. I don't want to think about him now.

The week after midsummer, the last week before her holidays, she drives herself to work. It gives her a remarkable sense of freedom, sitting at the wheel, master of her own fate – instead of being ruled by bus timetables and crushed in among dozing, disgruntled commuters.

Perhaps that part about fate is overdoing it a bit, but she is surprised by the tingle in her body as she pulls away from Little Burma in the mornings and turns onto the 272 towards town. I could drive off somewhere else entirely. Forget the hardware store, fill the tank and head for Gothenburg instead. Or somewhere even further afield: Oslo? Copenhagen? Check into a hotel for the night and then move on somewhere else tomorrow. Out into the world. Out into life.

If I had the money.

They're not real plans, of course, just mellow daydreams, but they still fill her with a sense of vitality that is something . . . well, something new and entirely unfamiliar. But what about Billy then, what did you think you'd do with him? she asks herself, or perhaps it's Mutti doing the asking. I'll take him with me, of course, she says. No problem, why would there be?

Mutti doesn't answer.

Daydreams behind the steering wheel. But soon they'll be off to Öland for their camping holiday, she and Billy; that's no daydream. It's good enough in itself, and she could never have thought that the absence of Harry would mean so much. But then she's never really conceived of him as absent. He's always been with her, like some crusted scab.

And now he's been picked off. About time, after seventeen years.

She's noticed it at work, as well. Her way of interacting with the customers has completely changed. She isn't all timid and deferential like she used to be, but much more open. Frank even, with the occasional smile and twinkle in the eye. She thinks so, anyway, but it's easier to detect twinkles in other people's eyes of course.

Her store colleagues presumably think she's being brave.

Her husband is missing, but Ellen Helgesson is keeping her anxiety in check. It must be terrible for her, mustn't it? Not knowing, having to go round wondering what can have happened. Good grief, what *can* have happened? Sofia told her she was welcome to stay at home if she feels she needed to, but she said she would prefer to work as usual. It's easier than just being at home, brooding.

They nod, and say they can understand that. She thinks to herself that if there's one thing they can't do, it's understand.

Without her new sense of vitality, the Dream Boy episode would never have happened. She would never have dared. It would have been beyond her to meet his gaze in that natural, open way when he asks if she recognizes him.

Which naturally she does.

'Of course,' she says as she puts his screws and wire and isolation tape and everything else into a plastic bag. 'Nice to see you. How are things?'

'Good,' he says, but she can hear that he's lying. 'And you?'

She wonders whether he has heard about Harry or not. Maybe not; she hasn't seen Dream Boy for several years, didn't even know he was in town. He accepts his plastic bag, hesitates for a second and then asks her if she fancies going for a coffee.

She finishes work in five minutes' time, but Dream Boy can't possibly know that.

'Now?' she asks.

He gives a shy sort of smile. 'Yeah, but maybe you can't get away?'

Fifteen minutes later they're sitting in Star Pastries & Coffee on the square at Norra torg. She thinks to herself that this is the first time in her life she has sat in a cafe with a strange man. At the age of thirty-six, so it's high time.

Though he isn't a stranger, strictly speaking, not really. They spent that year in the same class at Kymlingevik School, but she doesn't think she has seen him since. He hasn't got the same good looks now as he had at the age of fourteen or fifteen, either.

Good-looking and sleepy, that was how he got his name. His proper name is Kenneth Something-or-other; it was one of the teachers who started calling him Dream Boy, because he always seemed to sit through lessons in a dream.

Dreamy and handsome. Long, thick dark hair that made you want to walk barefoot through its waves. She knows she was in love with him for a while, just as lots of the other girls probably were – but because she was a mouse it was nothing she admitted, even to herself. A mouse and a Dream Boy, it was kind of unthinkable.

The problem with Dream Boy was that he was far too weary to commit himself to anything; he doubtless found himself the subject of attention from all angles, but when nothing really made an impact, the girls grew weary, too. Dream Boy went on being a looker, but he was soon discounted as a worthy love object. His dreamy moniker slid inexorably downhill and was reduced to a mere nickname.

The way she remembers it, anyway. She was only in that group for a year, which was the same year she experienced petting for the first time in her life, and she certainly didn't want to think about *him*.

Far better to think about Dream Boy and Star Pastries & Coffee. In spite of all her sorrows.

*

So there they sit, and his long wavy locks are gone, but you can still see that it's him. Dark eyes, attractive mouth, weak chin; he's different from how he was twenty years ago, inevitably, but he still seems as introverted. She wonders what made him ask her out for coffee.

'Do tell me then,' she says. 'How are you doing? I don't think I've seen you since school, have I?'

And he says he's lived here and there over the years, but has just come back to town. That was why he was in the hardware store, getting a few things he needed for the flat he's moved into. After some sluggish small talk, it emerges that he's newly divorced and unhappy. Not at all sure he can face life any longer, in fact.

She doesn't know what to say. Thinks he must be genuinely lonely if he issues a coffee invitation to someone he hasn't seen for so long and barely knows, and then starts talking about something like this.

Killing himself, or whatever it is he's contemplating.

But it proves as hard to talk to Dream Boy as it was twenty years ago. Having finally told her about his divorce and his unhappiness, he seems to think he's said enough. He doesn't ask how she is, and they sit there facing each other like two slowly expiring candles. She tries a few topics of conversation, but he answers in monosyllables, avoiding eye contact. Maybe he regrets having brought her here, and after twenty or thirty minutes, once the coffee and cinnamon buns are finished to the last drop and crumb, she says she has to go.

Then he stretches his hands across the table and clasps hers. He looks her steadily in the eye for the first time and asks if he can see her again.

And she feels: well, yes, for the first time in her life she feels that this is a man she could love.

It feels like plunging into a well, a deep shaft opens up inside her, and her head feels as empty as a dead doll's. She takes a few deep breaths to pull herself together, looks into his sad black eyes and she is finally able to utter a yes, of course they can see each other again.

He lets go of her hands and the magic is broken. They stand up and he says he knows where she works, after all, and they go their separate ways.

It is hard to tell now whether it is just the onions causing the tears. As a matter of fact she has switched to leeks, and surely nobody ever cried over chopping leeks?

She never hears from him.

It is only when she returns from Hinseberg, twelve or thirteen years later, that she happens to find out that he actually did it.

Dream Boy took his own life that summer.

She looks out over the magnificent landscape. The sun has broken through the morning's veils of mist and she can see far into the distance. I wish I could relive my life, she thinks. Nothing has turned out the way it should have.

No, goes her next thought, if I got to rerun my life, I'd only mess it up all over again. And maybe that applies to everyone. We walk from darkness to darkness. We make the wrong decisions, we end up with the wrong people and, by the time we try to turn back, it's too late. *Don't stop at Burmavägen.*

It really is stunningly beautiful out there. Why can't we just take it in? she asks herself. Why isn't it enough for us? Why did Dream Boy have to do what he did?

No, things never go as they were intended, they truly don't. But is there anyone drawing up the overall plan? Is there any meaning? Some kind of point to it, at the very least?

Well, apart from Billy maybe?

47

He wakes up feeling as if he has been asleep under a mountain.

Opening his eyes is like pulling up two blinds made of solid lead by means of the thinnest of cords, and he closes them again. He can't think what purpose keeping them open can serve.

But someone is insisting. Waking him, shoving and nudging him and saying something he is too groggy to make out. Now someone is slapping him round the cheeks as well. Shaking him by the shoulders, refusing to leave him in peace, and he pulls on the cords again in another attempt to raise his eyelids.

The result is passable. Passable enough for him to feel the need to orientate himself. *Where am I? What time is this?* Fundamental questions, undeniably, and he takes them one by one. He is lying on his back in a room that he recognizes. But only vaguely; so far, it is a recollection divorced of context. Marianne? he thinks, but as the word forms in his mind, he already knows that she is no longer with him. She is dead. Gone forever.

The question still crops up every morning, a turnstile from sleep to wakefulness. And the answer: oh yes, I remember, that's how it is. Maybe that will be the routine every morning for the rest of his life. Why does time have to be so relentlessly linear? he wonders. Why can't I wake up one day and be twelve years old, another day fifty-two, another day twenty-four? Why can't the days of one's life be a bit more of a mix?

These are old thoughts, nothing he could generate in his current state, just some flicker in his returning consciousness. It isn't even morning at the moment, after all. It doesn't feel like it. It doesn't actually feel much like any other time of day, either, but he's lying under a blanket, fully clothed. Why would he have his clothes on, if it was first thing in the morning?

Then suddenly he surfaces.

Vilhelmina. The guest house. Ellen Bjarnebo.

He opens his eyes once more, someone evidently having shut them again. He becomes aware that there is a woman sitting on the chair near his bed.

It isn't the axe woman, and it isn't the guest-house proprietress.

She appears to be in her fifties and is wearing a white coat. She has a stethoscope round her neck.

'How are you?' she asks. 'Are you awake now?'

He rubs his hands over his face.

'Er, yes, thank you,' he says. It comes out as no more than a hoarse whisper and he suddenly feels a raging thirst. He drags himself up to a sitting position and discovers a carafe and a glass on the three-legged bedside table. He only has to look at it for the woman to understand. She nods and pours him a drink of water. He drains the glass and asks for another one.

'What time is it?' he has the presence of mind to enquire.

She looks at her watch.

'Half past nine.'

He doesn't understand.

'In the evening?'

'Yes.'

'I've got . . . I've got a plane to catch.'

'You've missed it, I'm afraid.'

'But why? I mean . . . why am I lying here?'

'You fell asleep.'

'Fell asleep?'

'Yes. You've been asleep for . . . well, almost twelve hours. Do you remember: you came up here to lie down this morning?'

'Er . . . yes, yes I did. I . . .'

'Yes?'

'I was just going to take a little nap.'

'And so you did. It lasted rather longer than you intended, that's all.'

He swivels round so he is sitting on the edge of the bed. A bit too fast, and he feels momentarily giddy.

'What's happened to me?'

She gives him a gentle smile. She has that benevolent look, he thinks, rather like a bereavement counsellor. Although *she* is a doctor, of course. Dark-haired, slightly enigmatic and, as he has already noted, about his own age. Her white coat is unbuttoned and under it she is wearing a polo-necked jumper and jeans.

'I don't really know,' she says. 'Mona called me and, seeing as I live nearby, I dropped round.'

'Oh?'

She sets aside a little booklet she has had on her lap and leans a bit closer to him. 'Your blood pressure seems normal, your pulse, too . . . I've been keeping an eye on you for a while. Everything seems normal, but I can imagine it might be some kind of reaction to stress.'

'A reaction to stress?'

'Yes. Is there anything that could have caused you to react like that? Anxiety or a panic attack, say?'

He sighs and thinks.

'Well, yes, maybe. But to sleep for a whole day?'

'Have you been exposed any kind of trauma recently?'

'How long have you been sitting there?'

'A couple of hours, on and off. I came up after I finished work down in the village. But I asked you if you'd had any traumatic experiences lately.'

'My wife died.'

She takes hold of her stethoscope and then lets go of it again. 'When was this?'

'A month ago. Just over.'

'Was it unexpected?'

'Yes. And no.'

She nods, and looks at him for a few seconds.

'You're a police officer?'

'Yes.'

'And you're back at work full-time? Is that wise, really?'

He doesn't know if it's wise. He doesn't know anything at all – or that's how it feels. Here he sits on the edge of a bed in a little guest-house bedroom at the furthest outpost of civilization and he feels utterly unanchored. Exhaustion and confusion are smothering his thoughts like a wet blanket, and he suddenly feels overcome by the need to sleep for another twelve hours. On top of what he has already had.

'What's wrong with me?' he asks.

'I doubt it's anything physical,' she says slowly, seeming reluctant to commit herself. 'If someone's run ragged mentally, that can cause this kind of reaction. I take it you're grieving deeply for your wife?'

'Yes, I am.'

'And you have children?'

'Yes. Five.'

'Five?'

'Yes, but they're grown-up. Some of them, anyway.'

'Maybe you ought to be with them, not up here?'

'I was only meant to be here for a day . . . though now it looks like being two.' He feels a sudden stab of panic on the subject. 'Do you know what time there's a plane tomorrow?'

'There's a morning flight. But you'll have to leave here at six.'

'That's fine. I'll take it. But I'm still so tired. It's crazy.'

She thrusts her hands into the pockets of her white coat and seems to be considering.

'My recommendation is that when you get back you make an appointment with your own health centre and get them to give you a thorough check-up. But I think you ought to cut down your working hours for the next little while, in any event. Shall I ask Mona to bring you in something to eat, then you can go to bed?'

He nods.

'And I'll get her to make sure you have transport to the airport first thing in the morning, eh?'

'At six o'clock?'

'Yes, six o'clock. Is that all right?'

He nods again, feeling like an idiot.

'If you could undo your shirt, I'll just have a listen.' He unbuttons his shirt and she listens to his chest, asking him to take deep breaths. Then she makes him track a pen with his eyes, from right to left and back again, without moving his head. She shines a little torch into his eyes.

'No,' she said, putting her stethoscope back into her pocket. 'Everything seems fine. I don't think you need to worry. I'll tell Mona about that bite to eat then, shall I?'

'Yes, please.'

He eats in his room because they've already cleared away in the dining room. Some kind of stew: fish and seafood this time. Rice rather than potatoes. He realizes he's ravenous and asks for another helping. A creamy mousse-thing for dessert. It is neither Mona nor Ellen who serves him, but a younger woman with a ponytail and a T-shirt bearing the message 'My husband's clean'. He wonders what it means, but doesn't ask.

He feels strangely empty-headed. Or as if this isn't his usual head, more like.

After his meal he sends a couple of text messages: one to the children, in which he blames his day's delay on a faulty aircraft; one to Backman, in which he says the same and that he'll call her the next day.

Then he goes back to sleep, and when the alarm on his mobile wakes him at a quarter past five he feels alert and rested. Relatively at any rate, but he can't escape the sensation that he has lost a day of his life.

As if somebody owes him something. He calculates that he has spent twenty-five of the last thirty-six hours asleep.

It is a bright but slightly chilly morning. An overweight young man is standing beside a black Volvo having a smoke as Barbarotti emerges onto the veranda with his bag. He assumes it to be Henning's brother. They give each other a nod. Barbarotti gets into the back seat and when they reach Vilhelmina airport an hour and fifty minutes later they have not exchanged a single word. Not even 'Malgomaj'.

And he never discovers whether Henning's brother has a name of his own.

He makes his calls before he boards the plane. First the children, then Backman; this is starting to feel like a routine. He tried to do it from the car on the way, but there was no signal.

He gets through to Martin and explains again that he's been delayed up north – without going into any details. Martin is on his way to something important and assures his dad that everything is under control at Villa Pickford. Backman doesn't answer at all.

He has various items to discuss with Backman – and she with him, he hopes – but he decides it will do no harm for him to gather his thoughts first. He tries to sort out in his mind which conclusions he has actually been able to draw. These aren't exactly fresh matters that Asunander has set him to investigate, after all. No one is likely to run away and hide, so there's surely no reason to deny himself the luxury of a bit of time for reflection for once?

Can we meet on Thursday morning? he texts to Backman. He's hardly likely to be back home in Kymlinge until late evening, after all. And he still isn't exactly feeling at home in his own head.

The plane is leaving on time on this particular morning, and as he shows his ID at the gate, he comes across a little business card in his wallet.

The Sisters.

Nothing else. No phone number, no address. Just those two words. He has no conception of what they mean or how the card got there.

The air hostess who serves him coffee on the plane asks him if he's on his way to Skansen for the traditional open-air celebrations of Swedish National Day. He looks at her in surprise and says he certainly hasn't got time for *that*.

FIVE

June 2012

August 2007

48

In Kymlinge and district, Thursday 7 June was a beautiful early summer day with a warm south-westerly breeze, and Eva Backman woke up with a splitting headache.

She instantly attributed it to lying awake and grinding her teeth in the early hours, which was in turn related to the fact that she had dreamt about her former husband and his new she-dragon, Blanche.

Could you summons people for disturbing your night's sleep? she wondered as she stood at the kitchen counter, taking two paracetamol and washing them down with apple juice. Why not? No harm in sounding out that lawyer about it anyway.

The previous evening she had spent a frustrating half hour on the phone to Ville. She had attempted to explain that she had engaged a lawyer who was looking at the claim that she was retrospectively responsible for the house, and that he would be getting back to her after the weekend. Could they leave it at that for now?

But the fact was, Ville had pig-headedly insisted, that he and Blanche had already signed a contract with the builder to start the renovations, so couldn't they come to some agreement without getting lawyers involved? They'd managed the divorce without any of that, after all.

I'd be happy to, Backman had replied in the end. You're the

ones who live in the house. I shall never set foot in it again, and I've no intention of spending a single krona on it. Are we agreed on that?

No way. Come on, old thing, don't be unreasonable, was Ville's response, and so it had gone on – but the most irritating thing of all was that every so often he had asked her to hang on while he had short, whispered exchanges with the she-dragon. In the end, Eva Backman had snarled that if he called again, she would put him away him for stalking, and hung up.

Then she had drunk two glasses of wine in her solitude, taken aback by the anger that the encounter had generated in her. White-hot, uncompromising anger. I could throttle her, she thought, appalled at herself. And what about Ville, whom she had lived with for almost her entire adult life?

Not throttle maybe, but she never wanted to see him again, even though he was the father of her children. Old thing! He had called her *old thing*. Christ almighty.

I need a therapist, was the last thing that went through her mind before she fell asleep.

And now this headache.

It reluctantly receded as she was eating her breakfast. On her way to work she got through to Kalle and Viktor on their mobiles and reminded them they were coming round to hers for dinner that evening. Kalle seemed oblivious to the previous night's telephone battle and she wondered whether Ville had had the good judgement to keep him out of it, in spite of everything.

She would naturally have been very happy to make dinner for her third son, too, but Jörgen was studying in Gothenburg.

He had a girlfriend, too, and all the signs were that he was hopelessly smitten; she hadn't seen him for more than a month. This is how it's going to be, she thought. In a few years' time they'll be spread far and wide. The Eva Backman–Ville Vuorinen project will be complete and consigned to the archives. Twenty-five years of her life.

Oh well, she thought as she parked her bike in the rack outside the front entrance of police HQ. Three viable individuals, out in the world on their own wings, and none of them addicts or Nazis; she really couldn't complain.

Once she got to her room, it was no more than twenty seconds before DI Barbarotti knocked on the door and came in without waiting for a reply. Things are starting to look pretty much like normal, she thought.

'I think I've got a theory,' he started, once they were sitting down over black coffee and one and a half Brago chocolate biscuits each, which was all that seemed to be available for the moment. 'You've got time, I hope? This is going to take a while.'

Eva Backman looked at her watch. 'An hour and a half, will that do?'

Barbarotti nodded and said that it would.

'How are you?' she asked, before he could launch in. 'I think you look a bit brighter.'

'That's just my make-up,' Barbarotti assured her. 'The kids helped me with it this morning. Right, are you ready?'

'For your theory?' said Backman. 'Fire away, I'm all ears.'

Barbarotti referred briefly to his notebook. 'OK,' he said. 'Maybe I'm barking up entirely the wrong tree here, and I haven't so much as a pimple of evidence.'

'Pimple?' queried Backman.

'Don't quibble. What I mean is that I'm starting to get a picture of how it might all fit together. I still can't fathom why Asunander wants me to rake over these old cases, but I intend to find out. It's certainly a strange business . . . well, two, really. But I don't think we'll need to open a new investigation.'

'I thought that was what you were already working on,' said Backman. 'A new investigation.'

'I don't know what to call it,' admitted Barbarotti. 'But as I say, I shall have to leave Asunander to decide that.'

'I see,' said Eva Backman. 'OK, let's just call it a strange business or two, for now. But your time in Norrland helped to clarify things then? When you got to meet her.'

'Yes and no,' said Barbarotti, and scratched his head. 'But it's interesting how much it means to be able to sit down and talk to a person face-to-face. I mean, we can amass any number of bits of information from all over the place – data and more data and all kinds of stuff – but when it comes to sizing up what someone may actually have done or not done, you have to get a bit closer. But then we've been talking about this for twenty years.'

'We have,' agreed Backman. 'You're thinking of Ellen Bjarnebo?'

'Yes, I'm thinking of Ellen Bjarnebo. When I finally got hold of her, there was no problem really. She wasn't anything like as intractable as I'd expected. I talked to her for about an hour and a half. I recorded it, of course, and I've listened through it again twice. And I think I can claim that . . . things are starting to get clearer, like you say.'

Eva Backman gave a neutral nod.

'I'm inclined to think that the investigation after the death of Harry Helgesson was rather too much a question of going through the motions,' Barbarotti went on. 'They merely followed procedure and stuck to their initial assumptions all the way through, and perhaps that isn't so surprising. But what happened at those two farms was definitely, well, it was definitely more complicated than the police ever opened their eyes to. There were things, and relationships, that they simply didn't bother looking at.'

'A shoddy job?'

'Yes, I'm afraid so.'

'But she confessed straight away,' Backman pointed out. 'They found her prints on the murder weapon, if I remember rightly.'

'Just so. And that was all it took. If you admit to a murder, the chances are you'll be convicted of it. Especially if it's someone close to you that you claim to have killed, and there's nothing to point to anyone else.'

'Yes, that's the way it goes,' said Backman. 'You and I both know that. But what are you actually trying to tell me?'

'I'm coming to that,' said Barbarotti. 'But I've been thinking about all those people at those two farms. Harry Helgesson's death destroyed everything for them; not immediately perhaps, but in the longer term. Did I tell you that Ellen Bjarnebo was having an affair with the cousin up at Little Burma?'

'With her cousin?'

'No, with Göran Helgesson, Harry's cousin. There was this kind of Big Claus and Little Claus thing going on between the two cousins and the two farms. At Great Burma everything they did went well apparently, but at Little Burma most things went badly from the word go. I think Ellen Bjarnebo must have been living in hell while her husband was still alive . . . pretty much, anyway.'

'Wasn't that why she killed him? There was never any question, was there, about her having a motive?'

'Quite right,' said Barbarotti. 'She clearly had a compelling motive. The problem was that she also had a motive for confessing to the murder, even though she hadn't committed it.'

'What?' said Backman.

Barbarotti swigged his coffee.

'You're telling me that . . . ?'

'That somebody else might have done it, but she chose to go to prison in place of the perpetrator,' said Barbarotti.

'Somebody else?'

'Yes.'

'Is that what she told you, up there in the mountains?'

Barbarotti shook his head. 'Absolutely not. And I can only imagine she was the one who dismembered the body. So she's guilty of desecration of a corpse, if nothing else.'

Eva Backman considered the matter.

'I get it,' she said. 'The boy. You mean it was the boy who killed his father?'

Barbarotti nodded as he munched on his half biscuit. 'Yes . . . and no. That was more or less what I concluded after I'd talked to them all. Billy himself and that nervous woman in Hallsberg, his stepmother, but particularly Ellen Bjarnebo herself, of course. And after listening to the tape again. She was . . . well, I don't really know how to put it. She had something . . . *impressive* about her, I suppose I'd say.'

'Impressive?' said Backman. 'For taking the blame for her son's actions herself . . . yes, I can see that. But how certain are you? What do you mean by *yes and no*? That was what you said, wasn't it?'

'Leave that aside for the time being,' said Barbarotti. 'She's got a sort of moral stature to her is all I mean – or something along those lines. I have to stress that. Just think about the sort of life she's led, yet there she sits in a completely calm and obliging way and lets herself be questioned about everything that must feel like a bleeding wound inside her . . . all over again.'

'Hang on, though,' said Backman. 'You're saying, then, that the boy kills his dad, his mum takes the blame and goes to prison so the boy can have a normal life . . . Do you mean he went along with it all? How must it have been for him to live with this?'

'That's what's worrying me,' said Barbarotti. 'I can't make it add up.'

'But you met him, you say? The boy?'

'Yes, I did. I met Billy Helgesson, but it's rather problematic, with him being as he is. You may recall that he was practically mute throughout childhood?'

Eva Backman nodded. Barbarotti took a deep breath and cleared his throat.

'So, this is how things stand: mother and son have very little to do with each other nowadays. He was taken into the care of some relatives when she was sent to Hinseberg, and his new parents saw to it that contact between them was restricted to almost zero. Ellen Bjarnebo only saw her son twice, the whole time she was in prison. We're talking about more than a decade; the boy was twelve when she went in, twenty-three when she came out. And they haven't been able to repair the relationship since. I don't even know that they've really tried.'

Backman pondered. 'So there was no reward for what she did?'

'Not for her, no. But Billy's married and lives in Stockholm. Things are certainly a lot better for him than they would have been if he'd been convicted of his father's murder.'

'Stop a minute. He was only a child. He wouldn't have been sent to prison.'

'No,' sighed Barbarotti. 'You're quite right. But you can just imagine the future prospects for a . . . a twelve-year-old patricide who is mute and lacking all social skills, can't you?'

'Hmm,' said Eva Backman. 'What is it that doesn't add up then? That was how you put it, wasn't it?'

'What do *you* think?' said Barbarotti.

'I don't know,' said Backman and thought about it some more. 'Morinder, possibly? Where on earth does Arnold Morinder fit into the picture? Though . . .'

'Yes?'

'Though why should he have anything to do with this? He doesn't need to come into the picture, does he, because that's a whole other story?'

'It could be,' said Barbarotti, leaning back and clasping his hands behind his head. 'But I've got a feeling the two are connected. I know we *want* them to be, because it's always more convenient to have one murderer than two. It's better to have a Thomas Quick than nine other murderers on the loose. But even without him – without Morinder – there's something not right about the theory that the boy did it. I . . . I just have a feeling.'

'You have a feeling?'

'Exactly. Anything wrong with that?'

'I thought you were opposed to intuition?'

'Only to other people's, not my own.'

Eva Backman gave a laugh. Then she sighed. 'You know

what, Inspector Barbarotti, now I'm starting to recognize you again. Incidentally, why did you stay that extra day up in the land of mountains? I don't think you've explained that.'

'Oh yes, I have,' replied Barbarotti. 'The flight was cancelled. A technical problem, isn't that what they always say?'

'That doesn't mean you have to say it, too.'

Barbarotti did not respond. Eva Backman sat in silence, watching him. She could smell a rat. It was presumably intuition of her own making itself felt, but as it was not a widely accepted authority, she let it drop.

For the time being, at any rate.

'So what's next on your agenda?' she asked. 'Morinder?'

'Arnold Morinder and his blue moped,' stated DI Barbarotti, his face assuming an expression of resolve. 'Give me one more day and I shall have it sorted. I've got a plan. But now it's your turn. How did you get on with What's-his-name? Fridolin?'

'Hans Fridolin Hansson,' confirmed Backman.

'Tell me all about it,' urged Barbarotti.

And Eva Backman did so.

49

After the conversation with Backman, Barbarotti returned to his room.

He sat down at his desk and for the first ten minutes he did nothing except take off his shoes and think. Then he stared out of the window for about the same length of time, still cogitating. Largely oblivious to the view before him: two blossoming lilacs, a chestnut in flower, half a public-prosecution office and – at least if he had raised his eyes a little – a big orange balloon rising gently into the clear, open sky, advertising Kymlinge's organic sausage factory.

But Barbarotti did not raise his eyes; it was not that kind of clarity he was seeking, but the inner variety.

Once this delicate undertaking was complete and the sausage balloon had risen out of view above the treetops, he made three phone calls.

The first was to Inger Berglund in Midsommarkransen. She confessed to being surprised to hear from him again – and all the more so when she heard what he wanted. But after casting her mind back twenty-three years in time, she recollected that it was exactly as he suggested. It had in fact been that very spring and summer that the remarkable thing came into being, and she assumed there was no point asking what he was hoping to achieve.

Inger Berglund was quite right on that point. He thanked her, wished her a pleasant summer and ended the call. Then he moved on to Billy Helgesson.

It took a while to get hold of him. He was on a building site out near Saltsjöbaden and didn't really have time to talk.

'Five minutes?' proposed Barbarotti.

'OK, but no more,' Billy Helgesson agreed.

Three would have covered it, registered Barbarotti when the call was over.

The last of the three calls went to a company called Pooly Co. Ltd, which by some quirk of fate had survived in Kymlinge for more than twenty-five years. A branch of it, at any rate; the head office was in Gothenburg. He spoke to someone called Wetterström, who couldn't tell him anything straight off, but said he would have a ferret through some files and have a word with a couple of colleagues who had been around in those days. He could ring back the next day, if that would do?

Barbarotti said it would do nicely, thanked him and hung up.

Having ticked off his three calls, he sat there for a while longer and tried to draw some conclusions. He found himself thinking that what he had said to Backman about needing to have people in front of your eyes didn't apply invariably. Not strictly speaking; if you had met them already, asking for a bit of supplementary information over the phone could work quite well. As long as you knew who you were talking to.

Satisfied with his morning's fishing in those murky waters, he put his shoes back on, went down to sign out a car from the police pool and took a punt on a visit to the Autumn Sun Retirement Home.

And it was on his way back from his chat with Hasse Fridolin Hansson that Barbarotti almost bought his first evening paper for five years. Had he done so, it would have been from Tadpole's kiosk on Vattugatan, where any passer-by could see that *Aftonbladet* and *Expressen* were for once in agreement on the hottest news story of the day:

> *HITLER LIVED IN SOUTH OF SWEDEN*
> *UNTIL 1950s. SENSATIONAL REVELATIONS*
> *IN NEW BESTSELLER*

ran *Expressen*'s placard.

> *ADOLF HITLER'S SECRET GRANDCHILD WRITES*
> *SENSATIONAL NEW SWEDISH NOVEL*

announced *Aftonbladet*.

Barbarotti braked to a halt by the kiosk. He rubbed his eyes, shook his head and slowly took in the fact that Axel Wallman *had not* been on the run from some kind of institution when their paths crossed at the airport. Instead it seemed to be . . . well, not to put too fine a point on it, some kind of reality: the literary super-agent with his yellow suit, straw hat and cane. As loud and charming a schemer as the villain in some old Danish film. How could it be possible?

Bettina Braun? Hitler in Skåne? The third rebus?

Why am I surprised? sighed Gunnar Barbarotti, letting out the clutch and driving on. The world is a theatre and people want to be taken in – that's the simple truth.

And who could blame the madcap Wallman? Stories are better than history.

There is no remembrance of former things; neither shall there be any remembrance of things that are to come with those that shall come after.

Axel Wallman knew what he was doing, and the old Preacher of Ecclesiastes had seen it all before.

The German whist tournament at Villa Pickford that lovely summer's evening lasted two hours and twenty minutes, all told – because everyone had to play everyone and the result had to be conclusive. They started straight after dinner, and by the time they had the final result it was past midnight. But since school was winding right down in anticipation of the end of term the following week, nobody had any objection. Johan wasn't on the early shift at his espresso bar the next morning, and the inspector's meeting with his boss wasn't until eleven o'clock.

And they were good hours. There were moments when he could sense the spirit of Marianne hovering above them. Smiling down at them from her cloud. It was claiming a lot, maybe, but he could tell that the rest of them were aware of it, too. That's amazing, he thought. Thank you.

But they were only moments. And the whole evening was a walk across thin ice, of course; there were surface tensions and gaping cracks, but they were still taking steps in the right direction.

The tournament itself didn't turn out very favourably for the head of the family. Villa Pickford's rules for German whist allocated points, as for chess; a game could end with either a 1–0 victory for one of the players or, in the case of an equal number of tricks to each, which was more common than you might have thought, in 0.5–0.5. With six people taking part, that meant a total of fifteen games, five each, and when Lars, barely concealing his delight, read out the final scores, he was the winner. He had scraped together four points. Sara and Johan were in joint second place with three, Martin came fourth with 2.5, Jenny fifth with 1.5 and Dad Gunnar was sixth and last, with a single measly point.

Conclusive, just like they wanted it.

The boys took themselves off to bed straight afterwards, but despite the lateness of the hour, he stayed downstairs with Jenny and Sara for a while, and he soon became aware there was a closeness between them that he had not seen before.

His daughter, Marianne's daughter. There were six years between them, but it made no difference. It was very evident that there was a bond between them, an affinity. The realization that it was not only wishful thinking on his part almost brought tears to his eyes, and he decided to leave them in peace. As he climbed the stairs he took one last glance at the two girls in their wicker chairs in the bay window overlooking the lake, wrapped in blankets and the light summer darkness, nursing big cups of tea, and there was no doubt in his mind that they were under the protection of both Marianne and Our Lord.

These mood swings, he thought to himself. This sense of hope and trust that comes and goes as it will. As slippery as a bar of soap, he had thought many times before.

When he got to bed, he turned to Psalms and read numbers twenty-three and ninety-one.

Then he put out the light and turned on his side to sleep.

Five minutes later, with the time probably already after one, he switched it back on again. His body felt as if it had relaxed into sleep mode, but not his brain. He scrabbled for the case files lying on the floor beside the bed and started leafing through them.

At a quarter to two he finally found a name.

Börje Granat.

He got up, switched on his computer and went to one of the online directories.

And hey presto, there it was: the man appeared to be alive and still living in Kymlinge. His address was in Lilla Smedgränd and he had two phone numbers, a landline and a mobile.

Given the time, Gunnar Barbarotti accepted that further action would have to wait until the next day. He noted the particulars on a piece of paper and went back to bed.

Börje Granat is another person who won't be running away, he thought.

50

'Three forty-five point nine,' said Asunander. 'Does that mean anything to you?'

'Sounds like a fifteen-hundred-metre race time,' said Barbarotti.

'Dead right,' said Asunander. 'I never got below three fifty-five, and that's three seconds slower than Gunder Hägg. But then I gave it up before I was twenty-one.'

'Oh, did you?' said Barbarotti. He's really lost the plot this time, he thought.

'Never came in at under one fifty in the eight hundred, either, but I had promise, I want you to remember that. Exceptional promise.'

'I'm sure you did,' said Barbarotti. 'But I was under the impression we were going to talk about these cases I've been working on, and why you put me on them in the first place—'

'We're coming to that,' Asunander interrupted. 'But if it hadn't been for my brief career in athletics, you wouldn't be sitting where you are today.'

For a few seconds Barbarotti cast around for some comment to make, but failed to find one.

'Middle-distance,' Asunander continued unruffled, with a slightly far-away look in his eyes. 'The blue-riband events of the sport, as they're known . . . or actually I think that's just the fifteen hundred metres. Well, anyway, I was very involved in running, as a junior. I trained hard and competed for my home club in Halmstad. The reason I gave it up so early was that I started having problems with my periosteum. My periosteum and my knees. I would have carried on otherwise.'

'Hmm,' said Barbarotti.

'There's a time for everything,' observed Asunander, leaning across his desk. 'But this is where we find the reason for my asking you to look over the Morinder and Burma cases. Particularly the latter, but I wasn't in a position to make that entirely plain from the start unfortunately.'

'Not entirely plain from the start?' queried Barbarotti. 'I'm inclined to agree with you on that.'

Asunander appeared to be thinking. 'How can I put it? You see, what we're dealing with here is . . .'

'Yes,' said Barbarotti.

'Hrrm,' said Asunander. 'We're talking about a matter of a very private nature.'

'I was starting to think it must be,' said Barbarotti.

Asunander gave him a long look. 'Oh, you were, were you?' he said with a hint of doubt in his voice. 'But never mind, anyway. It's the year 1968 we're concerned with, the year I gave up running . . . although that was later, after the summer. I was twenty, and we had this exchange with an East German club. Dresden, the most badly bombed of all German cities at the end of the war, but by the sixties they had at least got their sports going again.'

He broke off for a moment, to check that Barbarotti was listening. Barbarotti nodded.

'We went there in the autumn of 1967, and in May 1968 they came up to Halmstad to pay a return visit. Training and a few competitions, and general promotion of good relations. I don't know how your knowledge of history serves you, but May 1968 was quite a tumultuous month. Practically a revolution in Paris, student demonstrations everywhere . . . yes, the leftist movement of '68 is a concept that ought to have filtered down to everybody, even if they weren't there. And then we had those young athletes visiting us for two weeks.'

He paused again, looking at Barbarotti for renewed assurance.

'I'm with you,' said Barbarotti. 'I was only eight, but I'm familiar with what was going on. In broad outline, at any rate.'

'Good,' said Asunander. 'And that was when I went and fell in love.'

Barbarotti surreptitiously pinched his arm to check that he was awake.

'Her name was Regina. Sprint and long jump, not a middle-distance runner like me. They were kept under close supervision, of course, but one evening we did it. It wasn't allowed of course, we were taking a huge risk, especially her.'

'You did it?' queried Barbarotti. 'You mean the good relations went, er, a bit further than intended?'

'I'm not giving you any details,' said Asunander tetchily. 'Suffice it to say that things happened, and two days later she went back to Dresden. I haven't seen her since. You're familiar with something called the Iron Curtain perhaps?'

Barbarotti made no answer. Asunander broke off again and looked out of the window.

'I've only got two weeks left in this job,' he said. 'I feel I can take a few liberties.'

He was clearly waiting for Barbarotti to comment. Or to say something, at least, and for the first time ever Barbarotti felt obliged to give his boss a helping hand. Felt he was . . . imploring him, somehow.

'What happened?' he asked. 'I mean, you've got to tell me how all this ties up with what went on at Little Burma twenty years later . . . or however long it was. Twenty-one?'

Asunander nodded. Stood up, did a circuit of the room and sat down again.

'And if I tell you that the girl's name was Regina Peters, does that ring any bells?'

'Peters?' said Barbarotti. 'Wait a minute . . .'

'I'm waiting,' said Asunander.

'Juliana Peters. I met her in Stockholm last week. She's married to Billy Helgesson, the boy from Little Burma.'

'Quite right,' said Asunander. 'Can you see any resemblance?'

'What?' said Barbarotti.

'Resemblance,' repeated Asunander. 'I asked if you could see any resemblance.'

'Yes, I heard you,' said Barbarotti. 'Resemblance between what?'

'Between her and me, of course,' said Asunander. 'She's my daughter.'

There was silence for a full five seconds. Barbarotti had no idea what was going through the chief inspector's head, but in his own it felt rather as if a fuse had blown. Or even two.

'Your daughter,' he finally managed to say. 'I didn't think you had any children.'

'Nor did I,' said Asunander. 'Until a few months ago, that is. That was when I had a letter from Regina Peters . . . who I was with just that once, forty-four years ago. It wasn't my sexual debut, but very nearly, incidentally. And she got pregnant, you see. Gave birth to a daughter in Dresden in February 1969, and now – well, now it's coming home to her that she probably won't live forever, she's decided that it's time to put me in the picture. She also told me they'd had quite a hard life, she and her daughter, but now she's in a sound financial position. Regina, that is. That was exactly how she put it: "in a sound financial position". In German of course, but I happen to speak the language.'

'Did you get in touch with her?' asked Barbarotti. I guessed javelin thrower, he thought. But she was a sprinter. I need to sharpen up my act.

Asunander shook his head. 'She was adamant that she didn't want any contact. She has another family and it would only cause problems, she claimed. But she wanted me to know of Juliana's existence. Especially as the girl moved to Sweden some years ago.'

He leant back and crossed his arms.

'And Juliana?' asked Barbarotti. 'Have you . . . have you contacted her?'

An expression he had never seen on his superior's face before was slowly spreading across Asunander's features. Summer skies, thought Barbarotti. Yes, exactly that – naked, all its defences down, those dense, virtually impenetrable defences that he had developed over almost forty years as a police detective. But now the mask was cracking wide open. Several peculiar seconds elapsed.

'I don't know if I dare,' said Asunander eventually. 'I know I've got to, but I thought I'd wait for my pension first.'

'Probably just as well,' said Barbarotti and swallowed.

'I set about locating her, with nothing to go on beyond that name in the letter, but it wasn't difficult of course. And then . . . well, I found out she was married to Billy Helgesson, of all people. They have a daughter, but you know that. Since

I was feeling a bit paralysed by indecision, I started looking through the old investigation – and the Morinder one: totally deplorable, the pair of them, I hope you've realized that. And as I was going through, I could see that events may well not have unfolded the way people assumed. Once I'd read it all through a couple of times, I found I could just as easily visualize a completely different scenario.'

'Namely?' asked Barbarotti.

Asunander tugged at both his earlobes before he answered.

'Namely, that it wasn't our infamous axe woman who killed and dismembered her husband.'

Barbarotti waited, his face giving nothing away.

'It was that damn boy who did it.'

Barbarotti cleared his throat. 'I understand what you're saying,' he said. 'And I can see the problem. Well, it was the axe woman who did the chopping up, I can promise you that, but as for the murder . . .'

Asunander leant across the desk and glowered. His expression this time was more than familiar. Less summer skies, more thunderstorm in the dark.

'Well, what do you say?' he said. 'You must see that I . . .'

'Yes?'

'That I want to know whether my daughter's married to a murderer or not?'

Barbarotti tried to muster his thoughts. He felt a sudden sense of frustration at not having been provided with this information from the start, but realized almost instantaneously that he could accept Asunander's tactics. What was more, he thought, it basically wouldn't have changed anything if I had known. Not helped matters, anyway; in fact it could have got in the way.

Asunander must somehow be reading his thoughts, because he let out a deep sigh and put up his hands. 'I'm sorry if you feel I've pulled the wool over your eyes, but I thought things would work better this way. And that wretched Morinder business deserved another look, regardless. Damn it, I couldn't simply go and start digging around in all this on my own.'

Why not? Barbarotti wondered, but suppressed that objection, too.

'You have a grandchild, too,' he pointed out, without really knowing why. 'Julia. You haven't just gained a daughter, you've become a grandfather as well.'

And suddenly a smile spread across Asunander's face. Barbarotti had never seen anything like it before, and he couldn't help feeling somehow . . . moved?

'I know,' said Asunander. 'They're . . .'

'What?'

'Well, I'd like to think they're named after me. Both of them. I used my other name in those days. Julius.'

'Julius?' said Barbarotti, feeling a muscle twitch in one of his cheeks.

'My middle name, as I say,' Asunander said quickly. 'But what I want from you is an answer: that's why we're sitting here. Has my daughter – who I've never met, and who I didn't know existed until three months ago – has she gone and married a murderer? Or not?'

Barbarotti glanced at his watch.

'I don't know,' he said. 'I honestly don't. But in an hour's time I'm meeting a man, and I hope that after I've spoken to him, we might see matters in a different light.'

'A different light?' asked Asunander, peeved.

'I shall definitely be able to tell you by then,' clarified Barbarotti. 'I think so, anyway.'

'You think so?' groaned DCI Asunander.

Barbarotti was on his way out of the door when Asunander called him back.

'One more thing,' he said. 'I would be grateful if this could stay between you and me. I don't want it circulating round the whole building.'

Would be grateful? thought Barbarotti. He isn't even saying, *I naturally assume.*

'Of course,' he said.

Asunander hesitated for a moment. 'No further than DI Backman, at any rate.'

'You have my word,' said Barbarotti.

51

5–6 August 2007

She heard the putter of the moped fade away and took three deep breaths.

She tried to get the tension inside her to loosen its hold. She felt as if her ribcage had shrunk. She had barely slept all night and had no idea how she had pulled it off.

Staying calm, that was to say. But perhaps she had greater resources than she had imagined. Perhaps she had acquired them in those years in Hinseberg; if there was one thing you learnt in prison, it was surely the art of waiting. Not to be too eager; it was utterly pointless being in a hurry if you were going to be locked up for ten years or more.

She went down to the lake shore. Kicked off her shoes and walked out into the water. Not far, only a few metres, until it came about halfway up her shins. The bottom of the lake was muddy and uneven, it wasn't the sort of place suitable for swimming, but if you simply wanted to stand there and cool off for a bit, it was fine.

And that was what she wanted to do. It was what the Mutti voice was trying to bring home to her. *Cool off and think. Make plans.*

Just so. Impose some sort of order on the whirling cacophony in her head and decide how she was going to proceed. Make the spin dryer stop.

Or did she already know, really? Perhaps. Perhaps there was only one way out, one definitive solution, and what was required was to plan the route, mark it out. Not the destination.

And as she stood there, looking out over the black water, the whole conversation came back to her, word-for-word, and perhaps it was not so strange that she should recall it in such detail. The question was rather whether she would ever be able to forget it.

'You mean to say you never realized?'

He sits there, leaning back against the wall of the hut with his feet up on the table. A beer in his hand. It is half past nine in the evening, there is the whine of mosquitoes, but only from a distance because they have a couple of pungent coils burning. He is a little bit drunk.

If he isn't drunk, he hardly ever speaks. Other women would find it disturbing that he is so uncommunicative, but not her. Quite the opposite, and she sees it as a legacy from Hinseberg. As for her, she has had two glasses of wine with her dinner and is on her third, and last.

And now he is talking. She decides to do the same.

'Never realized what?'

'What happened.'

'What happened when?'

'Come on, you know what I'm talking about.'

'No, I don't know what you're talking about, Arnold.'

He takes a swig of beer and looks out over the lake. He seems to be wondering whether to go on or not.

'I've never been able to work out whether you got it or not.'

She doesn't answer. She drinks some wine instead and tells herself it's a lovely evening anyway. For a couple other than this one, it would be the perfect setting for romance.

The thought dies instantly as he goes on: 'Harry, for Chrissake. It's Harry I'm talking about. Reckon it's time.'

'What do you mean?'

'I mean like the fact that you never thanked me.'

He gives a laugh as soon as the words are out. That is out of the ordinary, too. Arnold Morinder, talking and laughing at the same time. Maybe he is drunker than usual. She senses something is about to happen. A landslide; she has no idea where the image has come from.

'Thanked you for what?'

He pauses to take aim at a mosquito that has braved the fumes and reached his leg. He slaps it and misses.

'For killing him.'

She doesn't register it. The landslide happens and it all goes black and empty inside her head, the way it used to look in the cinema in the old days when the film snapped.

'That's what for,' he says.

The moments pass. They sit motionless. The mosquitoes whine and darkness falls over the lake.

'What did you say?' she asks finally. 'I couldn't hear properly.'

He knocks back more beer and takes his feet off the table.

'Give me strength,' he says. 'All I said was that you ought to be grateful to me for killing Harry.'

This time she hears. She is able to string the words together into an intelligible message and she also registers that he sounds pleased with himself. Slightly uncertain, perhaps, but basically pleased.

She is struck by how odd it is that every single thing – an

entire life – can be turned upside down in an instant, and that she can still sit there observing it. Observing it all as if it is nothing to do with her. But he could just be pulling her leg – though it would be a first, if so, because Arnold Morinder isn't really capable of joking with people. Or of being funny or sarcastic or ambiguous, come to that. If he says something, it is to underline that this is how matters stand. It is a quality in him that she has come to value. Arnold rarely says anything, but when he does open his mouth, he generally speaks the truth.

But this time she does not understand. It is impossible to understand.

'Go on,' she says, when they have been sitting in silence for a good minute. 'I don't really get what you're telling me.'

She can see that this is exactly what he was hoping she would ask him to do. Explain. She can also see that he is drunker and more pleased with himself than he ought to be.

'You mean you never realized?'

It is the third or fourth time he has expressed his surprise at the fact. She nods to him to go on. She never realized, what does he think? He hawks and spits onto the stony ground.

'Fuck!' he says. 'It was all over in an instant. I knew him a bit, did I ever say?'

'You knew Harry?'

'Well, I say "knew". I'd met him a few times. Played some poker. With Ziggy and Staffe and them . . .'

She doesn't reply. She has enough to do, trying to piece together his words and make them tally with a completely different story. Something she had *thought* to be a completely different story.

'Only that year, in fact,' he said. 'Yeah, I've liked you since we were at school – you bloody well remember that, don't you? We had something going even back then. I've had other birds, but you were, like, the only one that mattered, Ellen . . . Yeah, that's the way it's always been.'

She has never heard him say so much in a single breath, and at the same time it is as if she is rising from her seat. Floating up into the air, hanging there and seeing them from above. Her and him. And the slight intoxication she had been feeling simply runs off her.

'Go on,' she repeats, and from her new vantage point she is suddenly the alert and focused observer. All her feelings are stuffed into a sack under her chair, the one she has just vacated, but is still sitting in.

Arnold drains his bottle of beer, goes over to the water butt, fishes out a new one and comes back.

'Do you really want to hear?' he asks, but it isn't a real question because she can hear that he wants to tell her anyway. Perhaps it isn't as straightforward as him getting some enjoyment out of doing so, not entirely, but the thought is in her mind that he has been carrying this with him for a long time. It is a puzzle how he has kept it up, but Arnold Morinder is himself a puzzle. If she had not known it before, she knows it now.

But why now? Why choose this, of all evenings? It is beyond her. Or maybe it is pure chance, and it was bound to come out, sooner or later.

She nods. Sees herself down there on the chair, nodding, and is struck by how cool and relaxed she looks. Given the situation. Arnold takes a pull on his beer and starts his story.

'We were working on that swimming pool, yeah?' he says.

'Up at Great Burma. We were subcontracted to the company that was putting it in – whatever their name was. I'd already got a job to go to in Gothenburg after the summer. I moved there before . . . Yeah well, before you fucking owned up to it.'

Pause. Another mosquito. Another slap, another miss.

'So I just read about it in the paper. Never got why you confessed. Why the hell would you do that?'

Because . . . she thinks. Because, because . . .

But she isn't going to tell him. She can't tell anyone, and especially not him. And suddenly she feels a burning desire to know how it happened. How on earth could it be possible for Arnold Morinder to have delivered that fatal blow to her husband in the office out in the cowshed, when she had seen Billy with her own eyes, coming out of there with the sledge-hammer in his hands?

But even before he starts telling her, let alone gets to the details, she is sure that he is telling the truth.

And it isn't only because Arnold Morinder always tells the truth, but also because . . . because the boy is innocent.

Billy didn't kill his father. He's no murderer.

It's pure madness. But it's true. She has lived with the opposite truth for almost twenty years, and suddenly everything is turned on its head. Suddenly everything is rewritten and . . . and all those godforsaken days and nights, and torment and insomnia and meaninglessness, are punctured, and everything drowns in a stinking salvo of laughter from the underworld. *Stinking salvo of laughter from the underworld?* Has somebody else invaded my skull? Is it Mutti? No, it isn't Mutti, it's just my brain vomiting.

There is no need for her to urge him to tell her more. Arnold

Morinder himself wants it on the record now, that much is clear.

'Yeah, well, what the heck,' he excuses her. 'We were installing the cables for the underwater lighting and then I saw you come past. Jesus, I couldn't believe my eyes, and the next day I saw you again . . .'

Short pause. Swig of beer.

' . . . and that Saturday I thought I'd at least go over there and introduce myself, see if you remembered me. Say hello to Harry too, maybe, but then I saw the way he treated you, fucking bastard, and I went back to work. But later . . .'

'Later?' she can't help saying.

'Later, yeah, we kept at it right into the evening, even though it was a Saturday. But good money, with snacks provided and everything – all three of us thought so . . . And when we were done, the others went home, but I went over to yours again and decided I just had to have a quick word and check things were OK. You'd gone off somewhere, but I hung around and thought about it, and then I saw there was a light on in the barn and I went in and found Harry in that room.'

He stops for a moment, glancing at her before he goes on.

'He was pissed and he totally lost his rag. And I thought about you and what a nightmare it must be for you . . . and he swore at me and I saw the fucking sledgehammer lying there, and then he turned his back on me. Told me to go to hell, so I whacked him one and then he was dead. I left the sledgehammer on the floor and made myself scarce. Panicked, I suppose. I mean, I'd killed the bugger . . .'

He takes another swig of beer, belches and shakes his head. Just like Harry used to, she thinks, and as she shuts her eyes for a moment, the images of the two of them merge. The murderer and his victim.

More silence. He seems worn out by the effort of producing more words than he has said all summer; she can see that he isn't going to say any more. He is satisfied now. He is done.

'I was in prison for eleven years,' she says.

'You stupid cow,' he says, and tries to smile, so she will realize he is joking.

But Arnold Morinder can't do smiles or jokes, never has been able to. They sit out there for a while longer. Then he says he's had it with all these damn mosquitoes and he's going to bed. She says she'll sleep in the hammock. He has no objection; she'll simply have to douse herself in jungle formula. They haven't had sex for several months, neither of them seems to feel like it any more, and in any case it's virtually impossible in the cramped bunk beds in the hut.

All night she lies there under two rugs, and as a huge August moon sails slowly across the treetops and lake, the decision grows in her, as self-evidently and unresistingly as a well-tended tomato plant in a greenhouse. It's a duty, she thinks. An imperative duty, nothing more or less. You have to do justice to your own life.

And she has already served her time.

She has no intention of doing it again.

So the planning is crucial. She thanks her inner voice for her self-possession. She thinks about Billy.

She watches him as he parks the moped up against the spruce as usual. The evening paper under his arm; he gives her a lazy nod and goes in to fetch a rug. Spreads it out on the grass, lies down and makes himself comfortable and starts looking through the paper. They haven't said a word to each other all day.

She realizes they never will again.

A while later he has dozed off on the rug. The newspaper over his face, exactly as usual.

She goes indoors for the frying pan. It is cast iron, heavy and solid.

She stands over his head, her feet planted firmly. She's relieved the newspaper is there, so she doesn't have to see.

She takes a deep breath and swings the pan.

There are two sounds: one is the clang of the pan and the other is a sharp splintering, like when you break a branch off a tree. A line from a song comes into her head, and it is an odd one. *There is a crack in everything, that's how the light gets in.* Is it referring to Arnold's skull, or what? The idea that a bit of light has finally penetrated his darkened brain?

Presumably that single, powerful blow kills him. His arms and legs twitch a bit, then he lies still. But she stabs him in the belly five or six times with the carving knife. Just to be sure.

She lets him lie there bleeding for a while before she covers him with the other rug. She thinks it is as well they have no neighbours.

She thinks about Billy. Thinks about everything.

The rest of it will have to wait for the evening. She sits at the outdoor table drinking coffee, with Arnold just lying there. She does a few crosswords. It is a Sunday and in the afternoons there are usually a number of boats on the lake, so yes, she will have to leave it until evening comes. The frying pan is back in its place, the carving knife in its drawer. It's a simple thing, killing, she thinks. A couple of well-chosen kitchen implements do the job nicely.

She puts the rugs and the newspaper in the brazier for burning later. Not tonight, tomorrow will do fine. There is less of Arnold than there was of Harry; there is no need to joint the body this time, and she's grateful for that. She gets him into the boat without too much trouble. She takes the heap of old chains from the shed and wraps them several times around his body; they are long and must weigh ten kilos or more in total, but she nonetheless fixes on a tin bucket with a big rock in it. As an extra sinker. She bends in the sides of the bucket so the rock can't float out. An old padlock, a metre of wire and everything's ready. At 10 p.m. she rows out onto the lake with her load.

Round the reedbeds and off to the right, that's where it is deepest, Arnold told her. No place for pulling up pike. Fifteen metres at least, maybe twenty.

The ideal location for Arnold himself. She heaves everything overboard, loses an oar but manages to grab hold of it again, and once she has rowed back and pulled the boat up onto the shore, she feels nothing but deep gratification.

She doesn't take the moped in the boat, however, it simply wouldn't work. She waits another hour. Then she pushes it the 300 metres up the track to the road before she starts it. Gloves on her hands – she's thought of everything. She doesn't reckon any of the nearby huts and cottages are currently occupied, but it would be stupid to take the risk.

The risk that somebody might have heard Arnold coming back from the filling station has already been taken. She'll have to live with that. She will never reveal that he came back that afternoon, and she doesn't think anyone else will give evidence to the contrary.

There has to be some kind of balance in what happens. She put her faith in a higher power of some sort, though she has no real idea what.

She rides randomly west for half an hour. She meets no oncoming vehicles, but is overtaken by a little van with Norwegian number plates. She turns onto a narrow forest road when she thinks she has gone far enough, and is able to get the moped a good way into the trees. She leaves it sinking into the edge of a bog. The mosquitoes provide an accompaniment. The moon emerges from time to time to shine on the operation, but stays largely hidden behind restless clouds. As she covers the long stretch back home, it starts to rain, too, and for her this is excellent; it will certainly be enough to wash away all traces round the hut.

There is no traffic this time, either, but why should there be? By the time she is back and getting into the narrow lower bunk, it is half past one.

It's over, the Mutti voice tells her. *Sleep well.*

And she sleeps dreamlessly for eleven hours.

52

'On the whole, then?' enquired Rönn. 'On the whole, can we say you're feeling a little better?'

Barbarotti considered the matter. 'I heard something about grief,' he said. 'It was Jenny, my daughter, who told me. She'd read it somewhere and I thought it sounded spot on.'

'And what was that?' said Rönn.

'Well, you visualize grief as a room inside you, and it's all about the door. It has to be kept closed. We're either inside the room or outside it. But we always carry it with us, and we can go in and out of it at will.'

Rönn nodded. 'Whenever we need to. Yes, it's a good idea not to leave the door swinging . . .'

'But it does, doesn't it?' said Barbarotti. 'At the beginning, it does that all the time.'

'We learn,' said Rönn. 'And in your case it's only been . . . how long is it now?'

'Forty-one days,' said Barbarotti.

Rönn smiled. 'Not long,' he said. 'In my case it's been twenty-five years. Almost to the day, in fact. Shall we say I'll see you again next week? Perhaps we can talk a bit more about faith and trust?'

'Certainly,' said Barbarotti. 'Would Tuesday afternoon be all right? After work?'

'That'll be fine,' Rönn assured him, making a note in his diary before they said their goodbyes.

Barbarotti emerged into an early Saturday evening. They had been scheduled to meet on the Friday, but Rönn had wisdom-tooth problems and postponed their session until the next day. The fact that it was considered a Saturday made no difference, he said. The soul knows no distinction between weekdays and weekends.

He had parked at Norra torg, and since he had half an hour to spare, he decided to leave the car there. It was a fine evening and a walk along the river would do no harm. There were some thoughts he needed to gather together before he saw Eva Backman, that was clear.

Assuming she wanted a full account, and he guessed she would. It probably wasn't the most important reason for their meeting, but still.

But once he started turning over a few things in his mind, he realized that there were really only two things he wanted to withhold from her. Or maybe only one, depending on how you counted. Those two phone calls.

He had made them a few hours before, twenty minutes apart, and it struck him that he ought to keep them separate, rather like that room for grief that he and Rönn had been talking about. Keep the door closed.

And maybe go so far as to lock the door as well. From the outside, in this case.

His reason for making the calls was the dream he had experienced at the guest house. He was nonplussed by the fact that it had lurked there unnoticed for four days before suddenly coming back to him as if someone had started replaying a film. But you never really knew where you were with dreams and the subconscious – that wasn't news to anybody. And it would have to be a different kind of door, presumably, with a different kind of doorman.

It was just after his lunch with three of the kids, plus Johan's girlfriend, at Henry's Inn. That was when it whirred back into life. They all had things to do after lunch and disappeared in various directions, some of them in a hurry. He had given each of them a hug, lent Martin 200 kronor and stayed at the table to wait for the bill.

And then he remembered. The voice. The jab in his arm. The message.

And the little card he was carrying in his wallet suddenly assumed significance. *The Sisters*.

The first call he made was to the medical centre in Vilhelmina. He asked about the doctor who had come to see him a few days before, but said he couldn't recall her name.

'What do you mean, "her"?' a woman's voice with a distinct Norrland accent had answered. 'We only have the one doctor and he's called Markström. He's definitely a man.'

He thanked her and hung up, then thought hard for five minutes. After that he rang DI Gunvaldsson. It took a while to get hold of him on his private mobile number, but he found him in the end.

'How's the hay fever?' he asked.

'Improving daily,' declared Gunvaldsson.

In fact it was so much improved, he went on to explain, that he was currently sitting at an outside table at one of Karlstad's better restaurants with a lager. To what did he owe the honour?

'If I say The Sisters,' Barbarotti asked. 'What's your response?'

At that moment, the line went dead. He tried twice more, but could not get through.

He reached the bascule bridge and stopped in the middle for a while before continuing to Pampas on the other side. He leant his elbows on the railing as he looked down at the sluggishly flowing water and tried to conjure up Ellen Bjarnebo's face in his mind.

The murdering axe woman of Little Burma?

Like hell she was.

The Sisters?

Well, so be it, thought DI Barbarotti. A closed room. For now, anyway.

Eva Backman's balcony was a real godsend. The flat she had moved into after the divorce from Ville was on the top floor of one of the newly built blocks in Pampas, and sitting up there gave you a real bird's-eye view. The whole of Kymlinge was spread out below: the river and the town forest, the old town with the two church spires at its heart, the residential districts to the west and north, Rocksta and Gårdinge, the industrial areas to the south. The water towers, old and new, and away in the distance a dark hint of Lake Kymmen in the early-evening light, the forests and the farmed fields on both sides, and as Barbarotti sank into the reclining chair he forgot everything else for a moment and simply looked. He thought back to when he had stood up by Slussen a week before and looked out over Stockholm, and he had to admit that this town really wasn't too bad, either.

It was not the first time he had been up here, of course, but he could not remember any summer evening like this.

'You could rent this flat out for the summer,' he said. 'Or even just the balcony.'

Eva Backman nodded. 'I know. I've considered bringing the bed out here, but I'm not sure I can get it through the door. Thank you for coming, finally.'

'Sorry,' said Barbarotti. 'I've been too wrapped up in myself, but Rönn says that's allowed when you're bowled over by grief. And how are *you*?'

Eva Backman hesitated for a moment. 'Do you want a polite answer or a true one?'

'True, please,' said Barbarotti.

'Well, in that case, let's have a drop of wine first,' said Backman. '*Skål* and welcome.'

They drank, and at the same moment the church clock began striking seven.

'I feel pretty rubbish,' said Eva Backman, putting down her glass. 'To be honest, I'm sick of myself. It's as if I don't recognize myself any longer.'

'Well, I'm having no trouble recognizing you,' said Barbarotti.

'It's good to hear that you can remember my name,' said Backman. 'But I get so frustrated and worked up about everything nowadays, and I really don't know where it's going to end. Of course it's mainly Ville and his new dragon, but there are other things, too.'

'I get the sense that there's some kind of female zone women reach at your age,' Barbarotti suggested cautiously. 'But maybe I've got that wrong. Marianne used to say I misunderstood everything about women that could possibly be misunderstood.'

Eva Backman gave a brief smile. 'But you feel more able to handle it now? Not your own lack of understanding, but the fact that she's gone. I think I can see it in you.'

'Well, it depends what you mean by handle,' said Barbarotti.

'There are times when I feel as if I can, but sometimes it all feels as dark as night.'

'I can understand that,' said Eva. 'Maybe we shouldn't be launching straight into the topic. Help yourself from what's on the table, and there'll be something coming out of the oven in a few minutes. But now I want to hear about the closing stages of the Bjarnebo affair. Have you got all the pieces of the puzzle in place now?'

'It's not impossible, actually,' said Barbarotti modestly, and popped a chunk of mozzarella in his mouth. 'Mmm, nice. But the case is closed, just so you know.'

'What you told me about Asunander sounds like . . . well, I wouldn't like to say what. Some kind of fable?'

'Perhaps,' said Barbarotti. 'It was really quite . . . touching, almost. Anyway, I established what he wanted me to establish.'

'That the boy was innocent?'

'Yes.'

'And the axe woman was innocent, too?'

'Of the murder of Harry Helgesson, yes.'

'But not . . .'

Barbarotti sighed and threw up his hands. 'No, I imagine she killed Arnold Morinder, in fact. But it's only guesswork and I'm not intending to take it any further.'

Eva Backman waited while Barbarotti ate four olives and a breadstick.

'So, this is what I *think* happened,' he said, looking out at the view of the town rather than at her. 'It was Morinder who killed Harry Helgesson. He happened to be up at Great Burma for a few days around that time. They were having a pool put in and I expect he was working on the electrics. I'm not thinking of trying to clarify any details, but Ellen must have thought the boy had done it. He was more or less mute, as you know, and that was no doubt part of it. She assumes responsibility, they don't talk about it at all and, when I come to think of it, that's quite natural, really. Or at least entirely credible, in view of how he was . . . and is. She thinks it's the boy, he thinks it's her.'

'She thinks it's the boy, and the boy thinks it's her?' repeated Backman, frowning.

'I can't see any other explanation,' professed Barbarotti. 'She pays the penalty to spare the boy, and long afterwards she discovers Morinder was the perpetrator all along . . .'

'And she just happens to be living with him?'

'If she *hadn't* been, she would never have found out. And that was exactly why Morinder killed Harry Helgesson, don't forget: for being married to her . . . You remember there was something between them, way back in their schooldays. One shouldn't speak ill of those who have gone, but he was a rum customer, that electrician.'

Eva Backman shook her head and tried to digest all this information.

'I've no idea how she found out,' Barbarotti went on, 'but my guess would be that Morinder simply happened to let it slip. And that drove a coach and horses through everything she'd thought and done for eighteen years.'

'What do you think she did? With Morinder, I mean . . . if that's what happened.'

'Haven't a clue. Maybe he's somewhere at the bottom of Lake Kymmen. What's left of him, that is. But that's . . .'

'Yes?'

'That's something I'm not going to lift a finger to find out.'

Eva Backman leant back and reflected. 'I see,' she said.

'Crime and punishment. Everyone got their just deserts, you mean?'

Barbarotti shrugged and drank some wine. 'In any case it's uninvestigable, as they say.'

'OK,' said Backman. 'I can buy that, I suppose, though possibly with the minor reservation that we don't have the death penalty in this country.'

Barbarotti gave this his due consideration. 'Morinder's fine where he is,' he said finally. 'If we assume that's what happened. He committed murder. He said nothing when the woman he loved was convicted of the crime. He caused a permanent rupture between mother and son. I spoke to this man called Börje Granat and he claimed that Morinder and Harry Helgesson knew each other a bit. They'd played poker together, and so on.'

'You mean Morinder planned it?'

'No, hardly. I don't think he knew Ellen was at the farm until his job happened to bring him into the vicinity. It must surely have been a spur-of-the-moment thing; I don't know what took place between those two gentlemen that evening. And I don't think we ever shall know. Be that as it may, Morinder started hanging around Ellen Bjarnebo on her return to Kymlinge. He had come back from Gothenburg about the same time . . . or a couple of years earlier maybe. And things developed as they did. And I think in this case there was an element of planning.'

'He doesn't sound very pleasant,' said Eva Backman.

'No, and I haven't heard or read a single good word about him, so I think that's right. Why she agreed to them moving in together is a mystery, but if she hadn't, the truth would never have come out. Would it?'

'The truth?'

'Let's make that assumption.'

Backman nodded. Barbarotti was silent as he looked for the right words.

'There was something,' he said. 'Something about that woman . . . when I talked to her up at the guest house. Something that seemed – well, in balance, is all I can say.'

'In balance?'

'Yes. A sorrowful kind of balance, if you can say that, but we need to leave her in peace now. Her life hasn't been easy.'

'It's just as well we don't teach at the police training college, you and I,' said Eva Backman after a moment's reflection. 'For their sakes, as well as ours. Do you want to hear the end of the Fängström story, by the way? It resolved itself a couple of hours ago.'

'A couple of hours ago? You told me yesterday it was an accident.'

Eva Backman nodded. 'And indeed it was. But the detail that resolved itself was where the offending mushroom came from. Guess.'

'The forest?' hazarded Barbarotti.

'Clever cop,' said Backman. 'Exactly right. And it was none other than Lill-Marlene Fängström herself who picked it, that's the icing on the cake . . . To think that I still say that: the icing on the cake? It probably isn't really appropriate here, but it was an expression my dad always used.'

'So what was the icing on the cake?' asked Barbarotti.

'Oh, sorry, yes, back in the autumn Mrs Fängström and her boyfriend went on a trip over to Estonia and Latvia, and they took the opportunity of picking a few carrier bags full of mushrooms. Plenty of them over there, evidently. They took the bags home to Sweden and put them in the freezer. They gave a batch to our Sweden Democrat, and around eight months later, when he came across the bag in his freezer, he ate a portion, with fatal consequences. There are a couple of other bags on the loose, by the way. Wennergren-Olofsson's hunting them down.'

'Extraordinary,' said Barbarotti.

'Yes,' said Backman. 'But the file's closed on all that now, too. And I'm on holiday next week. A chance to do something about my grumpy frame of mind, I hope.'

'I'll drink to that,' said Barbarotti. 'There's a delicious smell coming from the kitchen. What are you making for us? Hang on, don't tell me it's a . . .?'

'Don't worry,' smiled Eva Backman. 'Not so much as a chanterelle.'

53

Three hours later they were still sitting there. The sun had gone down and Eva Backman had lit some candles and turned on her gas patio heater. Red wine in their glasses, a bit of cheese, a bit of chocolate.

'Where are your brood today?' she asked.

'You think I ought to get off home to them?' said Barbarotti.

'Perish the thought,' said Backman. 'I just wanted to be sure you hadn't forgotten them.'

'They're all off on ploys of their own,' said Barbarotti. 'Can you imagine that? The boys are with their mum in Gothenburg. Not sure what's on the programme, but she will insist on dragging them to the funfair. Johan's with his girlfriend – a student party or something. Sara and Jenny were going to the gym or for a jog, I think, and then to a film . . . Yes, I've got tabs on them all, see. Do you know what yours are up to?'

Eva Backman shrugged her shoulders and looked slightly mournful for a moment. 'Oh yes,' she said. 'Jörgen and Viktor have gone sailing with a couple of friends, or that's what they told me anyway. But they've moved out now, in any case, and they don't expect to be kept tabs on. Kalle's here at home with Ville and the dragon, poor boy. Or maybe he's taken himself out for the evening, to leave them in peace.'

'You really dislike that woman, don't you?'

She nodded and bit her lip. 'Yes, and that's what scares me. I ought to be able to handle it, but maybe I'm starting to turn into a real bitch? Someone said something about a female zone a few hours ago, don't you remember?'

'No idea what you're taking about,' said Barbarotti, but he could see that Eva Backman was serious now. Serious and sad. It's odd, he thought, we've known each other for goodness knows how long and I don't think I've ever seen her barefoot before.

It was an unexpected thought, and now she had donned a pair of thick socks to keep out the evening chill. But there was no denying the fact that they had been work colleagues for twenty years, and it struck him that there could scarcely be any other person in the world with whom he had exchanged so many thoughts.

'Do you remember how frightened I was when Marianne had her first aneurism,' she said. 'And that fear stayed with me, as if I . . . well, as if I knew that this was going to happen, too. That she was going to die. And do forgive me for saying that.'

He nodded. 'I remember. I think fear is the worst monster. That's what can really break us. Maybe . . . yes, maybe that was what I found so remarkable about Ellen Bjarnebo. She was somehow beyond fear.'

'Beyond fear?' said Backman. 'Sounds great. I do hope I can find my way there. Sorry to be so gloomy, Gunnar. The idea was for me to try to cheer you up a bit. But I feel so . . . lost?'

Barbarotti nodded but did not reply.

'Fifty years old, lost and alone. If I were to write my CV today, that one-liner would honestly cover it.'

'I thought you were only forty-nine.'

'I feel older,' said Backman.

She broke off a square of chocolate and chewed it for a while. 'Even the chocolate's bitter nowadays. And they make it like that on purpose, isn't it weird? I would never have accepted that sort of stuff when I was a child.'

She laughed and he couldn't help thinking that if there was one sound he would be able to pick out in a high-spirited crowd of a hundred, it was Eva Backman's laugh.

'Well, I've got a little plan in fact,' he said and cleared his throat.

'A plan?' queried Eva Backman.

'Er, yes, actually, hrrm.'

'Let's hear it then.'

'It came to me yesterday after my chat with Asunander. All that about his daughter and so on, you know . . . ?'

She nodded, and a look came into her face that could almost be described as uneasy. But it was getting quite dingy on the balcony now, so perhaps he wasn't seeing properly.

'Anyway he told me he didn't know if he dared, but he felt he had to do it. Introduce himself to his daughter, that is. It wasn't anything that special, you might think, but it was the way he said it . . . and his expression. And of course it was all the more striking because it was coming from him.'

'Go on,' said Eva Backman.

'Well, in the end I sort of couldn't stop thinking about it, and finally I realized why. I've decided to go and look for my father.'

'Your father?'

'Yes.'

'The one you've never met? The Italian . . . ?'

'Exactly. He may be dead, but in that case I'll find his grave instead. I'm planning to take a week off in September. Go to Italy and get to grips with this . . . I know his name and where he was born, after all. I think I can pull it off.'

Eva Backman smiled. 'Good,' she said. 'You're doing exactly the right thing there, Gunnar.'

'And there's one other thing,' said Barbarotti, running his hands a touch nervously over his knees.

'Yes?'

'I was thinking of asking you if you'd like to come with me.'

Eva Backman had just raised her wine glass to her lips, but set it back down on the table. She put her hand to her mouth and regarded him with a look he found well nigh impossible to interpret. As if she had seen something that had been swept under the carpet and been hidden there for so many years that she could no longer identify it. Or perhaps it was entirely the opposite: something utterly new and incomprehensible. Five seconds passed. Then she started to laugh.

Then she started to cry.

Have I gone and misunderstood something again? wondered Barbarotti. Or is it something else?

But instead of trying to understand that, he turned his gaze up to the delicate, transparent June sky. And it wasn't at all hard to see them up there: Marianne and Our Lord. They were sitting together on an old park bench; it looked like ancient oak, worn smooth by the ravages of time and a fair amount of sitting, and they were attentively watching and listening to everything under discussion down below them, on that godsend of a balcony in that fictional town, where a woman was just holding out her hand to a man.

'From up here, it looks as if things are turning out quite well,' said Marianne.

'Well, it's obvious your husband wasn't created from the rib of an orang-utan,' said Our Lord. 'But then I've never really understood that whole evolution lark.'

Marianne smiled.

'Human beings are inscrutable,' added Our Lord. 'Just like me.'

Thank You

The author wishes to express his heartfelt thanks, firstly to S and L, the two women at Hinseberg who gave him extremely useful information about various aspects of life there, and secondly to the Granlund brothers, who provided chauffeuring services up in southern Lapland and were significantly more communicative than their counterparts in the novel.